T0157550

Reflection City

JESSE P. WARD

authorHOUSE®

AuthorHouse™
1663 Liberty Drive
Bloomington, IN 47403
www.authorhouse.com
Phone: 1 (800) 839-8640

Published by AuthorHouse   07/28/2015

ISBN: 978-1-5049-1762-9 (sc)
ISBN: 978-1-5049-1761-2 (hc)
ISBN: 978-1-5049-1760-5 (e)

Library of Congress Control Number: 2015909431

Print information available on the last page.

Prologue

Brumble was born in Reflection City. He was perhaps the only person who knew the entire story of this strange but wonderful place. It all began years ago when his grandfather was a young knight. His grandfather, whose name was Dexter, was returning from battles with the eastern people. As he climbed the steep trail to his city, he was extremely burdened about the fruitlessness of fighting all the time. Even on the return to his home he had been attacked by bandits. He had left the northern front because he had received news that his young wife had died. The extreme winter had been more than her frail body could stand. Now he was returning to mourn her death and to make arrangements for the care of his child.

As he approached the lake that bordered his city he heard the sound of someone in pain. As he looked to the side of the road, he saw a fox with an arrow in its back. He stopped his horse. He thought how sad that someone would shoot a fox. They were no good for food and such lovely animals.

He picked up the poor fox and pulled the arrow from its body. He built a fire and made a mud pack for its wound. He covered the fox with a blanket, and he then fell quickly asleep.

The next morning to his surprise there was no fox under the blanket but a man. Dexter was so amazed that he could not speak, but the old man put him at ease when he said, "I am a wizard. I had turned myself into a fox to enjoy the country and was shot by hunters. I was too weak to return to my human form. I am so glad that you came along, or I am afraid that arrow may have been the death of me."

Dexter introduced himself and told the sad story about the loss of his wife.

They spent the rest of the day talking. The wizard's wounds were completely healed by evening. As Dexter mounted his horse, the wizard said, "Make a wish."

"I don't believe in wishes."

"You heard me; Make a wish."

Dexter didn't believe in magic but had seen the wizard turn from a fox into a man. He looked at the wizard and said, "I wish for the people of my city to be free of this world and all its cruelty. I would want for my people to have no fear of war, no fear of weather, no fear of men who take your property. I would wish for a place where animals are safe and people only hunt for food and not pleasure. I would want this for my people until this world is a better place." Dexter then rode away.

The wizard watched as Dexter disappeared from sight. "He is such a good man. I will grant this wish, and Dexter will have such a grand city. I will show the people of this city to the world only every fifteen years and only the people who are intelligent and have love in their hearts and want a better place can go there. I will give the people of this city a key. Any person who wants to leave must leave during the reflection time. This will be my gift to Dexter."

That night Dexter made camp next to Reflection Lake just outside the city. He would wait until morning and then ride around the lake and see his child. He learned of his gift in a dream. The wizard told him that the city would be invisible and protected by a key. Anyone who wanted to leave should leave during the reflection month. When he awoke the next morning he had a key around his neck and he could not see the city but only its reflection in the clear water of the lake. The dream was true, and he used the key to open the door to the city.

He told the people the story, and said if anyone wanted to leave they could but must leave during the reflection month. No one left the city and the city enjoyed many years of peace. It was not long until the city was forgotten and was only remembered as a fairytale. The only reminder was the appearance of the city's reflection every fifteen years.

King Joel Learns of the Capture

* *

Sitting atop the South Tower of Regstar Castle, King Joel could see some of his kingdom but not all. He and his wife enjoyed coming to the top of the tower so much that they had built a small garden in one corner of the tower next to the inner wall. They had planted roses in the garden and included a variety of colors. They had christened their little paradise Rainbow Garden. His wife had enjoyed coming up here so much when she was pregnant that he had included a small fireplace so she could be warm. Now she was gone. She had died in childbirth and he now missed her more than ever.

Now he was alone, and he felt alone. Joel had become king at a very young age. His father was at war, fighting in the north, when an arrow ended his life and made young Joel king of Regstar. Joel had surprised everyone by not seeking revenge for his father's death. Instead he had made peace, but it had been an uneasy peace, and Joel feared war could come to Regstar at any time.

That night Joel was in the large eating room. He did not like eating alone in such a large room, but this was expected. The room had very few decorations but had several heads of animals that had been killed on hunts by Joel's father. He had promised himself that he would remove them when he became king, but they had belonged to his father, long forgotten trophies of past hunts. There were two doors that opened into the room and one large window at the end of it. The window was open but could be closed if the castle was ever attacked. There was a large fireplace at the other end of the room, but the room was always cold. This day it was extremely cold. Joel walked to the window and looked across the land that made up his kingdom. On the horizon he could see the smoky haze that rose above the mountains that bordered the northern lands.

He was worried. His daughter was not late. In fact, she was not due to arrive until next day. Something was bothering him. Should he be concerned, or was this normal for a trip of this nature? He reviewed his decision to let her go. She so much wanted to see her aunt, and the trip would be so refreshing. She had left the kingdom very few times in her fourteen years. The coolness and humidity gave the air a hint of snow, but Joel did not feel this was a peril to his daughter's safety. So why this anxiety? What of this uneasy feeling? Was it just a father's concern for the safety of his only child? He turned back inside the room and walked to the large fireplace, held out his hands to try to warm his body. Then he walked back to the window.

The next day came and left, still and Donella did not arrive. Joel did not become too concerned, but the next day she did not arrive. That night he did not eat. While he was standing in front of the large window, in the distance he noticed a rider. His horse's gait was slow. Surely, if there was any trouble, if the rider had information about his daughter, the pace would be quick. There appeared to be no urgency with this rider. As the rider approached the castle he stopped. He dismounted his horse and stood next to his mount. He stood there motionless and stared at the castle. The king studied the rider and could see that he was tall, extremely tall. He could see that he wore a beard. This man a was knight, but not of his army. Joel alerted the night watch to keep an eye on the stranger but not to approach him.

That night as the king ate, his thoughts returned to his daughter. The castle was cold and the large fire in the eating room did little to warm the air. The warm food and liquid did warm his body, but did not warm his heart. He still had the feeling that something was wrong. He went to the window and saw the knight was still standing next to his horse. He had built a fire, and the embers' glow made this stranger look even taller. *Did this man have information about his daughter?* He ordered his horse to be made ready. He also sent for two knights to accompany him.

When Joel approached the rider he saw that he was not a young man. He was old. He stopped his horse several feet away from the man but did not dismount.

"I am Joel, the king of this land. State the purpose of your visit."

The old knight didn't move and said just loudly enough for Joel to hear, "We have taken her back."

Suddenly a pain shot through Joel's heart and pierced his entire body.

He knew this man. That sudden realization and what he had said increased his pain. He dismounted his horse and quickly walked to the knight.

"I thought we would never see each other again. I hoped that we would never see each other again. Come to my castle and tell me your story. Is she safe?"

The old man's face did not change. "I cannot come to your castle. The time is short. I came only to give you this information. She is gone, and she will not return."

When these words were spoken the old knight went to his horse.

"Enjoy your memories of her. There will be no more. She was yours, but we have taken her back. There is nothing you can do." He mounted his horse, and as he did, Joel pulled his sword. The two knights with him did likewise.

The old knight turned his horse to face Joel. "What good will killing me do? She is gone, and as I told you there is nothing you can do. I can give her a message if you wish."

Joel dropped his head. "Tell her I love her."

With that, the old knight turned his horse north and rode away. He felt bad that no message to Donella was going to be delivered.

Joel's mind was spinning. Should he ride after him? What could he do? Both escorts wanted to pursue the old knight, but Joel said no. His words had been true. There was nothing he could do, and he knew his daughter was in no danger.

When King Joel returned to his castle he didn't know what to do. He had worried that this might happen, but not to Donella, his daughter. When he married Phylass fifteen years ago, he had worried that this might happen to her, but not to Donella.

Joel Calls for Asher

* * * * * * * * * * * * *

Asher was a young man who had grown up in the castle and had been a good friend to Joel's daughter. His father was Pike, a knight and trusted friend to Joel. His mother was Calie, the royal librarian. She had given birth to Asher one month before the birth of Donella. When Phylass had died in childbirth, Calie had become the wet nurse to Donella. When Pike and Calie had been killed, Asher was three years old and Joel became like a father to him. He grew up in the castle and was like a member of the family.

While they were young, Donella was much taller than Asher. He would often call her the little giant because she was much taller than most of the children her age in the castle.

Asher and Donella were close and played together almost every day. Then came the day that Asher turned twelve years old. He had caught up to Donella in height. He and Donella had crossed the fixed bridge and were standing on the barbican when he looked up to see King Joel standing on the bridge. He motioned for Asher to join him, and both he and Donella walked to the king.

"Leave us, Donella. I need to talk to Asher alone."

Donella could see that her father was serious. He was always smiling while in their presence, because he was so proud of them.

When Donella was gone, he turned to Asher. "It is time you started your training to become a knight. You will need to say good bye to Donella because you are leaving the castle to be the page of Sir John. He is a good man and a better knight. He will train you well. You will be living in the barracks at High Oaks. After you have said your good bye to Donella, pack the things you need, and meet Sir John at the lower bailey near the well."

Asher did not know what to say. He just extended his hand to Joel and said, "Thank you sir, I will make you proud."

Joel did not take Asher's hand but extended both arms around the boy. "I know you will make me proud, and I know you will make both of your parents proud. Go see Donella."

As Asher stepped back from Joel he looked him in the face to see that the king had tears in his eyes. He quickly turned away and went to find Donella. He found her standing at the well, just below the keep.

"I know you are leaving," she said.

"Little Giant, I don't want to leave but this is what is expected of me. I want to make you proud as well as King Joel. I don't know when we will see each other again."

She smiled, "When we see each other again, don't refer to me as Little Giant. You are now taller than I am."

They walked slowly back to the main building without talking. Then Asher said, "Don't forget me."

She laughed. "How could I?"

Asher's training was consuming, and he only saw Donella a couple of times during the next two years. When they did meet, it was obvious they were changing and drifting apart.

King Joel loved Asher. It had been his hope that his daughter and Asher would fall in love, and together rule the kingdom of Regstar after he died.

As he waited for Asher, he wondered what he could tell him. *Was it fair to Asher to place such a burden on him?* The wait for Asher seemed forever.

When Asher came into the large room he could see the concern in Joel's face. He was just a boy, but he knew bad news was about to be spoken.

The king looked at the boy. "You are my only hope. They have taken Donella. You must know the entire story."

Joel and Phylass

* * * * * * * * * *

It had happened fifteen years ago when Joel was twenty-three years old and had just become king of Regstar. He had gone hunting alone in the northern mountains. He enjoyed hunting; however rarely killed an animal. He just loved to be outside. He had climbed the mountains and had discovered a beautiful lake. It was crystal clear and gave the most brilliant reflection of the mountains he had ever seen. As he looked across the water, it was as if the land went up and down at the same time. The reflection was as clear as the view. He had decided to camp by the lake, and the next morning the most extraordinary thing happened. He could see the reflection of an enchanting castle in the water of the lake. It was beautiful. When he looked across the lake he could see only a rock wall that bordered the lake. He looked back into the water and could see the castle distinctly. All day he just looked and admired the castle. He took from his pack a piece of parchment and with a charcoal drew the image. When he finished he noticed something bizarre. While scanning the rock wall and looking at its outline, there appeared to be no entrance.

After about two days of exploring the rock wall and looking for an entrance, the young king left his camp and went to a small village nearby. The leader of the village, Silas, welcomed him and invited him to eat. That evening, Joel told his story of the reflection.

Silas didn't seem surprised.

"I know of this reflection. It appears only every fifteen years, and only then for one month. I have seen it twice. "When I was a young man, I was traveling in the mountains and came across a knight who had been attacked by wolves. He was badly wounded, and I brought him to my camp. He lived for three weeks, but before he died he told me he was from Reflection City. He said that he must return as quickly as possible to his people. This is how I know that it returns every fifteen years. I have a key to this city. The knight had it around his neck. I went to visit this city and to return the knight's body but could only see the refection. I saw it disappear just as the knight said it would. Fifteen years later I returned but could only find a rock wall, while the reflection was clear in the water."

The next morning, Joel asked for the key. The old leader gave it to him and said, "There is no gate. Enjoy the refection, but there is no way in."

The young king spent days looking, but he could find no way to enter the castle. Maybe it was really in the water. He searched the rocks. He even dove into the clear water but found no castle and no gate. He looked at the key. It gave no hint of how it was to be used. There were no markings, just a plain key. That night the moon was bright and he looked at the reflection in the dark water. As he looked at the reflection he thought, *I will never get in, and I must return to my own castle.*

The next morning he bathed and shaved in the lake. He was using his mirror when suddenly he noticed the reflection of the wall on the water was gone. Through the mirror, he could see the faded outline of the castle among the rocks, but the reflection on the water did not show. With his back to the lake and looking through the mirror he could pan the image on the rocks. Suddenly, there is was. A very large door. He could see the entry was higher in the rocks than he would have thought.

He was so excited he could hardly dress. He ran around the edge of the lake to the rock wall. He climbed high up where the reflection of the door was and noticed a small hole just large enough for the key. He trembled as he placed the key in the hole and turned. He heard a loud click. Then he pushed the rock open and found he was standing high on ground overlooking a large valley. He could hear the sound of people from a distance but could see no one.

It was a long climb down to the city sounds. As he entered the city, he could hear people moving, talking as if selling goods. It sounded as if he were in the center of a marketplace. Yet he could see no one. Surely if he could not see these people they would not be able to see him either.

After his fear subsided, he decided to explore this strange land. Then he had an idea. He reached inside his pouch and pulled out a small mirror. He held up the mirror and looked. The city was a sight to behold. The market where he had entered was alive with sound and was a beautiful place. As he moved about the city, he could feel the presence of many people. Shops were made of marble, and silk, or what appeared to be silk, lined each and every one. Just the other side of the marketplace, he found a quiet garden. In the center was a large lake. It was surrounded by beautiful pink trees. He looked into the crystal blue water to see his reflection. He bent to take a drink, and suddenly he heard someone say, "Who are you? Why are you in the water?"

He looked, and standing next to his image was the most radiant girl he had ever seen. She had long straight, dark brown hair which came almost to her waist. Her skin was tan. She was dressed in a golden dress and showed no fear of him.

As he looked into the water he said, "I am Joel, and I am from the Sovereignty of Regstar. I mean you no harm."

He stood and looked around. He could see no one. He looked back into the water, and she was still standing next to him.

"You must be from the outside world," she said. "That is why we can't see each other. I have been told this by the great knight Brumble who has been outside our walls. Why have you come?"

Joel did not know what to say. He just said, "I am Joel. Who are you?"

She did not answer his question but repeated, "Why are you here?"

He told her of seeing the reflection and how he had found the opening and how he had received the key.

"So that is what happened to Lucas. He disappeared before I was born. He left to explore outside the kingdom and was never heard of again. Since then no one has left the city with the exception of the great knight Brumble."

They sat in the green grass close to the water so they could see each other. He told more of his story and about his kingdom.

She looked into the water right into his eyes and said, "Tell me more of your land. I want to know."

She had been listening, but suddenly her face changed, and she said, "You can't stay here. If my father finds you, he will kill you. No one from the outside is allowed to stay. I think this is true, but no one from the outside has ever come to our kingdom before. Meet me again at this time tomorrow. I must go."

He spent the rest of the day exploring the great city. That night he left and returned to his camp. He didn't know how long the city would be visible and was not sure what would happen if he were inside the city when it disappeared.

He was restless during the night. He thought of the girl. What was her name? She was so beautiful, and he could not wait to see her again. The next day he returned to the city. He went quickly back to the garden and sat by the fountain. It was not long until he heard her voice.

"Joel are you here?" She appeared next to him in the water.

"I am Phylass. My father is Rue the king of Reflection City."

She sat down beside him, and they looked at each other in the water. She started to tell him about her land and the kingdom she loved.

They talked for hours, she telling of her world and he telling of his.

Then she said, "Your world sounds wonderful, but the great knight Brumble says it is a cruel world and we must never go there. He has told my father about men who kill animals for pleasure and about men who live along the road and take the property of others. He says the air is sometimes extremely hot and other times extremely cold. He says it is not a good world and we must be thankful that we are only visible to it every fifteen years."

Joel told her that some of what Brumble had said was true. He said the air changed with each season and wasn't bad but wonderful.

They continued to meet each day, and she marveled as he told her of flowers of spring, the birds of summer, and frost of fall, wonders of the snows of winter. She reached to touch him in the water and suddenly pulled back her hand. He noticed it too. As they looked into the water, their images were almost transparent. They were fading.

"What is happening?" she said and as they looked toward each other and could see that they were slowly becoming visible.

Suddenly Phylass was pulled away from the water, and Joel heard her scream. He turned and looked into the pool to see a very large knight.

Brumble was pulling his sword when Joel heard Phylass say, "Please let me go. I love him so much. You must let me go."

The face of the knight softened. Joel could tell he was devoted to this princess. He could not make out what the knight and Phylass were saying, but knew the knight was no longer a threat to him. Then he saw the transparent figure of Phylass coming toward him, and behind her he could see a very large knight.

"Knight Brumble is my protector. He would not have harmed you. He only wanted to frighten you away from me. He has told me that the only way we can see each other is if we love each other. He says the reflection of the city will soon end. You have a key and can leave. I can leave if I truly love you or have a key. I love you, and I want to leave."

Joel felt the warmness in his heart. He knew if Brumble was willing to let Phylass leave, he must love her very much and want her to be happy.

Brumble looked at Phylass and said, "You know you cannot say goodbye to your father. He will never let you go. If he commands that I keep you here, I will have to obey.

Joel looked at Phylass, and she was no longer transparent but was now fully visible. She was even more beautiful than the image he had fallen in love with in the water. She was wearing a black dress trimmed in gold. The water had not shown how dark brown her hair really was. Her eyes were dark brown, almost black, and she had a glow about her. As they embraced, Brumble said, "Stay in the garden. Do not leave. You have much to discuss. I will return with provisions for your trip outside the kingdom. When I return, if you both really want to go, I will help you leave."

The old knight turned to Joel. "I can see you and you, can see me. The reason for this is that when this city was enchanted, provisions were made for people from the outside to join our kingdom. When you love someone here you can see the people and they can see you. Are you sure you want to leave? You know you can stay."

The old knight then left them alone in the garden.

Joel looked at Phylass. "Are you sure you want to leave?"

She looked at him though her teary eyes. "Yes, I want to be with you."

"You must be sure. This city will not be visible for another fifteen years."

He then knew how much she loved him. She was willing to give up everything to be with him.

Joel held Phylass in his arms and waited for Brumble to return. She was soft and warm. She smelled like fresh flowers in spring.

When Brumble returned he had packed a horse with things for Phylass to take on her trip.

"I have put some of your clothes and two blankets in the pack. There is food and drink. I found you a coat in case the weather is cold." He then turned to Joel. "Do think you will need anything else?"

"I left my supplies outside the gate and have even more at the local village. We will be fine. We need to go to the gate."

They left the garden and made their way on foot to the gate that led outside. Brumble led the horse and did not speak. Joel and Phylass held hands up the hill and when they arrived the young king used his key and opened the gate.

Brumble looked at Phylass and said, "Are you sure you want to leave? This can't be undone for fifteen years."

He was an old knight, but Joel sensed he was strong and very able. There was also a gentleness to the man.

The knight said, "I have let you take the future queen of this land to be the queen of your land. You must promise me that you will protect her with your life. You will not see me again. If you do, I will have given this land back their queen."

Joel turned to Phylass and said, "We need to go. We will try to return here when the reflection reappears." He took her by the hand and led her though the door. Once outside Reflection City the air had a slight chill, and Joel held her close to him. She looked at him and thought, *I love this man more than he could ever know.*

Joel and Phylass returned to his castle where they were married. It was a year later that Donella was born.

Phylass only got to see her daughter once and then she was gone. Joel held Phylass in his arms.

"I am sorry I took you from your land, and I will devote my life to our daughter," he said. "I want to tell your father and the people of your land about the life we had and how much I loved you and about our daughter, but I don't know how."

Joel did not have to tell the people of Reflection City that Phylass had died. A terrible pain had shot through Rue's heart at the moment of her death.

****

Joel looked at the young man as he finished the story. The young man looked bewildered. "How do we get her back?" he asked.

"I am not sure we can. I still have the key, and if we can get inside, we have to find Donella. We must do so before the city disappears."

The king and the young man left the castle of Regstar and rode three days until they reached the northern mountains. On foot they traveled up the hills, at just about nightfall they reached Reflection Lake. As Joel and young Asher looked at the beautiful reflection of the city, they saw it disappear.

As they walked back down the mountain, Joel wondered if he had made the right decision. Maybe if he had told Donella about her mother and made plans to visit the city when it reappeared, things might have turned out differently. Now he would have to wait fifteen years to see his daughter.

Donella's Trip

* * * * * * * * * *

It had been a long day for Donella. She was fourteen years old and had been raised by her father since her mother had died in childbirth. She was going to visit her aunt Para. She didn't get to see Para very often. Now she was making the long trek to Para's castle. Their castles were miles apart, and the trip involved some risk. The visit had been a secret--as much of a secret as possible. The trip would take about three to four days. If anybody knew the daughter of Joel was away from the castle it might be dangerous to her. She was going to spend nine days with Para who was twice her age. She had not seen her aunt for a couple of years, but they had become very close through the letters they often wrote to each other.

Donella traveled in one coach with about twenty troops in her escort. Half the troops were dressed as workers, and the others were in uniform. They were to look like a small detachment of troops on a return from some detail.

As they travel Donella was instructed to keep her window closed and not to be in view of anyone. The people of Regstar loved Joel and Donella, but the people of the north might have spies that would do her harm.

She was excited about the trip to Arsi, and that excitement made the journey less of a burden. She pulled back the shade of the window to see the beautiful landscape. They were out in the country, and she felt no one would see her. The red and green hues of the country passed by her window. She could hear birds singing, and as they passed a large lake, she could see ducks swimming. She loved the outdoors and wished she could open the window for a better view and to get fresh air, but she had been warned not to do so. She sat back, closed her eyes, and thought of her coming visit with Para.

It was late in the day and Donella had drifted off to sleep when she was awakened by shouting.

She heard the driver call to someone on the road. "Yield the road, yield the road."

She leaned out and saw a very large man moving to the side of the road. He was dressed in a brown robe' and his head was covered with a hood. As they passed their eyes met and she saw the face of this tall stranger change as the carriage went by. She had never seen this man before, but she could tell that he knew her.

How could he know me? Perhaps he had seen her riding. But she was not bothered by the fact that he seemed to recognize her. It was his face as they passed that troubled her. It was a look of shock. She looked out the back window and the old stranger was standing in the road looking at her carriage. She gave this encounter little more thought, and she again turned her attention to how she would spend the days with her aunt.

The man watched as the caravan moved out of sight. Another group of merchants was following about a half mile behind the caravan, and when they arrived at his location, he stopped them.

"Halt. I just passed a caravan of troops on the road. Is Regstar at war?"

"No, troops often travel this road in search of bandits and to protect people like us."

"There was a young lady inside the carriage."

One of the merchants answered, "I don't know but it could have been princess Donella. There was a rumor that she was going to spend some time with her aunt, Queen of Arsi. My sister works in the castle. This is what she told me."

"Do you know how long the princess is going to be at Arsi Castle?"

"My sister said that the staff at Regstar had been told to help her pack for a nine day visit."

The large man let the merchants pass and then he walked into woods where he had left his horse. He took off his brown robe, mounted his horse and rode as fast as he could.

Two days later he was standing in front of his king.

Brumble lowered his head. "I have sad news that I must tell you."

Rue looked at his first knight and friend. "I know what you are going to tell me. On your trip, you found out my daughter is dead. I have known this for a long time. But you have something else that you want to tell me. What have you found out?"

Brumble told his story about meeting the carriage on the road and when he finished the king was excited. "What will you need?"

"I will need about fifty men and several days. She is traveling with an escort of about twenty. Some were dressed as workers, but they all could be knights. I need twice their strength."

The king looked at the knight and said, "Great Knight Brumble, you are my only hope. Take what you need. Go get her, and bring her to me. Time is short. You must move quickly."

The great knight Brumble took his men and returned to the place of the sighting. They established a camp in the woods. That night Brumble sent a spy to the Arsi castle with instruction to find out when the caravan would return to Regstar.

When Donella arrived at the castle of Para she was greeted by her aunt. They embraced and giggled like two little girls. Donella looked at her aunt. She was a beautiful woman, maybe the most beautiful woman in the kingdoms. Para was the younger and only sister of Joel. Her real name was Parazilla, but through the years it had been shortened to Para. She was simply known as Queen Para. She was tall and slender, and she wore clothing that made her look even taller. She had blonde hair, and it was cut short. This did not make her less feminine. Her skin was tan, almost bronze. Her breasts were perfect for her size, and her small waist would make every man stare at her. She was married to Alnac, who was older than Para, if fact 10 years older. They had met when she was only sixteen and had been married since she was 18. Para had spent most of their married life alone. In the ten years of marriage Para had been with her husband only five months. While Alnac was away, she took an active role in ruling the kingdom. Donella thought that Alnac was a fool to leave her so much. They had no children, and the Kingdom of Arsi was without a direct heir.

While visiting with Para, they spent much of their time talking, with Para showing her the large castle. Both liked to read, and Para's castle had a large library. Often they would get a book each and sit in front of the large fireplace and read. Both also liked to take rides and almost every day they would ride south of the castle and enjoy the countryside. While Para didn't seem to have any friends, she did have Epson. Epson was a tall thin wizard.

He had a long white beard, but didn't look like a wizard. He looked more like a grandfather. No one knew how old he was. He seemed kind, and there seemed to be a special bond between him and Para. Donella thought it strange that Para and Epson were so close. Para had told Donella that Epson was teaching her magic. Donella thought that this meant card tricks and sleight of hand. She thought this strange and could not understand why Para had any interest in these types of skills. Yes, the trip had been wonderful and the nine days had passed quickly, and soon it was time for her to go home.

During the visit, Epson spent little time with Donella. They had very few conversations. When they did he was polite. In one conversation, he asked her about her father. She found it strange that he did not inquire about her mother.

Just before Donella was to start the trip home, she and Para were eating in the garden.

"Did you know my mother?" She looked at Para to see her response.

"Yes, but not very well," she said. "I understand she was a very good woman, and Joel loved her very much. I can't really tell you anything about her. I just don't know anything."

This was not true. She had gotten to know Phylass very well. They had become very good friends. She was living at Regstar when Donella was born, but Phylass was now gone, and Joel would not speak of her, so Para respected his wishes.

"You need to ask your father."

"I have, and he will not say anything. It puzzles me."

"Be patient with him. He loved her very much, and someday he will tell you about her."

They dropped the conversation and started planning the trip back to Regstar.

The next day the caravan had been assembled, and Para and Donella were standing by the coach. Both women were crying as Para promised she would come to visit her in a couple of months. They hugged, and Donella started for the coach, then rushed back to Para and hugged her again. Donella then got into the carriage leaned out the window, and watched Para as the coach left the castle. She pulled her curtain to cover the window. *This has been one great trip, but the ride home is going to be long and boring.* She thought of her father and looked forward to seeing him.

Danger

❋ ❋ ❋ ❋ ❋

Donella had been gone from the castle for about two days. Para was thinking of Donella when she felt a pain shoot through her body. *Something is wrong. Something is going to happen to Donella.* The pain left her but a feeling of confusion stayed with her.

She heard steps coming down the hall and then Epson stepped into her room. He looked at Para as if he knew something was wrong.

Then Para said, "Do you sense it too? Donella is in danger."

"Donella is not in danger. Reach deep inside yourself. Is it danger you feel or is it something else?"

"I don't know what it is, but something is not right."

Epson looked at Para. "What you feel is change, a change that will hurt the people who love Donella. That is what you feel. You feel your own pain, and it is not letting you see what is happening. She is not in danger. She will not be harmed in any way, but the change that is coming will cause pain to the ones who love her. That includes you and your brother and others."

Para started to speak again, but Epson took his finger to her lips and said, "I will meet with you tomorrow. I think by then you will be able to see what is happening. You need to do this on your own."

After Epson left, Para took out parchment and started a letter to Alnac telling him of the wonderful visit she had had with Donella. She did not tell him of the feeling of danger she had.

The Long Ride Home

Donella was getting tired. Her thoughts again turned to Para and the wonderful time they had had talking about the two kingdoms. Yes, it had been a wonderful trip. She then thought of the tall stranger she saw on the road. Why had he acted so strangely? Just then she heard the driver of the coach call back, "We are stopping for the night. We should be able to make the castle tomorrow. Stay in the coach while I pull into the woods. Then you can get out and stretch your legs while the men put up your tent."

While the men were putting up her tent and setting up camp she walked around the woods shaking off the long trip of the day. She noticed there was always a guard close by. *Why do people want to rob and hurt other people?* It was not long until her tent was ready, and she went inside. She brushed her hair, and put on some evening clothes which she covered with a long green robe. It was not long until a guard brought her supper. She quickly ate and was soon sound asleep.

Donella was awakened by the sound of swords clashing. She was scared and did not look out of the tent. When it got quiet, she left her tent and found that she was now a prisoner of some strange men. She did not recognize their clothing. She saw a tall knight. He was the same man she had seen on the road days earlier. She was afraid, but she didn't think the men would harm her. She looked around and several of her soldiers were now captive, and like her, they were prisoners.

The tall soldier approached her and said, "I am Brumble, do not be afraid. No harm will come to you."

She started to speak, but Brumble stopped her. "Go to your tent and change into clothes which are suitable for riding a horse. You are going with us, and where we are going the coach can't go."

Para and Epson

* * * * * * * * * *

After Donella left, Para felt more alone than ever. She had gone to the tallest tower of the castle and watched the carriage and escorts until they were out of sight. She continued to watch even after she could not see them but could make out the cloud of tan dust rising from the road. When she went inside she realized she had seen something strange. When the coach left the castle there had been rider in front of the coach. He did not wait for the coach but rode off quickly and left the caravan behind.

Para had mentioned to Donella that Epson was teaching her magic, but she did not tell her that she was becoming a powerful wizard in her own right. Epson had told her that she had magic in her, and he was teaching her how to use it. She loved her lessons with Epson but did not think she was making any progress in the world of magic. She found that she could do many things-- but nothing like Epson. Epson would tell her each day that she was becoming more and more powerful, but she felt that he was only trying to encourage her. When Donella was out of sight, Para returned inside the castle and called for Epson. When Epson came to Para, he said nothing. She look at him and smiled.

"I am sad," she said. "Teach me something new."

With a smile on his face, he said, "I cannot teach you anything. As I have told you many times all the magic is in you. All I can do is help you discover the power that you have. The power is there, I can feel it. Soon you will know your power and you will need me no more. When that day comes, I will leave."

"You could never leave me. You know you are my only friend, I won't let you go." She knew she could not stop him if he chose to leave. She would just have to hope that he would not leave.

Epson took Para's hand and said, "Do you see the flowers growing in the pot on the window's edge?"

"Yes."

"They have no blooms. Do you want them to bloom?"

"Yes."

"Look at them, and concentrate. You want them to bloom."

Para looked at the plants and felt a change in her body. Then she saw the blooms appear. The plant had red and yellow flowers in full bloom.

"We have done this before. This is not new."

He let go of her hands. "This time I did not help you. This time it was completely you. I am going to leave you now. I need a nap. When I go, see if you can make the blooms go away."

After Epson left, Para looked at the plants. All she did was think of what she wanted. She concentrated and the blooms were gone. Then she brought the blooms back. Every time she repeated the process it became easier and quicker. She felt her power, and she had pride in what she had done.

The Story of Epson

* * * * * * * * * * * *

The next morning, Para looked out the large castle window as the morning sun rose in the sky and thought of Alnac. Her first three years of marriage had been very lonely. She had thought that she loved her husband, but she wasn't sure anymore. After the first few years of being alone she had met Epson. He was a very old man, and their first meeting had been one brought on by pity. She had been riding outside the castle and found him sitting under a tree. He looked frail and weak. She stopped her horse and walked over to him. Without saying anything she offered him her canteen. He took the water without saying a thing and gulped it down. She returned to her horse, took some food she had packed for her ride, returned to Epson and spread the food on a small cloth in front of him. She looked at him and smiled. "Won't you join me for lunch?"

Again Epson did not speak, but looked at the food that was spread before him. He smiled and said, "my name is Epson. I sit under this tree every day, but you are the first to offer me food and drink."

It was her turn to smile. "My name is Para. I am glad to share my food with you and keep you company."

When they had finished the food, he said, "Let me give you something." He waved his hand in the air and produced a flower and held it out to Para. "This is for you, my queen."

"How did you do that?" she said, as she took the flower.

"Magic."

He seemed so lonely, and he had no one. Each day she would visit him and bring food. After several weeks she began to notice that there was more to Epson than met the eye. Their friendship grew, and she had become his student of magic. It wasn't long until he had moved into the castle and had become a part of Para's life.

Alnac had no idea that Para, with the help of Epson, was growing more powerful as a wizard, and with each lesson from Epson, she loved him less. Epson had made her life less lonely. She looked forward to the lesson each day. He had become her friend and advisor. When she turned to him for counsel, he never gave her direct advice. He would ask her questions and soon she would make her decision that came from within. She was always curious about Epson, and her many questions brought very few answers. At their first meetings he seemed to be so helpless, but this was not the case.

It was Epson who had arranged the meeting with Para. He was living in a small cabin in the swamps west of Arsi when he felt a change in his power. *Someone else also has magic.* His search for this person had led him to Arsi Castle and Para. He had to know if her magic was dark.

Epson had arranged the meeting with Para, and her acts of kindness passed his first test. Accepting him as a friend was the passing of the second test. When he was arrested by the palace guards and Para came to his rescue she had passed the third test. During their daily meetings he learned she was extremely intelligent, and this was the fourth test. She was kind, she was loyal, and she was intelligent, but most importantly she was the descendant of the old world order. She had magic in her soul and he would bring it out. She would become his new pupil, and he would pass to her his knowledge.

Epson had now been working with Para for almost three years. She learned the craft very quickly and was eager to learn more. She had no idea how much magic she had and lacked confidence in her ability. She had only stopped her lessons because of the visit of her niece.

The Four Kingdoms

* * * * * * * * * * * * *

The Four Kingdoms

Salados was northeast of Regstar. Salados had been in a war with Rhodes, and King Joel had made peace by becoming neutral and not supporting either Salados or Rhodes. Salados was led by King Andrew. Andrew was a very strong king but was not to be trusted. To the west of Regstar was Arsi. Arsi was ruled by King Alnac. Joel did not know what to think of Alnac. He was a very likable man, but he seemed to like fighting. Joel thought that Alnac could make peace if he wanted but preferred life on a battlefield. This created a problem for Joel because King Andrew was not sure if Joel would honor the peace because Joel's sister was married to Alnac of Arsi, and Arsi supported Rhodes in the war. Joel had no trust in Andrew because he knew Andrew was a cruel man. He had his first wife put to death because he desired another woman. He had even proposed marriage between Joel's daughter, Donella, and Prince Geoffrey, when she became of age. Both Salados and Rhodes wanted the lands of Regstar because of the rich soil and abundant water. Regstar and Arsi controlled the only outlet to the sea. About one third of Rhodes and Salados were barren rock land, and they had trouble producing enough food to support their people. They had to rely on trade and they both wanted the port at Edgewater, which was controlled by Joel and Alnac. Joel was willing to let both Salados and Rhodes use the river to get to the port but Rhodes was blocked by Salados.

Rhodes was to the north of Regstar. It was led by King Karnac. Karnac had no children; he was not even married. Joel thought he was a weak king, and it was said the real power of the kingdom was in the hands of Clive, the minister of Rhodes. Joel had dealt with Clive when he secured the peace between the two kingdoms. He had never secured peace with Salados, but with Rhodes east of Salados and Arsi on the south they were no threat to Regstar as long as the war continued.

As Joel sat in the Rainbow Garden, he mused. *This is a phony war, three kingdoms are at war and have been for ten years. They don't seem to do as much fighting as they do moving their camps to various locations to block the movement of each other's troops. It is like a chess match with there being only about one battle a year and sometimes less. Maybe it will go on forever, and they will leave Regstar alone.*

The four kingdoms were all about equal size. They all bordered the Diamond River which was large enough for boats to travel. The river created a natural border between Salados and Rhodes and a border between Arsi and Regstar. Diamond River emptied into the Silver Sea. The port on the sea was Edgewater. Edgewater was a town that was divided by the river with half in Arsi and half in Regstar. The four kingdoms had several other rivers, but the largest was the Diamond River. This river was the reason the three kingdoms were at war. They all wanted to control the river. Most of the fighting had taken place along either side of the Diamond River. The river had only four bridges. One bridge was Midway Bridge. It connected Arsi and Regstar. The second bridge, which connected Regstar and Salados, was near Centerville. The third bridge was at Edgewater. The bridge in the north was between Salados and Rhodes. It was located near a fork where a second river flowed into Diamond River, thus its name, Two River Bridge.

King Joel could not understand why Alnac had joined the war. He could have remained at peace by not choosing to join Rhodes against Salados. The border between Arsi and Regstar was mostly rolling hills and there was much trade between the two kingdoms. The people of Arsi and Regstar could move freely across the border. There were border guards, but they were there to keep bandits in check. Most of the bandits came from Salados. King Andrew had ignored pleas from Alnac to help with this problem, and this was one reason that Alnac had joined with Rhodes.

Donella and the Hidden City

⊛ ⊛ ⊛ ⊛ ⊛ ⊛ ⊛ ⊛ ⊛ ⊛ ⊛ ⊛ ⊛ ⊛ ⊛ ⊛ ⊛ ⊛

As they left the camp Donella discovered that she was the only prisoner her captors had taken. Brumble had released Donella's soldiers, but they had left them without horses or weapons. Brumble and Donella with the rest of the knights of Reflection City traveled into the mountains and in a couple days stopped at Reflection Lake. Brumble looked at Donella. "I can see by your face that you are scared and have many questions. Your questions will be answered shortly."

It was then that Donella saw the reflection of the city in the water, and her fear lessened. She felt that she belonged to this strange place. The men took her across the lake and climbed the stones. Brumble produced a key and open a large stone door.

Suddenly, Brumble took her by the arm and took her through the door. When she was inside the wall she heard the large door shut. Donella looked and saw the most beautiful land she had ever seen. She looked up at Brumble only to see him disappear, and a great fear came over her. She could still feel his strong hand holding her by one arm. What was happening? He led her down the side of the great mountain. She could hear the sound of hundreds of people as if they lined the streets on both sides but could see no one. As they traveled further inside the city, she could still feel the strong grip on her arm but could not see anyone. She listened to the sounds of the people and realized that these people were cheering. She started to relax, and the fear lessened. She suddenly noticed that she could see faces of people along the road. At first there were a few and then she could see hundreds. They were becoming more and more visible, and her fear was leaving her. These people were glad to see her, these people loved her. She looked to her right and could now see the large knight holding her with one arm and waving to the people with the other.

When they arrived in front of a marble palace, she heard the knight yell to the people, "She is home! She is home! She is home!"

She was taken into the palace and placed in a large room decorated in red. She felt very comfortable. Since she had been left alone, she explored the room and its contents. A large painting caught her eye.

How could these people have a painting of me?

"I never had a dress like this," she said to herself, and at that moment the door opened. A very old man entered the room, and she knew he had to be the king.

"Do not fear my child," he said, and his voice was so kind she knew she had nothing to fear.

"My name is Rue, and I am the king of this land. You are my granddaughter."

She did not reply. *How could this man be my grandfather?*

She knew that her father's father had been killed in a battle with Northern people. She knew nothing about her mother's people. She had asked her father many times, but he had never told her anything. She only knew that when she asked her father about her mother he became very sad, and she had concluded that her mother was a woman he loved very much and the pain of speaking about her was more than he could endure.

Her first words spoken surprised the old king. "How do you have this painting of me?"

"That is not you," he said. "That is your mother. You are much like her. The great knight Brumble discovered who you were several weeks ago. He had left Reflection City and had seen you on the road. The people told him of you and how your mother had died during your birth. Your mother's name was Phylass, and she was taken from us many years ago. Brumble let your father take her because she was in love with him, and he wanted her to be happy. We miss her and would like you to know of her land and her people. We want you to stay with us for a few days. Visit with us, get to know me before you return to your castle. I will send Brumble to your father to tell him that you are safe. I have never met your father, but he must be a good man or my daughter would not have fallen in love with him. I am surprised he never told you about her. Please stay and get to know her and your people."

"How come I could not see anybody when we came through the gate? I could hear voices, but only after I was here for a while did they appear."

"This is a magic land. We are invisible to people outside our kingdom. We all live a very magical life here. Because your mother was born here, it did not take long for you to become visible. Tonight you will dine with me. I will tell you the whole story about this land and your mother."

She felt completely at ease. She wanted to stay. She would now get to know her mother, and she felt anger at her father for never telling her of this land and people. "Yes, I will stay for a few days," she told the old king.

As he turned to leave, he felt sorry for deceiving this child. In three days, Reflection City would disappear and Donella would be trapped inside. His only hope was that she would grow to love the city and its people.

Donella and Evan

* * * * * * * * * * *

The years passed slowly for King Joel. He had aged beyond his years. His only child was gone and there was no way to get her back. If only time would pass quickly. But what would she be like? He looked out the window of his palace. Six years had passed since he had told his story to Asher.

Asher had grown strong and was now the strongest knight in the kingdom. Joel could see him below coming back from his daily ride. He was tall and lean. He had become the favorite of the people. The women admired him for his good looks and the men for his strength and ability as a knight. Joel turned back into his castle and thought of his daughter. She would now be twenty years old.

Donella had at first been crushed by the news that she was trapped in Reflection City, but over the last five years the people had been kind to her, and she knew her grandfather truly loved her. It wasn't long until she began to love him and the people. She often thought of her father and how much her mother must have loved him in order to leave such a great place.

Donella soon began to think of Reflection City as her home. She was learning about the mother she had never known. She found that she was just like Phylass in every way. She looked so much like her mother that some of the people even called her by her mother's name.

Rue was a powerful king, and his people loved him not only because he was king but also because he was such a good man. Every day she was in Reflection City was another day she missed Regstar less.

Each day Donella would go into the city. At first Brumble would always go with her but with the passing of time she was allowed to go on her own. She loved the walks and the visits to the city. She would go to the market, buy fruits and nuts and spend hours just talking to the people. She was truly the princess of Reflection City.

One day as she was walking around the castle, she noticed a young man walking toward her. He looked to be about her age, was clean shaven and dressed like a knight. He walked right up to her and knelt. He looked up and smiled. She told him it was alright to rise. He did not speak until she spoke to him.

"Are you a Knight?" she asked.

"Yes, I am." he said.

"I thought that the great knight Brumble was the only one."

"No there are other knights in the kingdom. Brumble is the first knight of Reflection City."

He went on to explain that even though there was no war in Reflection City and no outside force could enter the city, young men were still trained to be knights.

He then laughed and said, "Each year we have a big celebration and we parade through the city. It is all for show, and it reminds the people what we have. A city that has no need for knights."

"I know that there is a celebration each year. I have never been."

"Why is that?"

"I don't know, I just have never come. My grandfather asks me each year, and I have always said no. Perhaps it would remind me of my other home and how much I miss it. I have no good reason."

Donella smiled as he looked at her. He had never seen a more beautiful girl. She blushed a little as she returned his gaze.

"What is your name?"

"I am Evan, the great grandson of Dexter."

Donella had heard the name Dexter and knew he was a very important man, but she did not want Evan to know she really did not know who he was.

Donella and Evan walked around the city, and he explained everything even though she already knew about everything he was explaining.

When they had finished their walk, she looked at Evan and said, "Thank you for such a lovely afternoon. I hope we can do this again." She smiled and went inside.

Evan turned and walked away. *Is this what love feels like? If it is, it is wonderful.*

Asher

* * * *

Asher was now the most powerful knight in the kingdom of Regstar. He had proven himself in battle. He was well educated and was the most eligible bachelor in the land. He had not thought of taking a wife but had often thought of Donella. Because they had grown up together, her loss was like that of a sister. She would be almost thirty years old before he would even have a chance to see her. He often wondered if she would marry someone in Reflection City.

The air was cold and Asher hugged his arms together to break the chill as he walked back to his barracks. He was the commander of the knights, and even though he lived in the barracks he had private quarters. He opened the door and went straight to the fireplace. He picked up the iron poker and gave the logs a healthy poke, and the flames came to life, lighting the room and giving off wonderful heat. He soon realized he was not cold from the night air but from his commitment to attend Joel's yearly celebration of the Regstar harvest. He dressed quickly, half thinking the quicker he got there the quicker he would be done with it.

When he arrived at the large banquet hall, music was already playing, and the sound of laughter and music blended together, and you could not really make out either. Inside the hall he quickly went to the king's table. Joel was talking to someone he did not know and just gave him a quick glance.

After a few moments Joel turned to Asher and said, "This is Clive, minister from Rhodes, and his wife Kira. They are here to ensure our peace."

Asher looked at Clive, gave a quick glance to his wife, and silently extended his hand.

Clive looked at Asher, and said, "I understand that you are leaving for the northern border in a couple of days."

"Yes, I will leave in five days."

"I have been talking to Joel. We will have some important information to be given to Alnac," Clive said, looking toward Joel.

"The king's wishes are my commands."

Asher took his seat at the king's right. There was something he did not trust about Clive. He just didn't know what it was.

There was very little conversation. He watched the serving maids bringing the food and drink. Jesters were about the room entertaining the guests.

He was looking down at his food when he heard a voice. He looked up as a young lady was saying, "I am sorry that I am late, the time just got away. I was in the library reading and lost track of time."

She then glanced over at Asher but said nothing.

Clive rose. "This is my daughter, Kala," he said. "Please excuse her tardiness. She likes to escape in her books."

Joel and Asher rose to their feet and greeted Kala.

Kala was tall and blonde. Her hair was long, almost to her waist. Her eyes were blue, and she looked at Joel and Asher, smiling. "Please don't get up for me." She took her seat next to her mother.

Asher returned to his food, but he occasionally glanced over at Kala. This for the moment took his thoughts away from his distrust of Clive. He had not had any interest in a woman, not until now. Kala was beautiful, and he wondered if she was spoken for, or would she have interest in him?

Asher continued to eat, looking at the chicken on his plate, and when he looked up, Kala was standing in front of him.

"Would you walk with me, young knight?"

Asher quickly rose to his feet. He bowed slightly and took Kala by the hand, and they walked though the banquet room and onto the large balcony overlooking the gardens.

Kala spoke first. "Did you know that when I arrived, I found out that every young lady in this castle only talks about you? Why is this so?"

Asher smiled, "They have little to do."

"They say you are the youngest knight ever to lead the knight's brigade, and that you have no fear and travel without any reserve to the northern border and now you are going again."

"I am not sure about going to the north. Joel has to make that decision. If he commands it, I will go."

"My father says there is important information that needs to be sent, although he won't tell me anything more. Before you go, would you spend some time with me and show me Regstar? I want to know more about this kingdom."

Asher smiled and said, "It will be my pleasure." Kala took his arm, and they returned to the dining hall.

The next day Asher met with Joel.

"We have an important message to be sent to Alnac. You will need to leave in the next couple of days. I am sending you alone, and I know the danger of this trip. You must stay off the main roads, which will take you longer but should be safer. Alnac is my brother-in-law, and he has sided with Rhodes against Salados. This is dangerous for Regstar. The message will be in code, and only Alnac can read it."

"Is this message from you, or is it from Clive?"

"From me. Clive will send a message also. His will also be in code, and I am not sure what it will say. I don't trust him and he is not to know that you have a second message from me to Alnac."

When Asher left Joel, he knew that he was wise indeed not to trust Clive. Perhaps he would find more about Clive when he visited Alnac.

The next day Asher met Kala and they rode out to visit the nearby village and forest. As they went from shop to shop, Kala showed some interest but was more content just to talk with Asher. They purchased some cheese, wine, and bread and rode to the nearby forest. They stopped their horses near a waterfall deep in the woods.

It was Kala who spoke first. "This is beautiful. How did you know this was here?"

"I was born in this kingdom and as a boy explored it all. There is very little that I don't know about this kingdom."

Kala smiled at his boast. "My mother says that there was a chance you were going to be king of this land because it was rumored that Joel wanted you to marry his daughter. Is this true?"

"I don't know. Donella and I were close as children, but we drifted apart when I started my training to become a knight. She has been gone now for over five years, and now I know nothing about her. I do know that Joel treats me like his son and for that I am honored."

"Tell me about Donella."

"I don't know much. Even she did not know who her mother was. When she was taken, Joel told me that her grandfather took her. We tried to follow and bring her back but could not find them."

Kala looked at Asher. "What do you remember about her?"

"She was fourteen when she was taken. She had dark brown hair and very dark brown eyes. She was beautiful, the kind of young lady you could not take your eyes from."

"Did you love her?"

Asher did not answer. His thoughts were far away trying to remember Donella as a fourteen year old girl, and what she might look like as a woman of twenty. Yes, he loved her. She was his friend, and if she had not been taken, she might have been even more.

"I don't know. We grew up together in the castle. When my mother and father were killed, Joel let me live in the castle."

"How were your parents killed?"

"They had gone to Centerville and were attacked by bandits on the way back. Everyone in the party was killed."

"Is this why you go out on patrol to hunt for bandits?"

Asher changed the subject. "Tell me about you and your parents?"

"Like you, I was raised in a castle. My father has been the minister of Rhodes for as long as I can remember. My mother is from the village of Torex. It is not far from Rhodes Castle. Her mother worked in the castle. She met my father there. After they were married, they lived in the castle, and that is my story."

Kala and Asher placed their bread and cheese on a rock close to the falls. They spoke very little during the meal, and when they finished, Asher spoke. "Why has your father come the Regstar?"

Kala looked surprised. She had not anticipated such a question. Her heart sank, and she answered with a question. "Is this why you agreed to show me the kingdom, to discuss politics?"

Asher smiled knowing the question was unfair. "You are right. I have no right to ask such a question." He extended his hands to her and pulled her to a standing position. "Let's walk around the lake." He held her hand as they followed the narrow trail that bordered the lake.

They would stop, smell the flowers and make small talk.

When they stopped he turned and faced her. "Will you be here when I return? I will be gone for several days, maybe even longer. I really like you and want to see you again. Tomorrow I will meet with your father in the morning, and in the afternoon I will meet with Joel. The next day I am leaving before sunrise."

Kala leaned over on Asher's shoulder and said, "I want to be here but don't know how long my father intends to stay. If I am gone, will you come to Rhodes to find me?"

He looked into her face and in a whisper said, "Yes."

Donella

* * * * * *

Donella and Evan had spent several days together visiting the village and exploring the countryside. Even through the kingdom had closed boundaries, it seemed to go on for miles.

One day while out riding they stopped their horses near a large oak tree that seemed to go up forever. Evan helped Donella from her horse, and they sat at the trunk of the large oak.

"Do you think you might one day want to leave this city and return to the outside world?" he asked.

"I might. I miss my father very much and now have so much more understanding of his love for my mother. I love it here, and my grandfather is so kind. Nevertheless, I have several years before I can even make such a decision. I will almost be thirty when this city becomes visible again. I can think about this later."

"Did you have someone special in the outside world?" he said with a shy grin.

She paused before she answered. "There was Asher. He was my childhood friend. We played together almost every day. He was my friend, but we were never lovers. He became busy with his training to become a knight, and we went our separate ways. Anyway he was fourteen when I left Regstar and he will be about twenty now. I would not know what he even looks like, and by the time I am able to get home he will be married."

"Home. You called Regstar your home. Is this not your home?"

"It is my home. I guess I have two homes, Reflection City and Regstar, my father's home and my mother's home. They are both part of me."

Evan took Donella by the hands. "Do you ever think this could become our home?"

Donella was not shocked by Evan's question. She knew by his actions that he was falling in love with her. She was just not sure if she was ready to make a commitment. She was not sure of her feelings for Evan. She liked him very much, and her answer was simple and to the point. "Maybe. I just need some time. Can we go riding again this week?"

He smiled and said, "Yes."

Asher

* * * *

Asher did not see Kala again before he was to leave. On Tuesday he met with Clive. When he entered the room, his feelings of distrust were stronger than ever.

"Come in and have a seat. We have much to discuss."

Asher took a seat in front of Clive. "I understand that you and my daughter have been seeing quite a lot of each other."

"Yes, she is a lovely young lady, but I don't think this is why you wanted to see me."

He looked at Asher with a grin. "It is not, but you know of a father's concern for his only daughter."

"I can only imagine. You have done well. She is a beautiful woman. She seems so happy and full of life. I can only hope that you will allow me to continue to see her once I return."

Clive turned his back to Asher. "Yes of course, she is very fond of you."

Clive went to the window and looked out. *I don't plan for you to ever come back. For you, my dear Asher, this is a one way trip.*

Clive turned back to Asher and reached into the desk pulling out a packet. "This is a dispatch to Alnac. It is my hope that this will help end the war of the northern kingdoms. It explains how Salados and Rhodes have made peace and marks out our plans to help bring the war to an end. I can't explain everything, but when Alnac gets these plans, he will know what to do."

Taking the dispatch, Asher left Clive and went to meet with King Joel. Joel was standing in front of a painting of Donella. "I wonder what has happened to her. She is now twenty years old. Look at the painting, she looks just like her mother. Losing them both has been almost more than I can bear."

Asher went to King Joel. "You are a wise king and we the people of Regstar are happy you have been our leader. You must be patient. When possible, I am going to get Donella and return her to this kingdom. This kingdom is where she belongs."

Joel turned to Asher. "Now to the business at hand. I have a message for Alnac. This is important. I don't trust Clive. It's important to give my message to Alnac first and make sure he reads it before you give him the message from Clive. Tell him that my message is in code. He will ask for the code, and you tell him it is the code of a brother and a sister. He will know what that means. Ask him if there is a message he wants you to bring to me, but it must be verbal. Tell him not to write anything down. When you start back, you must take care. There are those who don't want Alnac to send me any messages."

Asher looked at Joel and said, "I will do what you have commanded me to do."

Joel took Asher's hands and looked him in the eyes. "I am sending you on a dangerous mission. If there were anyone else I could trust I would not send you. Please take care."

Asher looked at Joel and smiled. "I know how you feel because I feel the same way. I will be careful. I will be back in about eight days." and with that said, he left the room and returned to his barracks. He wished he had time to see Kala once more, but time was short, and he needed rest for the long journey ahead.

The next morning he was on his way. As he left the castle he could smell the wood fires that were heating the homes and the castle. The air was cold, and frost covered most of the ground as his mount carried him through the gate and on the road to Alnac's camp. After about an hour on the road, he stopped and began to talk to his horse.

"You feel it too. We are being followed." He guided his horse to a grove of trees and waited. It was not long until he heard the sound of hooves and then he saw five mounted men.

So you are looking for me and now I am behind you. After the men had passed, he guided his horse back onto the road and followed the men for about half a mile. At that point he left the main road and continued his journey. *This will take longer, but at least I will be safe.*

As he traveled the narrow path with low hanging limbs and holes and rocks just about everywhere, he thought, *I don't know which is safer, the trail or the main road. You can get killed on either.*

Donella

* * * * * *

The sound of laughter and music filled the air. The fair was a once-a-year event and Donella had loved going each year when she lived in Regstar. She was seated in the royal tent and could see the jousting area. She heard the sound of trumpets which announced the next event. The knights entered the arena, but unlike in Regstar, the knights only carried wooden swords. Then she caught a glimpse of Evan. He was looking at her and smiling. He was so proud.

The first two knights entered the arena and began to fight with their wooden weapons.

They were skilled enough, but Donella thought to herself, *I hope this kingdom never comes under attack from the outside. If it does, we are all going to die.* She then laughed out loud. That was never going to happen.

Rue, who was seated next to her, smiled and said, "What is so funny?"

Donella looked up at her grandfather, who was seated higher than she was and said, "Nothing, I am just happy."

Next, Evan and other knight took the arena. She was surprised that Evan was very skilled. He bested his opponent very quickly.

I wonder if he would be a match for Asher. Surely he would be a knight by now. She had no idea that not only was Asher a knight, but a knight at this moment entrusted with a secret mission, a mission that had put his life in danger.

The next match brought two more knights into the arena, and it was not long until just two knights were left: Evan and another knight who was bigger.

Is this the end of Evan? she thought.

The match started and the larger knight had more skill, but Evan had more speed and after a very long match, Evan was standing over his opponent in victory. To the sound of cheering Evan approached Rue and Donella. Evan kneeled before Rue, and Rue placed a silver medal on a chain around his neck. Evan then rose to his feet and faced Donella.

She rose to her feet, came to Evan and gently kissed him on the cheek. She smiled and said, "Good luck in the next event. I hope you become grand champion."

The rest of the events passed quickly. Evan was skilled in all areas of combat and won each of his events. When he was awarded the medal as grand champion, he approached Donella and she took his arm. They left the arena and made their way to the banquet hall.

Once they were seated, waiting for the food to be served, Donella spoke first. "You are very skilled, and I am so proud of you."

"I have been trained by the great knight Brumble. He says if my skill continues to improve, I might someday accompany him outside this city. He tells me that fighting with a wooden sword is a lot different from fighting with one of steel. We have steel swords that we wear when in full gear, but we have only trained with the ones of wood."

Donella thought to herself, *I hope I never see a time when a steel sword is needed.* But she knew outside Reflection City, steel was used in war, but it was also used to keep the peace.

Asher

* * * *

It took Asher four days to reach the camp of Alnac. One day longer than if he had stayed on the main road. As Asher approached the camp, he could see smoke beyond it. *There must have been a battle,* he thought to himself. He was glad he lived in Regstar which was maintaining its peace with Salados and Rhodes.

As he neared the camp he heard these words: "Halt, who goes there?"

He stopped his horse. "I am Asher, from Regstar. I carry a message from King Joel to Alnac."

Two knights with their swords drawn approached him and stopped on both sides of his horse. Asher placed his hand on his sword but did not draw it.

"Do you have any identification?" one of the knights said.

Asher reached into his bag, pulled out the message to Alnac, and pointed to King Joel's seal. Quickly the knights put their swords back in their sheaths and said, "Follow us." They then led Asher through the camp.

When they arrived at Alnac's tent, they stopped outside.

The tent was large and was of red. He then looked around and noticed that all the tents were red and there was no difference in Alnac's tent and the rest of tents in camp.

Asher thought to himself, *Very clever. If this camp is attacked they would have trouble finding the king's tent.*

After a short time a man came out and motioned for Asher to enter. When he went into the tent, he found himself face to face with Alnac, king of Arsi. He was tall, and he had a black beard. Asher could tell this man was a skilled fighter and would be a match for most men.

"Well how is my brother-in-law Joel?" Alnac said with a smile.

"He is fine. He sends you his greeting."

"Has he ever had any word from or about Donella? Did you know that I have never seen her? Para often would talk about her. She said she looked exactly like her mother. I know Joel has never gotten over this loss."

Asher studied the face of Alnac and could tell this was a regret in his life, to have never met his niece. "There has never been any word, but Joel looks forward to the day that the city will reappear. He knows how to get in, but the waiting is slowly killing him. Six years have passed and there are still nine to go."

"Why has Joel sent you to me?"

"I carry two messages from Regstar, one from King Joel and one from Clive, minister of Rhodes. King Joel insisted that you read his message first. It is in code, and he says you will know how to decode it if you use the brother and sister code. He says you will know what that means."

Asher handed both dispatches to Alnac. "Do you want me to leave you alone with these messages?"

"Yes, go with my servant, his name is Mason, he will see that you are fed and give you a place to stay."

Alnac called for Mason, and he quickly entered. "Take Asher and give him food and drink and a place to stay."

Mason motioned for Asher to follow him and the two men left the tent.

Alnac took the dispatch from Joel and smiled. Brother and sister code was a simple but effective code that was created by Para and Joel to communicate things that they didn't want their parents or anyone else to know. Para for fun had taught him the code but had never used it.

It took Alnac about an hour to decode the message. And then read it.

Alnac, your life and kingdom are in danger. The kingdoms of Salados and Rhodes are making a secret peace. Both our kingdoms are in danger. Regstar has not maintained a great army. Your army is not up to full strength. I have sent this message with my best knight. He has two messages. The other is from Clive. Don't trust that message. This is from a reliable source. I have started to strengthen my army. I don't want to go to war but I feel I must be ready.

Alnac was alarmed and not sure what to do. He had sided with Rhodes against Salados. He had fought at the border of Salados for many years. What plans did Salados and Rhodes have for his kingdom? Would they attack Regstar as King Joel feared?

Alnac took out the second message. It was coded in the military code of Rhodes. He had read many messages from Rhodes and could read it without decoding it.

Alnac, This message carries the great seal of Rhodes and can be trusted. Salados and Rhodes are meeting to make peace. They want Arsi to be a part of this peace. There will be a meeting of the three kingdoms in about three days when the moon is full at Diamond River near Desert Point. Choose fifty of your best knights to come with you. Fly three flags for safe passage across Salados. Two white and a middle flag of blue.

Alnac was confused. Didn't Joel's message give him the same information? Joel said not to trust the message from Clive, but they included Arsi in the peace, and he wanted this. He thought of his wife Para and longed to see her. This could be his chance.

The next day Asher started his long journey back to Regstar. He met with Alnac and asked if he had a message for King Joel.

"Tell him I am going to take a chance on peace."

What does he mean that he is going to take a chance on peace? "You take care and remember that neither Joel or I trust Clive." Asher then left Alnac, mounted his horse and started for home.

The Witch

* * * * * * *

Para was alone in her library looking in the stacks for a book of poetry. Suddenly she felt pain run through her heart and she sank to her knees. When the pain left her, she rose to her feet, rang the bell, and was soon greeted by a voice.

"My lady, are you Okay?" It was Gemma, her maid and friend.

"Go and find Epson. Tell him I need him."

Gemma started to leave the library, and there stood Epson.

"I am here my Queen. Gemma leave us."

When Gemma had left the room, Epson turned to Para. "I felt it too. Alnac is in grave danger."

"Why do we feel it now? Alnac has been in danger ever since he left Arsi. We are at war. Why now?"

Epson took Para by the hands and looked her in the eyes. "What do you feel now besides danger?"

"Betrayal. We must warn him."

Para and Epson were not even sure where Alnac's camp was located and the day after Asher had left, Alnac assembled his most trusted knights, gave them instructions, and started to Diamond Point. The trip would take about two days. He had the three flags, two white and a middle flag of blue leading his convoy so that they would be safe when they entered enemy territory. As he mounted his horse he turned toward Dorian, the first knight of Arsi. He had been with Alnac from the beginning of the war. He was a skilled fighter and was loyal to the king. Unlike Alnac, he did not like war.

"You are to stay here. Take command. If I do not return in six days, move the troops back to the border."

"I feel I need to be by your side, but I will do as you say. If you are not back in six days, I will move troops to the border and set up camp at the pass."

Alnac turned his horse north. As Alnac rode out of camp, he questioned his decision. *Was Joel right? Could Salados and Rhodes be trusted?*

After two days of travel his convoy encountered the first troops from Salados. When they saw his troop of knights, they waved three flags, two white and one blue. Alnac now knew he was expected and the journey to Diamond Point would be safe.

Time passed quickly, and they saw no more knights from Salados.

On the next day they were at Diamond River, Desert Point. His troop of knights was greeted by troops from Salados and Rhodes. Alnac noticed his troops were greatly outnumbered. He dismounted his horse, and there standing in front of him were Andrew, king of Salados, and Karnac, king of Rhodes.

Andrew spoke first. "Welcome, King Alnac, we have met many times in battle, but this is the first time we have met in peace."

Alnac took his hand. "I hope we shall have many more such meetings." He turned to Karnac. "Greetings friend. When I got the message from Clive, I was unsure of this meeting, but now that you are here, I feel very good. It is my hope that we can create a lasting peace."

Karnac took Alnac's hand. "I know that you must be tired after such a long journey. We have prepared a tent for you down by the river. My servant will show you where it is. Your men can camp near the trees about your tent. We shall meet in the morning. I will send a servant to guide you."

The two men smiled at each other and Alnac nodded to Andrew then left with the servant.

That night Alnac was tired. He thought of Para. He wanted to see her, and there was something he needed to tell her. He stretched out on his cot and quickly went to sleep. During the night, Para appeared to him in a dream. Her voice had concern. "You have been betrayed. Wherever you are, you must quickly go to safety."

Alnac suddenly woke from the dream to see a large knight standing over him with a sword pointed to his heart. Before he could move, the knight plunged the sword into his heart. With his last breath he said, "Gwen, I am sorry."

The next morning Para knew that her husband was dead. Throughout the day she had to stop whatever she doing and cry.

What could she do? She was the queen of Arsi, but now she was also ruler. She decided not to tell the people of Alnac's death until the news came from the war. Five days later it came. It was from Dorian, second in command to Alnac. The message was simple:

Alnac is dead. Salados and Rhodes are no longer at war. It is my fear that they will attack Arsi. I am moving the army back to Arsi.

That night, Para met with Epson. "I need to be more powerful than I am. I need magic to protect this kingdom and to avenge Alnac."

Epson looked at Para. "You did not ask me to protect your kingdom. Why?"

"I know you would never use your magic in such a way. This is something I must do."

Epson took Para by the hand. "You have all the magic you need to protect yourself and this kingdom, but your cannot use magic for revenge. It will change you forever. You will become a witch, and your focus will change from doing good to doing evil."

Dorian

٭ ٭ ٭ ٭ ٭

Dorian was now the head of the army of Arsi. He felt it was his duty to move his army back to the castle to protect the people and most of all to protect Para. Like Alnac, he had been fighting for years against Salados. All the fighting had taken place inside the kingdom of Salados with neither side gaining any advantage. Now, with Rhodes out of the picture the fighting would shift to Arsi. His spies had told him that the army of Rhodes was moving toward Regstar. Dorian saw this as both good and bad. He would only have to face one army at Arsi, but he feared that Regstar would not be able to defend itself against Rhodes.

As he sat on his horse at the head of the army, he thought of Para. She was now the ruler of Arsi. She would have to rely on his counsel. He had only met her once. Several years ago, he and Alnac had returned to Arsi, and the three of them had eaten dinner together. He could not forget that evening. She was a beautiful woman, and he could not take his eyes from her. Her blonde hair, her beautiful skin, and her tall slender body made her look like a goddess. He thought to himself that he should not be thinking of her this way at this time. He had other concerns. How would she take to him as a leader? Would she even keep him as head of the army? Of course she would. She knew nothing of the military. As he made the trek back to Arsi, he started to plan his defense of the castle.

When the army of Arsi marched into the castle, there was no cheering. The people were quiet. A powerful army was moving toward them, and they had every right to be scared.

Dorian dismounted his horse, gave it to his squire and went to meet with Para. When he entered the castle, he was met by Para's servant.

"She is in the chapel, and she is expecting you."

As Dorian walked toward the chapel, he wondered how he should approach her. Should he console her about the death of Alnac? He was not sure.

When he entered the chapel, he could see Para seated on the front pew. He went directly to her.

"Your majesty," he said.

When she spoke, her words shocked him. "I have a plan."

Joel

* * *

When the news of the betrayal reached Regstar, Joel was outraged. The peace was surely going to be broken. He knew that Andrew was marching to Arsi, and he would have no choice but to join forces with his sister. She would have to be protected at all cost. He did not know how long he had or how many men he could send to her aid. He could not lead the men because he would be needed to protect Regstar. As he pondered his next move, he was informed that Clive wanted to meet with him.

"Send him in."

As Clive entered the room, Joel could sense the power that Clive was feeling.

"What is it that you want?"

"I don't want anything, but Rhodes wants your kingdom."

Joel moved closer to Clive and looked into his eyes and said, "I could have you arrested and executed this very day. I could put your daughter and wife in prison and you stand there telling me Rhodes wants my kingdom."

"My wife and daughter have already left your castle and are on the road home. As for me, I have something to bargain for my life."

"And what could that be?"

"Andrew is moving his army on Arsi as we speak. Alnac's army is weak, and Andrew's army has been reinforced with knights and archers from Rhodes. Arsi will fall very quickly. Rhodes is moving toward your border, and you can't send troops that would get there in time. What I have to offer is the life of your sister."

Joel's anger almost overtook his judgment. "Get out of my castle, and get off my land."

Clive turned and walked away. He was free to return to Rhodes.

Para

. . . .

Dorian looked at Para, still shocked by what she had said.

"My Queen, I have a plan for the defense of the castle. We have food and water and can stave off any attack for several days. This will give King Joel time to reinforce us and then we can drive Andrew from our land."

"You and Alnac have been gone forever. You and my husband abandoned this castle, and you know nothing about how much food and water are here. We would be lucky to last two days."

"We could use the time we have to bring in food and water. You must let me guide you in this matter."

Para did not answer but thought back to her last meeting with Epson. She knew that Epson had left the castle, and her power had increased. She did not know if Epson had increased her power or if it had increased because of the death of Alnac. All she knew is she now had power, and she was going to use it. She would protect Arsi and she would then seek revenge on Salados and Rhodes.

She looked up at Dorian. "King Andrew is not going to set one foot on Arsi soil. How many archers do we have?"

Dorian was not sure how to answer her. Should he tell her or continue to argue for his plan to protect the castle?

"My Lady..."

She stopped him in mid sentence. "How many archers do we have?"

"My Lady, Andrew is only about four days away. We must make plans to defend this castle."

"Dorian, do not underestimate me. How many archers do we have?"

"About two hundred."

"How many arrows do each of the archers carry?"

"Twenty, but could have twenty-five if needed."

"They will be needed. Assemble the archers. We are moving to High Yellow Pass as quickly as possible."

"The army of Andrew will have defenses against an arrow attack. They carried shields, and they can see arrows coming. There are defenses in which several soldiers can get together and surround themselves with shields where no arrow can get through."

"I know that," she said.

Dorian started to protest, but Para rose to her feet and said, "Just do it."

"We cannot defend High Yellow Pass with just two hundred archers. The pass is too wide. Andrew will outflank us with his ground troop and knight support. It is too great of a gamble."

"We will have the high ground and that is all we need. Do not stand here and argue with me. Do as you have been commanded, or do I need to send for Bailee?"

Bailee was second in command. He too was an able knight and like Dorian had been very loyal to Alnac. Dorian knew that if he did not do what the queen had ordered, Bailee would.

"Your lady, I will assembly the archers. We will be ready in about four hours."

In two days, two hundred archers were two deep and spread across the high end of the pass.

When Andrew and his men came into bow range the archers would be about one hundred feet higher and would be just out of range of the Salados archers.

In the distance Queen Para and Dorian could see the vast army of Andrew.

Andrew could also see the archers on the high part of the pass. He knew that his archers would not do him any good in the battle, and he called his leaders together and said, "We cannot use our archers at the start of the battle. Move the infantry forward, and when they are in the range of the archers, charge them. Make sure they are prepared for the arrow attack. Move our archers in behind the infantry. Once the infantry attacks move the archers into bow range. We will then move our cavalry to the right and left of their flanks and engulf them."

Para could see the army moving closer and closer. "Bailee, have one of your archers send a flaming arrow to mark the distance of our range."

"A flaming arrow will not shoot as far as a regular arrow. It will fall about one hundred feet short."

"That will tell me what I need to know. Make it so."

Para watched as the arrow landed and could see that the enemy was within about three hundred feet from the bow range. She walked out in front of the bow men and raised her arms uttering words that no one could understand. The soldiers of Salados were getting closer, they were almost in range.

Para again raised her arms and repeated the chant.

Dorian and Bailee were almost in shock. A fog began to rise at the feet of the infantry of Salados. When they were within bow range the fog was well above their heads and they were going into battle blind. They could not even see the man next to them. Para turned to Bailee. "Turn your archers loose."

The first wave of arrows that fell into fog was followed by screams of pain and death. Wave after wave of arrows fell on the confused army.

In the fog, Andrew was not sure what to do. He took his knights and charged straight up the hill hoping to break the archers' ranks.

Again, wave after wave of arrows rained down into the fog and on Andrew's army.

Dorian raised his arm and waved to the archers to stop. Para looked out on the bank of fog. The sound was that of a defeated army with moans coming from every direction.

As the fog lifted, Dorian, Bailee, and Para could see an army in ruin. The men who were not wounded were helping those who were wounded flee the battlefield. Para walked down to the edge of carnage and there she saw Andrew with two arrows in his chest. Para walked up to the dying king and quietly said, "This was not revenge for you killing my husband. It was me protecting the people of my land."

Dorian watched as the army of Salados retreated back north. Their king was dead, but he knew that Geoffrey would want to avenge his father. *We have traded one enemy for another,* he thought. He estimated that Salados had lost about four hundred men in the battle. When they reorganize they would still be the most powerful army in the land. He turned to Para. "We must keep this pass guarded at all times. I fear the worst is yet to come."

Asher Is Wounded

Asher had left Alnac's camp unaware of the betrayal. He was on his way back to Regstar riding at a slow pace to rest his horse. He let his mind drift back to Kala. *Would she still be in Regstar?* He thought of how lovely she was and how she made him feel. If there were peace between Salados and Rhodes, he could go to Rhodes to visit her. Did she feel about him the way he was beginning to feel about her?

Suddenly he felt a strong pain in his left leg. He looked down and saw the arrow in his thigh. He looked up, and he was surrounded by four men all with swords and one with a bow. Before they reached him, he quickly drew his sword, and with one mighty blow one of the men was dead. The other four attacked him, pulled him from his horse, but he then quickly regained his footing before they could kill him, and two more of the five attackers lay in front of him dead. The other two were running for their lives. Asher pulled out his knife and quickly threw it into the calf of one of the fleeing attackers, bringing him to his knees. The last of the attacking men escaped.

Asher walked over to the attacker with his knife in the back of his leg and with his sword pushed him face first to the ground. He pointed his sword to the back of the man's neck.

"Why, I can see by the way you are dressed that you are soldiers from Rhodes."

The captive man said nothing, and Asher pushed the point of his blade about one half inch into the skin on the back of his neck. Blood began to flow.

"We were ordered to kill you before you could return to Regstar. Alnac is dead. Rhodes and Salados will take both Arsi and Regstar. I beg of you, take this information in place of my life."

Asher pulled his knife from the back of the captive's leg and said, "Get up and go."

Quickly the bleeding man jumped up and limped off into the brush.

Asher could feel a pain in his leg, and he looked down and saw the arrow. He pulled it from his leg, mounted his horse, and rode to a nearby lake. He had lost a lot of blood, and he felt sick and weak. With the strength he had left, he doctored his wound, ate some dried beef, and drank water from the lake and then went to sleep.

The next morning he was too weak to mount his horse so he stayed by the lake and rested. He was worried for Regstar and Joel. He looked at his leg which was still bleeding. He closed his eyes and again went back to sleep. When he woke up, it was still morning, but he did not realize that he had been asleep for two days. He felt stronger and cleaned his wound. It did not look good, but it was no longer bleeding. He got up and tried to walk. He was in much pain, and when he made it to his horse, he found he did not have the strength to mount. He made it back to his campfire and resigned himself to spending the remainder of the day resting.

That night he lay in front of his fire. It was a peaceful night, and he watched the sparks float gently into the sky and disappear. He watched the refection of the moon dance on the water. He began to think of the story that Joel had told him of seeing the city reflected in the water. He remembered being a boy and seeing the city disappear. He thought of Donella and wished he could bring her back to help Joel get strong again. Suddenly the reflection of the moon disappeared. Where did it go? Then he realized the moon had just gone behind a cloud and was really still there.

He thought, *It is really still there.*

Asher quickly sat up. "Is it possible that only the reflection of the city is gone but the city is still there?"

The next morning, even with the pain in his leg, he continued his trip back to Regstar. He was excited to tell Joel about his observation and what it might mean. He arrived in Regstar three days later.

Joel

※　※　※

Before Asher had returned from Alnac's camp, Joel had already received the news of Andrew's defeat at the Battle of High Yellow Pass. He did not rejoice at the death of Andrew but was relieved that he would not have to face both Salados and Rhodes. His forward observers had told him that Rhodes had withdrawn their troops from the border, and there was now an uneasy peace between them. He did not understand why Rhodes had withdrawn their army from the border. Maybe it was because of the death of Andrew, and they were unsure of their strength.

The news of Para's magic was shocking. He had had no idea she had acquired such power. In Arsi they were calling her a saint; in Salados she was referred to as a witch.

Joel had sent word to his sister that they should meet, and she was now on her way to Regstar. There was much to discuss. With the death of Alnac, Donella was now in line to be the queen of three different kingdoms, Regstar, Arsi, and Reflection City, but she could not be contacted.

Joel could hear the excitement outside his window. He looked outside and could see Asher approaching. Joel was excited too. Asher was his son, not by birth, but nevertheless his son, and he was relieved he was back.

When Asher entered Joel's chamber, he knew the theory about Reflection City would have to wait. His concern was for Regstar and the attack that might come from Rhodes.

"Sir, I have news."

"So do I," Joel said. "I think I know your news so you hear mine. Alnac is dead. Andrew has attacked Arsi. His army has been defeated and he has been killed. Rhodes has moved its army away from our border, and I am waiting for Clive to make a new peace."

Joel then looked at Asher. "Is your news any different?"

"No, my news is outdated and not nearly as good."

Looking down at Asher, Joel could see the hole in Asher's trousers and the blood-stained material. "You have been wounded." He turned and called a servant. "Go and bring the royal physician, quickly."

A few minutes later Asher was stretched out on the couch in Joel's room, and the doctor was looking at his leg.

"How is it?" Joel asked.

The doctor did not look up. "Not too good. It is a deep wound, and there is some infection. He will need rest. Too much movement and it could start it bleeding again." The doctor finished dressing the wound and said, "Try not to move too much. You need lots of rest."

After the doctor left, Joel said to Asher, "My sister is on her way here. The defeat of Andrew may not be a military victory."

"What do you mean?"

"Some are calling Para a witch, others a saint, but whatever she is called, she has the power of a wizard. You can stay here, and when you feel like it, you can be moved to your quarters."

Joel left, and Asher quickly went to sleep. He had a dream of Kala. He awoke and found himself still thinking about her. Did the betrayal of Regstar and Joel end any chance they had to be together? He decided now was not the time to worry about this. He did wonder if she was coming back to Regstar with Clive.

When he had been moved back into his quarters and he was on his bed, he heard a knock at the door. It was Joel with a servant. "I am going to leave Karlo with you. That way you won't have to move too much, and that leg can heal up."

"I am not staying. I am leaving Regstar."

Joel almost laughed. "Do you think that is a good idea?" Joel did not think that Asher was serious. "Your wound is not good and I remember the physician saying that there was some infection. Are you going to find Kala?"

"No, I am going to find Donella."

"How is that even possible? Do you have a fever?"

Asher told Joel of his experience watching the moon. "Did anyone say the city would disappear?" he asked the king. "Maybe it is just invisible."

The king's eyes became bright and hope returned to him.

"If you have your key and you said you had a drawing of the city on the rocks I will see if I can find the door and see if the key will open it and let me in."

Joel was excited. "I must go with you."

"No, you must not for several reasons. The first is you need to meet with Queen Para. We don't know how long this will take. Clive is coming back to Regstar, and we need a sound peace. Secondly, they are not to going let Donella go. They know who you are, and if there is a fight, better me than you. And lastly, Donella may not want to come back. She has been there for six years. It is now her home. There is a chance she is married. Also the people of the city will be able to see you. They will not be able to see me. I will be able to move about inside the city freely."

Joel was quiet for several minutes and then said, "You are right. I am needed here, and you may be able to enter the city and no one be the wiser. They would be able to see me. What all do you need?"

"I need that key, and a drawing of the city on the rocks, and I will also need a small mirror."

"It is a couple of days to the lake. I will have the servant prepare food for six days. Two to get you to the lake, two if you need food inside the city and two for your return here." Then he thought. "If you have Donella with you, you will need extra food on the return."

Joel left, but in about an hour he returned with the provisions and the drawing. He took the key from around his neck and gave it Asher. "The mirror is with the provisions. Go find out if the theory is true, and if it is bring Donella back to us."

Donella And Evan

* * * * * * * * * * *

In the days that followed the tournament, Donella and Evan spent almost every day together. She found she liked him very much and wondered if marrying him would be in the best interest of Reflection City. Then she thought, *Is this the best reason to marry a person? Shouldn't there be more?* She knew he was going to ask for her hand any day now, and she must be prepared with her answer. She knew that she would not have to give her answer to Evan, but to her grandfather. Custom would dictate that Evan go to Rue first. She had both dread and excitement and her thoughts turned back to her father. *What has happened to him in the past six years? Is he well, has he remarried?* She didn't know, and she started to cry.

She was in the garden, and she thought she was alone but Evan had entered and was quickly coming toward her. When he was about ten feet away, he stopped. He could see that she was crying. "Are you alright?" he asked.

She looked at him and smiled through her tears. "I miss my father and wish I could see him. It seems so unfair that I am here and he is so alone."

Evan came closer and took her in his arms. "Would you leave Reflection City if you were given a choice?"

Her answer was a simple one. "I don't know."

After her tears had dried, they sat beneath the willow tree which extended into the reflection pool in the garden.

"Tell me what it is like outside Reflection City. You have told me some things, but tell me more. What is it you miss?"

"What I miss most is my family. I miss my father and my aunt. I miss knowing what has happened to them." She leaned over on his shoulder. "Outside these walls is the worst, best, most horrible, wonderful place you can image. There is evil, but also good. You know the weather here is always warm and the rain is a gentle rain. Outside Reflection City we sometimes would have gentle rain, but sometimes it would be a storm. The wind would blow and lightning would strike the ground, and there would be loud thunder."

"What is thunder, and what is lightning?"

"Thunder is a loud sound you hear when lightning strikes, and lighting is a powerful light that flashes across the sky. Sometimes it hits the ground and it, causes fire."

"That must be awful."

"No, it's just nature. You know, I kind of miss the seasons."

"Tell me about seasons?"

"It is kind of hard to explain. There are four. In spring everything is green, and it rains a lot. The air is cool. In summer it rains but not as much, and the air is hot and sometimes the green turns to brown. In fall the air starts to turn cool again, and all the leaves get this wonderful color before they fall to the ground. In winter the air turns cold, and snow covers the ground."

"What is snow?"

"That is enough questions for one day. I miss my family and my friends."

"Do you miss your friend Asher?"

Donella noticed the bit of jealousy and laughed. "I told you he was a childhood friend, and I don't think I would know him if he walked into this garden."

Evan smiled at her answer. "I need to talk to your grandfather."

Reflection City

* * * * * * * * * *

It took Asher two days to find the village that was near Reflection Lake. It was already night when he arrived.

The village was about one mile from the lake. He would keep the purpose of his trip a secret, so when he found Silas, the leader of the village, he told him who he was and that he was a knight in the army of King Joel.

Silas was delighted to meet him.

"How is Joel? It has been a while since I have seen him. He used to come here often but not so much anymore."

"The king is well. There are some problems with Salados and Rhodes so you may see some troop movement toward the borders. If fighting breaks out and you are concerned about the safety of your people, move them to the castle."

"I don't think we will need to do that, but I shall keep your offer in mind. Is this the reason you have come to our village?"

"No, I have come to explore the forest and rocks around Reflection Lake. I have been in battle and was wounded. King Joel sent me to heal. He said the lake seemed to have healing power, but the truth is he knew if I stayed at the castle, I would be working and preparing the knights for a possible invasion."

"I don't think the lake water is going to help you heal any faster. Joel is right, you need to lie on the bank of the lake and rest. Yes, rest is what you need." Silas looked at Asher. "You are dressed like a knight."

"This is where I need your help. I want to leave my horse here. I want to change my clothes and dress like a hunter. I will take only my sword with me for protection. I will also need some help getting to the lake."

"When do you want to leave?"

"In the morning."

That night he thought of the story that King Joel had told him and made his plans. He placed several small items in his pack. The most important was the mirror.

The next day several of the men in the village took Asher to the lake. They had loaned him a horse, and when they arrived, they said their goodbyes and asked when he wanted to leave.

"Not for several days. I hope that when my leg heals I can walk back to your village."

Later that morning, he climbed the rocks where King Joel had drawn the door. It was there, just where Joel had said it would be. He took the key from around his neck, gave it a kiss for luck, put in the hole, and turned it. The door opened, and Asher was now inside Reflection City. He slowly worked his way down the mountain and soon, like Joel, he could hear the sounds of the marketplace but could see no people. He remembered that Joel said that they could not see him. He took his small mirror out of his pack and turned his back to the sound of the people. He looked through the mirror and could see hundreds of people in the marketplace, and they were happy buying and selling their goods. *If only all marketplaces were like this,* he thought. He always hated the marketplaces in Regstar because people were always trying to get the best price for their goods and always thought they might be cheated. He would explore this city. As he walked through the marketplace. He had some trouble finding his way using a mirror and sometimes to their surprise he would bump into a person to hear them say "Excuse me," and then see no one.

Inside the Great City

* * * * * * * * * * * * * *

As Asher traveled about the city he grew more and more fond of Reflection City. The sounds he heard were sounds of joy and contentment. After exploring the marketplace and palace garden, he went to the forest which was about a mile from the palace. He found several tall trees near a stream. There he made his camp. All the movement had made him tired. He checked his wound, and his leg was starting to bleed again. He took fresh bandages from his pack and redressed the wound. He needed rest, and he needed more time to heal. As he stretched out against a large tree, he began to wonder how he was going to find Donella. If he found her, would she be willing to leave with him? Could she leave? It was not time for the reflection. As he leaned against the tree, he took out the mirror and scanned the countryside to see if any people were nearby. He saw none. He then looked into the mirror at his own image. He had not shaved since he had left with the messages for Alnac. He had a full beard, but it was short. He thought to himself. *Donella will not recognize me, because I don't recognize myself.*

He had spent way too much time moving and not giving his leg time to rest. He looked, and his leg was bleeding, and he felt very weak. As he sat against the large tree, he thought, *I think I am going to be sick.* He then fell asleep.

Donella loved to take long rides in the country. She needed to think. Evan was going to see her grandfather and she knew why. What would her answer be? She loved this land. She wished that her father had never taken her mother from it but had remained with her. Her mother might still be alive, and she would have a family.

Her grandfather was a good man. Her father and grandfather had never met. If they had, maybe something could have been done to bring the two worlds she loved together. *"I am a prisoner here, but if I were not, I think I would stay.*

As she rode back to the palace, she decided she would stop at the forest. She would let her horse rest, eat a lunch, and enjoy the breeze. She dismounted from her horse, and suddenly she saw him asleep against the rock. This man was not of her kingdom. She didn't recognize Asher, her childhood friend. He was so tall and wore a beard. She was afraid, but she didn't run. She studied him. He was extremely good looking. Then she saw that he had sword made from metal next to him. She knew he was not from this land. Why was he here? How was he here? It was not time for the reflection.

Asher awoke and saw her staring at him. He knew that it was Donella. She was a beautiful woman and not the child he had grown up with. He also recognized her fear, and that she didn't know who he was.

"Who are you?" she said, but it barely came from her lips she was so afraid.

"I am stranger in this land, "he said," I am resting in your forest. I am returning from the northern lands. I am wounded. I need time to heal. I don't know how I got here." He didn't think now was the time to be completely honest.

"Give me time to heal and I will leave." He started to get up but was too weak.

"How can you leave? You don't even know how you got here."

He looked at her. She was tall, perhaps as much as five eight. Her hair was dark brown, almost black. She had a beautiful figure and was wearing a black riding dress.

He stood up but fell back down. He smiled. "As I said, I need a few days to let this wound heal."

She studied him. He was so familiar.

"You can't stay, this land is forbidden to those of the outside. If you are discovered, it will mean trouble."

She walked closer to him. "How are you injured?"

"You know that walking in front of an arrow thing. It happens."

She did not find his attempt at humor funny. It just confirmed that he was from outside the wall, and outside the wall was cruel and dangerous.

She stopped for a moment and asked, "Could the people of this land see you?"

"No they could not. I came through the market, bumped into a few people, and they were more surprised than me."

He told her that he could hear people, but she was the only person he could see. He asked her why she was visible although he knew the answer. She told him that she was born outside the kingdom. This is why they could see each other.

She sat down beside him and somehow knew she had nothing to fear.

"You have a sword and a knife. You won't need those here. If you are discovered, people can't see you. All you need to do is hide and stay away from anything that would reflect your image, water, mirrors, something like that." She thought for a moment and then said, "You must stay for a little while. You must let your wounds heal, and I must know of Regstar."

She looked at him and said, "I must go. I will return tomorrow, bring food, and tend to your wound. Don't leave until we can figure this out."

He started to answer her but when he moved the world started to spin. He closed his eyes, and everything went dark.

She looked at him and saw he had passed out, and that his leg was bleeding. She really didn't know what to do. She needed help, but could not trust anyone not to turn him in to her grandfather. She made him as comfortable as possible. On her horse she had some wine left from her meal. She brought it to him and held up his head and poured it on his lips. He instantly swallowed down several ounces of the wine. She laid his head back down. "I hope you don't die until I can return." She went to her horse and rode away.

Para

* * * *

As Para and her caravan moved toward King Joel's castle, she had time to reflect on the past several days. She had lost her husband, won a major battle, and become a powerful priestess of magic. She thought about Epson's warning about not to using her magic for revenge, because if she did, it would turn dark.

She had also noticed that those around her were now acting differently. Were they afraid of her? In her mind, she was no different.

That night in her camp, she sent for Dorian. When he arrived, she was sitting in front of a mirror combing her blonde hair. He had the urge to take her in his arms. She was so beautiful, but she did not look at him.

"Tell me about my husband. Why did he return to Arsi so seldom? Was he not in love with me?"

Dorian looked down at his feet. "How could he not be?"

She turned and looked at him. "I saw him only five times after we married. He came home only five times and spent only five months with me. He came home and took me. Was this because the only purpose I served was to produce him an heir?"

Dorian struggled to find the right words. "Alnac had a passion for the war. It consumed him. To answer your question, no he did not come often, but that does not mean he did not love you."

Para turned in her seat and faced Dorian. She had on a white dressing gown, and the top of her breasts were slightly exposed. She knew that Dorian was looking at her. "Did he have other women?"

He was not sure how to answer her. "Most fighting men do when they are away from home for long periods of time." He knew she already knew the answer.

"Did you?"

"I am an unmarried man. I think the questions you ask are unfair. Alnac, your husband and my friend, is dead. Let him remain dead. I will answer no more questions."

She looked at him and said, "Have you forgotten who I am?" Then she turned back to the mirror. She knew this was not like her, and the harshness of her voice made even her uncomfortable.

"You are my Queen, but I will answer no more questions. I hope we can become friends. I will serve you in every way, but not this way."

She continued brushing her hair. One question more. "Did he have one woman that was special?"

Dorian turned and walked out of the tent.

Para assessed what she had learned from the conversation. She knew that her husband had other women, and one was special. She could tell that Dorian had a desire for her and wanted even more.

Donella

* * * * * *

The next day Donella found Asher where she had left him. He was still asleep, but for a moment she thought that he might be dead. She gave him a gentle shake, and he awoke. He was quiet, and she could tell he was very sick. She gave him water and offered him something to eat.

"I don't think I can eat," he said.

"You must, you have to get your strength back, and the wound has to heal." She helped him pull down his pants, and she took the bandage from the wound.

"The wound is bad. We don't see many wounds here, but I know that it is bad. What is your name?"

He looked at her, her dark hair falling on the bare skin of her shoulders. He knew she had no idea who he was so he decided not to tell her anything. "I am Jason."

She doubted that Jason was his name but accepted his answer. "And where are you from Jason?" She continued to clean the wound. She had brought fresh bandages and quickly dressed the wound.

He knew he could not tell her he was from Regstar. "I am from the kingdom of Arsi."

"So you know Queen Para and King Alnac."

"Yes." He was not sure how much he should tell her. "You said you were not born here, where are you from?"

"Regstar, I was born in Regstar."

"How did you get here?" He knew they were playing games with neither wanting to tell the other very much.

"It is a long story, and I don't want to tell it to you. Tell me what is happening outside this city."

"So you can ask questions and expect answers, and I cannot."

"I know it seems unfair, but this is a special place. No one leaves to bring information from the outside world. We never get any news. The people living here don't care. They were all born here. I was not. There are people I care about living outside the walls. Please give me some information."

She was about to cry and he said, "Are you a prisoner here?"

"No, it's not like that. If I could leave I would not. So please tell me what you can about what is going on outside the walls."

He looked at her. He wanted to take her in his arms and hold her as he told her the latest news from Arsi. "If you are not willing to leave, are you sure you want the news of Arsi?"

"Yes."

He started to tell her the news. "Salados and Rhodes had been fighting for years and years, and somehow they formed an alliance and decided to attack both Regstar and Arsi."

Her heart began to race, and she was now scared for the safety of her father and her aunt.

Asher could see that she was now shaking. "Are you sure you want me to go on?"

"I am alright." She gathered her composure. "Please go on."

"King Alnac had been an ally of Rhodes for at least several years, but they tricked him and murdered him in the peace camp. King Andrew led his army against Arsi, but he did not know that Queen Para was a witch, wizard, or whatever and she led her archers to defeat Andrew's army and kill him. She is on her way to meet with King Joel and the Minister of Rhodes to discuss a peace."

Without asking, she now knew that King Joel and Queen Para were alright, and she began to relax. She looked at him with concern. "How can you know all this? Are you a knight in the army?"

Again he lied to her. "No I am a simple hunter, and I supply the royal kitchens with food. I hear all the news. I was hunting when someone mistook me for wild game. So here I am."

"Why do you carry a sword?"

"The roads are full of bandits. It is a necessity in my line of work."

She picked up the sword. "This is a knight's sword."

"Yes, it is. My grandfather was a knight." This time he told her the truth.

"Why were you on Regstar land hunting?"

"Who says I was?"

"Reflection City is in the kingdom of Regstar."

"I must go where there is game. I have permission to hunt given to me by King Joel."

"You know King Joel?" Her heart skipped a beat.

"Yes, we have met several times. He does not like to hunt. He only kills animals for food, and it gives him no pleasure."

Donella studied his face. She knew that he did know her father because she knew what he said was true.

"Tell me about King Joel. What is he like?"

"Why all these questions? Do you think that I am some sort of spy?"

"You might be," she said.

Asher looked at Donella. "What is your name?"

"I am Donella, granddaughter of Rue, King of Reflection City. Are you going to capture me and hold me for ransom?" She said this with a smile. She knew he was too weak to move and was really no threat to her.

"No, I am going to lie here hoping my leg will heal so I can go back to Regstar and then home."

"You said that you were from Arsi."

"I am from Arsi, but as you pointed out Reflection City is inside Regstar. And that is where I was hunting."

"Were you hunting by yourself?"

"Yes, I always hunt alone."

"Then who shot you?"

Asher thought for a moment. "The truth is I was not shot by another hunter. I was attacked by bandits. One shot me, but I escaped. I climbed the rocks next to a lake to hide and fell down a hole and here I am."

Donella looked at him. She knew he was not telling the complete truth, but she decided to question him no more.

She went to her horse and brought a small basket of food. "This is all I could slip out of the kitchen. I will bring you more tomorrow. Stay off that leg."

He wanted her to stay because he was dizzy and weak. While she was walking back to her horse, she looked back, and he had fallen back to sleep. She went back to him and decided she could not leave him alone. She reached for the wine, raised his head and let the wine touch his lips. He instantly swallowed the wine but did not open his eyes. Donella studied his face. He had to get well. She had to know as much about Regstar and her father as possible. She gave him more wine and laid his head down on the rock. She folded a blanket and made him a pillow. He was breathing peacefully so she decided it was safe to leave him and return to the castle.

Regstar

* * * * * *

Joel was excited to see Para. He was standing atop the keep watching for her convoy. In the distance he noticed some dust, and it wasn't long until they were in sight of the castle. He decided he must act like a king and not like a brother, and he went to the lower bailey to form a welcome committee. When the convoy arrived, he noticed that Para was not in a coach but was astride a white horse. On each side of her were two knights. She rode right up to him and smiled as he reached for her reigns.

Enough of being king. This is my sister.

When Para dismounted they embraced. It was a long embrace, and he could feel her crying.

"I am so sorry about Alnac," he said.

"I am so happy to see you my dear brother." They released each other, and he led her by the hand into the main building. People were still cheering as they disappeared behind the main walls.

"I know you must be hungry," he said, leading her into the small dining hall.

Para then turned to the two knights at her side. "This is Dorian, my first knight and Bailee, second in command. I want Dorian and Bailee to join us."

"I will have food and drink served in the main dining hall for all your men, but I thought we should be alone for a while. I just want to visit with you. Tomorrow we shall have an official meeting, and your men can join us then."

She agreed.

They were seated in the small dining area, and food and drink were brought to the table.

"This is good. Did you go on a hunt?"

"You know me better than that. I don't hunt anymore. Most of the food we eat is domesticated here at Regstar."

"It is very good. It is delicious."

"You don't know this, but I tried to warn Alnac about the betrayal. I don't know if you remember Asher or not, but I sent Alnac a coded message by him to warn him not to trust Clive's message. I did not know that Rhodes was involved in the plot, but Clive was here, and I had reason not to trust him, but there was no proof. Clive is coming back. He will be here tomorrow."

For a moment Para said nothing. She looked into Joel's sad eyes and said, "Don't be sad. I know you tried. I tried to warn him also, but we were both too late."

"How did you know about the betrayal?"

"I did not know, I only knew that his life was in danger. I felt it, and I appeared in his dreams to warn him, but I was too late."

"Yes, I know you now have magic. You know that Grandmother had magic. She did not use it but I know she did."

"I do remember Asher. He was Donella's friend. When Donella was a child he was always close by. What happened to him when he went to warn Alnac? Was he killed too?"

"Asher is no boy. He is the best knight in this kingdom. He was attacked and wounded on his way back, but he is fine."

"Bring him to the meeting tomorrow. I must thank him."

"He is not here. When he returned, he told me that he thought he had found a way to bring Donella back. I may have made a mistake. His wound had not even begun to heal, but he insisted on trying to find Donella and left immediately. He left the castle several days ago. He was due back yesterday. I worry about him, but he is very capable. If he does not return, there is nothing I can do, and I may have lost the key that will get me back inside Reflection City when it reappears.

Para was excited with this news, and she reached over and hugged her brother and said, "I hope this is not true, and Asher will return soon. I hope that he makes it inside the city and brings Donella home. I miss her too." She knew that if Asher had made it inside Reflection City there was nothing she could do to help him.

Evan

* * * *

When Donella returned to the castle, she asked where her grandfather was. She found him in the study. She gave him a big hug and said, "I love you so much, but I would love to see my father."

"That won't be possible for several more years. Meantime, you will have to put up with me. Evan came to see me this morning. I think he has been looking for you all day. Where have you been?"

"Out riding. What did Evan want?"

"You know what he wants. He wants to marry you."

"Yes, I do know that. What did you tell him?"

Rue turned his back to Donella and walked over to the fireplace. "I wish these fireplaces were still needed. Sometimes we need the weather to change. It rains, but it is always warm here. I think I will light it tonight just to watch it burn."

"Grandfather, what did you tell him?"

"I said I would have to think about it. I wanted to give you more time and to discuss it with you before giving him an answer. You two have been spending a lot of time together. Do you want to marry Evan?"

She walked over to Rue, hugged him. and laid her head on his back. "I think I do? When I leave here, I am going to find him and talk to him."

That is not the answer I wanted to hear, Rue thought. *A woman in love should not say "I think I do."*

Donella found Evan in the garden. He was standing with his back to her looking into a fountain of blue water. He looked somewhat sad.

"Hello Evan. Are you looking for me?"

He turned, smiled and walked to her. "I have missed you today. Where have you been?"

She did not like the tone in his voice but decided to let it rest. She knew he was only confused about his discussion with Rue and now had to face her without having the blessing from Rue he wanted. "I have been out riding, and I packed some lunch, and decided to just clear my head. I needed to be alone. I have talked to Grandfather. He did not say yes, but he didn't say no."

"I thought this would be easy. I know he likes me so why didn't he just give us his blessing so we could start planning a wedding?"

She tried to reassure him. "You know grandfathers. They don't want to give up their little girls. This is complicated. I have a father who is still alive. I want him to give you and me his blessing. I know this is not possible, but this is still what I want. Getting married should be the happiest day of my life, but it is going to be sad without my father being here."

Evan took her in his arms and said, "I know this is something you want, but you really don't know if your father is dead or alive."

Donella spoke quickly. "He is alive."

"How could you know this, Donella? I know you were very close to your father, but feeling he is alive is not the same as knowing he is alive."

She decided not to discuss her father any further. Giving Evan any more information might give away the fact that she was hiding a stranger from Arsi in the woods just a mile outside the castle.

Evan and Donella spent the rest of the evening making small talk and when Donella said she was tired and wanted to go to bed, he kissed her gently and said, "I will see you tomorrow."

That might not be true, she thought. She was going riding again tomorrow.

After Donella had left him, Evan thought about their evening. Something did not seem right. She was just a little different, but it was nothing he could put his finger on.

Healing

* * * * * *

The next morning Donella rode into the forest and found Asher standing next to the small stream that ran through the woods. After she dismounted her horse, she came to him and said, "I thought I told you to stay off that leg. Sit down on that rock and let me look at it."

"It itches."

"Good, that means it is starting heal." She knelt in from of him, and he exposed his legs. He was somewhat embarrassed, but she took little notice of his modesty. "It looks better but I can still see there is a small amount of infection here." She went back to her horse and brought two bags with her.

"I hope there is food in one of those bags because today I am hungry."

"There is, but what we need first is in this bag." She opened it and took out a small jar of salve. "This will help take care of that infection." She spread salve on the wound, and started to put a clean dressing. Her hands were cool to his leg, and he squirmed a bit.

"Be still. I have to get this wound covered, and you are going to have a scar."

"That's okay, only my wife will ever see it."

She look up sharply. "You have a wife?"

"No, I don't have a wife, but I hope to have one someday."

She could tell he was feeling better, and when she looked up at him, he was smiling.

"Do you have a lady that is special?"

"Yes and no."

"What kind of answer is 'Yes and no?' You either have someone special or you don't."

He decided to distract her by turning the same question on her. "What about you? Do you have someone special?"

She laughed, "Well yes and no. It is complicated."

"Well," he said, "You tell me about your complicated friend, and I will tell you about mine."

"Okay, you go first."

He sat back down on the rock. "Well, her name is Kala. She is very beautiful. We only met a short time ago. Once we met, we started seeing each other almost daily. I think she is in love with me."

Donella was almost jealous. "How is that complicated? If you love her, it seems a simple matter to get married, and when you can get married, she can see your scar."

He laughed and almost slid off the rock. "As I said, it is complicated."

"Well, is she already married?"

"No, she is not." Now he thought some half truths might be in order. "I told you I am from Arsi. She is from Rhodes. There is a chance that when I return Arsi and Rhodes will be at war. I will go from a simple hunter to a warrior in the army. I don't see how our relationship could have a happy ending."

"You are right, it is complicated. I don't know what you are going to do when you get home. Maybe you will be lucky and Rhodes and Arsi will have made peace. If Arsi and Rhodes go to war, that will mean that Regstar will also be at war. King Joel will support his sister. Your special person is more complicated than my special person."

"Your turn to tell me about him. What is his name?"

"His name is Evan. He has lived in this kingdom his entire life. I have only been here for six years." Donella decided to tell Asher the truth. "I did not come here of my own free will. I was kidnapped, but I was kidnapped by my grandfather. My mother was from Reflection City, and my grandfather, who is king here, wanted me to know about her. Once I was here, I fell in love with this land and just about everything in it. I got to know my mother for the first time. I don't know why, but my father would tell me nothing about my mother. I am going to tell you something, and you must promise me you can say nothing about it if you ever get out of this land. Do you promise?"

Asher agreed to keep what she was going to tell him a secret, but he also knew she could not tell him much he didn't already know.

"My father is King Joel of Regstar."

Asher tried to act as if this was new to him. "Gosh, I can see how this could get complicated. How does, what is his name, oh yes Evan fit into all of this?"

"He wants to get married. Just yesterday he asked Grandfather for my hand in marriage."

"Do you want married to Evan?"

"Well, here comes the yes and the no part. Yes, I want to get married, but I feel it should be my father's right to give me in marriage."

"Maybe so, but if you stay here and you feel this way, you will never be married."

She moved over to the rock to sit next to Asher. Not having slept very much the night before, she laid her head back and said, "I must be a fool. Here I am telling all this to a complete stranger, who for all I know may be a spy, or a bandit, or who knows what."

"Trust me, I am none of those." He then laid his head on the rock next to Donella. He could smell her perfume and see her chest rise and fall as she breathed. *What in the hell am I going to do,* he thought, as they both drifted to sleep.

When Donella woke up she found that she had fallen over on Asher's shoulder, and he had put his arm around her. Did he do this on purpose or was it involuntary while he was asleep? Nevertheless, she felt good lying there listening to him breathe. She could feel his heart beating. Who was this young man? Moving his arm, she got up without waking him and thought of a way she could find out more about him. She would write him a note. If he could read it, it would tell her that he was educated. If he could not read it, it would be evidence that he might be who he said he was. She went to her horse and retrieved pen and parchment. She began to write:

Jason

I must get back to the castle. I am going to meet with Evan, and my grandfather is giving a banquet tonight. I cannot come back until tomorrow. Keep out of sight. I will see you sometime in the afternoon.

When Asher woke up and found her gone, he saw the parchment lying on the bag of food she had left. He picked it up and quickly read it. *Why is she telling me to stay out of sight? She knows no one can see me.* He thought to himself. This was a sly way to get information about him. Should he let her know that he was educated and most of his education had taken place with her seated next to him? He was not sure what to do. When should he tell her who he was?

Regstar

* * * * * *

The next day Joel and his advisors and Para with her advisors met in the great hall. Joel spoke first. "Thanks to my sister and the army of Arsi, Salados has been defeated. Their army is weak. I don't think they are any threat to Arsi or Regstar at this time. With Andrew dead, the new king will be Geoffrey. Geoffrey will want revenge for his father's death. He will do one of two things. First, he may take what is left of his army and join Rhodes, or second, he may wait until he has rebuilt his army and then march on either Arsi or Regstar. Clive should arrive any day now. When Clive arrives, let your men visit with his men. They may pick up a clue as to what Rhodes' intentions are. Regardless of what Clive says, we cannot trust him."

Dorian spoke first. "Salados may not be as weak as you think. They have always had a powerful army. When Arsi and Rhodes were fighting together, we could not defeat them. My information tells me that they would be too strong for Arsi to defeat, but if Regstar would join us we, could march on Salados and end any threat to either kingdom."

Several of men around the hall shouted in agreement.

Joel spoke again. "There can be no doubt that we need to end this threat, but an attack on the castle at Salados would cost us many men and much time. During that time if Rhodes marches on Regstar, we could not get back in time to defend our land, and our army would be tired and weak."

Para stood up and faced Dorian. She was speaking right to Dorian, but her words were meant for all in the room. "We cannot do anything until we are sure what Rhodes is going to do. Last night after meeting with my brother, I went to sleep and had a dream. It did not tell me much, but I found out how to know if Clive is seeking peace with us. If he has his wife and daughter with him, he is not to be trusted. He will be giving the impression that he is a family man and has concern about his wife and daughter's future. This will not be true."

A knight from the back of the hall shouted out. "How can you know this? This is not something you could know. You are only guessing."

The large room grew quiet. Para walked to the center of the room and said, "If you had been at the High Yellow Pass you would know my power. I know this dream to be true."

The knight stepped toward Para and said, "I don't believe you have any power. You were lucky that a fog just happened to cover the valley during the battle. You have no experience in leadership, and you don't need to be at this meeting."

Joel rose from his chair, but Para raised her hand, and he sat back down.

"I was trained by the great wizard Epson. I don't have Epson's power, but I do have magic. I do not have the power to affect the outcome of a great battle, but I do have magic I can use to help give us an advantage."

The knight took a step toward Para and then stopped. "Show us you have magic."

"I will not do simple tricks for your amusement. I cannot demonstrate my power without hurting you."

"Then use your magic to protect yourself." He pulled his sword and started toward her.

Before anyone in the room could react, Para turned toward the attacker and pointed to him. He flew across the room into the wall. Everyone in the room was stunned, including Para. She went to the knight who was lying on the floor against the wall. He looked at her and said, "I would not have hurt you, but I had to know."

"I am sorry," she said. "I did not want to hurt you, and I don't know what powers I really have. I hope you are not hurt." Para could sense that most of the men in the room were now scared of her but, they were glad that she was on their side.

Joel came to his sister's side and said, "I believe what Queen Para has told us to be true. We will wait for Clive and then meet and decide how to best handle this."

No More Pain

* * * * * * * * *

The next day Donella came to the woods to see Jason. "Has anyone come into the woods," she asked.

"Yes, they come and go but, they see nothing."

"Did you get my message?"

He thought for a moment and decided to play the game. "What did it say?"

He looked at her face, and she seemed disappointed. "It said that I could not come to visit you until this afternoon." She looked at him, and he was smiling.

"You just wanted to know if I could read. My mother worked in the castle. She was educated, and she taught me to read and write. Did you think that if I could read and write, I might be someone more important than a hunter?"

"I still don't know if you are a spy or not. I wanted all the information I could get about you, and you don't have to be so smart about it. Let's take a look at that leg."

"I have already taken care of the leg and changed the bandage and used your magic salve. I even took a bath and cleaned my clothes in the stream. I feel if we are going to sleep together, I should at least be clean."

She did not like his humor. "We slept together, but we did not sleep together, thank you very much."

He looked at her smiling and then they both started to laugh.

"How was the banquet?"

"It was fine. In fact, I have a treat for us today. I have brought some leftover food from the banquet." She walked back to her horse and took the sack of food she had brought from the castle kitchen. As she walked back toward Asher, she looked at him. He was tall, about six two, and had medium length blond hair. His short beard was darker than his hair. His deep blue eyes seemed to penetrate her. *He is rather good looking.* She felt very at ease around him. It was almost as if she had known him for a long time.

Sitting down, she spread the food on the rock that they were now using as a table. "Look what I have: roast hen, which is today going to be served cold, baked venison, served cold, and we have spinach tarts, gyngerbrede, and plum tarts. To drink, we have buttered beer."

"You really did have a feast last night. How did you manage to get all this out of the kitchen?"

"After a banquet, Grandfather always gives the food to the workers and anybody who comes by. I just told them I was taking food to a friend."

"Are we friends?"

"For lack of a better term, that will have to do for now. I hope we are not enemies? Tell me about my father."

"What do you want to know?"

"Everything you know."

"I don't know much." Another lie. "I know that he is a very kind man, and the people of Regstar love him as a king. He has done much for the kingdom and has successfully maintained "the peace" for many years. He once invited me inside the castle when I came to visit Regstar to go hunting. He took me into his living area, and I saw a large painting of you when you were younger. I asked him who you were. Yes, I know what you are going to say. I did recognize you when I first came here. I found it better to say nothing about it. When I asked him about the painting, he became very sad. He said, 'This is my daughter. She was kidnapped. It is my wish to see her again someday.' Then he quickly changed the subject."

Donella started to cry. "I miss him so much, but I love it here. There is nothing but peace here. Do you think if you can ever leave this kingdom you could do me a favor?"

"I think so. What is it that you would have me do?"

"I want you to go to my father and tell him I am okay and that I love this land. Tell him if you can get in and maybe get out, the two of you could possibly find a way in again."

Asher thought for a minute; again, he did not tell her the truth. "If I find my way back to Regstar, I will do this." He knew he could leave Reflection City anytime he wanted. He now knew the secret of this city.

A little later they were both stretched out leaning against the big tree. "I have eaten too much. You must have really good cooks in your kitchen. I must thank them sometime."

"I am full too. I am also sleepy from this large meal and the beer, but I am not going to fall asleep today. I am going back to the castle."

Para

* * * *

After the meeting in the Great Hall, Para felt bad. She had used magic and was not even aware that she was calling on it. She had almost killed a knight of Regstar. She went to her room. She had to think. She sat on the edge of her bed and then fell over on the pillow and buried her head in its soft feathers. So much had happened in the past several days. She had lost her husband. Her magical powers had increased. She had won a major battle, and she had used her magic to kill hundreds of men and even the king of Salados. "Where are you Epson? I need you." Then she fell asleep.

When she awoke, she felt somewhat better. She sent a message to Dorian.

We need to talk. Please dine with me tonight.

That night Dorian and Para met in the small dining room. She had told Joel what she was doing and that she wanted to be alone with Dorian. She chose a medium low cut blue dress with a wide gold ribbon that outlined the square cut it formed around her chest. It fit tight at the waist but was full at the bottom.

When Dorian arrived he was taken by her beauty. "You are beautiful my queen." He then felt awkward. This was not a courtship. It was a dinner meeting to discuss what had happened in the Great Hall and how they would meet with Clive when he arrived.

She smiled. "Thank you Dorian."

After the food had been placed on the table, she opened the conversation. "I hope you don't feel that I don't need your counsel. I know how loyal you were to Alnac. I know you had made great plans to defend our castle, and I also know you did not agree with my plans at High Yellow Pass. What you did not know is that I have enough power to defend our home, and I am not like Alnac. I don't want Arsi to spend the next ten years fighting. I am like my brother, I want peace."

He looked at her. He was surprised at the gentleness. It made him feel much better about the last few days. "I am here to serve you and the people of Arsi. How can I help?"

"I need you by my side. At my last meeting with Epson, he warned me that I cannot use magic as a tool to seek revenge. If I do, my magic will become dark and this will destroy who I am. This is hard. I know that Andrew and possibly Karnac had my husband murdered at a peace meeting. A knight from Regstar was attacked and almost killed after he delivered a message that warned Alnac not to trust King Andrew. You must guide me and help me make decisions that will protect Arsi and Regstar and not involve me in any type of plot to seek revenge for Alnac's death."

The Woods

* * * * * * * *

That night after she had asked Jason to help her get a message to her father, Donella had dinner with Evan. As they ate, she said very little. She could not stop thinking of Jason. She needed to help him escape from Reflection City. Her father had to know that she was safe.

"What is wrong?"

She looked at him and forced a smile. "Nothing, I think my ride and being in the sun has made me tired."

"Maybe you don't need to take your rides for the next couple of days."

"I am not sure I am going to ride tomorrow. I am going to the market. I need a few things and a change in my routine."

"Do you need some company?"

She laughed. "I know that you don't want to spend the day at a market. After all, you are a man, and I don't think that this is a man thing. I may spend the entire morning looking for and trying on dresses."

"Alright, you win. Should I talk to King Rue again?"

"Not yet. Give me some time and let me talk to him first."

He gave her a big smile. "Don't wait too long."

The next day Donella entered the market. She quickly ducked inside a tent that sold men's clothing. A large woman of about sixty greeted her.

"Princess Donella, what brings you into my shop?"

"I need a couple pairs of pants and two shirts and a pair of boots."

"Okay, what size will you need?"

"I am not sure. He is medium built and about six-two in height."

"All the clothing on that table should fit. They are not going to fit Evan."

She looked at the fat woman and saw she was smiling. "You know about me and Evan."

"The whole kingdom knows about you and Evan, and we are so excited for you."

Donella looked through the clothing and found a pair of light grey pants and a black shirt that pulled over the head. She also found a pair of light tan pants and a brown shirt.

"Do you want me to deliver these to the castle?"

"No, I will just take them with me." And with that said, she paid for the clothing and left the tent.

The old lady thought to herself. *Why is Donella buying shirts and pants for a man?*

Donella decided she would not visit with her hunter from Arsi this day. She knew he would wonder where she was and why she did not come. She knew his wound was getting better and that he would be safe. She needed to spend some time with Evan. He was getting suspicious.

That night they walked around the garden and made small talk. "Have you talked to King Rue?" he asked.

This made her angry but she suppressed it. "No I have not."

He looked into her face, and she could see that he was disappointed. "Promise me you will do it soon."

"I will," she said. The truth was she was not going to talk to Rue about a wedding until she was sure that Jason could contact her father.

She looked at Evan and said; "You must give me some time and you must trust me. I will talk to Grandfather soon."

Evan reached out and lightly touched her arm. I know you want to contact your father, but that is not possible. You must be content with what you have here."

Donella turned toward Evan and gave him a hug. As she laid her head on his chest, she thought, *It is not only possible but very probable that I will see my father soon.*

As she raised her head from Evan's chest, she said, "I have had a wonderful night but I am tired and going to bed."

As Donella lay in her bed that night she thought of Jason more that she thought of Evan.

She didn't know who he was but knew that she liked him very much and felt she had known him all her life. Then for some strange reason she thought of her childhood friend, Asher. *Whatever happened to him?* He would be a knight now, and she wondered what he would look like. If she had not left Regstar, would they have become more than friends? Maybe not. After all they had not seen each other but two times in the last eight years and not at all in the last six. Then she heard the rain begin to fall. Poor Jason, he is going to get wet. Then she laughed out loud. She realized she was enjoying the sexual tension between them. She looked forward to seeing him again.

Evan

Evan could sense that he was losing Donella. The last several days, she had been distant. She had not talked to her grandfather and she went out riding almost every day. She had often taken long rides but not every day. How could he find out what was going on? Was she seeing someone else? No this was not possible. Maybe he should just ask her. Would she tell him? Was she having cold feet about getting married? Would she marry him without getting her father's permission which was impossible to get? His head was spinning with all these questions. He decided to go see Brumble. Maybe someone had gotten into their kingdom. Donella's father had gotten in and had taken her mother from the city. After all, Brumble had kidnapped Donella and brought her here. He had been outside the city. He knew Joel, and he had let Joel take Phylass from Refection City.

The Kiss

⊛　⊛　⊛　⊛　⊛　⊛

Asher had been walking around the forest and was returning to his camp when he saw Donella coming through the trees carrying two packages.

When she saw him she began to laugh. "You look like a drowned chicken," she giggled.

"I hope you are enjoying yourself. You were not here trying to sleep with the rain coming down. I thought the night would never end. You are not carrying food. What do you have?"

She laughed again. "I thought if we were going to continue this pseudo romance you were going to have to clean up. You need clean clothing. I picked out a few things for the up and coming hunter. How is the leg this morning?"

"Wet."

She reached into her pocket. "Look what I have. Soap. Get undressed and bathe in the steam."

He did not say anything, but just looked at her.

"Don't be so modest, I will go beyond those trees and it is not like anyone else is going to see you." "Put on the grey and the black. It might make you better looking." She handed him the packages and quickly went behind the trees.

Asher set the packages on the large rock, opened them, and took out the grey and black outfit. He was surprised that she had included underclothing and a towel. He quickly got undressed and took the bandage from his wound. It looked good and the infection appeared to be gone. He waded out into the water. It had been cooled by the rain, and this gave him a slight shiver. The water was about two feet deep and he sat down, splashed water on his face and hair, and began rubbing the soap on. It felt good to get the oil from his hair, and when he rinsed it, he could feel the squeak in his hair. He quickly soaped the rest of his body. He wanted to stay in the water longer, but knew that Donella was waiting for him to finish. Leaving the stream, he took the towel and dried off. The water had made his wound look redder so after putting on his underclothes he redressed the wound.

"Hey Mr. Modest, how long does it take to take a bath in a creek?"

"Not long. You should try it sometime."

"Can I come out from behind these trees? I am getting lonely sitting back here."

Is she flirting with me? He put on the shirt and then his pants. He took the belt from his old clothing and secured the shirt to his body. "I wish you had brought some scissors. I need to trim my beard and maybe my hair."

"Who are you trying to impress? Nobody can see you but me."

"I am finished, and I am starved. I hope you brought some good food."

"You come to me. I like it over here."

Asher walked to the sound of her voice, and when she came into view, she was standing in front of a blanket with food and drink placed on it.

She looked at him and thought, *He is one good looking hunter.* The clothes suited him well. She loved the lean look the black shirt gave him.

He walked up to her and got extremely close. Donella did not back away. He bent down and lightly kissed her on the cheek, and then faced her and gave her a quick kiss on her lips and said, "Thank you."

She did not step away but returned his kiss to his lips and said, "You are welcome."

They stared at each other for several moments and then she broke the silence by saying, "Are you not starving. Let's eat."

They ate without much conversation. Both were thinking of the kisses. When they finished their meal and had packed up the blanket, she said, "How is the leg?"

"It is looking good. I don't think my future wife will be ashamed of me."

He looked across the field and could see farmers working in the field just beyond the forest. His heart started to race. If he could see them, they could see him. He knew what was happening. He turned back to face her. He would not tell her what was happening. He was falling in love with her, but was she falling in love with him?

"You know I must leave. I have to get back. My leg no longer needs healing. Tonight I will look for an opening or door that will take me back to Regstar."

"Why do you have to search for it at night? The people here can't see you. Wait until tomorrow. I can come early, and I will help you look."

He didn't "tell" that he did not have to look for the gate. People could see him and when he left it would have to be at night.

"You cannot leave without telling me goodbye." She had a slight tremor in her voice. "After all, I have been your nurse and provider these several days."

Asher looked at her and could tell she cared for him. "I will not leave without saying goodbye."

"Good, I will see you tomorrow. By the way, there are some scissors in the package with your clothes. You can trim that beard of yours." She packed up her blanket, got on her horse and rode away.

On the way back to the castle, she suddenly had a feeling of guilt. She really had developed feelings for him, but what could she do? She felt that she was being unfaithful to Evan. He had asked for her hand in marriage, and several days ago she would have accepted. Now she was not sure. Was she in love with a hunter from Arsi, in love with a man who was going to leave and might never return? *What a mess.*

Evan and Brumble

* * * * * * * * * * * *

That afternoon when Evan and Donella were together, she was more distant than ever. Their conversation was polite, but the excitement they had shared in previous conversation was gone. Her mind was somewhere else. When she left him to meet with her grandfather, he was sure she was glad their meeting was over. She did not tell him "goodbye" or "see you tomorrow". She just walked away. He was sure something was wrong.

As Donella walked away, Evan decided to go see Brumble. He found him in his private quarters in the barracks.

Brumble was surprised to see Evan. "And what brings you to my humble home?"

"I need to talk to you, and I need to ask you many questions."

Brumble looked at Evan and could see he was a troubled young man. "I'll help you the best I can. What is bothering you?"

"Can I ask you about Reflection City?"

Brumble looked surprised. "Everyone knows the story of this city. Why are you asking what you already know?"

Evan walked over to the large window and looked out. "I want to know if it is possible for someone from the outside to get into our kingdom."

Brumble knew the secret of Reflection City, but he was not going to tell Evan, so he gave a vague answer. "I don't think so."

"King Joel, Donella's father was able to get in."

Brumble went to Evan and laid his hand on his shoulder. "King Joel came to this land during the month when our walls were visible to the outside world. He had a key. Joel and Phylass both left when the wall was still visible. No, I don't think that anyone can get through the wall." *He knew this was not true.* "Why do you ask?"

Evan didn't answer Bumble's question. "Does King Joel still have a key?"

"Yes, he does have a key. So I ask you again, why these questions?"

"It is just a feeling. I feel Donella is wanting to go home. The last couple of times we have met she is distant. I just feel that she is leaving and someone is helping her."

Brumble thought for a minute. "Everyone knows that you two are getting married. She may have gotten cold feet. It happens to young brides. She will be okay."

"Something just does not feel right. Will she need a key to leave this kingdom?"

"I think so, but I don't know. To my knowledge there are only five keys to the hidden door. King Joel has one, Rue has three, and I have one. The only one that is not secure is King Joel's. Donella was not born here, and it may be possible for her to leave without a key, but someone would have to open the door for her. I see Donella from time to time. I think she is very happy here, and I don't think she would leave."

"Maybe so but I think you should talk to her. Ask her about her father and if she misses Regstar." Evan started toward the door. "You may be right; I need to leave. Thanks for talking to me." Evan left the room and walked toward the great hall thinking to himself that maybe Brumble was right. "Just a case of cold feet." He would see her tomorrow, and things would be alright.

The next morning Donella was up and singing as she dressed. She fixed her hair and chose a blue riding dress. Then she thought, *What am I doing? Why am I fixing myself up for Jason? I know he likes me. but he is leaving and we might never see each other again.* Then she dismissed the thought and looked forward to seeing him. They could have breakfast next to the stream. She would get more information from him about Regstar and Arsi. She wanted to know more about her aunt and how she was doing after the loss of her husband. He might not know, but she had to find out as much as she could before he left.

She went to the kitchen, where several workers were preparing food for Rue and other members of the royal house. Margo, the head cook, looked up and said, "Here you are again. You are going riding again and want more food. As much food as you are eating on these trips you are going to get fat. Better marry that young knight quick before that figure is gone." Then she laughed and helped Donella pack the food.

Donella lingered and talked to the kitchen staff a bit and then picked up the pack and headed for the door. She went directly to the stable. She had sent word to have her horse saddled and ready to go.

Her horse was tied to a stall near the front of the stable. She threw the bag over the saddle horn and mounted the horse. Riding toward the gate, she saw the draw bridge. She thought, *I have never seen the bridge up. I wonder if it still works? This is a great place, no war, no winter.* As she approached the gate she saw Evan standing on the bridge. She pulled on the reins and brought her horse to a stop. "What are you doing here?"

Evan took the horse by the reins. "Where are you going?"

"You know I go riding every day. What do you want?" She knew she sounded cold to Evan and wished she had not been so short with her response.

Evan let go of the reins and said, "We need to talk."

She looked at him. "I am sorry Evan. I know that I have not been myself lately. This is why I go riding. It clears my head. I can stop by the stream or go into the woods, eat, and read, and it makes me feel better."

"Are you concerned about us getting married? Is it me that is making you confused?"

"I am going riding. I will be back after lunch. Let's eat supper tonight and then we can talk."

He stepped back and she rode out of the castle.

Donella and Asher

. . . .

When they met that day he embraced her and said, "I know how to get out of this kingdom. I think I have found a way."

She couldn't believe he had found a way in and now he had found a way out. "You are going to leave," she said. She could see the sad look in his eyes.

"I can stay no longer. I have stayed longer that I should have. I must return to my home. I need to know what is happening with Arsi and Regstar. They could be at war, and if they are, I am needed."

Why would he think he's so important to a war effort? she thought. *He is just a hunter and not even trained for combat.* "Don't leave until I have checked your wound and made sure you are safe to travel. I want to talk to you about many things, please stay until tomorrow. I can get you food for your journey, and it may be cold outside this kingdom. We have much to plan. You just can't leave."

He smiled at her. "You act like you are going to miss me. Let's eat. I am starving." They spread the food out on a big flat rock near the stream. As they ate, he looked at her. Her hair was shining; the blue dress she was wearing was stunning and he knew that he was in love.

"Tell me about what's-his-name."

"You mean Evan."

"Yes Evan, the man you are going to marry after I leave."

She could tell he was teasing her. "Evan is a great knight. He is very good with a sword and has just won the tournament. He might be as good as Brumble."

"Is he good looking? You are not going to marry someone ugly are you?"

"He is very good looking and well educated."

"Looks like you struck gold."

She needed to turn the tables on Jason. "Tell me about your girl, Kala. Do you think she will be waiting for you? Will she be content to marry a hunter?"

"Do you mean, will she be content to marry just a hunter?"

She looked at him and realized she had belittled his station and pointed out that she was royal and he was a commoner. "I am sorry for saying just a hunter. Please forgive me."

"I don't know. That may be a problem. Would you marry Evan if he were just a hunter?"

"I would marry anybody that I am in love with. Back to my question. You just can't leave. I need you to let my father and aunt know that I am okay and that I am happy. If you leave will you be able to come back and bring me news about them and how the war is going? I need to know if my father can visit me. There is so much that needs to be discussed. Please give me one more day."

At first he did not say anything and then he said, "You know you could come with me. You could visit your father and aunt. She was on her way to Regstar just before I left."

Donella fell silent. Her mind began to race. *If I left, would Father let me come back? Does he hate Brumble and Rue for taking me? Would he force Jason to show him the way into Reflection City, and would he bring troops to attack us?* There was too much to work out. She needed to buy more time. Should she talk to Rue and Brumble? "I need more time. I am not sure what to do. Please be my friend and give me some more time."

"Time is what I do not have. Every day I am here is a day that I run the risk of being discovered. I don't know what that means for me or you if I am." Asher was not sure what to do. Maybe he should tell her who he was and that he had been sent to bring her home. He wasn't sure how she would react. He decided he would continue to deceive her.

Donella looked as if she were about to cry. "I have to leave; Evan is acting very strange. Don't make this our goodbye. I will be back tomorrow. Please tell me you won't leave at least until then."

As she rode back to the castle, she thought about her dishonesty with Jason. She didn't want him to go because she had fallen in love with him. She did not know how to let him go, and she was too scared to go with him. She didn't even know how he felt and if he would even want her to go.

She wanted to see her family. If he would ask her to go to be with him, that would be different. Or would it? She had obligations to Reflection City. She would be the next queen of this land. Then she realized she had other issues to deal with. She was also in line to be the next queen of Regstar and maybe the next queen of Arsi. *Gee,* she thought, *what a mess.*

When Donella got back to the castle she went to the library. She was confused and had to make some sense out of what was happening. If she told Rue and Brumble about Jason, would they understand and help him leave or would they keep him here in order to protect the secrets of the city? Would Evan understand why she had kept Jason a secret? Could she leave and come back? Would her father let her come back? She had to come up with some plan to delay Jason from leaving. But what?

Para

* * * *

The next day Para decided to take a ride to clear her head. While she ate breakfast with Joel, she told him of her plans.

"I need some fresh air. I am going riding this morning. It will help me think. I have some problems I need to deal with."

Joel look puzzled. "Is this something I can help you with? You don't need to be riding alone outside this castle."

"Don't you think I can't protect myself? You saw what I can do."

"Yes I did, and you need to keep your magic in check. People fear magic, and you don't need to use it unless..." Then he stopped. "I can assign you an escort."

"I don't need you to assign me an escort. I have my own men."

"If you leave the castle, you need an escort of at least four men, and you need to ride only in the south. That is where it will be the safest, and if you are getting a southern breeze, it will be much warmer in that direction.

"Okay if you insist, but I will choose my own escort."

Para asked Dorian to get her a four-man escort but was somewhat surprised when she found that he was one of the four. They left the castle and as promised headed south.

The southern part of Regstar was made up of green rolling hills. Most of the hills had been cleared off for farming, but all the roads were surrounded by beautiful trees. There were lots of creeks, most of which were very small, and they too were surrounded by trees. As they traveled, they passed farmers on the road hauling their crops from the fields to storage areas. All were friendly and waved as they passed.

Para thought to herself, *These people have become so accustomed to peace, they are friendly to soldiers from outside their kingdom.* After a short ride they came to one of the larger creeks. It was away from the farm land, and they stopped to water their horses. Para dismounted, and Dorian did the same. They left their horses with the other knights and walked up the creek just out of earshot to others.

"I am sorry that I talked to you the way I did the other night. I put you on the spot with my questions about Alnac. You were right to refuse to answer me, but I am going to ask you again. Before I do I am going to explain why I am asking the questions. I am not a jealous woman trying to find out about my late husband's infidelity. Alnac and I have no children. There is no heir to the crown of Arsi. Donella, the daughter of Joel, is in line should something happen to me. If there is a chance that Alnac fathered a child outside our marriage and this is known, things could get complicated, especially if it is a boy. If Geoffrey takes Arsi in battle and later finds out there is a child of Alnac, the child will be killed. If I die without a child and the people know that Alnac fathered a child, it may split the kingdom. Now I ask you Dorian, was there another woman in Alnac's life?"

Dorian looked at Para. She was dressed in a gold riding dress and he thought to himself, *How could anyone be unfaithful to such a woman?* Her short blonde hair and tan skin made her look like a goddess. He looked down and said, "Yes." He felt that he was betraying his friend, Alnac.

Para gave no look of surprise. "Do you know her name?"

"Yes."

"Will you tell me?"

"Her name is Gwen. She lives in the town of Pan, which is in Salados. We fought a battle near this village and stopped there to get food and other supplies. This is where Alnac met her. She is about twenty five years of age. When we left Pan, she came with us. I think that Alnac loved her. The last time I saw her, she was leaving to go back to Pan.

"How far did she live from camp, and how often did Alnac visit her?"

"He did not have to go visit her. She lived in our camp."

"After the death of Alnac, you moved the army back to Arsi. What happened to her?"

"She left the camp because she was with child." Dorian felt he was saying too much. "Are you going to kill her and her child?"

Para walked in front of Dorian, got extremely close to his face, and looked him right into his eyes. "You really have no idea of who I am, or you would not have said such a cruel thing. Let's get back to the castle."

Distrust

* * * * * *

The next morning the only plan that Donella had was to try to get Jason to stay another day. She only brought food for their meal, and she rode out to see him unaware that Evan was watching her as she left. She did not sense that he was following her as she made her way quickly to the forest were Jason was hiding. He had gone to the barracks and secured a metal sword. *If she is meeting someone from outside this kingdom, I must be prepare.*

When she dismounted from her horse, she took the provisions and walked to where Jason had his temporary camp. As she approached, she saw Jason standing in the pathway. He was wearing the brown outfit she had given him. Somehow he looked different. Then she saw it. He was wearing his sword. He was leaving. She ran to him.

"You can't leave yet. I need you to stay just a couple of days longer. I promise I will ask no more."

"You can't know what you are asking of me. There may be a war going on outside this kingdom. I have been here far too long. There are people who care for me and do not know what has happened. You are asking too much." He then looked deep into her eyes. "Can you give me a reason I should stay other than that you want your father to bless your wedding? There is a chance that when I return to Regstar, Arsi, Salados, and Rhodes will be at war. Your father will be in battle. As much as he would want to, he could not come to this land at this time." His voice calmed. "If there is peace, I will let your father know you are safe. It will be his choice if he wants to come to this land."

"If there is peace, will you come back with my father? He must not know that you can get into the kingdom without it being the time of the reflection. I know that if he knew, he would have been here already."

"I think what you say is true. He did not know. I will tell him about how I got into Reflection City, and I will come back with him."

Donella took him by the arm, and they walked down the path toward the lake. "I agree, and you do promise you will come back with him."

Evan was watching from behind a small bush. *So she is seeing someone else, but who is he?* he thought. He was tall and wearing a sword; he was not dressed like a knight. Seeing Donella walking with him, holding his arm, made Evan's blood boil. As he watched he could hear what they were saying. They stopped near the stream and faced each other.

Jason spoke first. "You know I cannot stay. I am putting you in danger, and I am also in danger. I know you are afraid that if I leave and that I know the secret of Refection City, it will put the whole kingdom in danger."

She looked into his eyes but said nothing.

"I am going to let your father know you are alright. While I am gone, you must talk to Rue. You must tell him that I have been here and that I will not tell anyone except your father the secret of the city."

"When are you going to leave?"

"Tonight."

"Are you sure you will you come back?" She fought back her tears.

"I am not sure. If coming back puts this kingdom in danger then the answer is no."

This time a tear ran down her cheek and she looked down to the ground.

Jason bent over and kissed her forehead. "You have been a good friend. I will miss you more than you could ever understand."

She raised her head and kissed him on his lips. It was not a passionate kiss but one that expressed how much she cared for him. "Let's eat and make some plans. If you come back, you will need to know how you will contact me."

"Don't worry. I will find you."

Evan could take no more. He pulled his sword and stepped out of the bushes and started toward Asher.

Asher knew the sound of a steel sword being pulled from its sheath. He quickly drew his sword and pushed Donella to the side in time to deflect Evan's first blow. Evan's second blow was met with all the skill of an experienced knight. Asher took the blow and gave his sword a twist that sent Evan's sword sailing away. Asher quickly fell to one knee as Evan moved past him. With the flat edge of his sword he struck him across the back of his knees and Evan fell to the ground. Asher quickly rose to his feet and now had the tip of his sword pointed to the back of Evan's neck. The battle had lasted no more than five seconds. If they had not been in Reflection City, Evan would now be dead.

Then he heard Donella scream. "No, don't kill him!" She started toward the two men.

Asher instantly glanced at her and said in a tone that left no impression of who was in charge, "Stand back Little Giant, this man tried to kill us. I will decide what is to be done with him." Asher knew as soon as she heard his words they were a mistake. She would know who he was.

Donella stopped in shock. He was not Jason, he was Asher. She did not move.

Asher pulled his sword back from Evan's neck and allowed him to turn over and face him.

Evan looked up and again felt the sword against his neck. For the first time in his life he was scared.

Asher glanced over to Donella. She had not moved. He thought, *She now knows who I am.* He looked back at Evan. "My name is Asher. I am from Regstar. I am First Knight of the legions of knights of King Joel, and who may you be?"

Evan was looking up at him but said nothing. *Here I am, considered the best knight in this kingdom and was bested by a knight from outside of this kingdom in less than three blows of a sword. Is he going to kill me?*

Asher put his sword a little further into Evan's neck but did not break the skin. "I am not going to ask you again. Who are you, and why did you attack us?"

Evan paused. "My name is Evan. I only attacked you. I would never harm Donella."

Asher pulled his sword back from Evan's neck and stepped away. He walked over to Evan's sword, picked it up and tossed it to Evan. "Put that away. If you pull it again, I will cut off your hand." He then turned and walked over to Donella who had said nothing. "I guess I have some explaining to do."

Donella was trying to recover from her shock. *Why was he really here? Is he going to kidnap me and take me back to Regstar?* She was scared. He was not Jason; he was Asher. How much of Jason has actually been Asher? Then it hit her. Evan could see him. This could only mean one thing. She loved him, and he loved her, but how could she love this man who had deceived her, and she was now scared?

"I knew after I called you Little Giant that I had made a mistake. You would know that I was not Jason, but Asher."

Again she was afraid to say anything. She didn't know what to say. She just stared at him.

"Aren't you going to say anything?"

"You came to take me to Regstar."

"I know," he said. "I came to get you to return you to your father and to our kingdom. Once I saw how happy you were I could not take you from this land. I am still leaving today. I will still contact your father to let him know you are okay. I will give him the message we discussed."

"What does Father know? Does he know the secret of how to get into this kingdom?"

Asher glanced at Evan, who was just standing there saying nothing. "I told him I thought I knew how to get in. Since I have not returned, he will not know what has happened to me. He will either think that I have been killed or that I have made it inside and that I might be a prisoner here. He knew that I had a severe wound. I was attacked by soldiers of Salados returning from Alnac's camp. I was not shot by another hunter or bandit. I had been to see Alnac carrying a message to him from your father. It was never intended for me to make it back alive from that mission. Kala's father tried to have me killed. See how complicated things are?"

"I do want to see my father, but there are many questions that must be answered before we put this kingdom in danger."

"I agree. If Evan is any example of your knights--and you said he was the best-- you would have no chance if your secret was discovered by an enemy."

He glanced over to Evan and felt sorry for him because what he had said was cruel. Asher turned to Evan and said, "I am sorry for what I just said. I don't know what your fighting skill can become. You have never had to face someone in real combat. It is much different from a tournament.

I have been in combat many times fighting for my life. I have also taken part in many tournaments. As you have found out, they are not the same. You need to help Donella and me decide what to do. Come and sit with us. We will come up with a plan that will keep this land safe. Do you agree, Little Giant?"

For a long moment she said nothing. Then, "Who are you?"

"As you already know, I am Asher. I was your friend as a child. I am now a knight in your father's army. Once I got here I could not tell you who I was. What I have told you is mostly true. You know the parts that are not."

Tears came to her eyes. "We have a problem, and I don't know the answers."

He looked at her. "Let the three of us talk it through. We can come up with something."

"You said you were the leader of the Knights Legion. It was my understanding that this position is held by the best and most experienced knight in the kingdom."

"That is my understanding too. Did you bring any wine? I think we need something to drink."

She went to retrieve her bag. As she did she again thought, *Yes we have a problem. Evan can see Asher, and there is only one way that can happen.*

Para Has A Dream

• • • • • • • • • • • •

Para was in her room when she heard the knocking on her door. When she opened it, there stood Joel. "Clive has arrived. His wife and daughter are with him. He wants to meet tomorrow. I have set up the official meeting for tomorrow morning. Would you want Dorian and Bailee to be there?"

"Yes, I would, but I will talk to them first."

"Do you want to dine with us tonight?"

"No, I need to meet with Dorian and Bailee before the meeting, and I will do that tonight."

"Then I will take my leave and see you at the meeting in the morning. I don't think we need to discuss anything before the meeting. We need to wait and hear what Clive has to say."

Para turned her back to Joel. "You know what I told you about if he brought his family."

"I do, but I still want to hear what he has to say." Joel then turned and left her alone.

Para pulled the cord to call a servant. When the servant arrived she said, "Send word for Dorian and Bailee to come to my room tonight. Tell them I want to have the evening meal with them and discuss what is best for Arsi."

That night Dorian and Bailee arrived at Para's room. They knocked on the door, and after a few moments Para appeared. She was dressed in green. Food and drink had already been brought to the room, and a table had been set up, and three chairs surrounded the table. Para took her seat, and the two men joined her. Servants poured the wine, and the three started their meal.

"Clive is here, and Joel wants us to meet in the morning with him."

"I know," Dorian said. "We saw his party arrive. He has his wife and daughter and about fifty knights with him. We cannot trust this man. It was he who set up the trap that killed Alnac."

Bailee, who was usually quiet, spoke up. "We have several knights with us and with Joel's help we could kill them all. We need to avenge Alnac. I think we could defeat Karnac and Geoffrey if they then declared war."

Para looked at the two men. "This is tempting but not what we are going to do. I would like to avenge my husband, but creating a lasting peace comes first. We should hear what Clive has to say. Then we will decide what to do. This is not what I called you here for. I want to talk about Gwen."

Both men looked surprised.

"When Alnac was killed what happened to her?"

Bailee spoke first. "It is my understanding that she went back to Pan when we moved the army back to Arsi, I have not seen her since."

Dorian did not speak. He suddenly did not trust Para and feared that she was going to do harm to Gwen.

Para sensed this. She reached over and touched Dorian's arm. "I am not going to harm her. I sense that she may be in danger. If Geoffrey and Karnac know what we know, they will take her and use her against Arsi. Dorian, I need your help. I want you by my side during the negotiation. Bailee, I want you to take a group of knights to Pan, get Gwen, and take her to my castle. This must be done in secret. Tell no one. Once you get her safe inside the castle, tell the servants that she is my cousin. Let her stay in my room. Bailee, I want you to stay near her and protect her until I return to Arsi."

"When do you want me to leave, my Queen?" Bailee stood.

"Right now, tonight. We cannot waste time." Then she smiled." You can finish your meal."

After Bailee had left, Dorian looked at Para. She had a very serious look on her face. The green dress accented her figure. He desired her, but he also loved her. It was the love that kept him at a distance. He did not want to do anything to hurt her in any way. Her husband had been dead for only a few days, but he knew that her husband's love for her had been dead for years. Again he thought, *How could any man not love her?*

They spent the rest of the meal making small talk, and when they were finished, she walked him to the door. She opened the door and to his surprise hugged him.

"Thank you for being my friend. I know this has been tough for you also. You were loyal to Alnac, and I have asked you twice to betray that friendship. Thank you for understanding."

He instinctively put his arms around her. He could smell her perfume and feel the warmth of her body. He released her and left the room.

That night Para went to bed early. The wine put her to sleep quickly. Then there he was. Epson was in her dream. "I have come to warn you. Clive plans to kill you. He knows you have power, and what happened at High Yellow Pass has made him scared. He has poison in his ring. If he gets close to you, he can prick you and you will be dead in one day's time. By that time he will be gone. You must stay away from him. For your sake and for the sake of Arsi and Regstar, do not let him near you." And then he was gone. She awoke from her dream, hot and soaked with sweat. She removed her gown and poured water into her wash bowl. It was cold and made her feel better. She thought about Epson's warning. She could feel what Epson had said was true. She could sense Clive's plans. *How could I have missed this? I must pay attention to what is going on.* She had let the death of Alnac and his infidelity with Gwen distract her, and this had made her careless. *I must buy some time.*

The next morning Joel, Clive, Dorian, and several officials were in the great hall waiting for Para. They were seated below the large window that overlooked the courtyard. Joel was wondering why she was late. Then she appeared at the other end of the hall, and all the men turned and looked at her. She was dressed in a golden gown which fit her tightly and came all the way up to her neck. It fit her body much as a glove would fit a person's hand. She had a four point crown on her head, and she did not wear any smile. The men could do nothing but stare. She was a goddess, and they were now going to feel her power.

"Clive," she said.

Clive stood up and starting walking toward her.

With one wave of her hand she stopped him in his tracks.

"There will be no meeting today, and there will be no meeting in the future with you present. If Geoffrey and Karnac want to meet to discuss a peace, then let them be present in this meeting. King Joel is here, I am here, but where are King Geoffrey and King Karnac? I want you on the road home before this day is over. Your wife and daughter do not know of your deceit. They will remain here until we have a meeting that involves all four monarchs. Then they will be released to go home." She then waved her hand and released Clive from her spell.

He turned to Joel. "Are you to let this bitch start a war? Geoffrey and Alnac will see this as a personal insult to them. They will want revenge for this insult."

As he made his statement, Dorian pulled his sword to defend Para's honor. Para raised her hand and stopped him. She took one step forward. "Revenge, you speak of revenge. Your deceit caused the death of my husband. If I wanted revenge, I would kill you right where you stand. You tell Geoffrey and Karnac if they arrive on this border or my own with an army, I will have my revenge and it will start with you. My brother wants peace. I want peace. It remains to be seen if the other two kingdoms want peace."

She then disappeared. The men did not know if she really disappeared or just stepped through the door and left the hall.

Clive walked over to King Joel and laid his hand on his shoulder. He then looked down at his hand and the ring was gone.

After the hall had cleared, Joel went to Para's room. He was angry and entered her room without knocking. "What is going on? We met and decided to hear what Clive had to say, and you come in late and shut down the meeting. You practically threw Clive out of the castle and say you are going to kidnap his wife and daughter. I repeat: What is going on?"

His face was flushed and Para had never seen Joel so angry. "Brother, you must know that I would not do anything rash unless I had information that made it necessary."

His voice now calmer, Joel walked to his sister. "What do you know that I don't know?"

"Clive was going to kill me."

"And how do you know this?"

"Last night Epson came to me in a dream. He warned me that I was going to be poisoned. They fear me and are afraid to attack until they understand how much power I have."

Joel walked over to the window. "You based all this on a dream. How was he going to poison you?"

"He had a ring that he could use to stick me with. The ring had a poison in it. If he had been successful, I would have died in twenty-four hours."

"I can't believe this."

Para pitched Clive's ring on the table.

Joel remembered seeing the ring on Clive's finger. "How did you get it?"

"I took it with my magic. When I left the room, I watched him. For some reason when he found he could not kill me, he decided to try to kill you. If I had not taken the ring, you would be dead."

Joel remembered Clive coming to him and laying his hand on his neck. He picked up the ring from the table and examined it. "I am sorry I doubted you. It won't happen again. My knights will follow your instructions. Clive will leave immediately, and his wife and daughter will stay here. Do you want to lock them in the tower?" He was kidding with his sister because he knew she would be kind to them.

She laughed. "No, I will speak with them after Clive has left. I know they will be scared. I will set their minds at ease."

Kira

* * * *

Kira did not know what to think. Her husband had left the kingdom and had said nothing to her.

What was going on? She had to know.

She went to Kala's room. Kala was looking out the window, and when her mother came into the room, she burst into tears.

"I think we are prisoners here," she told her mother. "Father is gone. I heard the servants talking, and they said that Queen Para forced him to leave. She is a witch, and she threatened to kill Father. What is going on?"

Kira took her daughter into her arms and held her as she sobbed into her shoulder. "Don't be afraid. I know Joel, and he is a kind and just king. He will not let anything happen to us. I will send word, and I know he will talk to us and let us know what is going on."

Kira stayed with Kala until she calmed down, and as she started to leave, Kala asked, "See if King Joel will tell you where Asher is. Tell him I need to see him."

When Kira returned to her own room, she called for a servant. "Am I a prisoner here?" she asked.

The servant looked surprised. "No Madam, you are not a prisoner; my instructions are to treat you and your daughter as guests."

"Send someone to King Joel. Tell him that I need to see him."

Joel did not respond to Kira's request right away. He had to plan how the meeting with her would go. He liked Kira. She was beautiful and smart. Like her daughter, her hair was blonde and fell almost to her waist. She had a good figure, and her blue eyes where large and round. Even though she was married to Clive, he was attracted to her. He finally decided that he would be completely honest with her and answer any questions she had with the truth.

He started to the wing of the castle where she was housed. Going down the hall, he met Para coming toward him. Should he tell her where he was going? He decided not to and greeted his sister with a warm smile.

Para spoke first. "I know you are going to see Clive's wife. I know you, and you will tell her the truth. She and her daughter are scared. I can feel it. They are good people, and they know nothing of Clive's deceit."

Joel was stunned. *Can she read my mind?*

She looked at him and smiled. "I know what you are thinking. You think I can read your mind. I can't. I know you, and you care about people. I knew as soon as you got a chance you would make Kira feel at ease. I can feel their concern. Make them feel at ease. Tell them anything they ask, but remember they may not believe anything you tell them. Kira is a wife, and Kala is a daughter. You may find that they know nothing of the deceit, and they will remain loyal as a wife and a daughter."

Joel smiled and continued down the hall toward the east wing. He would do the best he could.

Knocking on the door, Joel was greeted by a servant.

"Please come in; she is expecting you."

Kira was standing by the window with her back to the room. She wore a green dress with wide sleeves that completely covered her hands. It was trimmed in a light yellow, and when she turned toward him, he could see the square cut neckline. Her skin was light and very smooth, and he thought that she was stunning.

Joel spoke first. "You sent for me."

"Yes, I need to know what is going on. We come here with my husband on a diplomacy mission, and after we arrive, he leaves and says nothing to us about why. The rumors are that he was asked to leave, --no--, he was told to leave. Is this true?"

"Yes, it's true."

"Was he asked to leave or told to leave?"

"He was told to leave."

"How could you do this? He came here to make peace between our two kingdoms. This could mean war. If war comes, will Kala and I become prisoners to you and your sister? Are we prisoners now?"

Joel turned his back to Kira. "You are not prisoners, and if war does come between our two kingdoms, you will be safely returned to your husband. Meanwhile, I want you to be our guest. You can come and go as you please. You can even dine with my sister and myself at the evening meals, or if you prefer, I will have your food brought to your rooms. I prefer that you dine with me."

"You are very kind. I will dine with you and your sister, but I cannot speak for Kala. She is very upset. She asked about Asher. She wants to see him and know how he is doing."

Joel thought for a minute. Should he tell her where Asher was? If he did not then she would think he was spying on Clive or on some other military mission. "Asher is not within the castle walls at this time. Let me tell you something you might not know. I have a daughter. Her name is Donella. When she was fourteen years old, she was kidnapped. That was six years ago, and I have not seen her since. Do you know the legend of the hidden kingdom?"

She looked at him feeling sorry for a man who had lost his daughter. "I have heard the legend. They say it appears only one month every 15 years. This is just a legend, isn't it?"

"It is not a legend. I have been there. It is where my wife was born. I know that this is where Donella is. A knight from that city came to me and told me that they took her. She is the granddaughter of the king of this hidden kingdom."

Kira looked into Joel's eyes and could see the tears forming. She felt sorry for him. He had lost his daughter, and he was still one of the kindest men she had ever known. She wanted to hug him and comfort him, but she held back.

She reached over and touched him lightly on the arm. "I am so sorry."

He looked into her face and could see she too had tears running down her cheek. "Several days ago Asher came to me and said he thought he knew a way to get into the hidden city. At the time, he was wounded having been attacked by men of Salados. He had a deep wound in his leg. It was bad. I told him to wait, but he insisted on going to find Donella. I have not heard anything since. He may be inside the city, or he may be dead. I just don't know." Saying this, his voice broke and tears ran down his cheeks. "Asher is like a son, and I feel that I have lost both him and Donella."

He then turned and walked over to the fireplace and leaned on the mantel. "I am sorry," he said. "Please do not speak of this."

"Don't be," she said. And with that she did give him a hug and said, "I am sorry too."

They did not say anything for several moments, and then they separated.

"If you want to leave, I will have my knights escort you and your daughter back to Rhodes."

"I don't want to go back just yet. You have to tell me the truth. What did Clive do that made you ask him to leave?"

He looked her in the eye and said, "Are you sure you want to hear this?"

"I know my husband. He is sly and will do just about anything to attain his goals."

Joel walked over to the window. "Do you know that my sister has strong magic?"

"I have heard this. The men seem to be afraid of her."

"She has been trained by the great wizard, Epson. Somehow they still can contact each other. The night before our meeting, Epson came to Para in a dream and told her that Clive was going to kill her. He had a ring which contained poison. He was going to prick her sometime during the meeting. Knowing this, Para did not let Clive get close to her. She told him to leave the kingdom. After she left the meeting, Clive came to me and laid his hand on my shoulder. Nothing happened because my sister had magically taken the ring from Clive." He then reached inside his pocket and pulled out the ring. "This ring. I am so sorry." He then turned and started toward the door. "I don't know if you believe this or not. I do hope you will think about this and what it means for Rhodes and Regstar. Whether you believe this or not you and your daughter are not prisoners here, and I do hope you join us for our meals. Nothing more needs to be said, and if you and Kala want to leave, my offer still stands. Please do not tell Kala where Asher is gone. Just tell her he is not at the castle." He then left.

As Joel walked down the hallway back to his room, he wondered how Kira would take the news he had told her. He had not looked at her reaction and hoped she would understand the actions of his sister and himself.

Kira was shocked to hear what Joel had said. Could she believe that her husband was capable of murder? She reviewed what Joel had told her. She knew that Joel was an honest man, and she did not believe that he would deceive her. She knew nothing about Para. Was she the type of woman who would devise such a story to control Joel and seek power through him? Joel had said that Clive had a ring with poison in it. She thought back to that morning, she had seen Clive wearing the ring Joel had shown her. It was a ring she had never seen him wear before, and she had not questioned it. There was a chance that Joel was telling her the truth, and Clive had tried to kill him. She knew that Clive craved power and that the king of Rhodes had given him control of most of the kingdom. Was he seeking more power? She just did not know. She needed more information. She left her room and went to the garden hoping to find Para there. She was not disappointed. Para was sitting on a bench near a reflection pool. She walked up to her.

"May I join you?"

Para looked up, surprised to see her. "Of course."

Kira sat down next to Para, but did not say anything. It was Para who broke the silence. "You and Joel have talked. You don't know if what he told you is true, and you are seeking more information."

"Can you read my mind?"

"No, but I know people. A good woman would want more information. What can I tell you?"

Kira didn't say anything right away, but collected her thoughts. Then she spoke. "I believe that King Joel is a good man. He is a tender man, and he told me about his daughter. I could see the hurt in his eyes as he told me the story. I believe that what he told me about my husband he believes to be true. It is you I am not sure of. I need for you to tell me what happened and why you drove my husband from this castle."

Para told the story just the way that Joel had told it. This gave Kira no comfort. She still did not know if Para had told Joel the truth or whether she had a sinister plan to gain more power.

"Tell me about your husband. How was he killed?"

Para was surprised by that question. What could she gain by asking her about Alnac? "What do you want to know?"

"How was he killed?"

115

"He was betrayed by Karnac and Andrew. He was given a message by Clive to come to a secret camp to discuss peace, and he was murdered."

"Are you seeking revenge for his death?" Kira looked right into the eyes of Para as she asked the question.

"I want to. But the price is too high. I only want to protect my kingdom and my brother. I will use all the power I have to do this. If Karnac and Andrew are killed by me protecting Joel and Arsi then I will not shed any tears for them."

The two women sat for a few minutes, neither saying anything. Many thoughts ran through the mind of Kira. She wondered what Para meant when she said all her power. Was she talking about her army or her magic? Should she ask about the magic that Para had? Maybe she should not. She should change the subject. "Did you know Joel's wife?"

"I did. I was here when she gave birth to Donella. She only lived a few minutes after Donella's birth. After she died, Joel never spoke of her anymore. He did not even tell Donella about her mother or where she was from. I am somewhat surprised that he told you about her."

"You mean Donella did not know of the hidden kingdom when she was kidnapped?"

"No, she did not. I guess Joel told you that Asher has gone to try to bring her back. If he is successful, it may save Joel. He needs his daughter's love. I must go. Thank you for coming to talk with me."

When Kira was alone, she was confused. Joel and his sister seemed to be so honest with her. Perhaps Clive was on some mission of power. It was not Clive that she needed to be concerned about. Even if what Joel and Para had told her was true then it would be impossible to convince Kala.

Asher Comes Home

* * * * * * * * * * * * *

Asher, Evan, and Donella sat down next to the stream and used the large rock as a table. At first they were quiet, then Asher broke the silence. "You are Evan. I understand that you are going to marry Donella."

Evan was not sure how to answer. "That was the plan."

Donella did not like the conversation, and she steered them away from idle talk to the situation at hand. "We can be social some other time. We have to find a way to let Asher get back to Regstar and still protect this kingdom."

Evan felt some relief. She was going to help Asher leave, but she was not going.

She looked at Asher because she was not sure how he would react to her next suggestion. "I think we should bring Brumble here. I think he can help us."

"I think you call him the Great Knight Brumble. What if he decides the solution is to kill me?"

Evan took his hand to his chin and then looked down. "I don't think he will try to kill you. Besides, I think you might be a good match for him."

"I don't want to find out. I don't think we should involve anyone else. I need to leave as soon as possible. My purpose was to come here and bring Donella home to her father. I have failed in that mission." He then turned directly at Donella. "When we talked earlier, I told you I would bring your father back here. I am not sure that King Joel or I should return until there is peace in the four kingdoms. It would not be safe for the people of this land. I will not know what to do until I have assessed what is going on outside these walls."

Gwen at Arsi

* * * * * * * * *

Bailee and his ten knights rode almost nonstop to Pan. When they arrived outside the town they set up camp. The men were tired and needed rest. Bailee decided to spend the night in camp and find Gwen the next day. That night as he was sleeping Para appeared in a dream. "Bailee, Gwen may not want to go with you. She will be scared. I have placed a small bag of powder in your saddle bag. If she does not want to go, take the powder and blow it in her face. This will make her sleep. When she awakens explain everything to her. Let her know she and her baby will be safe at my castle."

When Bailee awoke the next morning he went to his bag and found the powder. He thought to himself, *Did she place the powder in the bag before he left Regstar or send it by some form of magic?*

He called his men together. "We are deep inside Salados. We need to do what we came to do and make for Arsi as soon as possible."

He chose two men and rode into Pan. He had been to Pan before and knew where to look for Gwen. She lived in the center of the town in a small house. He went to the door and knocked. A man on one crutch opened the door.

"What do you want?"

Bailee did not answer but stepped inside the door. Gwen stood near the kitchen. She was wearing an apron and had flour on her hands and even some on her face. Bailee turned to the man and said, "Leave us."

When he did not go, Gwen said, "Please Father, it will be okay. I know this man, and I know he will not harm me."

When the old man had left, Gwen said, "I know he is dead. I found out after I left the camp and came here. Did you come to tell me this news?"

Bailee did not say anything at first. "No, that is not why I am here. Queen Para has sent me." Before he could say anything else, he saw the terror in Gwen's eyes. He quickly went to her and took her by her hands.

"You are wrong. No harm is going to come to you or your baby. Para has sent me here to protect you. She wants you to come with me to Arsi. There you will be safe."

Gwen did not believe Bailee, and she stepped away from him. She wiped tears from her eyes and then sat in a chair, buried her face into her hands, and began to sob.

Bailee took her by her wrist and pulled her from the chair. "We are leaving and going to Arsi. I swear you will be safe."

He then remembered the powder. He reached into his pocket and took the small bag. When Gwen turned to him he blew the powder into her face. The magic of the powder did its job, and Gwen fell asleep. Bailee picked her up and started toward the door. Her father struck at Bailee with his crutch, but Bailee grabbed it, and the old man fell to the floor. He called for the other knights to join him. They helped Gwen's father up and let him sit at a table.

"I know you are scared for Gwen. Don't be. This is the only way she can be safe. I am going to take her to a place where she cannot be harmed. I will contact you when it is safe for you to visit. I know this is hard, but you have no choice but to trust me." Bailee carried Gwen to his horse and rode back to his camp.

When Gwen woke up, she was in a large bed. She was unaware that three days had passed. The bed felt so good she hated to move. She looked around the room and saw that it was stone and had a very high ceiling. There were paintings on the wall; none of which she recognized. The large window was closed and had drapes that extended to the floor; Strangely she felt safe.

Suddenly, the silence was broken by a maid coming through the door. "Well, it is about time you woke up. Bailee said you would sleep a long time. You must be starving."

Sitting on the edge of the bed, Gwen found that her voice was hoarse. and when she try to speak, the words barely came out. Trying a second time, her voice returned. "I am hungry, and I need something to drink."

The maid came to the edge of the bed. "Of course you are. Bailee said you slept all the way here, and he said you were ill. I have wiped your face and tried to give you some water. I am so glad you are feeling better." There was a pitcher of water next to the bed, and she poured a goblet full and handed it to her. The young woman drank it all and asked for another. When she finished, she set the goblet back on the table. "Where am I, and how did I get here?"

"You are at Arsi Castle, and Bailee brought you here. He told me as soon as you woke up to let him know. I will get you some food and let him know that you are awake."

When the maid left, two other servants came into the room with warm water and soap and helped her take a bath. They brought her clothing, and when she was dressed, she looked in the mirror and could not believe her eyes. She had never had clothing so elegant, and she looked beautiful.

When Gwen had finished eating, the maid returned, took the dishes, and said, "Sir Bailee is here."

Bailee entered the room, and Gwen again became scared. He had kidnapped her, and she was a prisoner of her lover's wife -- a wife who was queen and maybe a witch.

Bailee could see the fear, and to ease the fear, he bowed and said, "My lady, I am at your disposal."

This caught her off balance. She had not expected this, and she didn't know what to say. She just stared at the knight who was in front of her.

"You have questions, and I will answer them to the best of my ability."

"Am I a prisoner here?"

"Yes and no. You cannot leave, but you are going to be treated as a guest. You can come and go as you please within the castle walls."

"When I awoke, I was not treated like a prisoner. Why is this so?"

Bailee got to his feet. "You and I are the only ones who know you are a prisoner. The servants have been told that you are a cousin of the queen and have come to visit. They think your husband was a knight who was killed in battle fighting in Salados. They know you are with child, and you have come to have your baby at Arsi."

"Why did Queen Para do this, and how did she know about me?"

"Dorian told her about you, but I think she already knew. How she knew I don't know. She has power."

Gwen got up from the table and walked over to the large fireplace. The fire was dying down, and she was getting cold. She picked up the iron poker and moved one of the burning logs, and it started to flame once more. Looking into the burning fireplace she said, "Tell me about the Queen."

Bailee walked over and stood beside Gwen and felt the warmth of the fire. "I don't know how to describe her. She is nothing like Alnac described her back when we were in camp. He said she was beautiful, and she is. He said she was full of life, and always had a smile for everyone. Now she rarely ever smiles. She is so serious and when you are around her, you feel she can read your thoughts. She has magic, and it seems to be growing more and more powerful."

"What does she want with me and my baby? I am scared."

Bailee laid his hand on her shoulder. "Don't be. If she wanted you dead, you would already be dead. We have no choice but to trust her."

Donella, Evan and Asher

As Donella, Evan, and Asher made their plans; none of them brought up what was on their minds. Asher was now visible to the people of Reflection City, and he was not sure what to do. He could ask Donella to leave with him, but did she love him enough to go? What about Evan? If Asher left Reflection City without her, did she care enough about him to marry him? Would she wait for him to come back? He did not know how long that would be. A war that involved four kingdoms could take years. Asher had to force himself to get back to the matter at hand. Should he talk to Rue and Brumble?

Asher looked at Donella and said, "I don't think I can trust my fate to Rue and Brumble. Their first concern will be the safety of this city, and your safety. They may force me to give them my key and force me to stay here. This I cannot do. The key belongs to King Joel. It has to be his choice whether he wants to come here or not. When I get back to Regstar, I will explain your fears, and if Regstar is at peace, he can decide if he wants to come. I know what he will decide. He will come. If Regstar is at war, I will not return Joel's key until there is peace."

Donella looked at Asher with tears in her eyes. "Will you come back?"

Asher stood up and picked up a small stone and tossed it into the stream. "I want to come back. I will try to come back when Joel comes, but that is not the question you are asking. It is obvious what has happened here. I love you, and I think you love me. This has made me visible, and it is the magic of this city that is inviting me to stay. As tempting as it is, I will not turn my back on Regstar and other people I care about who live there even if it causes me great pain to give you up. I will not come back to live here unless I know that I am free to return to Regstar."

"What about my pain? For you to be visible, love has to come from both of us. What about my love for you?"

Asher looked at Donella and said, "When you came here, you loved me as a friend, you loved your Aunt Para, and you loved your father. You had no choice. You had to stay and you grew to love your grandfather and the people of this land. When I leave, ask your grandfather and ask Brumble whether they knew the door to this city could be opened at any time."

A look of shock came over Donella's face. "You can't be right."

Asher looked at Donella. She was crying. He turned to Evan. "I know you love her too. Take her back to the castle."

Evan took Donella by the arm and started to guide her to the horses. "Wait, what are you going to do? Will you wait until tomorrow? I will not talk to Grandfather until... Please wait until tomorrow."

"I am not sure what I am going to do. Go with Evan. We will talk again."

Donella mounted her horse. She interpreted Asher's words to mean he would wait, but she was wrong. He was leaving and going back to Regstar.

As soon as Donella and Evan left camp, Asher packed up his belongings and waited for dark. When darkness fell, he made his way back to the hills where the door to Reflection City was located. He quickly found the key and opened the door and left the kingdom. Standing outside the door he could see the moon reflecting on the lake. The air was cold and he quickly found his camp and put on his warm clothing. The cool air felt very good, but all he could do was think about Donella. He built a warm fire and waited for first light. He would then go to the village, get his horse, and start back to Regstar Castle.

When Evan and Donella arrived back at the castle, she looked at him and said, "I am so sorry." Then she went inside.

That night as she lay in bed she thought about Asher's words. *He is right. I have no right to hide away in this land being warm and safe while my kingdom may be at war. I love my father and I want to be with him to give him support. I love Asher and I want to be with him for the rest of my life no matter where he is.*

The next morning at early dawn, Donella was riding back to Asher's camp. When she arrived, he was not there.

Karnac and Clive

* * * * * * * * * * *

Clive had been back in Rhodes for less than a day, and he was sitting in the castle library with Karnac. Karnac had never shown much interest in running the kingdom and had given Clive authority to run the government of Rhodes.

"What happened? Am I to understand that you were told to leave Regstar and your wife and daughter are being held hostage. What did you do?"

"I did nothing. I was making a peace with King Joel when his sister came into the room and said she would not negotiate with me and that you had to be present. She then ordered me from the palace and forced my wife and daughter to stay. She says she will only meet with you and King Geoffrey. I don't trust her. You might not be safe. We need to move the army to the border and force Regstar to return my family, and if they don't, destroy Regstar."

"Just wait Clive. You speak in haste. I have had contact with King Geoffrey, and his message is we must be careful. He says that Queen Para has power. So much power that she destroyed his father's army with a much smaller force. He says that she lost no knights or archers while over a fourth of his army was destroyed. We cannot do anything against such power. I feel that Queen Para is right. I must meet with King Joel and Queen Para. Salados has been weakened, and my army cannot take on both Regstar and Arsi at the same time. I want you to send a message to Regstar that we will be there in about five days, and I will negotiate a peace myself.

Clive walked away from Karnac and turned to face him. "Joel will not give you access to the sea. Para will not give us access to the sea. We must find a way to take Para's power away. While Arsi has a strong army, Regstar has not been at war for many years. They will be no match for our armies."

Karnac lowered his head. "You might be right. I will go to Regstar to negotiate peace and trade rights to the sea. You go to see King Geoffrey and tell what I am doing. If I am unsuccessful; we then will have no other options but to declare war on the brother and sister. While I am at Regstar, I will see if I can get your family released to come home. I feel that Joel will grant us access to the sea and we will be able to use the port at Edgewater. Joel has offered us that before. Leave tomorrow for Salados.

Asher Returns

* * * * * * * * *

Para was reading in the library when Joel came into the room with a big smile on his face. "I have good news. King Karnac is on his way here to negotiate with us. The message says that he wants to make peace and have a treaty that gives him access to the sea."

Para looked up from her book. "Arsi controls as much of the river as Regstar. I might not be willing to allow boats from Rhodes to have access. Have you forgotten that Rhodes and Salados killed my husband. Tried to kill both you and me."

"I have not forgotten, but there is much at stake here. If they don't get what they want then there may be war. Many men on both sides will be killed. I don't want war if I can avoid it."

Para closed her book. "You think I want war? I spent ten years waiting for a war to end. My husband was gone for ten years -- yes ten years." She was angry. "Here you stand in front of me saying that I want war. I hate war, but I will not bow down to fear and give the enemy of my people an unfair treaty out of fear. I know what you think. I want revenge. Well I do want revenge. Maybe I will get, it but it does not figure into this negotiation."

Joel did not know what to say. He walked over to the fireplace and laid his head on the mantel. "I am sorry. The last several years have been sad years for both of us. I was so consumed by my own grief that I never considered yours."

Joel left the fireplace and walked over to Para. "Forgive me, I was unkind. Let us not make any decision until we hear what Karnac has to say. I will not give away the right of Regstar and Arsi out of fear of war. You and I will make this peace together, and we both will be satisfied."

Both Para and Joel stood and she placed her arms around him and gave him a big hug. "I am sorry too. Please forgive me. You are a good and kind man. I know that you and I will agree. We will make this peace together."

Para left Joel and walked to the window. She then turned and faced Joel. "Someone is coming. I can feel the presence of someone who is coming to the palace."

"It is too early for Karnac and his knights. Who is it?"

"I don't know. I can't make out who it is. It is a person who carries news. They won't be here for a couple of days. I don't know why I have this feeling. Oh my, I know who it is. It is Asher, and he has news of Donella."

Before Asher left his camp, he hid the key to the city. He would keep his promise to Donella and Evan and keep the city safe. No one was going into the city until he decided what to do. He loved King Joel, but he would not let Joel into Reflection City until he knew it was safe for both sides. He just did not know how to tell Joel. After hiding the key, he made his way down the mountain to the village. After a meal with the village leader, he mounted his horse and headed back to the castle at Regstar. He rode the entire day only stopping to give his horse a rest from time to time. As the day became late, the road became less visible and he started thinking of where he could spend the night.

Then, suddenly, in the road he saw an old man, and he had to pull hard on the reins to stop the horse. He was too late, and his horse knocked the old man down on the road. Jumping from his horse, he quickly went to the man who was lying on his back. Helping the poor man to his feet, he said, "I am so sorry. Are you alright?"

"I think so, but I am not sure. I seem to be somewhat dizzy. Please help me off the road."

Asher helped the man to the side of the road. "We can't stay here. It is late. Let us move beyond those trees where we'll be safe."

When Asher had the old man well off the road he went back, got his horse, picked up the old man's bag, and joined him in the clump of trees that hid them from view of the road. After taking care of his horse and making a camp, he sat down next to the old man.

"Are you cold? I can build a small fire. I don't think it can be seen from the road." He gathered up small wood, and it was not long until he had a fire burning.

"My name is Asher. I live in Regstar. I have been in the mountains and spent last night with the people of the village near the lake. They gave me a bag of food, and I will be glad to share." With that, he opened the bag of food and spread it out on a blanket. The two men began to eat with neither saying anything.

When they finished the old man spoke. "You are very kind. I am not hurt. My name is Epson."

Asher looked at the old man. "I have heard that name. Where are you from?"

"I have been living in Arsi for the past several years."

"You are a long way from Arsi."

The old man threw a small branch on the fire. "Like you, I have been in the mountains near the lake. I was visiting friends that I had not seen for a while."

Asher stretched out on the ground and put his hands behind his neck. "You should not be on these roads alone. We are close to Rhodes and many bandits cross the border into Regstar. It is not safe."

"You are alone. Is it safe for you and not for me?"

Asher smiled. "I am on a horse, and I am armed."

Suddenly they could hear the sound of many horses. Asher stood up and reached for his sword which was lying next to him. "I will see what is going on." He made his way to where he could see the road and could see about fifty or sixty knights riding by. He stayed behind the trees until they were gone, and then he went back to his camp.

"They are gone and we are safe. They were knights from Rhodes. What are they doing in Regstar?"

He sat back down next to the fire. "I have been gone for about a month. I wonder if Rhodes and Regstar are at war?"

Epson again took a branch and stirred the fire. "They are not at war. The group you saw was Karnac and his knights on their way to Regstar Castle. There is going to be a peace conference there."

"How do you know this?"

"There were rumors in the hills that Karnac was coming to Regstar. I just put two and two together. You must have been away from civilization not to know what's going on."

Asher stirred just a little. "It is complicated."

"Well, we are not going anywhere, and we have the night. You look like a troubled young man."

"Well, while I was in the mountains, I met this girl. She loves the village she lives in and its people. I live in a castle, and I would not want to live in that village, and she won't leave to live in Regstar."

"Did you ask her to leave and go with you?"

Asher kicked the fire and the ashes drifted into the night sky. "Not really."

"What do you mean not really? Did you ask her or not?"

"I did not ask her because I knew she would not come."

"So you just left, and you didn't even say goodbye. I can sense things, and I know that if you would have asked her, she would have said yes."

Asher gave the old man a big grin. "So you can sense things. If this is true, tell me about myself and we will see how good your senses are."

Epson looked at Asher. "Give me your hands and look into my eyes. You were born in the castle at Regstar. You have known the young lady that you love your entire life. She does not live in a small village, but in another kingdom. There is another young lady that you are fond of. The reason you did not say goodbye is because you were angry. You were not angry at the lady, but at yourself. You wanted to stay with her but could not because you are a man of honor and have responsibility to King Joel and the people of Regstar. Believe me, if you had asked the princess to leave with you, she would have."

Asher was in shock. "How could you know that she is a princess?"

"I told you I could sense things. In the next few months many things are going to happen. You are right. You will be needed in Regstar. Queen Para will soon be going back to Arsi. King Joel will need you more than ever. When you return to the castle, he will be angry with you, but your plan is sound. Protect the hidden kingdom even from Joel. His anger will pass."

Asher tried to speak but no words came out. He tried again and in a weak voice he said, "How could you know these things?"

The old man stepped into the middle of the fire. "I told you. My name is Epson." He then disappeared into the smoke.

Peace Maybe

* * * * * * * * *

It was not an easy night for Asher. He was not sure what to do. Should he go back and get Donella? After the restless night ended he decided he must first know what Karnac and the knights from Rhodes were doing in Regstar. After some long thought, he decided that he should not arrive at the castle the same time or even the same day as Karnac. He would wait one day.

Para was sitting on the edge of her bed when she heard the commotion outside. The drawbridge was coming down. *How strange*, she thought. The bridge had rarely been up, and now with a threat to both her and Joel the bridge had been up for several days. She walked to the window and looked down to see Karnac and some fifty knights crossing the bridge and coming into the castle. There were about one hundred knights from Regstar and another fifty from Arsi waiting to greet Karnac. She could see Dorian approaching King Karnac but could not hear what they were saying.

Is Dorian the official greeter? Who made that decision? Well I guess I will have to trust him more. He is the first knight, and Arsi is without a king.

Then came a soft knock at the door. It opened and in walked Joel. "It is time. Your conditions have been met. King Karnac is here. Once he and his men are settled, we will meet in the Great Hall."

"I will be ready. Do you know what he will want?"

"No, but with your permission, I want Kira there. I feel the first issue will be Kira and Kala's safety.

"As you wish."

Joel then left the room, and Para turned to the mirror. "Now what to wear." She choose a tight fitting full length black dress. It had full length sleeves and was tight round her neck. She put on a silver necklace and placed the crown upon her head. "I guess I look like a queen, but sometimes I don't feel the part. Today I am going to sit back and let Joel be the king."

When Para came into the Great Hall, Joel was already seated. Next to him on the left was Sir Richard. He was the chief advisor to Joel. He was about fifty years old, and Joel had told Para he knew the most about the kingdom of Regstar, and Joel had depended on him during his time of grief. To the right of an empty chair sat Dorian. She came in and took her seat next to Dorian. No one said anything. They just waited for King Karnac. When the door opened, it was not Karnac. It was Kira and Kala. They came in and took a seat to the left side of the room. After about ten minutes, the door opened and in came Karnac and five men. All stood up to greet him with the exception of Para. She just leaned over on her elbow and studied the king. He was a large man and had no crown but was holding his armor's head gear under his arm. He stopped in the middle of the room. It was King Joel who spoke first.

"Greetings, King Karnac, and welcome to Regstar."

King Karnac handed his helmet to the knight on his right. "By what right do you hold the wife and daughter of my minister captive and force me here?"

Para studied the king and his first actions. Maybe he was not as weak as she had been led to believe.

"We did force Clive to leave without his wife and daughter. They have been told that they could leave any time they wanted. They are here, and, if you and they want, you may leave in peace, but I would rather you stayed and let us work out a lasting peace."

Karnac looked to his left and saw both Kira and Kala. "Lady Kira, take your daughter and go to my tent. We will see that you and your daughter are returned to Rhodes."

Kira stood up from her chair. "King Karnac, what King Joel has told you is true. We are not prisoner and have been treated as guests. We could leave any time we wanted. In the absence of my husband I wanted to stay and help develop a lasting peace between Rhodes and Regstar. I truly believe that this is possible."

Kala stood up and left the room, and Karnac and his five advisors took their seats in front of Para and Joel.

Karnac looked at Para and thought to himself, *So this is the famous witch. She looks completely harmless.*

Para could feel the stares coming from Karnac but did not move or change her expression. She knew that he felt trapped and did not want to show any fear. She knew that he had concluded that his best option was to make peace with Regstar, but she did not know what he felt about Arsi. She would wait and see how things played out.

"We have been at peace a long time. I know that you want access to the part of Diamond River that flows through Regstar. Regstar only controls part of that river. I assume that you have a treaty with Salados that gives you access to their area of the river. I am willing to give you access to the area that Regstar controls. That leaves you with having to deal with Arsi. Queen Para is here. She will speak for Arsi."

Karnac shifted in his seat. "While there is currently no fighting, Salados and Rhodes are still at war with Arsi. I signed an agreement between Salados and Rhodes some days ago."

Para stayed calm. "You made this agreement and then killed King Alnac, my husband, whom you were allied with."

"I did not make that agreement. I had given my minister Clive that power. He did what he thought was best for Rhodes. Clive had realized that the reason that we did not have access to the river and Centerville was our own rivalry. Clive has told me that he did not think that Alnac would agree to the end of the fighting and would still deny us the use of the river."

Kira moved a little in her seat. *So it was Clive who conspired to have King Alnac killed. Did he try to have Para and Joel killed too?*

Para studied King Karnac and then looked toward Kira. "Then Clive has been running your kingdom."

"He has, but I have taken charge. He is on his way to meet with King Geoffrey. He is going to tell him I am here to make peace. I don't know what Geoffrey will do. I believe he will want to kill you, Queen Para. If we form a peace, I think he will have no choice but to agree to a peace. Arsi defeated King Andrew and his army at High Yellow Pass. King Andrew is dead. I have not met with Geoffrey. If I make peace today with Arsi, I do not know what this will mean for Rhodes. Arsi defeated King Andrew, but Salados is still strong. They will be a force to deal with. I can only hope that they will agree to a peace."

Para had not changed her position or expression. She continued to wait and let Joel deal with Karnac.

While Karnac was waiting for Para to speak, it was Joel who spoke. "How do you tend to deal with Geoffrey? Do we need to wait until you and Geoffrey have sat down and worked out a treaty between Salados and Rhodes?"

"That won't be necessary. As I said, I have sent Clive to Salados to let Geoffrey know what I am doing. I will wait here until Clive arrives."

For the first time Para, moved in her seat and said very calmly, "If Clive comes into my sight, I will kill him where he stands."

Karnac came to his feet and said in an angry tone, "Then you had no intention of making peace, and you want to continue this war." Karnac started to leave.

Para stood. "King Karnac, hear me out. Salados and Arsi have been at war for more than ten years. Clive and King Andrew conspired to have my husband killed, and Clive has tried to have both me and Joel killed. It was the war with Salados that took the life of my father. I want to make peace, but how can I trust the men who have taken just about everything from me? I trust you, but I do not trust Clive. I will not give him a second chance to kill me. If you want peace, send word to Clive that he is not to come to Regstar but to ask Geoffrey to come here and help us make a lasting peace."

Karnac turned and faced Para. "If you believe all these things of me, how could you ever want peace? You would want to kill me. If you were a man, I would challenge you to combat. We could settle this with the swords."

"I don't want to kill you, but if you want to settle this with combat, choose your champion." She then told Dorian to give her his sword.

Dorian did not hesitate. He had learned to trust her judgment and not question anything she did.

Karnac was smiling. He turned to the knight on his right. "Sir Robert, be my champion. Do not kill her, but just give her a scar that will teach her not to threaten any citizen of Rhodes."

Sir Robert drew his sword and walked to the circle in the center of the Great Hall. Para walked out to the circle to join him and said. "Sir Robert,

I do not know you and wish you no harm. You are going to try to disarm me and cut me to teach me a lesson. The lesson taught here will be yours."

Para waved her arm, and Sir Robert's sword few across the room making a clanking sound as it skipped several times on the stone floor. He fell to his knees and reached for his neck with both hands. "I cannot breathe." He then fell to floor and passed out.

Para walked over to the unconscious body of Sir Robert and placed the point of her sword on his back and looked at Karnac. "Shall I give him a scare to teach him that the people of Arsi are not seeking revenge but with Regstar are seeking a lasting peace? It is up to you, but if you do not want peace we can defend ourselves. Kira and Kala can leave and join Clive, but if he comes here I will kill him, not out of revenge but to protect myself and my brother."

King Karnac was speechless, but when he found his voice he said, "I will send a message to Clive that he is not to come here. Clive is with King Geoffrey and telling him that I am here to make peace. I will let him know that we need him to be present at our next meeting. Queen Para, I hope to win your trust and perhaps we can build a lasting peace."

"I too want a lasting peace. I know my brother does, and let's hope that King Geoffrey will join us. I am needed back in my kingdom. Maybe the next meeting can be in my castle at Arsi."

By this time Sir Robert had regained his wits and was struggling to his feet. "Did I win?" He looked at Para standing with a slight smile on her face. "I guess not."

Asher and Joel

* * * * * * * * *

Asher rode slowly back to the castle at Regstar. His thoughts were almost always on Donella and how he had left. He knew he could not ask her to leave with him because there was much that was uncertain. He hoped that Kala had returned to Rhodes and would not be at the castle. As he topped the hill, he could see Regstar Castle. The drawbridge was up. *Not a good sign*, he thought to himself. When he was about fifty yards from the castle, he heard the cry from the top of the wall. "Halt and identify yourself."

"I am Asher, returning from a mission for the king."

"Hold your position." The drawbridge started down, and when it reached the ground, five knights rode across and joined Asher. They recognized Asher, and handshakes and laughter could be heard as they welcomed their friend back home.

Trent, a knight of about Asher's age, reached across his horse and gave him a hug. "Let's go to the castle. We have much to discuss. Queen Para, King Karnac, and King Joel are discussing peace. After you have settled and cleaned off the dust of the trip we will meet, and I will bring you up to date."

"Is Kala still here?"

"Yes, and her mother too. Queen Para forced Clive to leave, and I am not sure if Kala and Kira are prisoners or guests."

They then rode across the bridge and into the castle courtyard. He could hear the drawbridge coming up as they entered the castle. Even with all the trouble he was going to face, he was glad to be home. He just wished that Donella was with him.

After Asher cleaned up and was presentable, he went to the barracks to meet with Trent.

"Are you ever going to get married and get out of these barracks?"

Trent smiled. "I would, but all the women are waiting for you. If you will get married then maybe I may have a chance with some of the other ladies."

Asher took a seat. "Tell me what is going on."

Trent suddenly became very serious. "It is rumored that Clive tried to kill Queen Para and King Joel. Para used her magic and saved both of them. She then forced Clive to leave and forced Kira and Kala to stay."

"So they are prisoners."

"No, they are not. King Joel told them if they wanted to leave, he would allow them to do so, and if they chose to stay they would be treated as quests. But wait, it gets even better. During the meeting today, Queen Para told King Karnac if Clive was ever in her sight again, she would kill him."

Asher leaned the chair back and said, "Could she do that?"

"Do you remember Sir Robert? He is one of the most powerful knights in Rhodes. He challenged Queen Para, and she bested him without lifting her sword. Somehow she made him drop his sword, and he passed out on the floor. She is one powerful witch."

"I don't think she is a witch. She is a good lady, and yes, she has magic. She must have powerful magic, or she could not have defeated King Andrew's army at High Yellow Pass. How are the peace talks going?"

"I think they are going better than expected. They are going to meet again. Queen Para is going to return to Arsi. King Andrew will be returning to Rhodes, but they are going to meet again in Arsi. Tell me about your trip. Where have you been?"

"I wish I could tell you. It is all a secret. I must return to my quarters and prepare to meet with King Joel. Wish me luck because it will be the hardest meeting of my life."

When Asher left the barracks, he sent word to Joel that he had returned and would meet with him when he was ready. He then returned to his quarters. When he opened the door, there stood Kala. He was caught off guard and simply said, "Hello Kala."

"Is that the best you can do?" She sounded both hurt and angry.

Asher tried to make some excuse. "I am sorry. I have been riding most of the day and have not had much rest for the last several days. I just came from a meeting with Trent, and he has been bringing me up to date, and I now must prepare for a meeting with King Joel. I did not know you were even in the castle until just a few minutes ago."

Kala quickly came to his side and gave him a kiss. "You are forgiven. Where have you been? You left and didn't even say a word. I have been worried about you. Did you know that Mother and I have been prisoners here at this castle, and Father has been banished and not allowed to return?"

"Yes, I know about all this. Trent told me everything."

"Where have you been?"

"I cannot tell you. I have been on a mission for King Joel. I must keep everything a secret until he and I meet."

Kala turned away and walked over to the window. She suddenly became very distant. "Arsi and Rhodes are on the verge of war. Queen Para is at the castle, my father has been banished, and King Karnac has been lured here. Have you been spying on Rhodes? Are Arsi and Regstar planning a war with Rhodes? Are you going to attack my homeland?"

Asher couldn't help but smile. "Has your imagination gone wild? It is my understanding that Arsi, Regstar, and Rhodes are trying to make peace. My leaving the castle the second time had nothing to do with that."

"You mean you have left twice? Why did you not stop to see me in between?"

"I had no time. Please believe me when I say I can't tell you more. King Joel sent me on two secret missions. You must trust me, I can't tell you any more than that."

Kala's face was flushed with anger. "You say I must trust you, but you won't trust me. I have been told that King Karnac is going back to Rhodes tomorrow. I am going with him."

Kala then started to the door, but she was hoping that Asher would stop her. He did not. She quickly opened the door and was gone.

Queen Para, King Joel, and King Karnac decided to eat the evening meal together. It was King Karnac who spoke first. "You say that you will give Rhodes access to the port of Edgewater. What do Arsi and Regstar want in return?"

King Joel looked to Para and then to Karnac. "We want much. We first want peace. We want the border raids stopped. We want free trade between the citizens of all three kingdoms. We want you to patrol your borders and arrest the bandits who raid from across the border. We want our border patrols to be allowed to cross the border in pursuit of bandits if necessary. We would offer Rhodes the same. It is our hope that a lasting peace will put an end to the need for border patrols."

"This sounds fair, but I cannot speak for King Geoffrey. I have been at war with Salados for many years. We just recently made a very unstable peace. I know that the first thing on Geoffrey's mind will be revenge for the death of his father."

King Joel rubbed his chin. "You said that at the afternoon meeting. It will be up to you to convince him that revenge is not an option he has. You must remind him that no one has a greater reason for revenge than Para and myself. Remind him that she has lost a husband and father, and I have lost a brother-in-law and father."

About that time Richard came up to the table. "Sir, I hate to disturb you at meal time, but I must inform you that Sir Asher has returned. He has been back for several hours but did not want to disturb you during your peace meeting. He awaits word from you on when you can see him."

Joel's eyes lit up. "Was he alone when he returned to the castle?"

"Yes, he was alone. He first met with his knights, and then had a meeting with Sir Trent."

Para could see the disappointment in Joel's face.

"Where is Asher now?"

"He is in his quarters. Shall I send for him."

Joel stood up from the table. "You must excuse me; I need to meet with Asher." He then turned to Sir Richard. "Don't send for Asher. I will meet with him in his quarters." He quickly left the dining hall.

After Joel left, Para could sense that King Karnac had become suspicious of what was going on. She knew that Karnac suspected that Asher was a spy, and she knew that King Andrew and possibly Karnac had planned to have Asher killed on the way back from the secret meeting. "Does it surprise you that Asher is still alive? He returned several days after he was attacked. He was wounded very badly. King Joel sent him to a lake in the mountains that is supposed to have healing power. He is very excited to see that he is back."

Karnac rose from the table. "Thank you for a fine meal. I hope that Sir Asher is okay. Could you not have healed Asher?"

Para smiled. "You forget, I was not here. I was at High Yellow Pass killing King Andrew."

Joel went straight to Asher's quarters. He knocked and then opened the door and walked in. Asher, who had been sitting in a chair, got up and the two men hugged and exchanged smiles.

Joel walked over to the fireplace and turned to face Asher. "I have been worried. When you left here, you had a terrible wound. I had visions of you dying somewhere on the road between here and the lake. You have come back alone so I assume that you were not successful in getting into Reflection City, and you have been recovering from your wound. I am glad you are home."

"My King, you need to sit down. I have an interesting story to tell you. I was not successful in bringing Donella back to Regstar, but I did get into the hidden city."

Excitement came back into Joel's eyes, and he sat down at the table near the center of the room. "You got into the city! Did you find Donella?"

Asher looked down. "I did get into the city, and I have let you down. Yes, I did see Donella."

"Could you not get her out? Do I need to take an army to recover her?"

Asher paused before he answered. "You have to hear the entire story. Once you know all the facts, I hope you will forgive me for not bringing Donella back."

"Tell me about Donella. What is she like?"

"She is the most beautiful woman I have ever seen. She is tall with long very dark hair, and she told me that the people tell her that she looks exactly like her mother. Here comes the problem. She is not a prisoner of Reflection City. She loves the city, and she loves her grandfather Rue. She does not want to leave. I could have forced her to leave, but then I would be the kidnapper. There were also other things to consider. While I was there, I was extremely sick. She nursed me back to health. I stayed outside the city near a creek. No one could see me, and she came each day with bandages and food until I could regain my strength. She could have turned me in many times but did not. We spoke each day. At first she did not know who, I was and she asked many questions about you and Regstar. It was clear that she loves you very much."

"Then why can't I go to her?" Joel slammed his hands on the table.

"Before I left, I had to make a promise that I would protect Reflection City and not let anyone come into the kingdom."

"My daughter asked this of you."

"No, I made this promise to Epson. I met him on the road coming back from Reflection City. I thought about asking Donella to come with me. If I had asked, I think she would have come. I needed to protect her. I did not know if we were at war with Rhodes, and if you come marching into Reflection City, the people would surely protect their secret door. I did not bring the key back with me. I will keep my promise to Donella and Evan that I will not bring anyone back to Reflection City until they are ready. You can't get in, but I am almost sure they can get out."

Joel laid his head over on his folded arms on the table. "You said that she would not leave. Who is Evan?"

"Here comes the good news. Donella is not married but is somewhat engaged to a young man named Evan. I think he is a good man, but Donella told me she will not get married without your blessing. I am sure the wedding is on hold until she has seen you. Before Epson left me on the side of the road, he told me when it would be safe to return to the city. The four kingdoms have to be at peace. Forgive me for failing you in this mission, but I feel everything will work out. When we have secured peace with Salados and Rhodes, I am sure we will be able to see Donella again."

Joel got up from the table. "You have not failed me. It is getting late. I have much work to do to secure this peace. Please dine with me and Para tomorrow night. There will be some other guests and it will be quite formal. Please do not discuss this with anyone. The only person who knows of your mission is Para, and I will bring her up to date." Then he thought, *Kira also knows about your mission.* "Thank you for what you have done."

Mother And Daughter

* * * * * * * * * * * * * * *

After Kala left Asher, she went directly to her mother's room. She found her mother brushing her hair and getting ready for bed. "Did you know that King Karnac is going back to Rhodes tomorrow?"

Kira stopped brushing her hair. "Yes, he told me."

"Do you plan to return with him?"

Kira looked into her daughter's eyes and said, "No, I am staying here."

Kala was angry. "Then you believe the stories they have made up about Father are true."

"Yes, I do. I know you love your father, but Clive seeks power and will do just about anything to get it. He is not the man I married. The man I married would not have left us here. He would have insisted that we be released to leave Regstar with him. Since he has been gone, we have received no messages from him. You know that we have been free to leave anytime we wanted to. I have not wanted to. King Joel and Queen Para have treated us well. I am going to stay here until the peace between Regstar and Rhodes is secure."

"Maybe Joel and Para are not letting him get a message through."

"I know that Clive met with King Karnac before the king came here. The king has not given me any message. I even asked him if there was a message from my husband, and he said there was none."

Kala walked over and kneeled at her mother's feet. "Do you know that Asher has returned to the castle? He has been on a secret mission for King Joel. I feel he may be spying on Rhodes. Rhodes is my home and your home. I love my people, and if Rhodes and Regstar go to war I will be there for my people. I am going home tomorrow. Please come with me."

"I don't think Rhodes and Regstar will go to war. It is just a feeling I have and I have some things to work out with Clive. I am going to stay here where Clive cannot get to me and try to sort things out."

Kala got up from the floor and said, "I am leaving, and I hope you change your mind." She then left the room.

When Kala got back to her room, Asher was standing at her door. "I am leaving in the morning with King Karnac. There is nothing more to be said."

Asher took her by the arm. "Yes, there is."

For a moment Kala thought that Asher was going to confess his love for her, and ask her to stay and perhaps even more.

Asher looked into the eyes of Kala. "I know that you are hurt, but before you go you must know a few things. You are right and I am going to tell you what I can. When I tell you this you will hate me, but I owe this to you."

Kala thought to herself, *He is a spy, and if he loves me, I can forgive him.*

"You were right. I was on two missions for King Joel. On the first I carried a message from King Joel, and your father to Alnac. I do not know the contents because they were in code. On the way back I was attacked by several men from Salados and in my escape I was wounded. As it turns out much more seriously than I first thought."

"Why didn't you stay here at the castle, and let your wound heal?"

Asher decided not to tell Kala the complete truth. "King Joel needed someone he could trust to travel to the Northern Lake. When I got there I spent the night at a local village, and the next day went to the lake and made a camp. My wound became infected and I was extremely sick. A local girl nursed me back to health and we have fallen in love. As soon as King Joel and Queen Para can make peace, I am going to return to her village."

Kala was looking down and tears were rolling down her cheeks. "I will still be leaving tomorrow. You understand. Thanks for telling me this."

Asher leaned over and kissed Kala on the forehead. "I hope we will always be friends." He then left and went back to his room.

Clive and Geoffrey

* * * * * * * * * * * *

On the trip to Salados, Clive became more and more determined to find a way to destroy Queen Para. She had embarrassed him before the court and forced him to leave Regstar. She had taken his wife and daughter prisoner and placed him in a position where he had very little power with King Karnac. His only hope was that King Geoffrey would want revenge more than he wanted peace. As the days passed, he made several plans about his revenge. They all would need the help of Geoffrey to work. By the time he approached the castle at Salados, he had become so driven with revenge and hate that he had given no thought to his wife and daughter. He needed revenge and would do anything to get it and his power back.

When he arrived at King Geoffrey's castle, he was greeted by King Geoffrey himself. Clive knew immediately that he too wanted revenge.

"My servants will take you to your room. We will take dinner together, and you can bring me up to date on what's going on in the east."

After Clive had settled into his room and changed into more formal attire, his thoughts turned to his wife. *What has happened to her, is she safe?* He almost wished that something would happen to her so he could use it to stir the people of Rhodes to revenge. If Para would put Kira and Kala in prison, King Karnac would have no choice but to declare war on Regstar and Arsi. Maybe he could arrange something to happen to her. He could sacrifice his wife for his plans but not Kala. He would think of some plan to get her out of Regstar. He had plans for Kala, and they did not include her being a prisoner. She would make a great queen for Geoffrey.

When Clive and Geoffrey finished their meal, it was Geoffrey who spoke first about what was going on in the east. "What is Karnac doing? You told me that he would be a strong ally in our quest to take both Regstar and Arsi."

Clive leaned over on his elbow and spoke softly. "I know, but things changed after the defeat of Salados at High Yellow Pass. He wanted the defeat of Para and Joel, and that would mean he would have access to the ports at Edgewater, but now he thinks he can gain the same thing with a peace treaty between Regstar and Arsi."

"Does he not know that Salados controls part of the Diamond River, and he would have no access without my approval?"

"He assumes that he has it. You remember that King Andrew had made peace between Salados and Rhodes."

"He made that peace with my father and not me. If he makes peace with Arsi, he will not have peace with me. When you go back, make sure that King Karnac knows this," Geoffrey said with anger in his voice.

Clive thought for a moment and saw the timing was right. "Just what do you want, Geoffrey? Do you want peace, or do you want revenge?"

Geoffrey did not hesitate. "I want revenge, and I want Arsi. I want to see Queen Para dead for what she did to my father and his men at High Yellow Pass."

Clive lit up. "Then you and I want the same. I want revenge for what that evil queen did to me, and I want Rhodes to have Regstar. I want this, but I don't know how we are going to get it. You know that if Rhodes signs a peace with both Arsi and Regstar, they will be much stronger than Salados and would control the river trade. We would have to submit to their will."

Geoffrey rubbed his hands together. "I have a plan. When you meet with King Karnac, see if he will go along with doing away with Para. If he agrees, I know an assassin who can kill Para. With Para dead, Arsi will have no real leadership and will be easy to take."

Clive shifted in his seat. "I tried to kill Para, and she somehow knew my plans. This is what got me put out of Regstar and why I can't return. She has power that seemed to warn her of what I was going to do. No one could have told her because no one knew."

"I have someone who can do the job. He has power to kill anyone, and they never know he is coming. He can make it look like an accident. When you have talked to Karnac we will put our plan in motion. If he agrees then Para will be killed, and I will attack Arsi."

"And what if he does not agree?"

"Then we will have King Karnac killed and make it look like King Joel was responsible. Then we will have her killed too."

Clive rubbed his chin and said, "Who is this assassin?"

"His name is Piper."

Queen Para Returns to Arsi

* * * * * * * * * * * * * * * * * * *

King Karnac and his men were waiting for Kala. It was not long until she appeared riding a white horse. She was wearing a black riding dress topped with a black jacket trimmed in white. "Did I keep you waiting? I am so sorry."

King Karnac dismounted his horse and took the reins of Kala's mount. "I want to talk to you. Your mother is sympathetic to King Joel. I don't think she would give me any information if I asked her. I don't understand why she is staying here."

Kala's horse shifted a little, and Karnac patted it on the head. "She thinks that my father tried to kill Para and Joel."

"Do you think he did?"

Kala shifted in her saddle. "I don't know, but if he did, I would like to think he had a good reason."

"Listen Kala. I need for you to stay here in Regstar. Joel and Para seem sincere about wanting peace, but I don't know. and I have to know. I cannot gamble the future of Rhodes until I know what their plans are. If you stay here, you can be the eyes and ears of Rhodes."

Kala did not say anything for a moment. It would be painful staying so close to Asher. But then again, maybe all was not lost between them, and she could help Rhodes and her king. "I am not sure I want to stay, but I will do what you ask. If I find out anything, how will I let you know?"

"There is a man who lives in the village of Onida who is loyal to Rhodes. If you find out anything go riding and pass though the village. Wear a red scarf, and he will contact you." He then let go of Kala's horse. "Go back into the castle and tell them you could not leave your mother alone."

Kala puts her horse back in the stable, and on the way to her room she meets Para.

"You have decided not to go back to Rhodes with King Karnac. I thought you might stay," Para said with a smile.

"How did you know that? Are you truly a witch? Can you read minds?" Kala had concern on her face.

Para smiled even more. "No, everyone asks me that. I can't read your mind. I just know that a bond between a mother and daughter is strong and that you care for her. I just guessed you did not want to leave her here alone."

It was Kala's turn to smile. "You are right. I know that she would be safe here, but it did not seem right to leave her."

As Para started walking away, she said. "We are having supper tonight in the great hall. Your mother, King Joel, Asher, and several of the knights will be there. Please join us."

That night, Kala put on her green dress with the long sleeves and the low cut neckline. As she looked in the mirror, she said to herself, *I will show Asher what he is giving up for a village girl.*

As she walked down the hallway toward the great hall, she wondered if Asher just owed the village girl some debt of gratitude and would tire of her and come back to her. *No matter,* she thought, *Asher is a spy and now I am a spy. What a wee bit of irony.*

She was late coming to dinner, and when she looked at the large table which was almost square, Para and Joel were at one end seated side by side. Her mother, Kira, was on the corner next to Joel, and across from her mother was Dorian sitting next to Para. On down the table was a knight she did not know but later found out it was Sir John. On her other side was the knight Trent, and at the end of the table was Asher. All stood up when she approached the table.

"Please don't get up. I am sorry I am late." She took the empty seat next to Asher. All again took their seats.

Kira spoke first. "I am so glad that you decided to stay." Kala could see that her mother's eyes were moist, and she felt bad that she had not given her the news herself.

Soon after Kala had taken her seat the food arrived. Boiled potatoes, carrots, and beans along with pheasant and several loaves of bread were set on the table, and the servants poured wine.

It was not long until Para turned the conversation to a more serious topic. "We are leaving tomorrow. Dorian has instructed our knights to be ready to leave by dawn so we can make as much distance as possible before dark. We know that Clive has gone to see King Geoffrey, and if he wants to meet, the meeting will take place at Arsi Castle. There are things that we must prepare, and I have some personal matters to deal with."

She then turned and faced Kira. "If at any time you and Kala wish to leave, Joel has promised to give you an escort back to your home in Rhodes. For the most part, I have enjoyed my visit here and invite all of you to visit me at Arsi."

Joel shifted in his seat and turned toward Para, then said to the entire table, "I am sending Asher and a garrison of men to High Yellow Pass. If Geoffrey wants peace then Asher and his knights will escort him to Arsi Castle. If he does not want peace and has an army behind him Asher, along with Dorian, can defend the pass until Para and I can have our armies there."

Kala listened to all that was being said. *They are keeping nothing a secret. I do believe that they truly want peace and have nothing to hide.*

When the meal was finished, Para left with Dorian, and the rest of the table went their separate ways. As Kala got up, she heard Asher say, "May I walk you back to your room?"

Kala looked toward the end of the table where Kira and Joel had not gotten up but were talking. "No I think I can find my way." She then left the room.

After all had left the room, Joel said to Kira, "I am glad you stayed at Regstar. I have enjoyed your company. If things do not go as planned. I will have to leave. If Geoffrey moves an army on Arsi, I will have to go to support my sister."

Kira laid her hand over on Joel's arm. "You might have it all wrong. What if Geoffrey does not accept peace and moves his army not on Arsi but on Regstar?"

"He does not have enough men to attack both Arsi and Regstar. Para and I have thought of this, and if this happens, she will bring her army to support me. The real problem is that we don't know what King Karnac will do. I believe he wants peace, but he had just become allies of Salados, and I don't know how much influence Clive will have in these matters. These are matters that are now out of our control. Let's talk about more pleasant things. Would you like to take a walk in the garden?"

As Joel and Kira walked through the garden, they made small talk about the flowers and the weather. "I can't believe these flowers still have blooms. It has been so cold, and winter is coming." Suddenly, Kira turned and faced Joel. They were close, almost touching each other. Joel could smell the sweetness of her perfume and feel the heat from her body. She laid her hands on Joel's chest and slid them up to his shoulders. "I don't want to go back to Rhodes. I want to stay here."

Joel was not surprised by her confession. "I don't want you to go. You can stay as long as you like, or if you like, you can stay forever."

He then reached down, lifted her chin and kissed her lightly on the lips. "I have not cared about any women since my wife died. I have feelings for you. I don't know what problems we are going to have. Somehow we will have to let Clive know that you want to stay. You will have to talk to Kala. I have a feeling she will not take you staying here with me very well."

Kira laid her head on Joel's chest. "We will just have to take one problem at a time. I am not going to tell anyone I plan to stay. We should keep it a secret until peace has been secured. Then we will deal with Kala, Clive, and Rhodes."

Joel kissed Kira on top of her head. "I agree. We will go on as if there is nothing between us, but I have a sister who can sense things. If I feel she knows how we feel toward each other, I will have to talk to her. Go to your room, and I will see you when I am free tomorrow."

The next morning the caravan was assembled and ready to move out. Para was on a big black horse and was wearing a black cape. Dorian was on a brown horse and was wearing his armor. Joel rode up and told his sister that he would ride a ways with her. She agreed, and the group left the castle.

After they were gone, Asher and his knights assembled with the archers and prepared to leave the castle. He looked up as Kala rode right up to him.

She smiled as she stopped her horse next to his. "I came to see you off and wish you luck."

"Thank you. I hope this mission does not take too long. I am glad you stayed. I need a friend, and your mother will need the company."

She moved her horse next to his, leaned over, and kissed him on the cheek. "I wish you luck, and please return safely. May I ride along with you for a while?" He agreed, and Asher led his knights and archers out of the castle.

As they rode toward Arsi, Asher and Kala made small talk. It was not long until they reached a crossroads, and Kala stopped her horse. "I am going to stop at Onida. I understand they make wonderful blood sausage. I may treat Mother to a picnic this week. Be safe."

Asher thought it might not be safe for Kala to be in Onida by herself. "Do you want me to send a knight to accompany you?"

"I am a big girl, and I can take care of myself. Thanks for being concerned about me." She then rode away.

Asher watched, and he wondered if he should send a couple of knights with her anyway. He thought better of it. *We are currently at peace, and she is close to the castle. She will be alright. It's strange she is wearing a red scarf. It stands out because it does not match her outfit.* He gave it no more thought and continued on his journey.

It did not take Kala long to reach Onida. There she dismounted her horse and took a leisurely stroll through the market. It wasn't long until an old man came up to her and said, "Lady with the red scarf, do you have something for me?"

Kala turned toward the man. "What do you mean?"

The old man grinned. "King Karnac said that if a lady with a red scarf came to Onida she would have a message, and I was to take the message and send it to him. Is the message in code?"

"No, I do not know how to use codes." Kala handed the message to the man, quickly went to her horse, and left the village.

After Kala had left and the old man found a private place, he looked at the message.

My King. Queen Para is returning to Arsi. King Joel has readied his army because he fears Salados may attack Arsi. He has sent about one hundred knights to High Yellow Pass to help guard the pass. This is important. I am sure King Joel and Queen Para want peace. They just don't trust King Geoffrey. I will continue to stay at Regstar until we have peace, or if for some reason, we have war.

Piper

* * * *

King Geoffrey was a smart man and knew that he could not defeat Arsi and Regstar without the help of Rhodes. The problem was that Rhodes was considering a peace with Arsi. This would put Salados without any ally and close the Diamond River to his kingdom. If he was to have his revenge, he would have to find a way to separate Arsi and Regstar and regain Rhodes as an ally. He sat down and began a message to Piper.

Piper was a warlock, but in fact he was much more. He had many skills and was always willing to sell these skills if the price was right. He had not been in Salados long. It was rumored that he had come from across the sea and had been responsible for many deaths. When he arrived in Edgewater, he found out quickly that he could not sell his skills to Arsi or Regstar. When he found out about the death of King Andrew, he had gone to King Geoffrey and offered his services. Geoffrey had told Piper to go to a cave in the mountains that separated Salados and Arsi and wait for his message. He had done so, and now he stood in that cave holding the message from Geoffrey.

I am willing to meet your price. Your tasks will not be easy. In a few days King Karnac will start his journey to Arsi. I will let you know when he leaves Rhodes. He will be going through Centerville which is in Regstar. There you will kill him, but you must make it look like it was done by an assassin from Regstar.

After you have killed Karnac, go to Arsi and kill Queen Para. Make it look like some type of accident. I will be sending Clive to Rhodes. Clive will be named as regent of Rhodes and move his army on Regstar. With Para dead and Joel at war with Rhodes, you are to join me at High Yellow Pass for our march on Arsi.

King Geoffrey knew that the people of Rhodes would be outraged and would want revenge for Karnac's death. Clive would be there to take control of the kingdom and lead the army against King Joel. Arsi would be thrown into a state of confusion because there was no heir to the throne. King Joel would be tied up with the war with Rhodes, and his army could then slip through High Yellow Pass and take Arsi. If his plan went well, he would have control of Arsi, Regstar, and Rhodes and have his revenge for his father's death.

He sent for Clive and told him of his plan. "I am sending word that I am going to attend the meeting in Arsi. King Karnac will be killed in Centerville. It will look like he was killed by an assassin from Regstar. It is important that you be in Rhodes before Karnac leaves for Arsi. You must be in charge of the castle when Rhodes receives word of Karnac's death. You will move your army to the border and prepare for war against Regstar. Meanwhile, Queen Para is going to die. When that happens, I am going to attack Arsi. They will be leaderless, and this will make for a quick victory. I will then move my army toward Edgewater and attack Regstar from the south as you move across the border from the north. After the defeat of Regstar, we will control the entire country. You must leave at once. Timing is everything."

It took several days for Clive to reach the castle at Rhodes. He went to Karnac and said, "King Geoffrey is going to the meeting at Arsi. The meeting will be in eight days. I assume you will be attending the meeting also."

"I have no choice because I am sure that Para and Joel both want peace. This could put an end to years of war and give us an outlet to the sea. I see good times ahead for the people of Rhodes. I will leave in the morning."

"My King," Clive said lowering his head, "I cannot attend this meeting and for that I am sorry. I will continue to serve you by taking charge of the castle in your absence. I will prepare papers for you to sign naming me regent while you are gone."

"You are right. Get the papers ready, and I will sign. But tell me, Clive, why has your wife not returned from Regstar? Does this not cause you some concern?"

Clive knew he must be very careful with his answer if he was going to keep Karnac's trust. He thought for a moment and said, "I fear that Queen Para has cast some spell upon her to punish me for some reason. She thinks I tried to kill her, which is not true. It is my hope that when the peace is signed and you return to Rhodes, Queen Para will release her from this spell."

"That will be my hope too. Prepare the papers and bring them to me. I must make ready for my trip to Arsi."

Para The Queen

* * * * * * * * * * *

Para was in sight of the castle of Arsi. The trip had been exhausting and she was so glad to be home. As she rode into the castle, she was surprised to hear the bells ringing announcing her return. She dismounted and handed the reins to the stable boy. When she turned around, Dorian was by her side.

"Get some rest Dorian; I know you must be tired from the trip. I am going to take a bath and rest. We need to meet tomorrow and make plans for whatever King Geoffrey decides to do. I don't have a feeling one way or another." She turned away and started inside only to be greeted by Bailee. "Walk with me Bailee and bring me up to date with Gwen."

Bailee took his place by Para's side, and they walked inside together. "I have placed her in the room across from yours. Everyone here thinks she is a cousin, but they are asking a lot of questions."

"What type of questions?"

"The servants know she is with child. They wonder where her husband is and why she has come to Arsi."

Para slowed her pace. "What have you told them?"

"Nothing, my lady. They only know that she is a cousin, and I have let it go at that."

Para stopped for a moment. "What is she like?"

"Bailee turned and faced Para. "She is one scared young lady. I have told her she has nothing to fear, but she does not believe me. She thinks that you are going to kill both her and her baby."

"What do you think?"

"I don't know. I have known you as a kind lady, but a lot has happened to you the last several weeks. Your husband has been murdered. You have attempts on your life and have found out that your husband was unfaithful and has fathered a child. If I was sure you were going to kill Gwen, I would have taken her far away and hidden her from you."

Para looked at Bailee and smiled. "I am not going to harm her. Thank you for being honest with me. Go tell Gemma to come to my room and bring lots of hot water. Once I have cleaned the dirt from the trip from my body, I will meet with Gwen and put her mind at ease."

Para wanted to stay in the hot water forever. As she reclined in the large brass tub, she wondered how the meeting with Gwen would go. How could she explain Gwen to the staff and to her kingdom? She would have to come up with something, and that something might need to be the truth. Gemma came popping into the room. "What shall I lay out for you to wear, my Lady?"

"I need something cheerful, get me my blue dress with the gold trim. I need to let my hair dry, and then I will call you to help me finish dressing. Right now I am just going to lie here and soak. I might need some more hot water." She closed her eyes and drifted off to sleep.

Gemma laid out the necessary underclothes and the blue dress and quietly left the room.

While Para was sleeping in the hot tub, Gwen was pacing back and forth in her room. She was scared. The servants had been kind to her, and she really liked Bailee. He had come to see her every day and had become her only friend. She had thought about asking Bailee to help her leave Arsi and go somewhere and hide. She even thought about going back to Salados and asking King Geoffrey for refuge. She did not because she felt that King Geoffrey would use her baby against Arsi. All she could do was wait. Then she heard a knock at the door. Her heart almost jumped out of her body. Was it Queen Para? She went to the door and opened it. It was Bailee. "I just wanted to see how you were doing. I know you are scared to meet with the queen. Don't be. She is a good person, and you don't have anything to fear."

"I keep telling myself that, but it doesn't help. I keep wondering why she has brought me here. You tell me it is for my own safety, and I am a guest, but I know that I am really a prisoner."

Bailee stepped inside the door. "If you were not here you would be back in Pan. You would be in a small drafty hut with no help. To the people of Pan you would only be an unwed mother and an outcast. You would have no help with the birth of your child. The queen has protected you from all that."

Gwen took one of Bailee's hands and rested her head on it. "You have been a good friend. I know what you say is true. The queen has given me a good home here, and you tell me I am safe. What I don't know is why is she doing this? She has every reason to hate me, and what I hear from the servants is that she can kill anyone with the wave of her hand."

Bailee placed his other hand on Gwen's shoulder. "I have been with Queen Para the last several weeks and only left her to come to take care of you. To my knowledge, she has not killed anyone."

"They say she killed King Andrew."

"You are referring to the Battle at High Yellow Pass. She did not kill King Andrew. She was protecting the kingdom of Arsi and created a fog to confuse the soldiers of Salados. King Andrew was killed by an arrow from one of our archers. She did not kill him. He killed himself by attacking Arsi. I must go. If you need anything, send for me." He turned and left Gwen standing alone at the door.

Gwen went back inside her room and took a seat. Her heart was beating faster and faster. She knew Bailee had told her she had nothing to fear, but she could not control the beating of her heart or the shaking of her hands.

When Para awoke from her sleep, she was sitting in her tub and the water was getting cold. She thought of calling for Gemma to help her get dressed but then decided she could do it herself. Quickly putting on the undergarments and then the dress and shoes, she sat down in front of the mirror and started combing her hair. *Now is the time to meet my husband's whore. That's unfair,* she thought. It was Alnac who had been unfaithful. For all she knew, Gwen might not even have known that he was a married man. She would wait and pass judgment later. She finished brushing her hair and sprayed herself with just a little perfume and rang for Gemma.

Gemma quickly entered the room. "Yes, my lady."

"Tell cousin Gwen I will see her now." Even she noticed the sarcasm in her voice.

"Shall I come back with her or just send her into the room?"

"I need to see her alone."

Gemma knocked on Gwen's door and then just let herself in. "The queen will see you now."

A minute later Para, heard a quiet knock on her door. It was so faint she could barely hear it. She went over and sat in a large chair near a fireplace. There was a second chair on the other side of fireplace. Gemma must have stoked the fire while she was asleep. The flames were leaping high up into the chimney, and the wood was making a cracking sound. "Please come in." The door opened. Gwen came into the room and stopped about twenty feet from Para's chair.

Para did not say anything but looked her over. She was about five foot five and was wearing a purple dress which came almost up to her neck. She had long dark brown hair. Her pregnancy was showing, and Para could see that her hands were trembling. "Come and sit, and we shall talk."

Gwen came over to the fireplace and took her seat in the other large chair but did not say anything.

Para was not sure how to start the conversion and searched for the words to open with. "Dorian tells me you are from Pan. Is that correct?"

Gwen looked at the queen and answered, "I am from Pan, that is correct. I was born there."

Para shifted in her seat. "Tell me about your parents."

"My mother was a housewife, and my father was a blacksmith until he got hurt. My mother had to work some odd jobs to put food on the table. She worked hard taking care of Father and me. She died about three years ago so I have been taking care of Father since her death."

"Dorian told me that you have been living in camp the last year. Who took care of your father after you left?"

Gwen could sense where the conversion was going. "Alnac gave my father money to buy the things he needed. I know this sounds like your husband bought me, but that was not the way it was. I had a choice. I did not have to go live in camp. I cared about Alnac. He was kind to me and my father, and I loved him very much. This makes me sound like a whore. I didn't even know about you until I had lived in camp with Alnac for about two months." Gwen lowered her head and started to cry.

"How did he tell you about me?"

Gwen wiped the tears away with her sleeve. "He had returned to camp from a battle. He had a wound on his left shoulder. It was not serious, but

I cleaned it and put a bandage on it. He turned to me as I was finishing dressing the wound and told me that he had a wife. He told me your name and that you and he had started to drift apart. It was that day that he told me that he loved me and was not sure what he should do. Over the next weeks, he told me everything about you."

For a moment, Para wished she had joined Alnac in his war camps. Maybe then she and Alnac would not have drifted apart. She knew what Gwen was telling her was true because she had also drifted away from Alnac. "What did Alnac plan to do about your pregnancy?"

Large tears rolled down Gwen's cheeks. "He did not know about the baby. When I found out, I went to Dorian and told him. Dorian swore to keep my secret, and I told Alnac I needed to see my father. Dorian took me back to Pan. A few weeks later I found out that Alnac had been killed. I stayed with my father until Bailee came and brought me here."

"So the only people who know about the child are Dorian, Bailee and me." Para waited for Gwen's answer.

Gwen was not sure how to answer Para but she decided to tell the truth. "My father also knows."

Para leaned forward in her chair. "If you father knows, does that mean that some of the people of Pan know?"

"I don't think so. I was just beginning to show when Bailee came and brought me to Arsi. My father was ashamed and wanted to keep it a secret. He had planned to take me to a village in the mountains to have my baby."

"Does your father know that I am childless and that your child could become the next king or queen of Arsi? Would he try to take advantage of this information?"

This time Gwen leaned forward in her seat. "My father is a good man. He would never..." She stopped in mid-sentence. "Are you going to kill him too?"

Para frowned. "I am not going to kill anyone. I am going to send a detachment of knights to Pan and ask your father to come to Arsi. Here he will be safe and can be with you."

"What if he won't come?"

"Let me put it another way. I am not going to ask him to come to Arsi. I am going to tell him to come to Arsi. If he won't come peacefully, I will force him to come. I hope he will come willingly, but he will come."

Para got up from her chair and said, "Stand up. I want to know if we are expecting a son or a daughter."

Gwen did as she was told and Para kneeled. She laid her head on Gwen's stomach and quietly listened. After a moment she stood up. "Do you want to know what the child will be?"

"Yes I do. Can you know by just listening to my stomach?"

"I can. I did not know that I had that ability until just now. But I do, and we are going to have a son."

"I don't understand. You said we are going to have a son."

Para grinned at Gwen. "Have you forgotten? For the time being, we are cousins and you are part of the family. We will decide what to tell the people of Arsi when our child is born."

Donella and Rue

* * * * * * * * * *

Looking at the camp, Donella knew that Asher was gone. Her first impulse was to follow him, but she did not know where the secret door was located. For a moment, she just sat on the rock and thought about the last several days with Asher. He was a wonderful person and cared about honor and his duty to the people of Regstar. It was then that she completely made up her mind. She was going to leave the secret city and go back to Regstar. She would talk to her grandfather. She would find out if what Asher had told her was true and she could have left the city long ago. She went to her horse and rode back to the castle at a full gallop.

Donella found her grandfather alone in the library. "Grandfather, we need to talk. You must be honest with me." She then threw herself on the floor at his feet, laid her head on his knees, and started to cry.

"Is this some sort of lover's quarrel?" Rue didn't really know what to say, but he sensed it was more than a quarrel.

He waited for her to stop crying, and when she looked up, she said, "I have met someone from outside the city."

Rue gave a quick smile. "You mean that you have met someone who works on one of the farms?"

"No, I have met someone who is not from Reflection City. Someone who knows the secret to come and go as he pleases and does not have to wait until the reflection time to come or go."

At first Rue did not say anything. Then he spoke. "Donella, that is not possible. I know that you must have met someone who told you that they were from outside the kingdom but it was not true. Someone has fooled you."

Donella got to her feet and walked over to a stack of books and then turned and faced her grandfather. "Is it possible that even you don't know that we are not safe from the outside world? I know the person I met is from outside this kingdom. He just came here a few days ago and now has gone."

For a moment Rue did not say anything. Then he said, "How could you know this to be true?"

"Because I knew this person before he came to Reflection City. I grew up with him in Regstar. His name was Asher. When I left Regstar, he was training to be a knight. He now is a knight and a very good one. Evan discovered me with him and attacked. Evan lasted about three seconds."

Rue was alarmed. "Did this knight, Asher, kill Evan?"

"No, he only disarmed him. But now both Evan and I know that this kingdom is not safe from the outside if others discover the secret."

Rue walked over to the door and called for a servant. "Send for Brumble and Evan. Tell them to come to my room and to come at once." He then turned back into the room. "Walk with me to my room. We have to work this out. You must believe me. I did not know we were not safe from the outside. Brumble will have the answers we need."

Evan and Brumble arrived at the same time. When they entered King Rue's room, they saw Rue and Donella seated at a small table with two more empty chairs. Rue spoke. "Take a seat, we have much to discuss." When Brumble and Evan were seated Rue first spoke to Evan. "Donella tells me that you two have met a knight from outside our protective wall. Is this true?"

Evan looked at Donella. "It is true. His name was Asher, and he is the most skilled knight that I ever saw. He could have killed me in less than five seconds but did not. I am not sure even Brumble has his skills."

How could you see this knight and how could he see you? Rue thought to himself, *This is going to get complicated.* He decided not to pursue this. Rue then looked at Brumble, "Did you know that a person from the outside could get inside our walls and it not even be reflection time?"

Donella felt better about her grandfather. He really did not know there was a secret way to get in.

Brumble put his elbow on the table and put his thumb and forefinger to his chin and leaned forward putting the weight of his head on his arm. He was quiet for a moment, and then he spoke. "I know that you can come into or leave our kingdom at any time. But we are protected. A person who wants to come and go in and out of this kingdom must have a key. If what

Evan and Donella are saying is true, this person who came must have a key. There is only one key outside this kingdom and that belongs to King Joel of Regstar. The key that Joel has once belonged to Lucas, the knight who left many years ago and was killed outside our walls. I have never had any fear of an attack from outside. King Joel did not know of this because if he did, he would have come and taken Donella back. I don't know how this young knight could have figured out this secret."

Rue took both hands to the side of his face. "That means that King Joel has sent a knight to our kingdom. This knight has now left. If he reports our weakness, we could be attacked by his army."

Donella reached over and touched Rue on his shoulder. "That is not going to happen. Asher has told me that he would protect our kingdom even from my father."

Rue looked at Donella. "Can we trust him?"

"I trust him, and I think Evan trusts him."

Rue then turned back to Brumble. "Why did you not tell me of this weakness in our kingdom?"

Brumble spoke very slowly. "You know me as a loyal servant to you and this kingdom. I wanted to protect everybody and so I kept this secret to myself. I have traveled outside this kingdom many times, and it was not the time of the reflection. I never thought that anyone would figure out that to see our door, you had to see the reflection in the lake by using a mirror. Even if they found our door, they would have to have a key. It was just not possible for that to happen. So I kept the secret to myself."

Rue looked at Brumble. "Not only is it possible, it has happened. Did you not realize that if something had happened to you, your key could have fallen into the hands of someone who might figure out our secret? You know this is what happened to Lucas. He was killed outside our kingdom, and that is how Joel came to possess a key. He was smart and figured out how to use it and stole my daughter. I fear he may come back and take my granddaughter."

Donella got up from her chair and stood behind her grandfather. "Dear Grandfather, my king, it is too late. I want to leave Reflection City. I have been here too long, and my time here has been wonderful. Asher has made me realize that I have responsibilities to the people of Regstar. If something happens to my father, I would become queen. I have to leave.

Now that I know the secret to this kingdom, I can come back and see you often. You might want to visit Regstar. Please, will you help me get back to Regstar?"

"I had feared that when the next reflection time came you might want to leave and check on your father. You know I don't want to let you go. If I say no, you will never be happy here again, and you may grow to hate me. I will help you get back to your father. I will open the door and send with you the two best knights of Reflection City. You must take with you Brumble and Evan." Rue then turned to Brumble. "You and Evan will escort my granddaughter back to Regstar." He then turned back to Donella. "When do you want to leave?"

"Tomorrow morning. I want to leave tomorrow morning."

Rue then spoke to his two knights. "You must promise to protect Donella with your lives. The three of you must dress as common travelers. No one can suspect who you are. Wear old clothing. Brumble, once you pass through our door, you must hide your key in the rocks. If something happens to you, your key will be safe. If you do not return in two months, I will open the door and retrieve your key. I will be with you when you leave and watch where you hide it. I will see everyone in the morning. Go prepare for your journey."

That night Donella went to her friend Rachael. Rachael was a servant of Donella but had become more that. They sat down together on a small couch, and Donella took Rachael by both hands. "What I am about to tell you, you must promise not to tell anyone."

Rachael squeezed both hands tightly. "I didn't know that anyone had any secrets here in this kingdom."

Donella almost laughed. "I have a secret, and you have to promise to keep it if I tell you."

"Don't tell me. You and Evan are going to be married."

"Are you going to promise or not?" Donella said with a frown.

"Okay, I promise." Rachael smiled. "I thought that I had guessed it. Tell me. I will not tell anyone."

"I am going to leave Reflection City. I am going to see my father."

Rachael was stunned. "How is that even possible? We won't be visible for another eight or nine years."

Donella let go of Rachael's hands. "Do you remember that I told you that I had a childhood friend named Asher? He has found a way to get in and out of the city. He has been here, and now I know that it is possible for me to leave. I have talked to Grandfather, and he has agreed to let me go visit my father. You must not tell anyone. Again, do you promise?"

Rachael gave Donella a hug. "I promise, but I don't want you to go. I have been told it is not safe outside our kingdom. Are you sure you want to do this?"

"I have fallen in love. Asher is a wonderful man. He is a brave knight and has made me realize that I have responsibilities to the people of Regstar. If something happened to my father, I would be queen. I cannot be queen of Regstar if I hide behind these walls."

Tears filled Rachael's eyes. "Your secret is safe, I promise. Besides, it might create panic if the people knew someone could get into our city."

"The people are safe. There are safeguards that keep people out. You have to have a key, and there are not very many. My father had a key. He gave it to Asher. Asher promised me that no one on the outside would know our secret."

Rachael seemed relieved. "How can I help?"

"I must travel incognito. I need some old clothes. I cannot travel as a princess. The older and the more ragged the better. Can you help?"

"Yes, I can. We have some old clothes we were going to throw out. They are not bad, and they will fit you. I will fetch them and be right back." Rachael then left the room but in no time returned with a small bundle.

Donella quickly tried on the clothes which included a dark gray cape with a hood. She turned and looked in the mirror.

Rachael walked up behind Donella and looked at her reflection in the mirror. "You have a problem. You are so beautiful that you are going to look like a princess no matter what you are wearing."

Donella turned and kissed Rachael on her cheek. "You have been a good friend. I will see you in the morning before I leave."

The next morning Rue, Donella, Evan, and Brumble rode to the rocky hills that overlooked the city. They dismounted from their horses and led them single file up a narrow path. Soon they stood before the great door to the kingdom.

Rue looked at his granddaughter. "You know you can change your mind."

"You know I must do this, Grandfather. I am going to find my father and ask him to come back with me. I want you two to meet. You are both kind men and good kings. I know you are going to like each other."

Rue rubbed his head. "I could send Brumble to bring your father back and you could remain safe behind our walls."

"Grandfather, I know you love me and I love you so much, but there are other reasons I have to leave. Please open the door."

Rue did not say anything. He knew that if both Evan and Donella were able to see this strange knight that his granddaughter had fallen in love.

Rue took his key and opened the mighty door, and the four led their horses through. On the other side, the air was cool, and it was cloudy, and the wind was blowing. Donella had forgotten the feel of brisk air and wondered if she had enough clothing on. Evan reached into his saddle bag and pulled out a cape, "Gee, is this what winter is like?"

Brumble laughed. "This is not winter. This is just a cool day. You will know winter when snow starts blowing in your face, and you beg for a good warm shelter with a fire." He then walked up into the rocks and hid his key. "It will be safe there. Please give us time to complete our mission and return. It should take no longer than a month to get Donella to Regstar and settled in, but there may be a war going on. It may take more than a month."

Rue agreed and then looked at Evan. "My boy, you are turning blue. I know I commanded you to make this journey, but if you want to stay in Reflection City, it will be okay."

"Sir, I don't think I am turning blue, but I am cold. I look forward to seeing Donella safe in Regstar and then returning to Reflection City."

Brumble gave the young man a light punch on his arm. "I know you are cold, and you are turning blue. There is a village not far from here. We will get warmer clothes when we get there. You may still be cold, but you won't freeze to death."

Donella hugged her grandfather, and then the three mounted their horses and rode down to the lake following the shoreline until they were out of Rue's sight. Rue went back through the door and closed it. Tears were rolling down his cheeks.

It took most of the morning to come down from the mountain that led up to the lake. Brumble had been to the village several times, and they stopped to rest and eat. The old man who was the leader of the village greeted them. He knew Brumble but did not know he was from Reflection City. "Brumble, welcome. It has been a long time."

"Greetings, Silas. It is good to see you. May we beg some food from your camp and catch up on the news?"

"Where have you been that you don't get the news?"

"You know us men of the mountains; we don't see many people and months pass between seeing strangers so we don't get much news. This is my niece and nephew. I am taking them to see the big castle of Regstar and maybe do some shopping at Centerville."

"We will take care of your horses. You come with me, and we will have a meal. My daughter will set a table. You clean up, and we will have food on the table when you are finished." The old man then pointed to a well with a bucket hanging on it. "I will meet you inside."

When they were seated at the table and food was being passed around, Donella broke the silence. "This looks good; is this pheasant?"

Silas looked at Donella and smiled. "Surely a mountain girl like you knows pheasant when she sees one."

Donella thought quickly and responded. "I am sorry, I was just being polite and was breaking the silence. Your pheasants look wonderful."

Silas was not fooled. He knew this young lady was no mountain girl but decided to keep the secret to himself. As they were eating, Brumble asked what was going on in Regstar.

"A lot is going on. My son has a small shop near the castle at Onida. Queen Para has been at Regstar and just a few days ago left. There is a rumor that she put Clive the minister to Rhodes out of the castle and took his wife and daughter prisoner. King Karnac has been to Regstar. There is talk of peace."

Brumble interrupted Silas. "I can tell by your voice that you don't think peace is going to happen."

Silas spoke very softly. "I have lived here a long time. For the last several years King Joel has kept us out of the war that involved Arsi,

Salados, and Rhodes. But I hear that King Andrew of Salados was killed by Queen Para. There will be no peace until Geoffrey or Para is dead, and if Geoffrey kills Para, well then Joel will avenge his sister. No, I don't think there is going to be peace--not for a long time. The good thing is, this village is so isolated that everyone leaves us alone."

Brumble looked over at Evan and could see he was still cold. "Do you have any warmer clothing that we could buy? We didn't think it was going to be this cold."

Silas smiled. "It's not cold."

Evan almost got choked. "I feel a cold coming on. I chill rather easily. If you have something, we would appreciate it."

"I have something that you can put under your clothing. The extra layer will keep you warm."

After the meal was over, Brumble, Evan, and Donella left the village and continued their journey to Regstar. The afternoon passed quickly, and that night the trio took shelter off the road and under a large overhanging rock. They had no sooner gotten under the rock than it started to rain. It was a cold, blowing rain, and the three of them huddled close to the fire. Brumble took a stick and stirred the fire. "You know this rain is a good thing. It means that there will be no movement on the road. We will be safe, and the fire will keep us warm."

"We may be safe, but I am not so sure about being warm. That cold wind cuts right through you. How does anybody live here?" Evan moved closer to the fire.

"You get used to it. I think I like this kind of weather. It is better than the heat of summer." Brumble made a motion like he was wiping sweat from his forehead.

Donella did not say anything. She was drifting off to sleep, thinking of the last camping trip she had made with her father. She was enjoying the cold rainy night.

Events Come Together

* * * * * * * * * * * * * * *

While Donella was still a few days from Regstar, King Karnac was already on the road to Arsi. King Joel was on his way to meet with Karnac at Centerville. They planned to meet in Centerville, and then travel on to Arsi together. Piper was already in Centerville waiting for the two kings to arrive.

King Karnac was the first to arrive, and he made his camp just outside the city. His men quickly set up tents and prepared to spend the night. While coming from Rhodes, they had spent much time in the rain, but it had now stopped. Karnac went inside his tent and stretched out on his cot.

About two hours later, King Joel and his knights arrived. They also set up camp not far from the Rhodes camp. King Joel sent word to King Karnac that they could meet for the dinner meal. When they met, they made mostly small talk and spoke very little about the peace. After the meal, they exchanged pleasantries and went back to their camps. When Joel entered the tent, he felt something was wrong. Someone had been there. Nothing seemed to be missing, but he called his guards and alerted them. His first thought was that a spy from Karnac's camp had searched his tent. He and the five guards went straight to Karnac's camp where they were stopped by Rhodes guards.

"Someone has been in our camp. My tent has been searched. I will see Karnac now."

The Rhodes guards escorted Joel to Karnac's tent. A guard from Rhodes called for Karnac but he did not answer. He called again and when he did not answer he went inside. There he found Karnac dead with a knife in his chest. He went outside and said to Joel, "The King is dead. He has been murdered. Take your men and go back to your camp."

Joel did not know what to say. He motioned to his men, and they returned to camp. "Put the camp on alert." As soon as he said that a guard sounded a horn and the entire camp came alive. In minutes, the knights were armed and had Joel completely surrounded. Then they waited. They soon got word that Karnac's camp was also on alert. It was not long until a group of knights came to Joel's camp.

A tall knight came to Joel. "Karnac has been murdered. He was killed with this knife. Some of my men have said that they have seen you with this knife."

Joel looked at the knife. He knew it was his. It had belonged to his father. "That is my knife. Surely you don't think I killed Karnac and left my own knife there. Something is terribly wrong here. I have no reason to kill Karnac."

The tall knight handed the knife to Joel. "I don't know what to do here. I am taking my men back to Rhodes. Minister Clive was left in charge. He will know what to do. I suggest that you return to your castle until this is resolved."

Joel thought to himself. *Clive in charge of Rhodes. This explains a lot.* As soon as the Rhodes knights left the camp, Joel gave the order to break camp and to head back to Regstar. He knew that Clive and Geoffrey had had Karnac killed in order to start a war. His troops would have to protect his northern border and would not be able to help Arsi if Geoffrey attacked. He knew that Rhodes would not attack Regstar but would move troops to the border. Geoffrey would then attack Arsi without his support. His sister would have to protect her own kingdom. A squire brought him his horse, and he mounted and led his knights back toward his castle. If Salados could take Arsi then Geoffrey would be at his western border. He needed to get back to his castle and send word to Para as to what had happened. As Joel led his knights away from Centerville, he passed a man in black standing under a large tree. The man in black watched the knights pass, then he turned into a raven and flew toward the castle of Arsi.

The next day, the rain had stopped, but it had gotten colder and was starting to snow. Evan didn't think he could be any more miserable. He hated the cold, and now snow was starting to blow in his face. *How do people live in this country,* he thought to himself.

They were riding three abreast down the road when they saw an old man standing in the middle of the road some fifty yards ahead of them. When they approached, he spoke. "Greetings, great Knight Brumble."

Brumble didn't say anything but recognized the old man as Epson. *If Epson is out here in the road, something must be wrong.*

Epson pointed to the side of the road to a small path. "Get off your horse and follow me."

Brumble immediately got off his horse and said, "Do as he says." Evan and Donella dismounted, and the three of them followed Epson deep into the woods until they came to a cave. The cave was large enough to accommodate the horses, and they all went in.

Evan attended the horses while Epson, Brumble, and Donella sat around a small fire which was burning inside a large opening inside the cave.

"Why did you stop us?" Brumble asked.

Donella started to speak. "I must get to the castle at Regstar. It is very important. If you knew who I was..."

Epson held his finger to his lips. He then turned back to Brumble. "You asked a question. Why did I stop you. Last night I was in the castle of Arsi when I awoke with a terrible pain in my heart. I sensed something was wrong, and then I had a vision that King Karnac was dead. I came to Centerville to find he had been murdered. I have no clue as to who committed the murder, but I know why. A war is coming. If you had stayed on the road, you would have met knights from Rhodes returning to their castle. I don't know who committed the murder, but I know who is going to be blamed."

Again Donella spoke. "You mean King Joel is going to be blamed."

Evan had finished with the horses and had joined the three others at the campfire. Epson turned toward Donella. "You say I don't know who you are. You are Donella, daughter of Joel and Phylass. You grandfather is Rue of Reflection City. I have seen you many times taking your rides outside the city."

Donella looked at the old man. "We have met before. When I was about fourteen years old, I came to visit my Aunt Para in Arsi. You were there. If you have been to Reflection City, you know the secret of how to come and go. Do you also have a key?"

"I don't need a key. I can come and go just about anywhere I please. But now I must tell you something. The snow is getting worse as we speak. It won't be long until the knights of Rhodes will seek shelter from the storm. I brought you here to be safe. The storm is going to last several days. That will give me time. King Joel will be safe back inside his castle, and he will send a message to Para to let her know what has happened. She too may be in danger. Whoever killed Karnac can hide from me. He must have the power of a wizard. If I can't feel his presence then I can't protect anyone from him."

Donella noticed that the hands of Epson had a slight tremble in them. "Are you okay?"

The old wizard looked at the young princess. "I am old. I don't have the strength that I once had. I must choose what I do carefully. I don't have much strength left in me to do my magic."

"You mean you can't protect Aunt Para. That is what you are saying, isn't it?"

"I am leaving here soon. I am going to my home where I am going to try to find out who this wizard is. You three will have to stay here for several days. Then the storm will end, and you can go on to Regstar. I hope by then I will have some way to stop this evil and maybe even avert a war."

Donella looked at Evan and Brumble then back to Epson. "How can you be so many places? You said you were in Arsi, in Centerville; you are now here. These places are days apart. You now tell us you are going into the storm that is so bad we can't leave. How can you leave?"

Epson looked at the young girl. "You do look just like your mother." He then stood up, turned himself into a hawk, and flew out of the cave.

Donella looked at Brumble. "Was that Epson, the man I met many years ago who my aunt Para said was teaching her magic?"

Brumble nodded his head. "Yes, it was the great and powerful wizard who created Reflection City."

Preparing For War

* * * * * * * * * * * *

King Joel and his knights had not been trapped by the snow. If fact, the snow seemed to stop a few miles outside of Centerville, and by the time they got back to the castle at Regstar, the weather was quite mild. The snow storm had just hit the high country along the borders of the four kingdoms.

Once inside the castle, Joel called for a meeting of all his advisors. He also sent for Kira and asked her to attend the meeting. Once all were assembled he said, "If you were not at Centerville, you don't know that King Karnac was killed, or should I say, he was murdered." A rumble of voices went through the great hall. "I am going to be accused of this murder. Karnac was found in his tent with my knife stuck in his chest. Anyone who knows me knows I would not murder Karnac especially when we were so close to peace, and I certainly would not use my own knife and leave it to be found there. I found out before I left Centerville that Clive was left in charge of Rhodes." He then turned and looked at Kira as if to say he was sorry. "Clive will use the murder of Karnac to start a war between Rhodes and Regstar. If it is snowing as hard north of Centerville as it was near the city, the knights of Rhodes are trapped in the mountains, and news of Karnac's death has not reached Rhodes. Clive will not move an army to our border until his knights return and give him the news. We must be ready and have our army on our northern border when the army of Rhodes arrives. I don't want war. But if Clive wants it, then he shall have it. Sir Richard, I want you to get the army ready to march on short notice."

Sir Richard stood up. "I will have the army ready to march in two days. How many troops do you want left at the castle?"

Joel turned back to the table and faced his advisors. "Divide the army into four groups. Have two groups ready to move to the northern border. Have a second group ready to march to the mountains north of

Reflection Lake. Sir Trent, take two knights and extra mounts and ride to High Yellow Pass. Tell Asher he is needed here. You take command of the knights under his command and tell him to make haste. I need him here as soon as possible. Sir John, I need you to send a message to Arsi. Let them know what has happened. Tell my sister to be on guard."

All the knights got up and left the room leaving only Joel and Kira. Joel looked at her and said, "I am so sorry. I hope you believe me. I believe that your husband and Geoffrey are behind this. Someone killed Karnac with my knife. I had hoped that someday you and I would have a life together. I don't see a happy ending to events that are about to unfold."

"I believed you when you told me that Clive tried to kill you and Para. I believe you now. The problem that I have to deal with is Kala. She will not see the evil in Clive. She will want to leave and join him. I want her to stay here. I think she will be safer here."

Joel looked at Kira. "For the next several days, she will have no choice. The mountain roads are blocked. Did you know that she has been spying for Rhodes?"

Kira was shocked. "How do you know this?"

"A few days ago she went to Onida. Caleb, an old friend of mine, saw her there and she met with an old knight of Rhodes. He saw her give him a note, and as soon as she left, the knight left the city riding to the north."

Kira lowered her head. "I am so sorry. Are you going to arrest her?"

"No, I am not. She has done Regstar no harm. We have nothing here that we wanted to keep a secret. You might ask her what message she sent. Tell her we want her to stay, but if she insists on going to Rhodes, I will provide her an escort to the border. Please dine with me tonight. Right now I need to meet with Sir John, and you need to meet with Kala."

As soon as Joel left, Kira went straight to Kala's room. She immediately went into the room after a light knock. "Have you heard the news?" she asked.

Kala was sitting at a small reading table and looked up from her book. "What news? I see that King Joel is back. Is that the news you are talking about?"

"No. The news is the reason why Joel is back. Karnac is dead." Kira watched Kala's reaction. She was shocked.

"Oh no," she said as tears formed in her eyes. "Oh no, what happened?"

Kira choose her words carefully. "He was murdered. You must listen to me carefully. Karnac and Joel met in Centerville to travel together to Arsi. That is where he was murdered. The knights from Rhodes said it was King Joel. That is not true."

Kala wiped the tears from her face. "How do you know it is not true?"

"I know it is not true for a couple of reasons. First of all, King Joel is not that kind of man. Second, if he was going to kill Karnac, he would not have used his own knife and left it in his body."

"If King Joel didn't kill him, who did?"

"I think your father had him killed."

"Why would Father kill Karnac? He was our king. Are you mad?"

"Karnac left your father in charge, and I know your father's ambition. He tried to kill Para and Joel."

"I don't believe any of this. I am going home."

Kira looked at her daughter and could see rage in her face. "You are not going home. There is a snow storm in the mountains, and the road to Rhodes is blocked."

"Who told you that? Would it be the same man who killed our king?"

"Yes, and he did not kill our king. He also told me that he knew you were spying for Rhodes. I guess you are going to deny this too. He could have you arrested and put into prison."

"Karnac asked me to stay here and make sure that Joel truly wanted peace. I sent him a report that said I believed that King Joel really wanted peace. Now it may be me that caused King Karnac's death. Do you think I am going to be put into prison?"

Kira went to her daughter and gave her a hug. "King Joel said there was nothing to hide. and you are not going to be arrested. Things may change if we go to war. If you are spying and Regstar is at war with Rhodes, and you are caught, you won't be just put into prison. You will be put to death. Promise me that you will keep your wits about you. I feel you are safer here than in Rhodes, but if you want to leave when the mountain roads clear, you may." She released her hug and stood back. "Remember I love you very much."

Kala looked at her mother. "I love you too, Mother, but I just can't believe that Father would kill King Karnac."

That night Kala and Kira joined Joel for the evening meal. Kala did not want to come, but Kira had insisted. It was silent as they sat around the table. Then Kala broke the silence. "I really thought we were going to have peace. I even sent word to Karnac that I thought you and Para wanted peace. What happened?"

Joel put down his drink and turned toward Kala. "There are evil forces at work. Sometimes men do things they think are right and something tips the scale and a series of events begin to happen. Salados and Rhodes were at war so long I don't think they knew why they were fighting. King Alnac joined Rhodes, and why, I don't know. Perhaps it was greed and he wanted to expand his northern border. I don't know. Para and I control the Diamond River to the sea. When Rhodes joined with Arsi they were able to get access to the sea, but Salados and Rhodes still shared about fifty miles of the river and that prevented Rhodes from getting to the sea. When Salados and Rhodes joined together and killed Alnac, that had nothing to do with access to the sea. They wanted to conquer both Regstar and Arsi. It was nothing more than conquest and greed. Para stopped Andrew at High Yellow Pass and Rhodes wanted peace to gain passage to the sea. Now Geoffrey wants revenge, and he wants land. He has allied with Rhodes, and it looks like war is coming."

"When you say 'allied' you mean my father." Kala's voice was firm.

"Yes, I am afraid I do. When the weather breaks in the mountains, I will provide you an escort to the border. I will send a message to Clive to meet you to give you safe passage on to the castle. I don't know what is going to happen. You can stay here until peace is restored."

Kala glanced at her mother. "I want to go home. Let me know when the weather is clear." She then turned back to Joel. "Why have you not arrested me?"

Joel rubbed his chin and said, "You have done Regstar no harm. I have a daughter about your age. I would not want her in prison because she loves her country."

Kala was shocked. She didn't know that Joel had a daughter. "Your daughter is not here. What happened to her?"

King Joel got up from the table. "She is gone." He looked to mother and daughter. "Thank you for dining with me." He then turned and left the room.

Kala asked her mother, "Did you know he had a daughter?"

"Yes, I did. She was kidnapped. It is a long story."

The Spider

❀ ❀ ❀ ❀ ❀ ❀ ❀ ❀

When Gemma entered Para's room, she was surprised Para was still in bed. She opened the curtains to let in some light, and she noticed Para did not move. She went to the bed and gave her a gentle shake, but again she did not move. She checked and could tell the queen was still breathing, but it was very shallow. She quickly rang for other servants, and as they arrived, she sent for a physician.

The morning passed slowly. The doctor's examination found a small bite mark on her neck. He had also found the spider and placed it in a small bottle. He did not know what to do but had concluded that Para was dying. When he came out of Para's room, he was confronted with Rachael, Gwen, Bailee, and Dorian. "I am afraid the news is bad. She is dying, and there is nothing I can do."

Gemma started crying. "This can't be. This can't be."

Dorian was in a state of shock. He loved Para, but had to keep his wits about him. "If she dies, there are things that need to be done." He turned to Bailee and said, "Come with me. We need to meet. Call the council of knights together. We will meet this afternoon. I will stay with Para. Call me when they are assembled."

Bailee left and Dorian rejoined the two women and doctor. "What can we do?"

"Stay with her. She is running a high fever. Keep her cool with wet towels, and if she can drink, give her some water."

Gemma went to get the water and towels while Gwen sat beside Para holding her hand. Dorian was standing by the fireplace. Suddenly the door opened and in walked Epson. He immediately went to Para's bedside and laid his hand on her forehead. He turned to Dorian. "I need to see the physician." Dorian went after him while Epson looked at the insect bite on Para's neck. He could see that she was near death. When the doctor returned, Epson examined the spider.

"Everyone leave except Dorian and Gemma." When they were gone he said, "The spider is a common house spider, but it has been changed by magic. This was made to look like an accident, but it is an attempt to murder her."

Dorian walked over to Para's bedside. "Can you save her?"

Epson joined Dorian next to the bed. "I don't even know what type of magic was used here. I cannot save her, but I can slow things down. That will give us some time." Epson got up and reached in his bag retrieving some powder from a small bottle. He said a few magic words and sprinkled the blue dust over Para. "This will slow everything down. She will go into a deeper sleep. We cannot leave her here. Tonight I want you to take Para to my cabin in the western swamp. I will be there when you arrive. Only the three of us will know where she is. If she dies, we must keep it a secret until we can be assured of stability in the kingdom."

"I don't know how we can maintain stability. Queen Para has no heir."

"She has an heir. Her niece Donella."

"Donella has not been seen for six or seven years. No one knows where she is." Dorian scratched his head as he spoke.

Epson faced Dorian. "Donella is in Regstar. She is not at the castle. She is on her way. If Para dies I will see that she gets here. Meanwhile we must get Gwen to safety."

Dorian thought for a minute. "We could send her and Gemma to South Castle. It has a small garrison of men under the command of Gaylord. He is a good man and can be trusted. It is only about two days from here. I will have Bailee take them there and then come back and take change of the army until I return."

Epson nodded in agreement. "Remember no one can know where you take Para. It is the only way she will be safe." He then took out another small bottle from his bag. He sprinkled the liquid over her. "This will keep any other wizard from being able to use their magic to find her. There is something else you should know. King Karnac has been murdered. Clive is in charge of Rhodes, and they are blaming Joel for the murder. I believe we are going to have war. Para's condition must be kept a secret to prevent our army from becoming confused and disorganized. Salados may attack us and Regstar cannot help. Go and make the preparations for the army and prepare for your journey."

The meeting with the knights took only about thirty minutes, and everyone knew what was expected. Dorian and Bailee packed their coaches and Bailee, Rachael, and Gwen left after dark. In secret, Dorian carried Para and placed her in the coach. He then turned to Epson. "What if she needs something? I will be driving the coach, and she could die without me knowing." Dorian was really concerned. "Besides, I don't know how to get to your cabin."

"She won't be alone. You will be with her. The horses will take you to my cabin. It will take you two days to get there. The horses will not stop until you arrive. You did pack food and drink for several days. I have a potion that will keep Para alive for a while. Every four hours, force her mouth open and pour about an ounce into her mouth. Force her mouth closed and she will swallow. I also have a potion for you. It will give you strength. It will also keep you awake. You will need to stay awake to take care of Para."

Dorian took the potion and quickly drank it down. He reached out and took Epson's hand and then got into the coach. Epson slapped the horse near him on its flank, and the coach was off.

Asher at the Pass

* * * * * * * * * * *

It had been four days since Joel had sent Trent to Asher's camp. It seemed like a month. He had built a fire in the fireplace and tried to read but just could not concentrate. He finally decided to try to get some sleep so he got into bed and watched the flames dance in the fireplace. Dark shadows looked like ghosts on the walls. How could he ever get any sleep? Suddenly he heard a light knock on his door, and then the door opened. He looked up, and there stood Kira. "I know I should not be here but I don't want to be alone tonight." She walked over to the edge of his bed.

Joel got back into bed, threw back the covers and scooted over to make room for her. "Neither do I."

Kira dropped her robe. She was wearing a blue gown. She lay down beside Joel and said very softly, "I love you."

He turned toward her and propped himself up on one elbow. He then leaned over and kissed her. "You already know that I love you also." He lay down on his back with the pillow supporting his head. Kira snuggled up next to him and laid her, arm across his chest. He could smell the sweetness of her body. He raised up, leaned toward her, and gave her another kiss. He raised his body up and he felt her body slip under his. He had not had this feeling for a very long time. He took his time, and they made love gently then fell asleep in each other's arms.

Joel woke up just before dawn. He had not slept that well in years. Kira moved slightly and then stretched her arms above her head. "Good morning," she said. "I am glad we woke up early. I don't think anybody should see me slipping out of your room."

He gave her a smile. "I guess we do have to keep this a secret; although I don't want to. You do not have to slip back to your room. There is a secret passage that will allow you to leave this room and go directly to your room. Very few people know about it."

"You mean you had this castle designed for your affairs." She was smiling and almost laughing.

"I will have you know that this castle was built before I was born. The castle was built by my grandfather. The secret passage leads to several places. I will show you sometime. Meanwhile, let's get you back to your room. I would hate to have to explain this to your daughter."

Asher was at High Yellow Pass and had no idea of the death of King Karnac or the attempt on Para's life. All he knew was that he had never seen a snow this early in the season. He was trapped and could not go anywhere. He thought to himself that this was good because King Geoffrey could not move his troops to the pass. Meanwhile Trent had gotten to the mountains. He was not trapped, but the road leading to High Yellow Pass was blocked with the heavy snow. He would just have to wait it out. He built a camp and waited. After three days the sun came out, the temperature warmed up, and the snow began to melt. He was only one day from Asher and his trip would be over.

That day was the longest day of Trent's life. It seemed that he would never make it to the pass, but he pushed his horses to the limit, and about sundown he was at Asher's camp. He identified himself and the sentries let him pass. He found Asher's tent and when inside. When Asher saw Trent he got off his cot and gave him a hug. "My friend, it is good to see you, but for some reason I feel uneasy that you are here."

Trent released the hug. "It is good to see you also, but you are right. I have news, and it is not good."

Asher could see that Trent was near exhaustion. There was a small table in the tent. "Please sit down. I will have food and drink brought to us, and you can bring me up to date."

It was not long until they were seated at the table eating in the small tent. Trent was hungry and was eating rather quickly. Asher had already eaten so he only had wine to drink. Asher then spoke. "What news do you have?"

Trent set his bread down on his plate. "King Karnac has been murdered. Troops from Rhodes think that King Joel did it. King Joel thinks that there is going to be war between Rhodes and Regstar. He also feels that King Geoffrey will attack Arsi. He wants you to return to Regstar and allow me to stay here to help protect the pass. I do not know what has happened the last few days. I have been blocked by the snow and lost a couple of days waiting for the road to become passable. He has sent you a message. It is in code and is sealed. He told me for you to open and read it in private."

Asher was shocked by the news. "We were so close to peace. You and I also know that King Joel would not murder anyone. He is the kindest man I know, and no one wants peace more than he does. Give me the message, finish your meal, and go to your tent. After I have decoded the message, we will meet again."

Trent finished his meal and left Asher alone. Asher opened the message and decoded it.

Asher

I did not kill Karnac. Clive is now ruling Rhodes. If he moves his army to our border I will consider it an act of war. I will not let that army cross into Regstar. I feel King Geoffrey will attack Arsi. Salados is not strong enough to defeat Arsi. I feel something is going on that I am not aware of. They feared the power of Queen Para and now they don't. I need you to return to Regstar and take the Legion of Knights to a small pass northeast of Reflection Lake. It will allow you to move your knights behind any troops posted on the border. I will tell you the plan once you return to Regstar. Make haste. The snow in the mountains has given us a little time but I need you here.

When Asher finished reading the message, he walked outside his tent and threw it into the fire and watched it burn. He then went to Trent's tent. "I am going back to Regstar. I will leave in the morning after I have made the men aware that you are taking charge."

The next day, Asher took an extra mount and supplies and left the camp. He knew he would have very little time to stop and rest.

Donella In Regstar

* * * * * * * * * * * *

Being trapped in a cave was not what Donella thought being outside of Reflection City was going to be like. Brumble had been very patient, but Evan had complained the entire time. She longed for a bath and clean clothes but sitting in the cave entrance and looking at the snow was refreshing. She hadn't realized how much she had missed the seasons and the changes in the weather. It had stopped snowing and the temperature had gone up. The road was beginning to clear. It was now time to head toward the castle of Regstar.

The horses were restless from being cooped up in the cave, but they soon calmed down when they were on the slushy road. They were only about a half day's ride from Centerville, which meant they were only another day from Regstar. The ride to Centerville seemed to take forever. It was just past noon when they arrived in Centerville, and Brumble said they would stay there until the next day. He did not want to spend the night on the open road to the castle. They found lodging in Centerville at a quaint little inn. They could only get one room which was on the second floor. Donella had warm water brought to the room, and she took a sponge bath while the two men had an ale in the tavern below. That night Donella slept in the bed while the two men slept on the floor. The next morning, they had breakfast in the tavern. No one seemed to pay any attention to them. They were just three travelers, perhaps a man and his son and daughter. After the meal was completed they went to the stable, got their horses and continued the journey.

Joel was looking out the window of the keep when he saw a pigeon fly into the message cage. Good news, he hoped, but knew it would not be. He waited, and in just a few moments a young boy came into the room with the message.

"What does it say?" Joel said with a nervous voice.

The boy handed the message to Joel. "I don't know; the message is to you, and it is in code."

Joel took the message from the boy and told him he could leave. The message was written in a very small hand, but he could make it out. He could read the code without taking time to translate it. The message was from Dorian.

Attempt made on Para's life. She is gravely ill. Epson and I have taken her into hiding. Witchcraft was used to poison Para with a spider bite. I am going to organize our army and move it to the northern border. I feel King Geoffrey is behind this. Protect yourself. An attempt may be made on your life.

Joel took the message and threw it into the nearest fire. *Enough is enough*, he thought to himself. He sent for Sir Richard. When he arrived, Joel asked, "How strong do you think the army of Rhodes is?"

"They are quite strong and battle hardened. They have been fighting for many years so they might be at their weakest. King Andrew and King Karnac may have made peace because both armies were getting weak."

Joel looked at his friend. "Our troops are fresh. I feel now is the time to move on Rhodes. When Asher returns, be ready to move your two garrisons to the northern border. We are not going to wait on Clive."

"Do you feel this is wise? If you make the first move, it will look like we started the war and you did murder King Karnac."

"You are right. But what you don't know is someone has tried to kill my sister, Para. She may die. I feel that Clive and Geoffrey are behind all this. We cannot sit back and wait. What do you suggest we do?"

"At best, Asher is four days away. If he was caught in the snow storm, it may take him another two days to get here. I will have our armies ready, and we will move them to just north of Centerville. We will only be one day from the border. I will also send an observer to the mountains that overlook the plains of Rhodes. When he spots movement, our army can get to the border just as they do. They will be unorganized, and their trip will be two days but ours only one. We will have the advantage."

"Now I know why you are my advisor, and I am only the king. It is a good plan. Make sure the army is ready, and we shall wait for Asher."

That night Joel, Kira, and Kala met in the great dining hall. Joel was quiet. He had whispered to Kira that he had received some bad news and that he would share it with her later. They were just about to start eating when a guard came into the room and came to Joel.

"Sir, I think you need to come with me. Something is strange on the horizon." They went to the window that faced to the northwest. In the distance, they could see a large knight standing next to his horse. He had built a fire, and he just stood there motionless against the orange night sky. The sun was going down, but he could be seen clearly.

Joel turned to the guard. "Get me a horse and two knights to go with me."

As the guard left, Kira joined Joel. "Are you sure you want to leave the castle with only two knights as escorts?"

Joel turned to face Kira. "I know who is out there. I must go. I will be safe. This man will have news."

A few minutes later, Brumble could see the drawbridge come down and three riders leave the castle. He turned, looked behind him, and said, "Stay close behind me. I told you that your father would come. This way we can get an escort right into the castle and not have to beg the night watchman to let down the bridge."

Donella was excited. "How did you know that my father would come when you built a fire and stood next to it?"

"Because I did this once before about six years ago. I came here to tell your father that you were safe in Reflection City. It was a sad day for Joel. I knew he would not forget it." Brumble then turned to see King Joel and the rider stop their horses about twenty yards from where he stood.

King Joel could not contain his excitement and blurted out, "Great Knight Brumble, tell me of my daughter. Is she safe?"

The old knight smiled. "She is more than safe. She is right here behind me." He then stepped to the side, and there stood Donella. Joel was speechless. He just stood there and looked at her. She looked just like her mother, and he started to cry. Donella ran to her father and threw her arms around him. They hugged for a long time with neither saying anything. Then Joel spoke. "I must get you back to the castle. I knew you were safe. Asher told me he had seen you and that he had gotten into the city. He had hidden my key and would not let me go to get you."

Donella squeezed her father even harder. "Then Asher kept his promise to me and Brumble. He said he would keep Reflection City safe -- even from you. Is Asher inside the castle?"

King Joel released his daughter and stepped back from her. "Asher is not at the castle. He is at High Yellow Pass. I don't think he will be back for several days." He could see the disappointment in her face. He then saw Evan. "Who is this young man?"

"This is Evan. He is from my city. He and Great Knight Brumble escorted me from the city to Regstar. We need to get him inside the castle. He does not like the cold weather of Regstar." She then turned and took Evan by the hand. "Evan, I want you to meet my father, King of Regstar."

Joel took the young man by the forearm. "Welcome to Regstar. Let's get all of you inside where it is warm." They then rode back to the castle.

It was completely dark as they crossed the drawbridge, and they could hear it squeaking as it rose behind them. They rode to the main door of the central building and were met by servants. King Joel got off his horse and said, "Take these guests to the east wing. Give them a room, and give them what they need. When they are finished, escort them to the great dining hall."

He then turned to Donella and again gave her a hug. "I will take you to your room. It is unchanged since you left." Turning to one of the servants, he said, "Go and get Lucy and send her to my daughter's room."

It was then that the servants began to buzz with excitement. They knew that Donella was back.

When Donella and Joel got to her room, Lucy was waiting. She screamed when she saw Donella and ran and gave her a big hug. She was rather large and not very tall and when they hugged she laid her head on Donella's chest. "I remember when you only came up to my chest." Tears were rolling down her cheeks.

Lucy released her grip on Donella, and the three of them went into her room. Lucy lit several lamps and the room brightened. Donella looked around the room. Nothing had changed. The last dress she wore was still lying across the bed. She then turned to her father. "I am so sorry for the past six years. It must have been terrible for you."

"It was bad, but I knew you were safe. I thought I would have to wait fifteen years to see you again. It was Asher who figured out how to get back into the city. He is one smart knight."

"That he is." She dropped her head and started thinking about him. She wished he had been here. She wanted to run and give him a big kiss.

Not because she loved him, but because he had solved the mystery of the city and had brought her and her father back together.

Joel broke the silence. "Lucy will see to your needs. I am going back to my rooms. I can see you can't wear your old clothing. I will pick out one of your mother's dresses and send it to you. When you are cleaned up and presentable, I will take you to the dining room, and we shall eat and drink and celebrate your return."

After several minutes Donella knocked on Joel's door. When he opened the door, her beauty took his breath away. She was wearing the black dress which fit her tight around the waist. It was cut low, had long sleeves, and was trimmed in gold. She took him by arm and said, "I am ready to meet the people of Regstar."

As they walked down the hall toward the great dining hall, Joel thought to himself, *Is Regstar ready to meet you?* He was so proud, and all the other problems had been temporarily pushed to the side. When they got to the dining hall, the servants opened the double door, and Joel and Donella walked through. The hall had been rearranged banquet style. There were large long tables down each side of the room with the main table at the other end of the room. When they entered the room, the whole room became quiet. Her beauty had stunned everyone. After a few moments, everyone stood up and started clapping and continued to clap until they reached the head table. Joel turned and faced the guests. "Please be seated. I am pleased to present my daughter who has been gone for about six years." Everyone started clapping again.

Donella turned and waved to the tables and then turned to the head table. She saw Brumble, Evan, Sir John, Sir Richard, and two women. She had no idea as to who they were. King Joel came up to her side. "I want to present Sir John and Sir Richard, and Lady Kira and her daughter Kala. Kira and Kala are from Rhodes." Donella spoke briefly to the two women and took her seat. She then looked back at Kala. *I wonder if this was the complication that Asher told me about.* Sir Richard was to her right, and her father was to her left. The food was served. Everyone was hungry: Brumble, Evan, and Donella because they had not eaten since breakfast and everyone else because they had had to wait for her to get ready. When the meal was finished, most everyone left with the exception of Joel, Brumble, Kira, Kala, Evan, and Donella.

After a few minutes, Kala came to Donella. "Where have you been the last six years if I may ask?"

"I have been living with my grandfather who lives in the north. He is old and I take care of him." Donella did not want to give this stranger too much information. "Why are you here?"

"I came here with my father. He has gone back to Rhodes. I will join him as soon as the weather clears in the mountains. I guess I need to be honest because you will soon know. Your aunt made me and my mother prisoners and forced my father back to Rhodes. You father told me I could go to Rhodes, and I will be leaving in the next couple of days."

Donella was perplexed. "That does not sound like Aunt Para. She is one of the kindest people I know."

Kala frowned and said, "I assume you have not seen your aunt for the last six years. She has become one the most powerful witches in the land. No matter, I will be soon going home."

"I hope I get to spend some time with you and your mother before you leave."

"Oh, Mother is not leaving. She likes it here. I do hope that we get more time together." Kala then tried to go fishing for more information. "Did you know Asher before you went to stay with your grandfather?"

The question gave Donella the information she had asked herself. Kala was Asher's complication. "Asher and I grew up together. I hoped he would be here, but Father told me that he was on a mission."

Not getting the information she wanted, Kala was about to ask another question about Asher when Evan came up to the two women. "Donella, will you introduce me to your new friend?"

"Kala, this is Evan. He is from my grandfather's village."

Maybe I can get some information from Evan. "And where is this village, Evan?"

"It is far to the north. Maybe you can visit sometime. I understand you are from Rhodes. I do hope you don't leave anytime soon. I would like to get to know you better."

"I would like to get to know you better also. Perhaps a walk in the garden tomorrow. Say about mid-morning. I will see you then. It is getting late. I will see both of you tomorrow." Kala left Donella and Evan then told her mother good night and left the room.

Everyone was soon gone leaving only Donella and Joel in the room. Donella gave her father a big hug. "Father, who is Kira and why is she here?"

"She is a friend. I will tell you everything about what is going on tomorrow. Right now I will walk you to your room. We will have breakfast tomorrow, just the two of us. All your questions will be answered." He let Donella take his arm, and they left the dining hall.

The next morning Donella and her father had breakfast together. He told about the death of Karnac and that there might be war. She was told about Para and her magic and that Clive, Kira's husband, had tried to kill both Para and himself. She was told of the second attempt on Para's life and that she was struggling to stay alive. He left nothing out except that he and Kira were sleeping together.

When he finished bringing her up to date. she looked at him. "Why is Kira not leaving with her daughter and going back to Rhodes?"

He decided to tell only a half truth. "She believes me that her husband is evil. She does not want to go back to him. She wants her daughter to stay here also, but I won't stop her from returning to Rhodes. Kira has become a good friend, and she is going to stay here until things are settled between Rhodes and Regstar."

Donella could sense that there was more between Joel and Kira but decided not to pursue it. After all, her mother had been dead for more than twenty years.

Joel then said, "Can you trust Evan to protect the secrets of Reflection City?"

Donella was surprised by his comment. "Oh, did you know that Evan and Kala are going to meet in the garden today? Don't worry; Evan won't say anything, and even if he does, no one can get in without a key. Evan and Brumble will be going back to Reflection City soon. When they return, the only key outside the walls of Reflection City will be yours, and only Asher knows where it is. I think we are safe."

When Kala and Evan met in the garden the air was cool. Kala was wearing a black cape. "Hello Evan. You look cold. You would think that a young man from the mountains would like this cool air and find it refreshing."

Evan's teeth were almost chattering, but he put on a good face and tried not to show how cold he really was. "I'm doing okay. The air seems different here."

Kala took his arm. "The air is different. They get a breeze that comes from the sea this time of year. That is why it is not really, really cold."

Not really cold, he thought to himself. "When are you going back to Rhodes?"

"I am not really sure. It will be soon. I miss my father." Kala then looked into the sky and saw a flock of birds. "They say that when birds flock up like that winter is coming."

They stopped at a fountain to watch the water. Then they continued their walk along the path. It was then that Kala thought the time was right to find out if her theory about Donella and Asher was true. "Have you ever met the knight Asher?"

Evan stopped walking and wondered to himself why she would ask such a question. He decided to be somewhat honest. "Yes, I have. He came to our village some time ago. He demonstrated his skill with a sword. I was most impressed."

"Did he come to see Donella? I understand they were childhood friends." She turned away as if the question was a matter of fact.

Evan wasn't sure why Kala was asking these questions but decided to hide the truth inside some half truths. "I don't know, I guess so. He was not there long. He couldn't see much of her because she and I were about to get engaged. I was going to ask her grandfather for her hand in marriage and she decided it would be best to come and see her father. When we left the village and found out that a war was about to start between Rhodes and Regstar, everything changed."

"You mean that you are not going to get married now. Is that why you agreed to walk with me in the garden?" Kala was flirting.

"I am not sure where I stand with Donella. I know I like you and wish you would stay a couple more days. I would like to get to know you better. I know you must be getting cold and want to get back inside. I need to talk to Brumble and see what our plans are. Could we dine together tonight?

Kala gave him a smile and then a quick kiss on his cheek. "Of course."

As Kala returned to her room she felt like she had the information she wanted about Donella and Asher. She was just not sure. She thought to herself, *Another meeting with Evan, and he will let it slip.*

Living in the Swamp

* * * * * * * * * * * * * *

Epson had placed a protection spell on Para so that Piper could no longer feel her. Piper assumed Para was dead and decided to go back to meet with Geoffrey and get paid. He again turned himself into a raven and flew back to Salados. He met with Geoffrey and told him the job was done. Karnac and Para were dead.

"Good job. I have your gold. How do I find you if I need more help from you?" Geoffrey pointed to the gold on the table.

"Contact me the way you did before. I will be in Edgewater for the next few weeks. I think by then everything you want will be decided. By the way, in Arsi they are keeping Para's death a secret. You are going to have to give that news a little help to create the confusion you want." Piper then walked over and looked at the gold.

Geoffrey watched Piper looking at his gold. "I have a way to take care of that. We have a problem with the weather in the mountains, but it is clearing. As soon as the weather clears, I will put my plan into action, and within a few days I should be marching on Arsi."

For about half the night and into the morning, Dorian held Para in his arms. He loved her both as a queen and as a woman. He did what Epson had told him. Every four hours he would open Para's mouth and pour in about an ounce of the liquid then he would force her mouth closed until she swallowed. About mid-morning, he found he was getting very sleepy. He forced himself to stay awake, but late in the afternoon he closed his eyes. *The potion that Epson gave me must not be working.* He then closed his eyes and went to sleep.

When he awoke, it was pitch black outside. He looked at the moon and guessed he had been asleep for about four hours. He gave Para another ounce of the liquid. He found that he was still very sleepy and feeling weak.

Para was asleep leaning against the side of the coach. He moved over and took a seat next to her and gently pulled her over so she could lean on his shoulder. He put his arm around her. *How could any man not love her?* He then went back to sleep.

When Dorian woke up it was still dark. He tried to look to the sky for some guidance on time but the carriage had moved into a heavy fog. *I hope Epson has some magic to guide these horses. You can't see anything out there.* He gave Para more potion and let her lean back against the side of the coach. He then sat back and wondered why he felt so weak. He forced himself to stay awake and watched the darkness turn to light. When it got light, he tried to see where they were, but the fog was too thick. He could not see anything.

For the rest of the day, the fog did not lift. Dorian found that he was getting weaker and would take naps between times to give Para her potion, but he always seemed to be awake in time to give her the drink. Epson had put some food and drink inside the carriage, and even though he was not hungry, he forced himself to eat and drink. After it got dark, he was about to go to sleep when he felt the carriage stop. He got out of the carriage, and in the fog he could see a small cabin. He could see light coming from an open door, and Epson stood in the doorway. He quickly picked up Para in his arms and carried her inside. He was weak, and she felt extremely heavy. He laid her on the bed inside the cabin and almost fell as he did so. Dorian glanced around. The cabin only had the one room. To the right of the door was the bed. On one side of the bed was a small table which had a lamp. On the other side was another table which also had a lamp, but there was a chair at the table. To the left of the door was a larger table. It had only two chairs and there were some dishes on the table. In the back of the room, he could see a bench and shelves which had many bottles on them. There was also a bookshelf loaded with large books and a door that opened to the back. To the right of the door was a fireplace which was burning logs. There was a small stove to the left side of the room.

"I will change Para into a clean gown. While I do that, there is a small barn about fifty yards up the road. Unhitch the horses and put them in the barn. There is hay and water already there. When you are finished, I will have her changed. We will then talk."

Dorian was really feeling weak but he put the horses in the barn and returned to the cabin. He took a seat at the table. "How is she doing? You didn't even ask if she was dead or alive when I brought her in. How did you know she was still alive?"

Epson kept a stern look on his face. "I saw that you had made the journey, and you were still alive. When you left the castle at Arsi, I gave you both a potion. It linked you two together. During the trip, Para was taking strength from you. You may have noticed you started to feel weak. She will stay alive as long as you are alive. But this is not a cure. She will continually take your strength, and if you die, she will die unless we can come up with some cure." Epson got up from the table and picked up a pot of stew from a small stove and put some in Dorian's plate.

Dorian was not angry that Epson had cast the spell. He would gladly give his life to keep Para alive. Epson had placed a bottle of wine on the table with two glasses. He poured wine into both glasses and took a drink from his.

"Have you made any progress in finding a cure?"

"No, but whoever did this made a mistake. They left the spider behind. I have used the spider to find out what kind of poison was used on Para. It was not from this area. It is from somewhere across the seas. I think I know the type of poison but cannot be sure. I have created a potion. If I am right, it will be an antidote and cure Para. If I am wrong, it will help kill her." Epson placed a small bottle of blue liquid on the table.

Dorian picked up the bottle and looked at the liquid. "You know if you are wrong you will kill me too."

Epson took the bottle from Dorian's hand. "I could break the spell that binds you and Para. I know you will not want me to. We need to give the antidote to Para right away. I have something that I need to tell you. I am not staying here. I can also use the power in the magic of the spider to find who did this. It is important to do so. It could stop a war and save hundreds, perhaps thousands, of lives."

"I understand. How will I know if the potion is working?"

"You won't. I am going to give you a potion to put you to sleep. If the antidote works, Para should wake up in about a day's time. If I am wrong, you and Para will die together, but neither of you will feel any pain. Let's get started."

The two men went to the bed and Dorian opened Para's mouth as Epson poured in the blue liquid. He then gave a second bottle of liquid to Dorian. "Drink this. If this works, you need to stay at this cabin for about five days before returning to the castle. Once you drink the liquid, you will fall asleep very quickly. I have only the one bed. You can stretch out next to Para." He then smiled at Dorian. "If we are lucky and she awakens before you, you can explain why you are lying in her bed. That is, if she doesn't use her magic to kill you first."

Dorian returned the smile. "I can die with that." He was already weak and tired so when he drank the liquid he almost fell asleep immediately.

Epson straightened Dorian's body on the bed. "Dorian you are good man. You are a better man than Alnac ever was." He fixed the fires so they would last about a day. He placed more wood next to the fireplace and stove. He then wrote a message to Para and left it on the table. He then opened the door and was gone.

The next day, late in the afternoon, the fires of the cabin had died down. Para opened her eyes. At first everything was a blur, but soon things started to come into focus. She was not in her room. She looked to her left and saw Dorian lying next to her. *What is going on? Has Dorian kidnapped me?* She turned and sat on the edge of the bed. She felt weak and thought she might throw up. She looked around the room and saw the table, but her attention was soon drawn to the bookshelf and bottles across the back of the cabin. She had never been there, but she knew she was in Epson's cabin.

She got up and made her way to the table. She saw the bottle of wine on the table and picked it up and took a drink, and then another. What had happened? Then she saw the note addressed to her. She picked it up and started to read.

Para

If you are reading this it means you are still alive and my antidote worked. You have been poisoned. I was not sure that you would live. Dorian and I brought you to my cabin. We wanted to protect you and keep what had happened to you a secret. Dorian can tell you what has happened. Dorian is a good man. He has saved your life. I linked the two of you together, and you were kept alive by drawing from his strength. If you had died, he also would have died. I will contact you tonight in a dream. There is some stew outside the door to keep cool to preserve it and some bread and cheese in the cabinet. There is also more wine in the cabinet, and there is a spring near the back of the cabin.

Para laid the note on the table and walked over and looked at Dorian asleep on the bed. She bent over and gave him a light kiss on his lips. "Thank you, my faithful knight. I owe you more than I can ever pay."

She then went over and found some bread and cheese in a cabinet. She was starving. She set the bread and cheese on the table. She picked up a couple of pieces of wood and restarted the fire in the stove. She also restarted the fire in the fireplace. It was not long until the fire was leaping, and the room was getting warm. She opened the door, got the stew, and put it on the stove.

She was busy stirring the stew when Dorian came up behind her. "What? Stew again? Is that all we are ever going to have?"

She quickly turned and without thinking gave him a big hug. "I am so glad you are awake. You may have to get used to stew. It seems that that is all there is to eat." She realized she was standing before him with just a gown on. She quickly walked over to the bed and grabbed a blanket and wrapped it around herself. Then she became serious. "Where are we?"

Dorian was still weak. "I don't know. I brought you here in a carriage. The horses knew the way. Epson was not with us. He was here when we got here. I know we are in a swamp, and it took two days to get here."

Para came over and sat down in one of the chairs at the table. "Would you serve our stew? There are forks and plates in the cabinet and a bottle of wine and some cheese."

Dorian dished the stew onto the plates and poured the wine. As they ate Para said, "Bring me up to date on what has happened."

Dorian told how she had been found with the spider bite and that Epson had suggested she be brought here.

"Who is in charge at the castle?"

"No one. We are taking a chance. Everyone who knows you are ill is no longer in the castle. Bailee took Gemma and Gwen to South Castle. He should be there by now and on his way back. It came an early snow storm in the mountains and the pass is blocked. Bailee should be back before it is opened. At least that is the plan."

Para took another drink of wine. "If we rest tonight and leave in the morning, we could be back about the time Bailee arrives."

Dorian took his last bite of stew. "What you say is true. But I don't know the way back. And if that heavy fog has not lifted, we won't be able to find our way back. Epson said to wait five days before starting back. I suggest we do as he said. In two days, we will have our strength back."

Para shook her head in agreement. "Did you or Epson think to bring me some clothes? I went to sleep in a green gown and woke up in a blue gown. How did that happen?"

Dorian did not answer. *I will just let her think I saw her nude.* "There are clothes in the carriage. I will get them for you. There is more you should know. King Karnac has been murdered. Clive is in charge of Rhodes, and they are blaming your brother for the murder. I know that you want to get back to Arsi as quickly as possible, but I believe we have time." He left to go to the small barn to get Para's clothing.

When he returned Para was still wrapped in the blanket. She had gotten some water from the spring and was cleaning her face. "If you sit in that chair and face the wall, I will finish bathing or at least wiping off. Just lay the clothes on the bed. When I finish, we will change places, and you can clean up a little."

When they both had cleaned up they sat at the table. "It is strange," he said. "I have slept all day, and I am still tired and sleepy. How are you feeling?"

"I am also very tired. I think I am ready to lie down on the bed. We could share the bed like we did last night."

Dorian felt uncomfortable. "I think it best that you take the bed, and I will stretch out in front of the fire."

Para lay down on the bed. "Thank you, Dorian." She then turned on her side and closed her eyes.

In her dreams, Epson appeared. "I know what you are thinking. You want to start back to the castle in the morning. That is not possible. You may not have realized it, but you have no power or magic. You lost it because you are so weak. It may take days for it to return, or it may not return at all. Wait four more days and you will gain some strength and during the trip back to the castle maybe your magic will return. I will meet you in four days at the castle. When your strength returns, I am sure we can find the demon who tried to kill you."

The next morning, Para woke up to the sound of eggs frying in a pan. She had slept with her clothes on, and she sat up on the edge of the bed. She could see Dorian busy working at the stove.

"What do you have?"

Dorian looked over his shoulder. "I found some chickens in the barn. They said I could share their eggs. I also found a side of bacon."

Para almost laughed. She did not know Dorian had a sense of humor. She got up and walked over and sat down at the table. "Too bad you could not find a cow."

"But I did. There was a cow in the field behind the barn."

"Did she share some milk with you?"

"She did, just about a gallon. It is sitting just outside the door. I am trying to cool it. It has not been too long so we may have warm milk with our breakfast. I also found a bow with some arrows. I will go hunting after breakfast to see if there are other animals who would like to contribute to our food supply."

After they had finished breakfast, Dorian took his bow and quiver of arrows and went hunting. Para looked through Epson's books of magic and found a couple she wanted to read. She sat in the chair at the table and began to read and waited for Dorian. He did not return until mid afternoon.

When he came in the front door he said, "I cannot believe I am so tired. The animals of this swamp don't want to share. I would have been back sooner, but I got lost. You cannot believe how thick the fog is around here."

Para smiled. She was happy to see him back. "I guess we will have to have bacon and eggs again."

It was his turn to smile. "No, we will have venison tonight. That is one reason I am so tired. I had to carry that thing for about two miles. He is hanging in the barn. When I catch my breath, I will dress him out and we will have steak and wine tonight. Did you find anything for lunch?"

"Yes, I shared some more eggs with the chickens."

After they finished their meal, they talked for a couple of hours. She found out more about Dorian and his mother and father. She found out that he had a brother who had been killed in the wars. She asked him why he had never gotten married, and he told her that he had fallen love with a beautiful woman, but she was already married, and he felt that she did not have the same feelings for him.

When she went to bed she fell asleep very quickly. In her dreams, Epson appeared again. "You should start to feel strength coming back in the morning. The horses will bring you back to the castle. It is very important that once you clear the fog that you and Dorian are seen by as many people as possible. A spy in the castle has spread the word that you are dead. There is much confusion. When you get to the castle go meet with your knights, visit the staff, and let everyone know you are alive. I have not felt any sign of the return of your magic If for some reason it does not return, rely on Dorian. He is a good man. It is safe for you to start back to the castle."

The next morning they cooked extra meat, took a supply of water and a couple of bottles of wine, and put them in the coach. The horses started the trip back to the castle. As Para watched the cabin disappear into the fog, she was sort of sad. She had enjoyed her time with Dorian. There was more to him than she had thought.

The Long Ride Home

* * * * * * * * * * * * * * *

Asher had made the trip from High Yellow Pass in about four days because he rested very little at night and kept changing mounts. He was now in sight of Regstar Castle, and it was past midnight. He rode up to the drawbridge and heard the guard call out, "Who goes there?"

He stopped his horse a bit short of the moat. "It is Asher, first knight of Regstar."

He had to wait several minutes, and when the gate came down, several men surrounded him with their weapons drawn. It wasn't long until he was recognized. He got down from his horse, a couple of men took the horses, and he walked with the group of men across the bridge.

"Don't wake the king. I will go to my room, clean up, and get a bite to eat and see King Joel tomorrow. I am worn out, cold and dirty." When he arrived in his room he heated some water, made a bath and settled in for a good soaking. After what seemed like an hour he climbed out of the water which was getting cold and fell onto the bed and then drifted off to sleep.

The next morning King Joel, Kira, Kala, Brumble, Evan, and Donella were eating in the small dining room. They were engaged in light conversation when they heard a commotion coming down the hall. The door opened and in walked Asher. He walked up to the table and looked at King Joel. "I have returned. I got back late last night. I hate to interrupt your breakfast, but I need to be brought up to speed on what has happened. I have not had any contact with anyone for about four days." He did not notice Donella at the table as she had her back to him.

King Joel got up from the table and walked around it to give Asher a hug. He then stepped back and said, "We will meet here as soon as you have had something to eat." The servants brought another chair. When he took his seat at the table, he saw her. She was dressed in blue and looked beautiful. She simply said, "Hello, Asher."

He returned the greeting, "Hello, Donella. You have returned from your grandfather's home." He was careful not to identify Reflection City, nor did he let on that he recognized Evan and Brumble.

"Yes, I arrived about four days ago. Brumble and Evan brought me. They are starting back in the next couple of days."

King Joel was careful not to mention where Asher had been. He told the guests around the table that Donella and Asher had played together as children. He introduced Brumble and Evan as if Asher had never seen them before.

Kala was perplexed. She still did not know if Donella was the woman that Asher had said he had met in the mountains. Then she spoke. "How long has it been since you have seen Donella?"

"Long time." He then quickly changed the topic. "Kala, I thought you were going back to Rhodes."

Kala glanced at her mother. "I was going back today, but I think I will stay a few more days. I am just getting to know Donella, and I enjoyed spending some time with Evan. Perhaps the four of us can spend some time together."

"That would be nice, but I don't know how much time I will have. I have been away for several days. I need to meet with my men. I have duties that will take most of my time." During the rest of meal he spoke very little to Donella or Kala.

When the meal was over everyone left to go back to their rooms, with the exception of Joel and Asher. They were joined by the rest of the king's advisors. "I need to bring you up to date. The truth is nothing has changed. Clive has not moved his troops toward the border. I have men watching for any movement in Rhodes, and I have men watching the border. If we get word that Rhodes' army is on the move toward our border, I want you to take your knights and move to River Shore Pass. You must be ready to leave in short notice. It will take three days to get there. From there you can move your men and come in behind Rhodes' army. I will attack from the front. That should give us an advantage and a win."

Asher looked at the map. "I will need more knights and archers than have been assigned to me."

"We are going to send one hundred archers and one hundred knights with you. I will have the rest with me."

"My men and I will be ready."

Joel held a finger to his lips. He then walked over to the door and opened it, and there stood Kala. She was caught off guard but quickly recovered.

"I think I left my bag at the table." She walked in and looked on the table and then in her chair. "No, I don't see it."

Joel called for a servant. "Escort Kala back to her room and help her retrace her steps so she might locate her bag. If you don't find it, come back here and let me know and I will expand the search."

Kala was turning a little red. *Playing this spying game is not easy. I must be calm.* "That is okay King Joel. I am sure I just left it in my room."

"If that be the case, William can come back and let me know." Joel turned back to the table and pretended to look at the map. William and Kala left the room.

Asher gave Joel a strange look. "You suspect that Kala is a spy?"

"I do. She has already sent a message to King Karnac about what we are doing."

Asher walked back to the table. "Why have you not arrested her?"

"She is the daughter of my enemy and the daughter of a good friend. It is complicated. She has passed no information that would do us any harm. She believes in her father, and I think Donella would do the same if the roles were reversed. She now has information that will not hurt us but help us. Forget everything I told you about River Shore Pass. That's not where you are going."

Asher scratched his head. "What plan do you have for me and my knights?"

"If we get word that they are moving toward the border then I want you and your knights to go to Cold Mountain Pass. From there you can move behind Rhodes' army and attack Rhodes Castle. If you are successful, they will return to the castle to try to protect it. We then will move our army across the border and attack their flank."

Asher looked at the map. "I never heard of this pass. Where is it located?"

"It is on the other side of the mountain not far from Reflection Lake. You can take the road to the lake, but it is easier go east to the other side of the lake. Brumble is going to show you where it is located. I have been there. It is sometimes called Dead Man's Pass. It is narrow and steep. When you see it, you will know why it is called Dead Man's Pass. There will only be enough room for one man leading his horse. You will be traveling light. There is not room on the pass for a cart."

Asher again looked at the map. "Why would Brumble agree to help us?"

"He has some idea that this will protect Donella. If Rhodes attacks our northern border and Salados attacks from the west, we may lose everything. You need to go now. Get some more rest. I will keep you informed about movement in Salados."

As Asher left the hall, he no intention of getting rest. He had to see Donella. He went straight to her room and knocked on the door. There was no answer. *Where could she be?* He looked in the library, the garden, other places she might be and finally gave up and went back to his room at the barracks. He opened the door and there she sat on his bed. He closed the door and said, "You know you should not throw yourself at me like this."

Anger came to her face. "Why is it that you always say the wrong things?"

He saw the flush in her face. "Let me try again. I left your father over an hour ago. I went straight to your room, looked in the library, the garden and just about all of the castle. I wanted to see you so badly I was going crazy. I am supposed to be this tough knight, but all I am is a man in love."

"When you were in Reflection City you told me you loved me. I asked you to wait another day before you left. You did not. Does that mean you love me a little but not enough to stay one more day?"

"It means that seeing you one more day was too painful. If you knew my obligation to your father and to the people of Regstar, you would understand."

Donella folded her hands into her lap. "What you are saying is that you did not love me enough to give up Regstar."

Asher turned his back to Donella. "I fell in love with you as Jason, a hunter without the duties of a knight. When I had to be Asher again, things changed. I loved you more that you can imagine, but you had already told me you would not give up Reflection City. So I guess you loved your city more than me."

"I am here. What does that tell you? I understand more than you know. While I have been here I have learned much more about you. You have the respect of everyone. People admire you. My father thinks of you as a son and even though you love my father very much, you deny him access to Reflection City choosing to protect the city even against Joel. I fell in love with Jason and that is not who you are. You are Asher. Before you left, you made me aware that being the daughter of Joel carries obligation. I came back to be princess of this land and someday queen. I also came back to see if I could fall in love with Asher the knight." She then stood up from the bed, put her arms around his neck and kissed him on the lips. When she finished the kiss she looked him in the eye. "Thank you, Asher, for coming to get me." She then kissed him again. "I don't think falling in love with Asher the knight is going to be hard."

Asher did not know what to say. He wanted to kiss her again. "Please have dinner with me tonight. Asher the knight wants to get to know Donella, the future queen of the land."

Donella thought for a moment. "Father expects us to dine with him tonight and your 'complication' is asking all sorts of questions. What did you tell her when you got back from Reflection City?"

Asher stepped away from Donella. "I told her that I was falling in love with a young woman from a mountain village. I thought she accepted that. When I left to go to High Yellow Pass, I thought she would be gone when I returned. When I came to the breakfast this morning, I was surprised that both Kira and Kala where still here."

"I do not know what is happening either. Kala told me she was planning to return to Rhodes, but Kira is staying. Why would Kira do that unless she is in love with my father? Your complication is becoming my complication. I think my father may be in love with Kira also. I guess we can let Kala think that I am the girl from the mountain village you fell in love with, and we can let father deal with Kira." She then smiled and said, "Do you think you can pretend to be in love with me until she leaves?"

"We will start tonight. We will have our dinner at the top of the South East Tower in Rainbow Garden. It will be a little cold but we can have a fire there. I will call upon you tonight."

News of Karnac's Death Reaches Rhodes

The news that Clive had been waiting for finally arrived. Karnac was dead, and the knights were telling everyone about Joel's knife being the murder weapon. Clive immediately called a meeting of the Council of Rhodes. He knew what he was going to say. When all twenty members were present he spoke. "My dear council. You have heard the news. Karnac has been murdered by King Joel. Karnac wanted to bring peace to our land. Joel tricked him into thinking that he would grant access to the river and an outlet to the sea and lured him away so he could murder him. He has formed an evil alliance with his sister, Queen Para of Arsi. To end the war, King Karnac had formed an alliance with King Andrew of Salados. King Andrew was killed in a battle at High Yellow Pass. His son Geoffrey is now king of Salados and has asked us to move our army to the border of Regstar. King Geoffrey is certain that Salados can defeat Arsi and then he will attack Regstar from the east. Then we can defeat this man who has murdered our king and is holding my wife and daughter hostage."

From the back of the chamber a voice was heard. "The council must choose a new leader. King Karnac left no heir. What you say may be true, but this council must appoint you or someone else as leader."

Clive was prepared for this statement. "What you say is true. I am not going to ask this council to appoint me as ruler of Rhodes. I only ask that you grant me the power to handle this crisis. Then the council can take its time and determine who you want as your new king."

The council asked Clive to leave so they could consider his request. He went to an outer chamber and waited for the council to decide. He knew he had support from ten council members. He only needed support from one more. After about an hour, he was asked to rejoin the council.

One member stood up. "Clive, you have served this country well for many years. This council has known for years that this day might come and we would be left without an heir to take the throne. After the issue with Regstar is settled, we plan to hold an official coronation and name you King Clive of Rhodes. Until then, we trust you to handle this crisis and keep us safe."

It was more than he had hoped for. He was now going to be king. "As my first act, I am going to meet with Hector. I will put him in charge of the army. He has more military knowledge than I. He and I will lead the army to the border and wait for King Geoffrey's support."

That night Clive met with Hector and his staff. "Looking at the map, we should have a broad front across the border. Hector, how powerful do you think Regstar's army will be?"

"We have been fighting for many years and are battle hardened. The problem is that we will not be strong enough to defeat King Joel unless he splits his forces. If I were King Joel, I would divide my army into fourths and move one half to the border to face us. I would leave one fourth to protect the castle and one fourth in reserve to be moved in once the battle starts. You say that King Geoffrey will attack his western border. I am not so sure that King Geoffrey can break through the pass. Queen Para is a witch. Geoffrey could meet the same fate as his father."

Clive looked up from the map. "I have received word that Queen Para is dead. They are leaderless, but what if we don't get the support we expect from Salados?"

Hector pointed to the map. "We could send a small raiding party across the border and attack his forces. When they retreat, his army would pursue them across the border. While this is going on, we could divide our army into three groups. The center group would retreat. As Regstar's army pursues our retreat, we will suddenly turn and fight. Their army would now be fighting from three sides. Regstar could not withstand this."

"We have a plan and a backup plan. How soon can our army be ready to move to the border?" Clive began rolling up his map.

Hector looked at Clive. "How many men do you plan to leave to protect the castle?"

Clive thought for a moment. "We won't need many. We will be between our castle and the army of Regstar. We have no threat from Salados. Only leave fifty archers and fifty knights."

Hector slapped his arm across his chest. "We will be ready in two days."

The Spy

* * * * * *

That night in Regstar, Joel and Kira were having dinner together. Kala and Evan were seated at a small table near one of several fireplaces in the great dining hall. Joel turned to Kira as he sat down. "Looks like we will be dining alone tonight. Why are Evan and Kala over by the fireplace?"

"It seems that Evan is a little cold. He is having problems adjusting to the sea breeze, or at least that is what he told Kala. Maybe he just wants to be alone with her. Where is Donella?"

Joel pointed up. "Donella and Asher are eating on the South East Tower in Rainbow Garden. I don't think the cool weather bothers either of those two. She told me they wanted to catch up on old times."

Kira watched the food being served. "You told me that Donella had been kidnapped. How did she get away? Asher told Kala that he was in the mountains and had met a young lady there. Did he go into the mountains to pay a ransom?"

Joel laid his hand on top of Kira's. "I wish it had been that simple. If so, I would have had her back many years ago. Donella was kidnapped by her grandfather. He decided to let her return. If you will come to my room tonight, I will tell you the whole story."

She looked at him and smiled. "Okay. Is this an official visit, or shall I come through the secret passage?"

"Come through the secret passage." His look was serious.

"What is it?" she asked. "You act as if something is wrong."

"Something is wrong. I am going to send Kala back to Rhodes."

Kira was shocked. "Why now? I was just hoping that she would stay. She seems to like Evan, and I feel she is safe here."

"It is not that simple. She will want to go. She has been caught spying. I should put her in the dungeon, but I am just going to send her home.

When I tell her she is leaving, she will want to go. She has information that she thinks her father needs to defeat Regstar. If she wants to stay, then I am wrong and I apologize to you and your daughter." Joel rubbed his chin. "I hope I am wrong."

They did not say much for the rest of the meal. When they finished, he sent a servant over to where Kala and Evan were seated and asked Kala to come to his table. When she arrived, she stood in front of Joel and her mother.

Joel stood up. "I have arranged for you to return to Rhodes. You will leave in the morning. I assume you want to be in Rhodes if war breaks out."

This was what Kala wanted. She was going to ask Joel for passage that very night. "Thank you. I will be ready to go. You must think the war is close. Mother, will you walk with me back to my room and help me pack?"

Kira left the table and walked back to Evan. "Well, I guess this is both goodnight and goodbye at the same time. By this time tomorrow I should be in Centerville. Why don't you ride along with me? You said you were going home, and this on the way."

Evan was not sure what to say. He needed to talk to Donella and Brumble. "I will talk to Brumble. If he is ready to leave, I will join you in the morning."

Kala turned to her mother. "Are you ready?" The two women then left together.

When they were in Kala's room, Kala spoke first. "I want you to come with me back to Rhodes."

Kira took her daughter's hand. "You know I love you very much. I want you to stay in Regstar, but that is no longer possible."

Kala was shocked. "What do you mean that is no longer possible?"

"Joel knows you are spying for Rhodes. If you don't leave, he will put you in prison and then on trial. You could be executed."

Kala was angry, and her voice rose. "Well, that makes us the same, doesn't it? When Rhodes defeats Regstar, you will be put on trial as a traitor. I don't think father will save you."

Kira shouted right back, "So you admit that you have been spying! Do you have information that could harm Regstar?"

Kala turned her back on her mother. "King Karnac asked me to stay in Regstar and spy for Rhodes. I assumed my father would want the same.

Do you think that King Joel would let me leave if had he thought that I had such information?"

"I don't know. I know he is a good man. He understands that you love your father and your country. How does he know you have been spying?"

Kala walked over and sat on the edge of the bed. "He caught me outside the door of the great hall listening to his plans. I don't think he thinks that I heard anything because he had me escorted back to my room. I told him I left my bag in the great hall, and he pretended to help me look for it. If he thought I had information, I would be in prison and not packing for home."

Kira rubbed her hands together. "Did you hear any of the plans of King Joel?"

"No, I know nothing, but if I did, I would take it straight to Rhodes and my father. I know that King Joel either killed King Karnac or had him killed. I don't have the faith in him that you seem to have."

"What about Asher? I thought you cared for him."

"I did, but he does not care for me. He left me to go off in the mountains to see Donella. He loves her, not me."

"Don't tell me you are doing all of this for revenge because if you are there is no one who has a greater reason for revenge that Joel. He lost his father to the war with Rhodes, his brother-in-law was murdered by Rhodes and Salados, and his sister is near death by a possible attempt on her life by Salados and Rhodes. When you see your father, you might just mention that despite all this Joel would still be willing to make peace."

Kala got up from the bed and got a trunk from the closet. "You don't think that King Joel killed King Karnac."

"Of course not, he is a kind man. I don't think he would harm anyone."

Kala looked back toward her mother. "Then your love or your lust has blinded you."

Kira walked to the other side of the bed so she could see her daughter's face. "My love for King Joel has made me see things clearly. This is not going to end well for us, Kala. If Rhodes wins this war, I have lost you and if Regstar wins this war I again will lose you. Tell your father I am never coming back to him. I am going to stay with King Joel and accept what fate has for me. Just remember that I love you."

Kala continued to pack the trunk. "You say you love me, but you don't love me enough to come with me back to Rhodes; Please go, leave me alone."

Kira left Kala and went back to her room. She fell across her bed and started to cry.

Later that night, Kira was lying in Joel's arms. Joel could tell that she had been crying and was unsure what to say. Then he said, "I am sorry about Kala. You know I can't leave her here. She is a daughter who loves her father and too much is at stake."

Kira sat up on the edge of the bed. "I am going to go with her. I am sorry, but I can't let her go back without me. Who knows what Clive will do?"

"That is the problem. We don't know what he will do. I don't think he would harm his daughter, but what about you? He will want to know why you waited so long to come back to Rhodes. You could be in real danger."

Kira turned and lay back down on the bed. "I have given this some thought. If Regstar defeats Rhodes, I expect you to come for me. If you can somehow make peace with Rhodes, I will come back to you."

"What if Rhodes defeats Regstar?"

"Then we have nothing anyway. Rhodes cannot defeat Regstar without the help of Salados. Things may change if Arsi can defeat Salados or at least delay them from attacking your western border. There are so many what if's."

Joel put his arms back around Kira. "You know I will come for you; somehow we will be together."

Geoffrey Invades Arsi

. . . .

The next day as Kira and Kala were leaving Regstar, King Geoffrey was meeting with his knights. "Now is the time for us to attack Arsi. Their queen is dead. We cannot give them time to organize."

There was rumbling among the knights. It was Sir Luke who spoke first. "They don't need many men to defend the pass. If we go through Pan and get around the mountains, it will take six days. They will know we are coming. If we attack the pass, they will see us coming, and it may take six days to break through--if we can break through at all."

Geoffrey laid his map out on the table. "I have a plan. I will send you and about two hundred men to the pass. About half your men will be archers. It will take you about a day and one half to reach the pass. I want you to arrive after dark. There has been heavy snow in the mountains. It is now melting. I know this pass. Fog will settle in after midnight. You and your men can sneak past the guard on the left side of the pass. The next morning, I will arrive with the rest of the army and attack. They will defend the pass and not know you are behind them. We have estimated that there are only about three hundred and fifty men guarding the pass. As soon as we attack from the front, you will attack from the rear. It should be an easy victory."

Luke looked at the map. "This could work. It will work if I can sneak my men past their camp."

"Make your preparations. I am going to send a message to Clive by bird to tell him it is time for him to move his army to the border. That will take King Joel out of the equation."

When Clive got the message, he knew that Geoffrey was moving toward the pass. He sent word to Hector to get ready to move to the border of Regstar. Even though Clive had never been trained to be a knight and had never been in combat, he put on armor and the colors of Rhodes. He would look like a king if nothing else. He would be seen by the people of Rhodes leading his army to take revenge on Regstar.

That night Luke and his men were moving up the side the mountain pass. The left side of the pass was lined with trees so he and his men stayed inside the tree line. Geoffrey had been right. There was a heavy fog, and they could barely see the fires of the guards who were stationed on that side of the pass. He was surprised by how easy it was to get his two hundred men past the encampment. Once they were through, they made a temporary camp in the trees. There they waited for morning and the attack of Geoffrey.

The next morning Trent, and the protectors of the pass could see as the fog lifted that the army of Salados was moving up the pass. Trent called for a rider. "Go to the castle at Arsi. Let Dorian know that we are under attack. I don't know how long we can hold out. He has at least a thousand men." The rider mounted his horse and rode quickly out of camp. He had only gone about one half mile when an arrow from the front took him off his horse. He lived just long enough to see Luke and his men preparing for an assault on the mountain pass. When Luke and his men made their assault the battle didn't last long. The archers took down over half of the army of Arsi and Trent and his men before they even knew they were being attacked from the rear. There were no survivors. Geoffrey then moved his army through the pass and into the open country, ready to move on the castle of Arsi.

When Para and Dorian arrived back at the castle, Bailee was already there. They did not know that Geoffrey had breached the pass and was only about two and a half days away. It was dark when they reached the castle. The drawbridge was up but Dorian gave the password, and it was not long before they were inside the castle. They ordered food and drink and met with Bailee and other advisors. Para said very little. She had decided to let Dorian take charge.

"What have we heard from the pass?" he asked.

"Nothing. We are blind. In the morning, I am going to send a rider to find out what is going on. We have to be ready. We have enough men at the pass to hold it for a while. If the snow has melted then Geoffrey could be on his way." Bailee then turned to Para. "I am glad you are okay. Gwen is safely at the South Castle."

Para only gave a nod. She had too much on her mind to worry about Gwen. The only way to keep her safe was to defeat Geoffrey. She knew if Geoffrey could successfully defeat her army, no one in Arsi was safe.

Dorian put both hands on the table and learned over. "How many men do we have?"

"We have about one hundred and fifty at the pass. We have about four hundred here and another fifty at South Castle. We also have another four hundred near the border not far from Centerville."

Dorian took his hands off the table. "Why do we have men there?"

Bailee walked around the table and spread a large map on it. "We put men there in case Geoffrey decides to come by way of Pan. We have over nine hundred men which I am sure is equal to Geoffrey's contingent. But he has an advantage. We don't know from which direction he will come so we are spread thin. If he breaks through at High Yellow Pass, he will outnumber us by as much as two to one. Should we send riders to bring the men on the border back to the castle?"

Dorian looked at the map. "We need information. We are blind. If we send a rider to bring our men back from the border, it would take at least four days to get them here. We need to know where Geoffrey's army is now. If he is still in his castle, we are safe. If he is on our eastern border, we need to move our army there, and if he is coming through the pass, we need to call the border troops home. We will meet again in the morning. I need to rest, and I am sure Para does to. It was a long ride here. Tomorrow we will be fresh. Let us hope that when we get up in the morning we don't see Salados outside our castle walls."

Para went straight to her room. She was extremely tired, and she was scared. She looked at the flowers on the table. She tried to use her magic to make some of them bloom. Nothing happened. She had no magic. On her bed she saw a note. She picked it up and saw that it was in code. She took the note to her table and decoded the message.

Para

I know that if you are reading this message then you are back at the castle. You have also found out that you have no magic. It will return, but I don't know when. You were near death, and it may take a long time. I can't be with you or give you help at this time. I will explain later. Meanwhile, here are two things you need to know if you are to keep Arsi safe. Your men at High Yellow Pass have all been killed, and King Geoffrey has moved his army though the pass. The second thing you need to know is that there is a spy on your staff. Be careful in whom you trust.

When Para finished reading the letter, she folded it and laid it on the table. She again felt tired. She rang for a servant and told her to send for Dorian. Dorian was still in the castle so it was not long until he was knocking on her door. She opened the door and told him to sit at the table. She handed him the note and asked if he could read it.

He took the note and looked at it. "I can." He then took his time and read the note to himself. "This is from Epson. We have a problem. This means that Geoffrey is close, and that we have lost one hundred and fifty men at High Yellow Pass. It also means that the men that Regstar had there are also dead. If we have a spy and don't know who it is, we have an even bigger problem. Any plans we make may be passed on to Geoffrey."

"We have an even bigger problem in the fact that I have no magic. I cannot protect this castle." She then walked behind Dorian and placed both of her hands on his shoulders. "I have to count on your wisdom and skill to protect us. I am so sorry."

"Don't be sorry. I am going to my room to work out a battle plan to save this kingdom. You get some rest. The note said your magic would come back. We need a plan that will buy you some time." He then got up and walked toward the door. "I will see you in the morning. Don't worry. I will figure out a way to get you the time you need."

Para walked to the door with Dorian and gave him a hug. "Thank you. I will see you in the morning. I don't think we are linked anymore because you are getting stronger." She released her hug and opened the door and he left.

Para lay down on her bed. She felt as if she could cry. She had not cried for a long time. She had not even cried when she got the news of Alnac's death. *Asher was at High Yellow Pass.* Her thoughts turned to Donella, and then she started to cry.

When Dorian got back to his room, he pulled his chair over in front of the fireplace, took his seat, and stared into the fire. He muttered to himself. "We have a spy; Salados is moving toward our castle and outnumbers us two to one. This should be an easy problem to solve. We need our four hundred men from the border near Centerville. We just don't have time to send for them. We need time. How can we buy time?" That night he continued to go though the various options. He could move Para and the army to South Castle, but South Castle was too small. It could just about house only two hundred men.

South Castle was about a mile from the sea. It was more of a summer home than a castle. It was surrounded by a wall, but the wall was not tall, just about twenty feet high. Its main defense was that the small castle was surrounded by a lake. Any attacking army would have to cross the lake by boat or traverse a small road that led across the lake to the castle bridge. The small road also had a second bridge at the center point. That bridge could be destroyed if South Castle was ever under attack. Moving the army to South Castle was not an option.

He could send Bailee to get the men at Centerville. That would take two days to reach the army and another two to get to Arsi Castle. If he could hold out for three days then he would have Geoffrey's army trapped between his army and the army of Bailee. He continued to go over things in his mind until he finally fell asleep.

Kala and Kira

* * * * * * * * * *

By the time Kala, Kira, and their escorts reached Centerville and were nearing their second night of camping on the road, they had grown tired. They had brought only two tents. The two ladies stayed in one tent, and the knights who were escorting them stayed in the other. Two of the knights slept while the third took his turn at the watch. It was cool and one of the knights had built a fire and heated some rocks and placed them inside the ladies' tent. Kala and Kira stretched out on the ground to sleep when Kala said, "Why did you decide to return to Rhodes with me, Mother?"

Kira, who had her back to Kala, rolled over to face her daughter. "After I talked to you the other night, I realized what you said was true. I was placing everything before my love for you. I have to be honest. I don't love your father anymore. That was gone a long time ago, but I can't imagine my life without you."

Kala raised up on her elbow. "I love you too, Mother. How do you think Father will react when you return? Are you going to be safe?"

"I don't know. He does not know why I have not returned from Regstar. He may think that Joel and Para would not let me go. I don't know what King Karnac told him. You father is now in position to be the next king of Rhodes. If he thinks me returning will help with that, I will be okay. Our problem is the coming war. Regardless of who wins the war, we are both in a difficult spot. We are going home. Let's change the subject. You spent some time with Evan. Did you like him?"

Kala lay back down on her pillow. "I did, but I didn't do very well with the men of Regstar. I invited Evan to ride along with us back to his village, but he chose not to. I thought Asher was falling in love with me, but he went to visit Evan's village and fell in love with Donella. I wonder why Donella was even in that village."

"If I tell you something, will you keep it secret?"

"What do you mean, Mother, what secret?"

Kira sat completely up on her blanket. "I mean you have to keep what I am about to tell you a secret. You can tell no one. Not even your father."

Kala sat up, crossed her legs and leaned her elbows on her knees. "I promise, but what do you know that I don't?" She giggled. "After all I am a spy."

"Have you ever heard of Reflection City?"

"No."

"You think that Evan didn't come because he did not like you. I know he told you that he wanted to go to his village but he is not from a village. He is from a place called Reflection City."

Kala shifted a bit. "What and where is Reflection City?"

"I don't know, but I do know it is a magical city. It is invisible. No one can see it. Once the people go inside, they become invisible. It has mountains for walls and a magic door that can only be opened with a key. It only becomes visible for one month every fifteen years. Joel met his wife there twenty-one years ago. She died when Donella was born. When the city became visible six years ago, Donella's grandfather kidnapped her. That is where she has been living."

Kala did not know what to say. Then she thought for a minute. "You mean Donella and Evan came from this invisible city. Did she and Evan escape?"

"No, Asher discovered a way to get into the city without it being reflection time. Joel sent Asher to get her. That is where he has been. Evan and Brumble are both from this city. Evan could not go back to Reflection City without Brumble. He would not be able to get back in."

"How do you know all this Mother?" Kala lay back down.

"King Joel told me the whole story. He has been a tortured man for the past twenty years. He now has his daughter back."

Kala pulled the blankets up around her neck. "Thank you, Mother, for telling me this. I wonder why Father did not send someone after us?"

Kira didn't say anything for a few moments. "I don't know."

Dealing With Another Spy

· · · · · · · · · · · · · · · · · ·

One half day after Kala and Kira left for Rhodes, Brumble led Asher and his soldiers toward Dead Man's Pass. They planned to push hard and make the four-day journey in three days. While Kira and Kala were spending their second night north of Centerville, Asher and Brumble had camped out at the foot of the mountains that led to the pass. They were one day away from the pass.

The next day Para got up from her bed. She had spent a restless night and still felt exhausted. She quickly dressed and went to the meeting. Dorian and Bailee and several of the advisors were already there. Para looked around the room. *Is one of these men a spy?* Then they all took their seats around the large table. Para didn't say anything. It was Dorian who spoke first. "We now have information that Geoffrey has taken the pass."

There was a rumbling among the knights. Dorian continued to speak. "We all had friends at High Yellow Pass. We mourn their loss. It also means that there are one hundred and fifty men we can no longer count on. Geoffrey and his army could be no less than a day away. I have spent the night trying to come up with a plan. I wanted to hear what some of you might suggest. Without the men from the border at Centerville, we are outnumbered two to one."

It was quiet around the table. Para was uncomfortable knowing that one of these men might be a spy, but she said nothing. When the silence was broken, it was Bailee who spoke first. "We could send a rider to bring our army from the border back here. I know that would take four days. If Geoffrey is a day away, we would have to hold the castle for three days."

Then another knight spoke. "Queen Para, we know you used your magic to save us from the attack by King Andrew at High Yellow Pass. Is there anything you can do?"

Para looked at her council. "As you know, I have been very ill. Someone tried to poison me. If it were not for Epson and Dorian, I would be dead. During my illness I lost most of my strength and all of my magic. It may or may not return. The plan to hold off Geoffrey may give me the time for my magic to return. I just don't know."

Before anyone could say anything, there was a loud commotion at the door. Darin, a young knight, came in dragging a man behind him. He walked right up to the table and pulled the man to a standing position. "This man had his ear to the door listening to what was going on."

The man fell on his knees in front of Para. "This is not true, my lady. I was getting ready to come in to see if anybody needed food or drink when this man attacked me."

Dorian did not let Para answer. "I had Darin posted to watch the door of this hall. If anyone came to the door, he was instructed to watch them for several minutes and if they didn't enter and appeared to be listening, bring them in. Let me tell you right now, I have more faith in Darin than I have in you. So it is my conclusion that you were spying. Do you have anything to say before I take you into the courtyard and chop off your head?"

The man faced Dorian. "I beg for mercy. My name is Merek, I am from a village in northern Salados. My son is in the dungeons of Salados. King Andrew sent me here to get information. He said if I failed, he would kill my son."

Dorian took out his sword and stood next to Merek. "Merek, I am going to ask you some questions. If you don't give me true answers, I am going to cut off your hand and then ask you some more questions. Did you hear from the door that Queen Para's magic is gone?"

Merek stayed on his knees and brought his hands together as if he were praying. "I did."

Dorian continued. "Her magic is gone, but she can tell when someone is lying. If you tell a lie she will know it and then I will know it. You know what that means. Let's continue. What information did you pass on to King Andrew?"

Merek kept his hands together as if in prayer. "I passed no information to King Andrew. He was killed at the pass before I could. After he was killed, I thought I would be safe but Geoffrey knew about me."

"What information have you passed to King Geoffrey?"

"None. I have had very little contact with him. There has been almost no one in the castle. I did receive information that Queen Para was dead."

"You were just caught spying. How were you to get this information to King Geoffrey?"

"There is a village just to the northeast of here. There is a barn there that has pigeons. I can send a message. I have sent no messages, but he has contacted me. I was told to spread the word that Queen Para was dead. I did that. I was going to send a message tonight about what I learned here and that Queen Para was still alive."

Dorian slipped his sword back into its sheath. He turned to Darin. "Take this man and lock him in the dungeon."

As Darin picked the man from up the floor Para spoke. "I am sorry that your son is in danger. I promise that when my power returns and this conflict is settled, I will try to save your son."

When the room settled and all were back at the table, Dorian looked to Bailee. "I thought about your plan last night. It might work, but it would be a gamble. I came up with a more radical plan, and you need to hear me out. As I thought about this last night, I remembered getting the message from King Joel that he could not give us any support because Rhodes was going to move their army to his northern border. Their plan is to divide us, and they have. I think Geoffrey wants to take both Arsi and Regstar. Once he conquers Arsi, he will move his army to the eastern border of Regstar, and he and Rhodes will attack at the same time. I say we need to send the staff and citizens of the castle to South Castle and abandon this castle. We will move our army to the eastern side of the Diamond River and wait for Geoffrey there. When we leave, Bailee can ride to our army at the border near Centerville and take command--ready to attack Geoffrey from the north. We will have almost as many men as Geoffrey and a much better position to fight."

Everyone was quiet for a minute. Then Bailee spoke. "How do we know he will follow us? He may just stay here or even burn our castle."

Dorian stood up from the table. "We can let Merek go. We can instruct him that we are leaving and have only four hundred men. He can tell Geoffrey that we are going to defend Regstar's western border. He will think he outnumbers us. I don't think he will stay at our castle. I think he has a commitment to Rhodes that he will fulfill. When he finds out Para is alive and has no power he will want to take her captive or possibly kill her."

Everyone looked to Para. "It is a good plan. Make it happen."

Clive, Kira, and Kala

* * * * * * * * * * * *

Kira and Kala were in sight of the border. They could see long lines of tents. The escort made a white flag and approached the camp. When they were spotted, they stopped. In no time, they were surrounded by knights for Rhodes. The two women and their escorts waited. They were joined by Clive and Hector. When Kala saw her father, she got off her horse and ran to him. Clive dismounted and greeted his daughter.

After Clive had hugged his daughter, he shouted to his knights, "Arrest these men."

Kira protested. "These knights escorted us safely to your camp. You can't arrest them. You must honor their white flag."

Clive looked at his wife and then his daughter. He knew that if he arrested the three knights, he might lose the support of his daughter and wife. He did not care too much about what Kira thought, but she could influence his daughter, and he knew she had information to share. "Let them go. Escort Kala and Kira to my tent."

When they were inside the tent Clive came in. He cleaned his maps off the table and ordered food and drink. He spoke to Kira first. "Why did you not come back to Rhodes after you were released? King Karnac told me that you could have returned with him."

Kira was defiant. "Why did you not send for us? We had no word from you. Why did you not send word to us?"

Clive had anger in his voice, and Kala sensed that she should intervene. "King Joel is moving his troops to the border. I would say he is about a day behind us, maybe two."

Clive smiled at his daughter. "We know that. If there is an attack, he will have to cross our border. We will not provoke him."

Kira spoke up. "You have already provoked him. His army is strong. You might not be able to win this battle."

Clive mocked his wife. "His army might be strong, but Salados is going to attack his western border. He will have to split his army to defend Regstar. Oh, by the way, you will soon be queen of Rhodes. As soon as Regstar is defeated, I am going to be named king."

Kala again spoke. "Father, there is something you need to know. Before I left Regstar, I overheard King Joel's plans." Clive turned away from his wife and called for one of his guards. "Take Kira to a tent. I ordered food, but she has not eaten. See that she gets something."

Kira started to protest but the guard ushered her out. Clive turned to his daughter. "Let us eat, and you can tell me about these plans. I don't think that your mother has any sympathy for our cause. She will be alright when this is over and she is back in the castle of Rhodes."

Kala felt a little uneasy but took a drink of wine. "King Joel feels that you conspired to have King Karnac killed. I think Mother and everyone else thinks it is true."

"What do you think? Do you think that I am that kind of man? I had served King Karnac for many years. I didn't always agree with some of his actions, but he was my king. What do you know of Regstar's plans?"

Kala was hungry and started to eat. "He will only bring part of his army to the border. His first knight is a young man named Asher. He is taking a smaller force across the river near Pan and is going to cross the river upstream behind you. When King Joel attacks across the border, he will attack you from behind."

Clive suddenly was concerned. "How much time will we have?"

"When King Joel's army is in sight, then you will know that Asher and his men are behind you."

Clive got up. "Guard, send for Hector. Thank you Kala. I will have a guard escort you to your mother's tent. I will deal with matters and come and see you later."

After Kala had left the tent and Hector came in, Clive told him of Kala's news.

Hector thought for a moment. "We have time. I will send a force to ambush them at the river. They will have to cross a small bridge. I will have my archers open up on them while they are on the river. Do you know how many men they will have?"

"I don't know. I would think no more than two hundred. Send an equal amount to the river. Surprise and the small bridge will give us an advantage."

When Kala arrived at Kira's tent she went in. Her mother was sitting at a small table. She looked at her daughter and said, "If it were not for me, King Joel would have had you put in prison and maybe executed. His love for me may have cost him his kingdom. What did you tell Clive?"

Kala was not sure of her actions. She cared about Asher, and her actions would mean that he might be killed. "I told them that King Joel was going to send part of his army across the river into Salados and come in from behind."

Kira was upset. "You know if Regstar wins the war, you are going to be executed, and if Rhodes wins this war, Joel and Asher will be killed or executed. We have no chance for any happiness from this war."

Kira started to cry. Kala came over close to her mother. "I am sorry, Mother. Rhodes is our country. Why do you think so much of Regstar?"

Kira wiped the tears from her eyes. "I have been in Rhodes all my life. They have been at war all that time. King Joel has kept his kingdom free of war the entire time. He loves peace. You say he killed Karnac to start a war. Does it make any sense that a man who loves peace would start a war? I am not sure Salados and Rhodes can defeat Arsi and Regstar even with your information, but if they do, in less than a month, they will be fighting each other."

Kala started to say something when Hector and Clive entered the tent with about four other soldiers. Clive turned to his wife but spoke to the soldiers. "Take my wife and daughter back to the castle. When you get there, place my wife under arrest for treason."

Kala started to speak in protest, but Clive left the tent. Kala started to follow Clive out of the tent but Hector blocked her way. "Be ready to leave in ten minutes."

When Kala and Kira rode out of the camp toward the castle, they saw about two hundred knights and archers marching out of camp to the west. Kala looked over at her mother. She was crying. "What have I done? I have destroyed everything."

Dead Man's Pass

* * * * * * * * * * *

Asher, Evan, Brumble, and several other knights looked at the descent into Dead Man's Pass. The pass cut along the side of the mountain and was steep and narrow.

Asher shook his head. "Are you sure we can get our horses down this?"

Brumble gave a hardy laugh. "I guess you can see why they call it Dead Man's Pass. You can get killed if you are not careful. The first part of the pass is steep and narrow. If we are lucky, we won't meet anyone coming up the mountain, but there are a few places that you can get by each other. The second half of the pass is not quite as steep but just as narrow. Make a wrong step or if your horse bolts, you might end up at the bottom of a ravine. Everyone will have to keep their horses calm."

Evan patted his horse on its nose. "How long will it take us to get through the pass?"

Brumble looked toward the pass. "It will take about two hours because we have to go slowly. We need to stay as close to the cliff's inside wall as possible."

Asher looked back at his men. He wondered if all would make it safely. He then turned to face Evan and Brumble. "You know that you don't have to go down this mountain. You are only about a day's ride from your home. This is not your fight."

Evan looked at Brumble. "I am just getting used to this weather. I think I would like the challenge of going down this pass."

Brumble patted Evan on the back. "You are becoming a man. I will lead the way. We need to stay about ten feet apart and remember to stay to the right as much as possible."

After Brumble, Evan started next and one by one the men, followed by their horses, started down the mountain. They had ten horses carrying supplies, and those were the last to be led down the mountain. As they went down, Asher looked over the side. It was at least a thousand feet to the ravine bottom. It was slow going down, and sometimes the trail seemed no more than three feet wide. As they got closer to the bottom of the mountain, the trail got wider and everyone breathed a little easier. When Asher looked back up the trail, he did not see the supply horses. Evan walked up next to him. "I believe they are okay. If something had happened, we would have heard and seen them fall."

Asher's face lit up. "There they are. We are all safe." He took out his map. "We are about a day's ride from the castle. We will rest here for a couple of hours. We will eat, but spread the word that we cannot build a fire."

As the knights and archers ate dried meat and bread, Asher gathered the head knights around him. "We will ride all the way to the castle today. We will stop only to eat and rest our horses. We should be within sight of the castle by midnight. We will then wait until morning to attack."

The March to the River

· · · · · · · · · · · · ·

Before the army left the castle of Arsi, Dorian had Merek brought to the courtyard. "I am letting you go. You can ride north and report to Geoffrey."

Merek was caught off guard. "What do you want me to tell him?"

"Tell him the truth. Tell him that Queen Para is alive, and that she has no power. Tell him that we are leaving and heading for the border to protect Regstar's western border. Tell him that we think we can keep him from crossing the river into Regstar at Midway Bridge. If you stayed at the door this is what you would have heard. Salados is moving toward us from the north. I would say they are less than a day away. You should meet each other in about a half day's ride."

Merek rode out the gate and headed his horse to the north. When he was out of sight, Dorian and Para led the army of Arsi toward the border, while Bailee and two other riders headed to the northeast to pick up the rest of Arsis' army.

As Merek rode north, he was not sure if he should tell Geoffrey how he got the information. If he told Geoffrey that he was given the information, he would not believe him. He decided to tell him he attained the information by listening at the door. This would convince Geoffrey that the information was real and protect his son.

Dorian was right. Merek had only ridden about a half day when he came into sight of Geoffrey's army. When Geoffrey saw him he was delighted, but it did not show in his face. "I hope you have information for me that made it worthwhile for you to leave the castle."

Merek turned his horse and rode alongside Geoffrey. "I do your grace, I was able to spy on their meeting last night, and I know their plans."

Geoffrey stopped his horse and with a big smile and said to Merek, "Let's hear them."

Merek pulled on the reins of his horse. "They don't think they have enough men to defend the castle. They have abandoned the castle and are moving to the Regstar border. They feel if they can get across Midway Bridge, they can hold you at the river."

"How many men do they have?"

"They have about four hundred moving toward the border."

"What about the other men? You sent me a message that they had another four hundred in the east."

"Bailee sent them several days ago to protect the border between Salados and Arsi. Bailee was sure you could not get through High Yellow Pass and thought that you might come by the way of Pan."

Geoffrey reached in his bag and pulled out his map. He looked to Luke.

"Once they reach the border, it will take them three days to contact King Joel and another three for Joel to make it back to give support. By then we could have defeated Arsi, and we could trap Joel between us and Clive and his army. Merek, how far are they ahead of us?"

Merek's voice was hoarse. "I have been riding for about one half day. They left just before I did. They are about one day ahead of you."

Luke pointed to the map. "If we don't go to the castle, and leave the road for about three hours, we could make up one half day."

Geoffrey looked at the map. "This is true, we need to turn our army to the southwest."

Merek reached for his canteen and took a drink of water. "Sir, there is more."

Geoffrey looked concerned. "More! What is it?"

Merek put the cap back on his canteen. "Queen Para is not dead."

Geoffrey looked at Luke. "This makes no sense. Piper told me she was dead and that he had killed her. If she is alive, why did she not stay and defend her castle?"

Merek again spoke. "I know why. She has been very ill, and she has lost her magic. There is nothing she can do. That is why she is trying to get across the border into Regstar. She is seeking protection."

The concern left Geoffrey's face. "Merek, go back to my castle. I will discuss your son when I return."

Merek watched the army of Salados turn to the southwest. After they were just about out of sight, he turned his mount to the north. He was three and one half days from the castle. He felt good. *If Geoffrey wins the battle, he will return and release my son. If Dorian wins the battle, Queen Para will take Salados, and my son will be released.*

As Geoffrey led his army toward the border he also felt confident. Even if Para was not dead, she would have no power to use against him. Her army was disorganized. She had troops at High Yellow Pass which his army had killed. Dorian had sent almost half his force to stop any attack from the border near Pan. Things were going according to plan. Clive did not plan to cross the border and attack Regstar. He was only there to occupy the army of Regstar. After Geoffrey had defeated Arsi, he would turn his army north and attack Joel's army from the south. Joel would be caught between his army and the army of Rhodes.

Dorian and Para led their army toward Regstar until it grew dark. Dorian called out, "Feed and rest your horses, and take some food and drink. We are going to rest for only four hours, and then we are going to continue on. Salados is less than a day behind us.

Para dismounted her horse and Dorian took care of both of the horses. When he came back to where Para had stretched out on the ground he said, "We are lucky that there is a full moon tonight. We will be able to see the road clearly. We should be at the river by noon tomorrow." He waited for her reply, but she said nothing. She was sound asleep. He looked and saw that Darin was close by. "Stay with her. I am going to check on the men." As he walked among his army, he was thinking of the coming battle. Geoffrey had a well trained army. If Bailee was delayed from the north, his army might not hold out against Geoffrey. He tried to think as to what Geoffrey would do. How did he defeat the men at High Yellow Pass so quickly? He wondered if he should defend the bridge from the Arsi side of the river, or the Regstar side of the river. The Regstar side would be a better defensive position, but the Arsi side of the river would be best to attack from when Bailee arrived. If Bailee rode all night he would only be one day away from the bridge. That meant he would only have to hold back Geoffrey for half a day.

He went back to where Para was sleeping. He told Darin to get some sleep, and he stretched out on the ground to get some rest. He wanted to sleep, but sleep did not come. When the four hours were up, they were quickly on the road again. He did not hear much conversation from his men. They were tired. If his men were tired, Geoffrey's men would be tired too. *This is good*, he thought. *We will have a half day's rest before Salados arrives. They may want to rest before battle. That would give us even more time.*

Para was extremely tired. She was almost asleep in the saddle. She wondered why she had not heard from Epson. Just the note, that was all she had. She felt like something was wrong. She needed him, and he was not there. She would have to rely on Dorian and his skill as a leader. She then fell asleep. When she awoke, she found that she was not on her on horse but was sitting on Dorian's horse in front of him. "What happened?"

"You went to sleep and were falling off your horse. I decided to let you continue your rest and hold you so you would not fall."

She felt good that Dorian was still taking care of her. "I am okay now. I want to return to my horse."

When she was back on her mount, she said, "It is daylight. Where are we?"

Dorian looked at the sun. "We are about four hours from the bridge. We are just about ready to stop to rest and feed the horses. We will rest for a couple of hours and then move on to the bridge. When we get to the bridge and set up our defense, I want you to continue on to the castle at Regstar."

"No, I want to stay with the army. If we lose this battle, we will have nothing left. Both Arsi and Regstar will fall."

He looked at her and spoke in a tone that left no doubt as to who was in charge. "If we lose this battle, then you become the only hope to save what is good about Regstar and Arsi. If we buy you time, your magic may come back. We will let you rest until Geoffrey is spotted. Then you and two knights will continue on to Regstar Castle."

She knew he was right. If she could get some rest, her magic might return.

Rhodes

* * * * * *

As Asher and his men were starting their journey toward the castle of Rhodes, Kira, Kala, and their escort were arriving at the castle. The guards took the two women to their rooms. When they stopped at the door to Kira's room, one of the knights spoke. "You are confined to this room until Clive returns. If you attempt to leave the room, you will be confined in the dungeon." They then took Kala up the hall to her room.

Before she went into her room she said, "Am I confined to my room also?"

"No, you may come and go freely. Only your mother is charged with treason."

"May I visit my mother if I choose?"

"I guess, I don't really know. I was given no instructions about visitation. I think it might be okay."

Kala then went into her room. She stretched out on her bed. She waited for about one half hour and left her room and went to see her mother. A guard had been posted outside the door. "I have come to see my mother. I was told that this was permissible."

The guard turned and knocked on the door. "Lady Kira, you have a visitor. May she come in?" Without waiting for an answer, he opened the door and let Kala in.

When Kala entered into the room her mother was kneeling by the fireplace and lighting a fire. "It is very cold in here," she said to her daughter.

"Mother, I am so sorry. This is all my fault. What are we going to do?"

The guard came over to the fireplace and struck the flint several times and finally got a spark to light the straw. He blew several times and the flame leaped beyond the straw to the small cuts of wood. "You will soon be warm. If you need anything, I will be right outside your door." He then left the two women alone.

"Maybe something good will come out of this. Your father was hurt that I had not returned. If he puts me on trial, there is no evidence that I have done anything wrong except I stayed in Regstar. If Asher had not rejected you, would you have stayed with him in Regstar even if he went to war with Rhodes?"

"I don't know, but I see your point. I have really made a mess of things. You said that maybe something good will come out of this. I have given information that my father will use to get both Joel and Asher killed. I wish I could live the last day over again. I would not have told Father of Joel's plans. I would have tried to convince him that we need peace."

Kira watched the fire now spreading to the large logs and making a popping sound. "There are some men who don't want peace; they want power. If Clive wins this war and becomes the new king, I think he will do away with the council. He will not want to share power with anyone. I just hope he puts me on trial before that happens. Will you spend the night with me? I am scared."

Kala went to her mother and gave her a hug. "I am scared too, but not for myself. I am scared for Joel, Asher, and all the men who will die because of me."

Rhodes Castle

* * * * * * * * *

As morning light approached, Asher and his men were hiding in the trees about a quarter mile from the castle. Asher was surprised that the drawbridge was down. He gathered his knights around him. "The bridge is down. They are not expecting us. We need to get inside the castle before their men can respond to us. If they see us coming, they will raise the bridge. We were not expected to take the castle, only to lay siege and force them to send their army back to defend it. I don't think they have many men here. If we can get inside before they know we are here, I believe we can take the castle. We are too far away to charge the bridge. They will see us and raise it. Anybody got any ideas?"

Brumble spoke up. "Evan and I are not wearing anything that would identify us with Regstar. We will ride up to the gate as if we are two peasants. Once we get inside, you can lead your knights in a charge toward the bridge. Evan and I will make sure the bridge stays down."

Asher looked at Brumble and then to Evan. "Sounds a bit risky. If you fail, you will die. Are you sure this is want you want to do? I could take Evan's clothes, and I could go with you."

"I prefer to keep my own clothes on. Brumble and I can do this. Just make sure you are not late. Once we are inside, it should take you no more than a minute to cross the open land to the gate. We will give you that minute."

Asher walked away from the group and then back to it. "We will do it. But not exactly the way you planned. We will dress up like hunters bringing food to the castle."

Brumble scratched his head. "You said 'we'."

"Yes, we. We will cut six long poles and make it look like drags. We will cover them, but instead of game each drag will have an archer underneath each cover. We will take Jevan and Jolis. They are our best archers."

Evan looked at Asher. "Who will be the third archer?"

"I will be the third archer. The problem is, we need to know the layout of the castle. Since we don't know, we will just about have to guess." Asher started to draw what he thought the castle might look like on the ground.

Evan took his foot and erased the drawing. "I know the layout of the inside. When Kala and I had dinner the other night I asked her what it was like, and she said it was almost the same as Regstar. She said the basic difference was the drawbridge tower. It has steps going up both sides."

Asher starting drawing on the ground again. "When we enter the castle, Brumble and Evan will be stopped, and the guards will look at their drags. There will be maybe two or three. You two will have to subdue these guards. When this happens, Jevan, you will cover the courtyard. Jolis will take the right side of the tower, and I will take the left side. We cannot let them lower the gate. Gaven, you will lead the attack through the gate. As soon as we are inside, I want the archers to take to the walls. If the alarm is sounded their knights and archers will come out of barracks which are located here and here just like the castle at Regstar. We won't have much time. They will have no more than ten men at watch on the walls. We must take them out quickly and get our archers up there. When their knights come out of the barracks they should be at our archers' mercy. Does anyone have questions?"

"Gaven, you prepare the men, and we will prepare the horses. I will be behind Evan, Jevan will be behind Brumble, and Jolis will be behind the supply horse. Let's get ready."

When all was ready, Brumble and Evan started their ride toward the gate. For the three men under the blankets it seemed like forever before they heard a guard call out, "Halt! Who goes there?"

Brumble answered. "My name is Brumble, and this is my son. We are hunters and hope to sell our meat to your kitchen. We have mostly deer, but there are a few ducks and small game."

Asher heard the guard call back. "Come through the gate and stop. We will have to examine your cargo."

They crossed the bridge and went through the gate. Once inside, one of the guards said, "Dismount and uncover your game." Asher heard the sound of steel against steel. He threw open his blanket and looked toward the tower. There was a guard next to the alarm bell. He quickly sent an arrow into the chest of the guard, and he fell to the ground. He looked to his right and Jolis was climbing the steps on the other side. A guard was running toward him, and Jolis quickly brought him down with his arrow. When Asher reached the top of the steps, he looked to his left. Two more guards were coming toward him. He stopped the first with an arrow, but the second was too close to use his bow, so he drew his sword and with two blows brought the second guard down. He looked down and saw Brumble and Evan fighting with the guards on the ground. Brumble was winning, but Evan was in trouble. Picking up his bow, he quickly sent an arrow into the neck of Evan's opponent. Asher looked to see where Gavin and the rest of the men were. They were halfway to the bridge. Another guard who was near the barracks started to blow a horn, but an arrow from Jevan brought him down.

Another started yelling, "We are under attack; to arms! We are under attack!" He was out of bow range. Asher could hear men yelling and the clanging of steel as they grabbed their weapons, shields, and armor. He felt some relief when his men came riding through the gate. The archers quickly dismounted and ran up the steps and down the castle walls. In no time, they had their arrows pointed to the doors of the barracks. When the doors opened the men inside rushed out and started to fan out to protect the castle. The archers sent a volley of arrows, and in less than a half minute, ten of the Rhodes men were lying in the courtyard. They started to retreat back inside, and a second volley took another ten.

In less than five minutes Rhodes had lost about twenty men. Asher and his men waited and again the door came open with soldiers coming out behind large shields. The archers were only able to bring down about five more before the knights of Regstar charged into the oncoming men of Rhodes. Fighting was fierce. Archers on the wall were able to continue bringing down some of the men of Rhodes. The men of Regstar were on horseback, and this gave them an advantage. The fighting continued for about a half hour and suddenly the men of Rhodes gave up and started dropping their swords. They had lost over half of their men in the battle.

A few minutes later they were on their knees in the center of the courtyard surrounded by men of Regstar. Asher was looking around to see how many men he had lost. He found Brumble and Evan, both with only slight wounds. He then saw Gavin. "How many did we lose?"

"Ten killed, fifteen with wounds, five of them severe."

"How many prisoners to we have?"

"About twenty. It looks like they lost over half their force. What do you want to do with them?"

"Pick out two that are not wounded and keep them in the courtyard. Find where the dungeons are located and put the rest there."

Asher then looked around the castle. The living quarters were lit up because those inside had heard the noise of the fighting and had lighted lanterns. Asher took about twenty-five men and headed into the castle. As he entered the great hall, he was confronted by several men and women. He stopped and said, "I am Asher from Regstar. If you have weapons, step forward and throw them down in front of you. Your men have surrendered."

Several men came forward and threw down swords and knives and then stepped back.

Again Asher addressed the group. "Who is in charge?"

A tall thin man stepped forward. "I am Thomas. I am the chief member of the council. I guess I am in charge."

Asher looked at the man for a moment. "I want all members of the council to step forward." It was not long until about twenty men were standing together and facing Asher.

Thomas said to Asher, "Why have you attacked our castle? There has been no declared war between Regstar and Rhodes."

Asher's face grew red with anger. "When you moved your troops to our border. That was an act of war. You drew your sword. Did you expect us not to react?"

Thomas raised his voice. "Your king killed Karnac who was trying to make peace. That was the first act of war."

Asher grew even more angry. "You have been deceived. King Joel has killed no one. Clive had Karnac killed so he could cause a war. While his army is on the border, he is waiting for the army of Salados to attack our western border."

"Clive moved the army to the border to protect us against King Joel. He felt that if he didn't, Joel would invade Rhodes."

"I guess you will also deny that Clive tried try to kill Para and Joel with a poison ring. It is useless to try to talk to you. Is Clive's daughter, Kala here?"

Thomas was surprised that Asher knew Kala. "She is here. She and her mother both got here yesterday."

Asher turned and faced the crowd of citizens of Rhodes. "I want you to go back to your rooms. You are to stay there until you hear my men sound the alarm. Thomas, you and the other ministers stay here. Where are Kala and her mother?"

Thomas pointed toward a door. "Their rooms are through that door. Kira's room is the first on the right and Kala's is on up the hall."

Asher motioned to his men. "Stay here while I get the women. When Asher got to Kira's door, the guard was no longer there. He had joined his men and was lying in the courtyard with an arrow in his leg. Asher opened the door and gently called out Kira's name before entering the room. There he saw the two women seated on the edge of the bed. He looked first at Kala and then to Kira. "Are you okay?" Kira nodded and Asher spoke again. "Both of you come with me." Kala said nothing.

When they were back in the great hall, Asher pointed to the meeting table and told the minister, Kala, and Kira to have a seat. He took a seat at the head of the table.

"I am not sure what is going to happen to you. I do know this: My men and I left about one half day ahead of King Joel and the rest of the army. I am going to send a message to Clive that his castle has fallen. If he starts back to retake this castle, King Joel will then cross the border and pursue his army. He is going to be caught between me and Joel."

Thomas spoke up. "Why are you telling us this?"

"Because when you see an army coming to this castle you better hope that King Joel is leading it. You are far better off under King Joel than any type of rule that Clive could offer."

Thomas pointed to Kira. "Why has Clive charged his own wife with treason?"

Kira stood up and faced Thomas. "I am charged with treason because I chose to stay in Regstar instead if returning to Rhodes. While I was there, I was treated with respect and I learned that King Joel had maintained a peace for many years. I found him kind, and he really cares for the people of Regstar. He only went to the head of his army and moved toward Rhodes because the people of Regstar were threatened."

Thomas was watching Kira closely as she sat back down. "Why did you come back to Rhodes?"

"I came because my daughter would not stay with me."

Thomas spoke again. "I take it your daughter does not share your feeling toward Regstar."

Kala stood. "May I speak?"

Asher looked at her with a stern look. "You may, but before you do, you must know that you are going to be taken back to Regstar to stand trial for spying."

Before she started to speak, she looked around the room. She saw Evan and Brumble standing together. "It is true; I did spy for Rhodes. I was asked to do so by King Karnac. I only sent him one message. I told him that I believed that King Joel was sincere in his efforts to make peace for all four countries. After King Karnac was killed, I continued to spy to help Rhodes. I believed King Joel killed King Karnac. I don't believe that now. I wish I had stayed in Regstar. I gave my father information that I believed might lead to the defeat of King Joel's army." Then Kala stopped talking and looked at Asher. "I thought you were going to lead the soldiers at Two Rivers Bridge. How could you be here?"

"King Joel knew you were listening outside our door. He let you hear false information. But that does not matter. You were spying, even though you were not very good at it."

Thomas joined the conversation. "Did Clive send troops to protect Two Rivers Bridge?" Kala nodded. "Do you know how many?"

Kala began to cry. "About two hundred I think."

Thomas shook his head. "That means that Clive will be outnumbered by King Joel's and your army."

Looking at the ministers around the table, Asher spoke again. "Go to your rooms and listen for the alarm. Then you can come out to get food and drink."

Then Asher turned to Gaven. "Give the two men we have in the courtyard a couple of horses and send them to Clive. Tell them to tell Clive I want to talk with him. They will tell the rest that we have taken the castle."

The two men rode the rest of the day and into the night. When they got to the camp, they were escorted to Clive's tent. Clive was in a meeting with Hector and was surprised by the two men. "What has happened?"

"We were surprised early this morning by an attack from Regstar. We did not have enough men to hold the castle. We lost over half our men, and the rest have been captured."

"How did you escape?"

"We did not escape. They let us go. Their leader's name is Asher. He told us to tell you that he would like to talk to you."

Clive was visibly upset. He turned to Hector. "We are going to have to retake the castle. If we don't, we will lose the support of the people."

"If we leave now, Joel will be able to attack us from our rear. We would need to put some space between our troops and his to have a chance. How many men did this Asher have with him?" Hector growled.

"He had about two hundred," the young soldier said.

Hector turned to Clive. "We won't have to attack the castle. I can get us inside and take it from the inside. We need to move out tonight. I can have the men ready to leave camp in about four hours. When Joel wakes up in the morning, we will be gone."

Joel had expected Rhodes to retreat back to the castle, but not during the night. The next morning he could tell that the camp was abandoned. It took about three hours for him to get his men ready to move out, and he guessed he was about a half day behind Clive. Asher and his men would have to hold out about a half day.

Battle at the Bridge

* * * * * * * * * * * * *

It was past noon when Dorian led his army to the bridge which crossed the river. He quickly organized his defense of the bridge. The archers took their horses across the bridge while the knights kept their horses with them. He set up two rows of archers, one on the eastern bank and one on the western bank. If they had to retreat across the river, they would have cover. Once everything was completed, he sat with Para.

Para was tired but tried to look otherwise. She was stretched out on a blanket not far from the river. "Our men are building fires. Is this wise?"

Dorian sat down beside her. "It's okay. Geoffrey knows where we are, and we need to have fires going. I have placed torches next to the bridge. If the battle goes poorly, I am going to bring my men across and set fire to the bridge. That will give us another three days. He would have to cross at the Centerville Bridge."

"Why don't we burn it now and move on to the castle?"

"We can't. Bailee is coming from the north. He would run right into Geoffrey's army, and he would be vastly outnumbered. We have to make our stand here. Are you cold? Do you want me to build a fire?"

Para lay back and closed her eyes. "No, I am fine. I am going to rest now. You need to get some rest too."

As Para lay on the bank of the river, she thought about how much things had changed in the past several weeks. She had lost her husband. Her niece had returned from Reflection City. She had found out that her husband had a mistress and a child on the way. There had been two attempts on her life. Her country was at war and was retreating from a hostile enemy. She had no idea what had happened to Epson. She had lost her magic. It was possible she and her brother were going to lose everything. The best thing that had happened was she had gotten to know

Dorian. He was a good man and a very capable military leader. She found she admired him very much. *I wonder how long he has loved me,* she thought as she drifted off to sleep.

Dorian did not go to sleep. He was too worried about Geoffrey and his army, Para and Joel. He wondered what was happening with Joel and Rhodes. *One thing is certain,* he thought, *tomorrow we will know.*

It was just about sunset when Geoffrey and his army came into view. Geoffrey quickly spread his army out about a half mile from Dorian's camp. He and Hector sat down and started to make their plans. "Shall we attack tonight?" Hector said.

"No, we don't want to attack tonight; let's make them worry. Our men need rest, and our horses need water and grain. Let us just make them have a rough night. Take about twenty-five archers in range and shoot a volley of arrows into their camp every so often. Have the men ready to attack at first light."

Dorian had just finished eating when a young knight came to him. "There is some movement not far from our camp." Dorian shook Para. "Wake up. We are going to have to move." Dorian knew what was going to happen. He looked at the young knight. "Quickly tell the men to move back away from their fires. Make it quick. We don't have much time. Tell them to cover themselves with their shields."

Para, rubbing her eyes asked, "What is going on?"

"Move to the bank of the river. They are going to harass us during the night." Para and Dorian had just moved down to the river when they started hearing the thud of arrows striking the ground around them. He quickly laid Para on the ground and covered her with a shield. Again they heard the steady sound of the thud of arrows striking not too far from them. In a few minutes they stopped. Dorian went to his horse and mounted it, gave Para a hand and she swung up behind him. He quickly rode his horse across the river safely to the other side. Once on the other side, he called for a knight. "Get Queen Para a horse and take her to the castle at Regstar." He then let Para slide off his horse to the ground. "I am sorry I let you stay on the other side of the bank. It was recklessly foolish of me. Forgive me, my queen." He looked down at her. She didn't look like a queen at this moment. She looked like a woman who needed to be protected. At that time, the young knight rode up pulling a horse behind him. As Para mounted the horse Dorian said, "You are two days from the castle. I will see you in three." He did not give her time to say anything. He turned and rode back across the bridge.

Para and the young knight rode away from the bridge. *It is going to be a long ride ahead*, she thought. Strangely, she didn't feel as tired. *Maybe my strength is coming back.* She looked at the young knight riding next to her. "Did you pack any food and drink?"

"I did your majesty. There is some dried beef on one side of your bag and some wine on the other. There is also a bag of water."

Para reached behind her and felt into the bag and came out with a piece of dried beef. She found she was hungry. *This is a good sign,* she thought.

The night passed slowly for Dorian and his men. He knew when dawn broke he was going to face an attack from Geoffrey's army. During the arrow assault during the night seven men had been wounded, but none killed. They had also lost two horses.

Dorian called his head knights together. "It won't be long until dawn breaks. He will move up all his archers, and they will rain arrows down on us before the knights charge. We have an advantage. It has been a clear night, and the sun will come up behind us. I want our archers to form a line between us and the river. Have them cover themselves with shields. Wait until the knights charge before shooting our arrows. We need to do the most damage to their knights. Shoot three volleys of arrows into the knights' ranks, and then run to the bank of the river. We will then charge and hope we can repel the attack. The archers will then deal with any of their knights that might get through."

As the sun came up above the horizon, Dorian could see that Geoffrey had moved his archers forward and his knights were on their horses behind them. What he had predicted was right. Salados archers sent wave after wave of arrows into their ranks. They tried to cover themselves with their shields and block as many arrows as possible, but several of his knights went down.

Then they heard the shouting of men and the sound of hoof beats as the knights of Salados charged. The archers of Arsi rose up and let their first volley of arrows fly, then the second volley, and then a third. They quickly retreated to the river bank. As his archers ran past him, he could see that they had not done as much damage as he had hoped. *We are in big trouble.* He was just about to give the order to charge when he noticed several of the knights of Salados fall off their horses. Then there were more. He looked to the right and could see two rows of archers sending arrows into the charging knights of Salados. It was Bailee and his group. When Geoffrey realized they were being attacked on the left flank, he called for his men to stop the attack and started to retreat. More of his men were falling because they were caught off guard. Dorian gave the order to charge. Bailee and his knights charged from Geoffrey's left. When the two armies came together, the fighting was fierce. The fight lasted for nearly two hours. Arsi was victorious. The men of Salados were throwing down their swords, falling on their knees, putting their hands behind their heads, and asking for mercy.

Dorian got off his horse and walked among the dead and wounded. In the distance he saw Bailee doing the same. Both sides had lost many men.

Dorian walked up to Bailee. "You got here quicker than I expected. You saved us." Then the two men embraced.

"Our camp was further south than we thought. We had luck on our side."

Dorian had taken a wound to his left shoulder. He was bleeding. "We need to see about your wound."

"I am okay. Bailee, we have been fighting for many years; what have we to show for it? I am going to hope that Joel has had our luck. If he has we, can put this fighting behind us forever. We need to see to our wounded, bury their dead and ours, and also be merciful to our prisoners. Do you know what happened to Geoffrey?"

"Maybe he is among the dead." Dorian started walking among the dead looking for Geoffrey. It was not long until they found Luke. He had an arrow though the neck. Then they saw Geoffrey. He was lying on his back. He was still alive. Dorian kneeled beside him and showed no mercy. "If you don't die I am going to kill you," he said. "If you could see all the deaths you have caused. And for what? You could have achieved everything you wanted with a peace treaty."

Geoffrey coughed, and then spit out some blood. "You will not get the pleasure of killing me because I am already dead. I only regret that Piper failed to kill Para."

"Where is this Piper?" Dorian pulled out his knife and held it to Geoffrey's throat.

Bailee touched his friend on the shoulder. "It is too late. He is already dead."

Dorian stood up. "We need to set up a camp on the other side of the bridge. We are going to stay here for a couple of days. We need rest, and we need to take care of our wounded. There is a small forest up river not too far. We can hunt and get fresh game. I need sleep. I am going to go down to the river, clean this wound, and then go to sleep. You do the same, my friend."

When Dorian got to the river, he built a fire. He then went to the edge of the river and walked right in. The water was very cold, but it felt good. He let the water clean the blood from his clothing and then came out. He cleaned and dressed his wound and then lay down by the fire. As he went to sleep, he was thinking about Para.

When Dorian awoke the camp was getting more organized. It did not take him long to find Bailee. "Do you have a report on our losses?"

"We lost over a hundred men. We have another twenty or so who might not make it. There are many with minor wounds. How is your wound?"

Reaching for his shoulder, Dorian said, "Count me among the men with minor wounds. I am going to be fine. I am going to take several men with me hunting later on. We can't move on to the castle until we are rested and well fed."

Bailee looked at his friend. "I don't think we can fight anymore. I think we should head back to the castle at Arsi. You should take about fifty men, go to Regstar Castle, and get Queen Para. If she is rested, bring her back to Arsi. We have other wounds to heal. I would like to go to South Castle and check on Gwen. What do you want to do with the prisoners?"

Dorian looked out at his men scattered along the bank of the river. They looked like a beaten army instead of one that had just won a great victory. "You are right. These men have no fight left in them. When we are rested, take the army back to Arsi. Tell the prisoners we are going to let them go. If they have wounded that can't make the trip back to Salados, take them to Arsi, and when they are healed, they can go back to Salados.

I just hope King Joel has a plan to defeat Rhodes because we are not able to help. How many men do you think Salados has lost?"

"I estimate that they have lost over five hundred killed and wounded. They will not be able to fight another battle for a long time."

Kala

* * * *

The next morning when the alarm sounded the people of Rhodes came out of their rooms. They moved around but were in fear. The men of Asher's army had taken over the kitchen and were preparing food for Asher and the rest of the men. Kira came into the great hall. She saw Asher, Brumble, and Evan sitting at a table talking. "May I join you this morning?"

"Of course," and the three men stood up.

Once they were seated, Kira spoke. "You understand that there is no way for this to end well for me. I am glad that you have taken the castle though I fear that my husband is on his way here to retake it. If he is successful, all of us will die. If you can hold the castle and somehow defeat Clive, there is a chance my daughter will die or spend the rest of her life in prison. I am not here to beg for her life. I am only telling you this because in war there are not any winners. Do you need me to help look after the wounded?"

"No, we were lucky and did not suffer a great deal of wounds, and we are dealing with those. You might talk to Minister Thomas and tell him we want to take care of his men in the prison. They need to be fed, and we need to see to their wounds also. Tell him we will escort him to the dungeon, and he can find out what they need. By the way, where is Kala?"

"She stayed in her room. She won't come out."

Asher looked at Kira with pity. "I will see that she has food and drink."

Evan stood up from the table. "With your permission, I would like to take the food and drink to Kala. She may be a spy to Regstar, but she is still my friend."

Asher nodded in agreement. "That will be fine. She needs a friend. Tell her that she is free to move about the castle, and that if she chooses to stay in her room, I will come and see her sometime today."

Evan gathered up several items of food that he thought Kala might like and went to her room. He knocked on the door, but there was no response. His first thought was that she might hurt herself in some way so he quickly knocked again. This time he heard her coming to the door. She opened it and saw Evan standing there with a wooden tray of food. She opened the door wider. "Please come in, you can set the food on the table. I am hungry, but I didn't want to come out. I have really made a mess of things."

Evan set the tray at the table and pulled out a chair, and Kala sat down. "Won't you eat with me."

"I ate with Brumble and Asher, but I will gladly keep you company. We are all playing the waiting game. We are sure your father will attack the castle, but we don't know how far King Joel is behind him. This must be painful for you. I know you love your father, and I think you care about Asher, and I hope you care about me. Someone is going to get hurt."

"My father will think I betrayed him. If he takes this castle, Mother and I will be put to death. Let's change the subject. I want to enjoy this meal; it may be my last." She then looked up and gave Evan a smile.

There was a gentle knock on the door. Evan went to door, and a young serving girl came into the room carrying a pitcher of milk and a goblet. "Just as you requested. Will you need anything else?"

Evan thanked the girl, and she left the room. Kala took a drink of the milk. "She did not treat you like the enemy."

Evan retook his seat. "We are not the enemy. I am not even from Regstar." He stopped talking realizing that he had said too much.

Kala stopped eating for a moment. "I know you are not from Regstar. You are from Reflection City."

He was surprised. "How do you know this?"

"My mother told me. She has told me the whole story of how Donella was kidnapped by her grandfather. She has told me that somehow Asher was able to breach the walls of your city. I know that you and Brumble brought Donella to see her father, and I want to ask you some questions that will help you understand what I have done. Do you love Reflection City?"

"I do," he said. "It is the greatest place on earth. I was born there. I knew about the outside world, but not until the other day did I know we could leave. The king of Regstar is Rue, Donella's grandfather. He may have had Donella kidnapped, but he is a good man and good king. When Donella decided to leave, he sent me and Brumble to keep her safe."

"You are not keeping her safe now. You are helping Asher defeat my father."

Evan shook his head. "Brumble says the only way to keep Donella safe is to help King Joel defeat Rhodes. Brumble seems to know people. He believes Joel to be a good man. I do too. I want all this to be over. I want to go home."

"When you go home, are you going to take Donella with you?"

"No, I have lost that battle. As soon as this last battle is over, I am going to ask Brumble to take me home."

"If something happened and Reflection City was threatened, what would you do?" She did not let him answer. "I love Rhodes, and I only wanted to protect my country. I didn't think things through. When I gave Father the information, I did not realize that if that information was true I was sending Asher to his death. I am such a fool."

Evan reached across the table and touched one of Kala's hands. "I understand, and I think King Joel may understand too."

"I don't think King Joel will show me any mercy, nor do I think my father will show any either. One sees me as a spy and the other as a traitor. I know my father will show no mercy, and King Joel will have to make an example of me. He will not want to put me to death because he loves my mother. He will do what he thinks is right for Regstar."

Evan did not know what to say. He just sat there staring at Kala.

Then she spoke again. "If my father attacks this castle before King Joel gets here, you are going to die."

Evan put his other hand across the table and laid it on top of Kala's other hand and said, "We can hold the castle for at least a day. I think Joel will be here by then."

Kala turned her hands over and took Evan's hands. "I like you very much, and I am not going to let you die in this castle. Listen to me and listen well. My father will not attack this castle. There is a secret way into the castle. He will be inside before Asher's army can react."

Evan let go of Kala's hands and stood up. "You mean there is a tunnel into the lower part of the castle. Do you know where it is?"

"While I was growing up I played with a young boy. His name is Adri. His father was a knight and advisor to the king. One day, while we were playing in the lower part of the castle, the area where they store wine, he showed me his secret. The large wine rack on the eastern wall will open, and it leads to a cave. It will take you to a forest. It has been a long time, but I think it is about a quarter of a mile to where it opens. The opening back then was covered with bushes and the opening was small, but you could walk through it. Once you get through the opening, the cave is rather wide and many men could slip through. Take this information to Asher. Tell him I expect nothing except for him to get you and Brumble and my mother out of here."

Evan walked over to Kala as she stood up. He knelt down beside her and took her hand and kissed it. "My lady, you are truly noble. I will take your information to Asher."

Evan found Asher meeting with a group of knights. He sat down at the table and listened to the conversation. Asher was telling them that they did not have enough arrows to repel too many attacks, and they should search the military storage to see if they could find more and to have the men pick up the arrows already used in their attack. After the men left, Evan told Asher he needed to talk with him.

Asher looked at Evan. "Does Kala need something?" He was almost sarcastic.

"No, she only wants to save your life."

"Right now my life is not worth very much if Clive is able to breach these walls before King Joel gets here."

"That is just it. He is not going to attack."

Asher started to leave. "Go back and tell Kala that she has already tried to deceive us once and that was once too many."

"She told me that there is a secret tunnel that leads into the castle. Clive can get inside this castle without attacking the outer walls."

Asher turned and came back to Evan. He thought for a moment. He knew that Evan was serious. "What does she want for this information?"

"She only wants one thing. She wants you to send Brumble, me, and her mother back to Regstar. She wants her mother to be safe."

Asher thought for a moment. "It is not a high price to pay. We will go back and talk to her. I will agree. It is a small price to pay to find out where this tunnel is located."

"I already know where it is located. Kala knows that regardless of the outcome of the coming battle, she is a dead woman. I think she would rather die a spy than a traitor."

"Kira is right. There is no happy ending for Kala. She is a spy and she is now a traitor. Show me where it is located."

The two men quickly found the wine cellar. It was dark, and they had to light torches. Evan turned to Asher. "Which one of these walls would you think is the eastern wall?"

Asher pointed. "I think it would be that one." The two men pushed on the side of the large wine rack, and it slid open. They entered the tunnel and found their way through to the outside. While they were outside Asher was thinking out loud. "Only one man can get through this opening. Twenty archers can hold this tunnel." He then looked to the ceiling. "If we pull down that beam, it will block the tunnel, and it would take several days to clear it."

Asher then turned to Evan. "When we get back inside the castle, go and get Brumble and Kira and meet me in Kala's room. I am going to make my men aware of this tunnel so they can plan a defense."

A few minutes later Asher was knocking on Kala's door. Brumble, Kira, and Evan were already there. "Pack food and drink for a five day journey. I'm sending you back to Regstar. I will let you have two pack horses. I think we can find a couple of tents and enough food for the trip."

Kira protested. "I am not leaving."

Asher looked at her. "Have you forgotten who is in charge? You are leaving. You can be sitting on a horse or strapped across it."

He then turned to Kala. "I have met your conditions. Pack your things; you are going with them." He saw the joy in Kira's face. "Be ready to leave in one hour. You four will leave by way of the tunnel. I will meet you on the outside with your horses and supplies. I don't want the people of this castle to see you leave. I will see you on the outside in one hour."

When Asher arrived at the cave entrance the four were waiting for him. "You must leave quickly, but before you do, I want to talk to Kala."

When they were alone, Asher said to Kala, "I want to thank you for what you have done. I know you want to save your mother. When we get back to Regstar, I will stand up for you if you face a trial. Joel is a fair man. He will do what he thinks is right."

"Thank you for letting Brumble and Evan leave. They are not a part of this. Thanks for sending Mother back to Regstar. You have saved her life."

"No, you have saved her life and the lives of all my men." Asher then went to his horse and pulled out a map. He called for Brumble, Evan, and Kira to join them. "Look at this map. If you head east, you will run into a small backwoods road. It may be no more than a trail. Once you find it, it will go to the southeast. In about a day's ride, you will be at Dead Man's Pass. Then you will know where you are. From Dead man's Pass, you are another three days from the castle. Good luck."

The four travelers got on their horses with Brumble pulling one pack horse and Evan pulling the other. Asher watched them until they were out of sight and then he headed back to the castle. After about a two hour ride, the four found the backwoods trail headed toward the pass. It was not much of a trail and some of it was grown over. Brumble, who was leading the group, had to use his sword to cut some of the brush out of the way. After another hour, the trail cleared and riding was much easier. Asher was right. Just as night was falling, they were at Dead Man's Pass.

Brumble pointed to a group of trees off the trail. "We will camp over there away from this road. I don't think anybody will come by, but let's be safe."

It didn't take long until they had the tents up and the animals fed and watered, and they were seated around the camp.

"We cannot be seen from the road; the trees are extremely thick. I think it will be safe to build a small fire." Brumble started to gather up some wood, and Evan began to help.

The fire helped but it was still quite cold. Kala and her mother sat close to the fire with blankets wrapped around them. Kala was able to find some humor in the fact that Evan was shaking with cold. Kala threw her blanket open and motioned to Evan. "I don't want you to freeze; come and share my blanket."

Evan slid over next to Kala. "How do you get used to this weather?"

Kala wrapped the blanket around them both. "So you don't have any winters in Reflection City?" She looked at Brumble. "How come you don't freeze like Evan?"

"I guess because he is a boy, and I am a man," he said laughing. "No, we have no winters in our city, but I am quite proud of Evan. He has given a good account of himself on this trip."

They broke out the food and ate and then went to their tents. Brumble took the first watch. Later that night, he was replaced by Evan. For the two women, the night passed quickly. The next morning they had a small breakfast and moved back out on the road. It was not long until they were looking at the narrow pass.

"Evan, I want you to go first. I will go last. Tie the two pack animals behind my horse. Kala, you go second, and Kira, you follow your daughter. If for some reason the horses panic, let them go and hug the wall. If we go slowly, we should not have any trouble."

Kira watched as Evan led his horse up the narrow ledge. "What if we meet someone coming the other direction?"

"We will just push them over the edge," Brumble said with a smile. "No, we are going to be lucky. We are not going to meet anyone. I hope."

Kira looked up the winding ledge. It seemed to go on forever. Every once in a while, she would glance over the edge. She could not believe she was doing this. Kala seemed to take everything is stride. She didn't seem to be bothered by the danger of the narrow ledge. There was no rest; they kept moving and after about two and a half hours they reached the summit. At the top, Kira sighed in relief. "That seemed to take forever."

Brumble checked the pack horses. "We will rest here a while. I must be getting old. I am quite winded."

After they had all sat down, Evan pointed to the trail ahead. "It is easy going from here on. It is all downhill."

"Not quite. We are not going down the mountain. We are going to turn west. We are going to take Kala to the safety of Reflection City. We are only a day away. We will stop there and rest for one day. Then I am going to take Kira on to Regstar."

Kala and Kira were in shock. Kala spoke first. "Why would you do that?"

"Because I don't want anything to happen to you. Inside the hidden city, no one can get to you. It takes a key, and I have a key. You can remain inside the city until all charges against you are dropped. It will not be easy for you inside Reflection City. You will not be able to see anyone and no one can see you."

Kala again spoke. "Will I be completely alone?"

"No, I am going to ask Rue to give you a room in his castle. You will be able to talk and be able to see the people there by using a mirror. If you want to have conversation just sit in front of the mirror and you can converse by talking to their reflection."

Kira spoke up. "You said you have a key, but doesn't Joel also have a key?"

Brumble looked at her and said, "He no longer has a key. He gave it to Asher, and Asher will not let anybody in that he feels is a threat to the city--not even Joel. Let us get started. We can be at the city by dark."

Rhodes

* * * * * *

When Clive and his army arrived at the castle, they went immediately to the tunnel. They quickly found that it was blocked. Hector looked at Clive. "They have found the tunnel."

Clive was extremely angry. "They did not find it. My daughter has shown it to them. When we take this castle, I am going to hang her in the courtyard for all to see what we do to traitors. We can still take the castle; it just won't be as easy."

Hector looked strangely at Clive. "We don't know how many men they have holding the castle. It might not be possible to take it before Joel and his army arrive. I feel we need to try to make peace with Joel. If we don't take the castle before he gets here, we may be in trouble. I don't want to lose my army."

Clive looked into the sky. "We have time. Have your men cut down a tree to make a battering ram. Create some type of cover to protect the men using the ram from the archers that will be on the walls. Move our knights to just out of archer's range and move our archers close enough to protect the men with the ram. We also must make a temporary bridge. Can you have this ready in three hours?"

"Perhaps, but I suggest that we turn our army west and go meet our men at Two River Bridge. I don't think that Joel will follow. He will stop at the castle. He may abandon it or only leave a small force to hold it. If he follows us, we will have the advantage. If he goes back to Regstar, we can retake our castle. You will be a hero."

Clive didn't seem to be hearing what Hector was saying. "You have your orders. Get the battering ram and bridge ready."

Hector rode away, but as he did he was thinking of his men. They could lose many men attacking the castle, and if they were attacked by Joel while they were attacking they could lose their entire army.

When the bridge was constructed and battering ram in place, they started moving toward the castle gate.

Asher and his men were on the wall. They watched the army emerge from the trees and could see the bridge and ram coming to the wall. The men of Rhodes had built a cover over the bridge and over the ram. It was crude--held together with leather strips--but it would stop arrows. Rhodes' archers sent the first volley of arrows toward the top of the wall. Regstar's archers returned in kind. Neither side did any damage. It wasn't long until the temporary bridge was in place over the moat and the battering ram was making a steady boom against the gate. Several men of Rhodes had come along- side the cover of the battering ram and were protecting the sides with shields. It did not take long until the gate started to give.

Asher decided that in order to buy some time, they should set fire to the gate. He had his men gather any wood in the courtyard and pile it on the gate. He spread oil over the wood and just as the battering ram broke though the gate, he set it ablaze.

Clive pointed to the gate and turned to Hector. "It won't take long for that to burn. Get your men ready to charge the gate."

Hector moved his men on horseback close to the burning gate, just out of range of Asher's archers. He moved his archers back. They would move up when his men made their charge.

Asher had moved back to the top of the wall. He could see that as soon as the gate finished burning Rhodes' knights would charge the gate. He knew the archers would again move into position and cover their charge, and that they were in trouble.

Just as the burning gate was about to collapse Asher saw the army of Regstar emerge from the trees. Joel and his knights were lined up three rows deep and ready to charge the rear of Clive's army. He moved his archers out to protect against any charge from the knights of Rhodes.

It was not long until the men of Rhodes saw that they were about to be attacked from the rear.

Clive rode up alongside Hector. "Turn the men and attack."

Hector reached out and grabbed the reins of Clive's horse. "I suggest you hold up a white flag. We need to buy time. Go see what terms Joel will offer. If we charge, the archers will cut us to pieces. I need time to get our archers in place to offset their advantage."

Clive was like a madman. "We don't have time. If we don't charge them, they will charge us." He then shouted and gave the command to charge.

Hector was right. As soon as the knights of Rhodes charged, the archers of Regstar let their arrows fly. Joel held his army firm waiting for the archers to cause disruption in the attack. The men of Rhodes were falling in great numbers.

Hector blew his horn to signal for his men to retreat. Clive was furious. "What are you doing; are you mad?"

"I am saving the army of Rhodes."

Clive pulled out his sword and was just about to plunge it into Hector's back when a young archer sent an arrow into Clive's back. Hector acknowledged the young man and told him to get something white. They quickly made a white flag, and Hector rode toward Joel's army waving it back and forth. His knights were passing by him. Ahead of him he could see countless knights lying on the battlefield. He could see that he had lost maybe one hundred to two hundred men, and Joel had lost none. Suddenly, he was by himself waving his flag. The archers of Regstar were no longer shooting. Then he saw Joel and two other knights riding toward him. He stopped and waited.

Joel rode up and stopped his horse just a few feet from Hector. "You are at a disadvantage. You have lost many men, and your knights are disorganized. I will not give you time to organize or move your archers forward. You can surrender now, or I will give the order to charge."

Hector did not hesitate. "We will surrender."

"Tell your men to throw down their weapons and to dismount from their horses."

Hector did as he was commanded, and the men of Rhodes began to disarm.

Joel watched as the men disarmed and dismounted as they were told. "Where is Clive? I will continue this surrender with him present."

Hector handed his sword to Joel. "Clive is dead. I will be spokesman for my army, but you will have to deal with the council inside the castle to make terms."

"What happened to Clive?"

"I was giving the order to retreat when he tried to kill me. One of my archers saved me. You will find his body back there."

Joel motioned for his knights to move forward. They began to round up the men of Rhodes and gather up their weapons throwing them into a pile. When the fire on the gate was out, they marched the prisoners into the castle and made a makeshift stockade in the middle of the courtyard.

Asher greeted Joel as he rode in. "Your timing could not have been better. That gate was just about to fall."

Joel smiled at his young knight. "I told you to attack the castle, I didn't tell you to take it. I need for you to assemble their council. I will check things out here. When they are ready, send for me."

After Asher left, Joel walked around to check on the prisoners. He saw that several had been wounded. He shouted out, "Anybody that is wounded bring them to me so we can see to their wounds." It was not long until fifty or so men were being treated for their wounds. Joel helped dress many of the wounds himself. Soon Asher came and told him that the council was ready. When Joel walked into the meeting hall, he was surprised to see not only the council but many of the residents of the castle were gathered along the walls, and many were in the balcony that overlooked the great hall. Joel's first thoughts were that he might need more men to keep control.

He stopped in the middle of the great hall, looked around, and then spoke. "I do not take any pleasure in what has occurred here. I know you see me as the aggressor, but Clive moved his army to our borders which created an act of war."

Joel's speech was stopped by Thomas. "We had no choice. You killed Karnac; that was the first act of war."

Joel heard the rumbling through the gallery. "I did not kill your king. In fact, I will show you that your king was killed by Clive and King Geoffrey." He pointed to the door, and two of his knights brought in Hector.

Hector looked toward the council. "What King Joel tells you is true. King Karnac was killed by an assassin named Piper. He was hired by King Geoffrey. Geoffrey coveted the lands of Arsi and Regstar, and Clive wanted to be king."

The rumbling of the crowd was very loud. The council was outraged. They were speaking to each other, and many were shouting. Finally, Thomas got control, and everyone got quiet. "King Joel, we are at your mercy; our castle is yours; you have beaten our army. What has happened to Clive?"

Joel glanced to Hector and then said, "He was killed in battle."

Thomas held up his arms to stop the talking. "What is your command?"

Joel walked up to the council. "My army and I are going to spend two days here. My men and I need to rest. In two days, we will leave and go back to Regstar. We will turn the castle and this kingdom over to this council." Again the council members starting talking among themselves, but Joel raised his hand to quiet them. "When you have formed a new government, I want you to know that the treaty which gives you access to the Diamond River and port at Edgewater is still in effect. I don't know what is going on with Salados and Arsi. If Salados has blocked the river at the Centerville bridge, your merchants will be allowed to use the road to Centerville to get to the river or take the road all the way to Edgewater. I will let the council talk this over. I will meet with Thomas tomorrow morning." He then turned, motioned to Asher, and the two men left the hall.

Outside, Joel turned to Asher. "Where are Kira and Kala?"

"I did not know if we could hold this castle until you arrived. I sent Kala, Kira, Evan, and Brumble back to Regstar by way of Dead Man's Pass. They should be through the pass by now."

Para At Regstar Castle

∗ ∗ ∗ ∗ ∗ ∗ ∗ ∗ ∗ ∗ ∗ ∗ ∗ ∗

Para had made her way back to the castle at Regstar. She did not know what had happened to her army and Dorian. When she had arrived at the castle, she was tired, so tired that after spending only about an hour with Donella she fell asleep. When she woke, she was in her room alone. She was hungry and thirsty, but she did not get up. She just lay there in the bed. She finally sat up and turned to sit on the edge of the bed. All of a sudden the door opened, and one of the servants walked in carrying a pitcher of fresh water.

"Oh, you are awake. We have been worried about you. How do you feel?"

"I am feeling oka. I think that I may have slept too much. My head feels heavy. How long did I sleep?"

The maid set the pitcher of water on the night table, picked up the wash bowl, and carried it out. "I will be back in just a moment. I need to empty this. Shall I have the cooks prepare you something to eat?"

Para, still seated on the edge of the bed, repeated her question. "How long have I been asleep?"

The maid stopped at the door. "You have been asleep almost two days."

Para was shocked. *Two days.* That meant the battle at the river was over. She was either still queen of Arsi or a queen in exile waiting for another invasion. "What time of day is it?"

"It is early morning, but just about everyone is already up. What about your breakfast?"

"Just bring something to drink. I will join the others and eat breakfast with them."

After the maid brought the bowl back and some milk to drink, Para cleaned herself up. The maid found some clothing she had left from her last trip, and when she was dressed, she left the room and went to the dining hall. There she saw Donella and several knights that she did not recognize. When Donella saw her enter the room, she got up from the table and ran to her.

"I was so worried about you. How do you feel?"

"I am okay. I don't seem to have much memory of getting here. I remember leaving our camp and Dorian but not much afterwards. I think I will be okay once I have something to eat. Can you believe I have been asleep for two days?"

The two women took their seats at the table. Donella introduced the knights seated with her. She could not remember any of their names with the exception of Brentley. Para could tell that he held rank over the others, but she still addressed her questions to Donella. They had no sooner sat down than the food arrived. There were eggs, sausages, and bread. As they ate, Para decided it was time to find out as much as she could. "When I left my army, they were under attack. Have we heard any news as to what has happened?"

It was Brentley who answered the question. "We have heard nothing from the west and nothing from the north. We are just waiting. Do you know anything as to how your men were doing in their battle?"

"When I left it was night, and we being attacked by archers. Dorian felt the main attack would come in the morning. We were waiting for support from Bailee. If Dorian could hold out until Bailee arrived, we had a chance. If not, I am afraid as to whom we will see come in sight of this castle first."

When they finished, Brentley asked a straightforward question. "My lady, do not think this forward of me, but everyone says you have some magic. Was there nothing that you could do to help your army?"

Para knew what Brentley was thinking. Did she have power to help Regstar if attacked? "I have been extremely ill; I almost died. I thought that when I healed and regained my strength my magic would come back. I feel fine, but I have no magic."

"I am sorry, my lady. I am glad you are better. King Joel is up on the border if he has not invaded Rhodes. He is at least four days away. Your army or King Geoffrey's army is only two days away. Let's pray to the gods that your army is the one we see first."

Para thought for a moment. "How long can you and your men hold this castle?"

"The castle is well built, and King Joel did not leave us without men. We can hold for several days. If Salados has won the battle, and they turn north to support Rhodes, they will be weakened after two major battles. It may be weeks before they get here. We just have to wait."

The rest of the day Para and Donella were together. They caught up on the past several years and Para gained an understanding of Reflection City.

"Why did you leave Reflection City? You were safe there."

Donella smiled and said, "I am like my mother. I fell in love."

"You fell in love with Asher?"

"I did, and Asher fell in love with me. But it is more than that. Asher convinced me that I had responsibilities to Regstar. Someday I will be queen. I will be queen of Regstar, Reflection City and maybe Arsi."

"Donella, I need to share some information with you. I don't know what is going to happen here, but I want you to know how important you are to me. You do not know this, but all the men at High Yellow Pass have been killed. I am so sorry. I know that Asher was at the pass."

"I am so sorry for the families of the men who were lost at the pass. "She paused. "Asher was not at the pass. My father sent for him, and he is with my father in Rhodes."

Para gave Donella a big hug. She started to talk and Donella stopped her. "You don't have to say anything. I love you too."

"There is something you need to know. You are not the only heir to the throne of Arsi. Alnac had a woman in his camp. Her name is Gwen. She is with child. I am not sure what I am going to do. When the child is born, I think I am going to be honest with the people of Arsi and let them know that this child is the son of Alnac and let them decide who should be the next in line for the throne."

For a moment Donella did not say anything. "You should do what you feel is right for the people of Arsi. Where is this Gwen now?"

"She is in South Castle. If Geoffrey wins the battle, it will mean very little. If he finds out about Gwen, he will kill her and her baby. If I had my magic, I could protect us all. I don't know what has happened to Epson. I have not heard from him for days. I fear something has happened."

"I met Epson on the road coming back from Reflection City. He told me that he had much work to do."

"Did he say anything else?"

"No." Donella walked over and looked out the window. "My life has been good; if Geoffrey takes this castle, I don't regret coming back. If Geoffrey wins, maybe he won't find out about Gwen. Are you okay with Alnac having another woman?"

"At first I was hurt, then I began to realize that our love had been fading away for a long time. You know Dorian is in love with me."

Donella walked over to Para and gave her a hug. "Do you love him?"

Para released the hug. "I am not sure it is love, like the love you feel for Asher. I admire him very much. He is a kind man. He is a born leader and cares about the men in his army. He saved my life by putting his life at risk. I feel good when I am with him. We will have to see."

The two women went up to the top of the North East Tower which was above the chapel and sat outside. The air was cool so they spread a blanket around the two of them. Suddenly they heard the alarm bell and the motion of men taking to the walls. The two women stood up to see who was coming and could see about twenty or so riders on the road to the castle.

Donella squinted to get a better view. "There are not enough men to be an army."

Para gave Donella's arm a squeeze. "Those are my men. I can tell by the colors. Are they all that's left, or are they coming to give us good news?"

As the riders got closer to the gate Para could see that Dorian was leading the men. She ran to the door and down the steps. When she reached the courtyard she waited and the gate came up. When Dorian saw her he rode up to her and dismounted from his horse and kneeled before her.

"We have won the battle. You kingdom is safe." He then stood up.

Para came to him and embraced him. "I was worried."

They held the embrace for several moments. "I was worried about you." For a moment he was just a man holding a woman he loved. Quickly he became aware of where he was and that he was the first knight in Para's army. He released the embrace. "We need to go inside. There is much you need to know."

A few minutes later they were in the small hall. Donella, Brentley, and several other knights had joined them. Dorian gave his report. "When you left we were under attack. Salados harassed us all night. They attacked us the next morning just as it was getting light. Just as they attacked, Bailee arrived and attacked Geoffrey's left flank. The fighting was fierce. We won the battle, but we lost a lot of men, but they lost more. Geoffrey was killed in the battle. We took two days to rest. I decided that we were not strong enough to help Joel. I sent the army back to Arsi."

Donella did not say anything. She knew the news was good but also knew that if Rhodes defeated her father, they still might be attacked.

Para stood up. "Thank you Dorian for what you and your army have done for both Arsi and Regstar. You were right to send the men back to Arsi. We will just have to wait to hear from Joel. We are not completely out of the woods but at least we do not have to face two armies. Get yourself cleaned up and get some food. We will meet later after you have rested."

That night, Dorian and Para sat together in the throne room. "What about your magic? Has it returned?"

"No, it has not. I feel fine. I feel rested. I worry a lot about what is going to happen, but I don't know why it has not returned. I have no idea where Epson is. I worry about him. There is no telling how old he is. He has been like a father."

"I don't know what to say about Epson. I hope he is okay. Don't worry about this castle. If Joel and Clive did battle, and Joel did not win, Rhodes' army will be like ours. It will not be able to lay siege to this castle. They will have to rest for at least two weeks, and they will have to march four or five days to get here. We can defend this castle for weeks if need be. Joel was wise. He left several good men here to defend the castle. We can add twenty-six to that count. We will be okay."

"I worry about Asher and Evan. Donella is very close to both of them. She is in love with Asher. If she loses them both, I don't know what she will do. I am not sure what to do about Arsi. We can't govern it if we are not there."

Dorian noticed that she said "we" but did not comment about it. "Bailee is a good man. He will take charge and take care of things."

"What happened to the men of Salados?"

"Geoffrey is dead. We sent them back to Salados; there was no reason to keep them prisoners. They are leaderless. They don't have a king, and unlike Rhodes and Regstar, they don't have a council. After we get through all this, and if Joel can keep Rhodes at bay, we will march into Salados and help them set up a new government, or you could annex Salados if you please."

"I don't want to annex Salados. I am happy with Arsi the way it is."

Dorian reached over and put his hand on Para's. "Think about it. The people of Salados would be much better off with you as their queen."

Para laid her other hand on top of Dorian's hand. "I don't think you are being completely objective. Thank you for being such a good friend. I am going to bed now. Maybe things will be better tomorrow."

Dorian watched her walk away. *I wish she loved me the way I love her. I guess I will just have to be content with being close.*

The next day Dorian met with Brentley, and they worked out a defense of the castle. They checked their supplies of food and water. As Dorian went to report to Para, he heard the gate start to open, and he saw Para and Donella standing in the courtyard. When the gate was open two riders came though. It was Brumble and Kira. *Is this good news or bad? Most likely bad,* he thought to himself.

Donella hugged Brumble when he joined the group and Kira gave Para the news.

Para turned to Dorian. "Kira tells me that Asher has taken Rhodes Castle."

"Asher took the castle?" He did not understand.

Brumble joined in the conversation. "Before King Joel left the castle, he sent me and Evan to lead Asher and about two hundred men through Dead Man's Pass. He knew that Clive would have his men on the border. He felt that if Asher attacked the castle, Clive would pull away from the border and be between him and Asher. It worked well, and Asher and his men were able to take the castle."

"Let's get inside; Kira and Brumble are tired. They can tell us the rest as they eat and rest." Donella took Brumble by the hand and led him inside.

As they sat around the table, everyone was to be asking questions at the same time. Brumble stopped eating and held up his hands. "We cannot answer all these questions at once. Let's start by letting Donella ask the questions. I am sure many of her questions will answer your questions."

Donella asked her first question. "You said that Asher and his men took the castle. Were there many losses?"

Brumble knew that Donella wanted to know about Asher. "Our losses were minor. They had not left enough men to defend the castle. They had left the gate down because they had not expected an attack. Asher didn't get a scratch."

"Did Asher think he could hold the castle when Clive returned?"

"He was not sure. That is why he sent me and Kira back. He wanted to make sure Kira was safe."

"Why did he not send Kala and Evan back?"

Brumble decided to sidestep the question. "Kala is a spy. She is not safe in Rhodes or Regstar. Her father will think that she betrayed him. She was not safe regardless of the outcome."

"You should have brought her back here. I would have begged my father for her life. Why did Evan not come back?"

"He chose to stay with Kala. We all owe Kala our life. She showed us a secret tunnel that might have been used for Clive's men to slip into the castle and surprise us. Asher was going to seal it and leave several archers there in case."

"Do you think Asher can hold the castle?"

"He only has two hundred men and about half are archers. He will need to have luck on his side. If Joel is only a half day behind Clive then Asher and Joel will have the army of Salados between them. Thanks to Kala's spying, Clive sent some of his men to the bridge at Two Rivers. They won't find any of Joel's army there, and he has made himself somewhat weaker. I think we have answered your concerns. Kira needs rest, and so do I."

That night Kira lay across her bed. She had lost her country, her husband, and might not see her daughter again. But somehow she felt content. She had really never loved Clive. Up until now, her life had been somewhat boring. The most exciting thing she had done was come to Regstar. She had been surprised when Clive asked her and Kala to join him in the trip. She had come to Regstar and fallen in love with Joel. He was everything that Clive was not. He was a wise king, he seemed to love everyone, he was honest, and he wanted peace. Now all she could do was wait.

The next day the men continued to prepare for the possibility of an oncoming attack. Everyone was so busy. When the sun went down, everyone gathered in the great dining hall. Brumble, Dorian, Brentley, Kira, Para, and Donella sat around a table together. In Joel's absence, everyone assumed Donella was acting as queen so they checked their ideas with her.

Donella stood up and addressed the room, "I know that I have not been here very long. My father is off fighting to try to regain peace. When he left, he placed Sir Brentley in charge of this castle's safety. I want to make it clear that until my father returns, he is in charge. We are most fortunate to have Dorian of Arsi here with us. With the approval of Sir Brentley, I would like to see that he is second in command. I feel the battle in the north is over, and any day we could see either a returning army or an invading army. I could have gone to safety. I could have returned to my grandfather's city, or I could have moved to Winter Castle. I have chosen to remain here. You are my people and this is my home. We will defend this castle because, like me, this is also your home. Let's just pray that the next days will bring us peace."

The hall was loud with applause. It was so loud that they almost did not hear the alarm bell. The applause stopped, and the bell became loud. The knights ran from the room to take their positions. Para, Donella, and their guests went to the highest point in the castle. They could see the archers taking their positions on the wall. They looked to the north and could see an army moving toward the castle. They were carrying torches and it looked like a thousand men. Dorian and Brentley move down to the walls to direct the defense. They just watched as the army came closer. Para put her arm around Donella. "They will not attack tonight. They will camp just out of bow range and attack in the morning."

They continued to watch the army, but it did not spread out to make a camp. They just kept riding toward the gate. Suddenly Donella shouted, "That is Father! He has come home! It is the army of Regstar. Open the gate! Open the gate!"

Kala and the Magic City

* * * * * * * * * * * * * * * *

Kala had had to make some tough adjustments in Reflection City. King Rue had welcomed her into his home. Once inside she could see the interior but still could see no people. He would talk to her every day. He had set up a mirror, and they had a morning conversation each day. He asked a lot of questions about Donella. She knew that he knew about the war going on between Rhodes and Regstar and was worried about her. Evan also came by every day. It was strange that once they came inside the gate Evan and Brumble disappeared. This talking to the mirror was going to take some time to get used to. Once she became more familiar with her new home, she started taking longer and longer walks. It was strange that the creator of this land made the people invisible but left other parts of the kingdom visible, and she had asked Rue about it. He had told her that if they were invaded, they would have an advantage. "The intruders could not fight us, and we could not fight them."

On her eighth day of living in Reflection City, she was walking just outside the castle when she saw an old man sitting under a tree. She was surprised. She had not seen anybody since she came to the magic city. She just stared at him. Then suddenly he spoke. "Move closer, my child, so I can see you."

Kala moved closer. "Who are you, and why can I see you?" She was just a few steps away from the old man. "Do you need food or something to drink? I could go to the castle and bring you something back."

"I don't need anything. My name is Epson, and I know you are Kala. I am the wizard who created this wonderful city. I am getting old and weak. My strength is fading. I have used what strength I have to protect the people I love. I don't have much time left."

"Let me take you to the castle. I can go and get some help."

"No, it is too late for that. I am going to do something for you, and then you can do something for me. First, let me give you some information.

265

The war outside Reflection City is over. Both Salados and Rhodes have been defeated. King Geoffrey and Clive, your father, are dead. Your father was killed by his own men. With Para and Joel in charge there will be peace for many years. Come closer, I need to give you something."

Kala reached out and took Epson's hand. "What do you wish to give me?"

Epson smiled at the young lady and said, "Look around."

Kala did not get up but looked back toward the castle. She could see people working and carrying out their daily routines. She was delighted. "Can these people see me also?" She leaned over and kissed Epson on his forehead. "Thank you ever so much. You said you wanted me to do something for you."

"I do. Queen Para is still in danger. There is a wizard who tried to kill her. I no longer have the power to protect her. I need for you, when you get a chance to leave this city and find her. I am placing a message inside you. When you see her all you have to do is give her a hug. She will then know my message. Can you do this for me?"

"I want to help you, and I will do this, but when I leave this land, Joel will have me arrested and maybe executed."

"Joel is a just and kind man. He has loved only two women in his life, Phylass, and your mother. I feel you will be safe. Explain to him that you have met me and that you carry a message inside yourself for Para and that she is in danger. You will be okay. I don't know where Para is. She could be in Regstar or back in Arsi. I do know this. I am almost certain that after a few days, Joel, Donella, and Asher will come here. Asher will not let Joel bring an army. You will be safe. You can talk to him then. There is not much time. Remember, only tell Joel that you carry a message but tell him no more. Give me both your hands."

As Epson held both of Kala's hands, he disappeared. As he did she felt her body tingle all over. She stood up and smiled to herself. *Now I can do something good.*

When she got back to the castle, the servants were staring at her and she felt very uncomfortable. She immediately went to see Rue. When she entered, Rue was behind a desk reading a book. When he looked up, he smiled. "You must be in love," he said. "I am so happy for you. Is it Evan?"

She returned his smile. "No, I am not in love except with you and this wonderful kingdom. I have to explain what has happened to me."

He got up and took her over to a davenport, and they sat down together. "Tell me your news."

"Today I took a walk near the side garden. There I met an old man. He was sitting under a tree. He did not say so, but I got the impression that he was dying. He said he wanted to give me something. What he gave me was the ability to see the people of this kingdom."

"Did the old man tell you his name?"

"He did. He told me that his name was Epson. He told me that he created this enchanted place. He also told me that he wanted me to do something for him. I have agreed to do this. That means that sometime in the near future I will have to leave this place."

Rue was alarmed that Epson was dying. His concern showed on his face. "Epson has been a wonderful friend for many years. It grieves me that he is dying. What did he ask you to do?"

"He wants me to give someone a message. He did not say, but I got the impression that I was to keep it a secret."

"When will you have to leave?"

"Not for a while. He also gave me a message which I need to share with you. He said King Joel, Asher, and Donella would be coming to see you. I was to remain here until their visit."

Rue's face turned to excitement. "Did he say when they would be here?"

"No. He told me that the war was over and that Arsi and Regstar had defeated Salados and Rhodes and that my father and King Geoffrey were killed in battle. He said that King Joel would rest and then come here, but he did not say when. I believe it will be soon."

"I hope it is soon. I miss Donella, and I want to meet Asher. King Joel and I have much to discuss. Have you ever met Asher?"

"I have. He was at Regstar Castle while I was visiting. He is a wonderful person."

"Now that everyone can see you, we need to let them know who you are and that you are our guest. I will also have to explain to the people how you got here. It is time they know that there is a way for people from the outside to come into this land, and it has nothing to do with our protection. We are only protected by who has a key. There are only two keys outside our kingdom. King Joel has one, and Brumble has the other."

Joel

* * *

The army of Regstar entered the castle walls and dismounted. They began to take care of their horses and move to their barracks and homes. Donella stood in the middle of all the commotion hugging her father. She did not want to let go. Then she saw Asher, and she let out a little girl scream and ran to him giving him a hug. When they released their embrace, he stepped back and just looked at her. "I am home my princess."

Donella was glowing. "You are home, my knight. I understand you are a hero. You took the castle at Rhodes."

"I am not a hero. I am just one lucky knight. Besides, Brumble and Evan had as much to do with it as I did. Are they still here?"

"Brumble is here, but Evan never came back."

"What about Kira and Kala?"

"Kira is here, but Kala is not. Brumble has told us very little about what happened to them, other than that they are safe."

Asher was somewhat concerned about the fact that Kala had not been returned to the castle. After the courtyard had cleared, King Joel invited Asher and a few other knights along with Donella and Brumble to meet with him and discuss their victory. He went to his room and had warm water and clean clothes brought to him. He had just finished dressing when he looked in the mirror and saw Kira standing behind him. He quickly turned and took her in his arms. "You were not in the courtyard to greet me."

"It would not have been appropriate for me to be hugging you in public. That would be hard to explain to your people. It is going to be hard enough to explain our relationship to your subjects with me being here and you defeating my husband's army. You know I have to know what happened to him."

"He was killed, not by my army or me, but by his own men. Hector, who was second in command, tried to stop the battle to save his men, but Clive wanted to fight on. He tried to kill Hector, and an archer shot him. I am sorry."

Tears came into Kira's eyes. She walked over and sat on the edge of Joel's bed. "I am so sorry that his life came to this. It will be difficult for Kala."

"Speaking of Kala, where is she? Asher said he sent both of you back to the castle."

Kira did not answer his question. Instead she asked a question of her own. "What is going to happen to Kala?"

"You know she was caught spying. If she had not been caught, things might have turned out very differently, and we might have lost this war. She did not know that Asher was going to take a force through an obscure pass to attack the castle. She thought he going to take his force to Two Rivers Bridge. Had that been our real plan those soldiers would have been slaughtered and Asher would have been killed. You did not answer my question. Where is Kala?"

"Kala did not return."

"You know where she is."

"We were on our way home. When we got to the top of Dead Man's Pass, Brumble told us that he would not take Kala to Regstar. He instead took us to Reflection City. We left Kala and Evan there. I loved my one day stay there. Rue is a wonderful man, and I would have stayed with Kala if not for you. I had to see that you were okay. Now I ask you again: What is going to happen to Kala?"

Joel walked over and sat down on the bed next to Kira. "You know I love you. As soon as we can find a way, I want to make you queen of Regstar. You ask me what is going to happen to Kala. Nothing, as long as she stays in Reflection City. Will you join me in the great hall? We have a celebration to attend."

It was a bittersweet celebration. Regstar and Arsi had lost several men, and it all could have been prevented with a peace treaty which Joel thought was going to be signed. There was laughter and some pats on the back, but it was late, and the meeting didn't last very long. Only Kira, Para, Brumble, Dorian, Asher, and Donella were left sitting at the table. They all knew the details of what had happened at both the battles at the border between Salados and Arsi and the battle in Rhodes.

Joel looked at the others seated around the table. He stood up and picked up a goblet of wine. "I want you all to know that you are my family. Here is to family." He took a drink as did the others. He then sat back down, brought his hands together, and placed them at his lips. He took his hands down and looked at Brumble. "Asher sent Kira and Kala with you back to Regstar. Why did you take Kala to Reflection City?"

Brumble spoke in a very soft voice. "I must with respect tell you that I am not a knight in your army. I only went to Rhodes because I felt this was the only way to save Donella. As for Kala, Asher told me to bring her here, but he also said to keep her safe. I felt those two orders were in conflict. If you lost the battle, she would not be safe, and if you won the battle, she would not be safe. She was only guilty of trying to protect her homeland. If it had not been for Kala, all of us would have been killed in Rhodes Castle. She told us of a secret tunnel that Clive and his men could use to sneak into the castle and take us by surprise. She did not ask anything for this information except that her mother be saved. Yes, I took her to the safety of Reflection City. She will remain there until you grant her a pardon."

Joel didn't say anything. He looked over at Kira and could see tears rolling down her cheeks. Then he spoke. "I hope that Asher, Donella, Kira, and I can go visit Reflection City. I have a long overdue meeting with Rue. I will decide what is to be done with Kala after I have had a conversation with her. It will not go unnoticed that Kala saved us in Rhodes. It is getting late. I think we all are tired. We shall meet again, but don't expect me to get up early tomorrow morning. I need to meet with Queen Para. Thank all of you for what you have done for Regstar and Arsi."

When the hall cleared, only Joel and Para were left at the table. Joel took his sister's hand. "You have been quiet. Are you okay?"

"I am okay. I have lost my magic. I don't know if that is good or bad. People are much more at ease around me. I am just not as sure of myself. If it had not been for Dorian, I don't know what I would have done. He saved my life; he took control of my army and defeated Geoffrey. I also think he is in love with me."

"Having someone love you is not so bad. If fact, it is a good thing."

"I know. I just don't think that I am ready to return his love. I am just not myself. I think if I let myself I could fall in love with Dorian. He would make a good king. There is another problem. Alnac is going to have a child."

"What do you mean going to have a child?"

"He kept a woman in camp with him. Her name is Gwen. I am keeping her at the castle. I like her. She did not ask to be a part of this, but her child will be in line to be the next king of Arsi."

"What do you plan to do?"

"I plan to wait until the child is born and then ask her for the child to be raised in the castle and tell the people who she is and who the baby is."

"Are you sure this is what you want to do?"

"It is not what I want, but it is the right thing to do."

"You know you are still quite young. You could get married and have a child. Your child would be in line to be the ruler of Arsi.

"I have thought about that. I not sure that I can have children. Alnac and I never had a child. The problem was not with him. It was with me. If I could get my magic back, I would feel more under control."

Joel pushed back from the table. "Let's go to bed, little sister. We will both feel better tomorrow. You have had a very trying ordeal. You were near death. Give yourself time to heal. Your magic will come back."

Para gave her brother a hug. "Something is wrong. I have not heard from Epson. I feel something has happened to him. I must be honest. I don't think my magic will come back. I believe that Piper did something to me to destroy it."

Joel kissed his sister on her forehead. "It does not matter if you have magic or not. You are a great queen either way."

Asher was walking down the hallway heading back to his barracks. When he passed one of the large support columns, he heard a soft voice say, "There are things we need to say to each other that can't be said at a busy table."

He turned back and smiled at Donella who was leaning against the column. "You know there are things that can't be done at a busy table." He walked to her and kissed her on the lips. "You know, the trouble with Reflection City is that when you fall in love everyone knows it. How do you think your father is going to react to this news? He may banish me from the kingdom."

"You sure are dumb for such a smart knight. He sent you to Reflection City. He expected you to win my love so I would return."

"I know this is true, but he didn't say that I would fall in love with you."

Asher put his arms around Donella and pulled her close. "It has been a wild ride the past several weeks. Your father has more to worry about than just me. He has to contend with Kira, and that becomes complicated with Kala. If King Joel pardons Kala, it will look like one reason he invaded Rhodes was to steal Clive's wife. It is obvious that Kira and Joel are in love."

Donella stepped back from Asher's embrace. "How do you feel about Kala? Do you think Father should give her a pardon?"

"I can see the problem that Joel has. I can't be objective with her. You know she was my complication I told you about in Reflection City. I have to be honest. I care for her. She did save us in Rhodes. To answer your question, yes I would, but I am in love with Joel's daughter, and Joel has the problem of Kala's mother and public opinion. In the eyes of the people of both Rhodes and Regstar, he must look like a man who defended his kingdom and people and not a man who went to war because he lusted for another man's wife."

"So you are saying that my father can't be kind and just. He will have to sacrifice Kala to maintain stability in the kingdom."

"What would you do?"

"I would ask her to come back to Regstar and make her a hero. After all she did to save you and your men."

"She did save me and my men, but in the war both sides lost hundreds of men. Rhodes lost more than Regstar. If Joel makes her a hero, she will be an outcast in Rhodes. Rhodes may also try to capture her and bring her back to stand trial. Even worse, someone may put a bounty on her. There is no way out of this. The only safety Kala has is to stay in Reflection City." Asher again put his arms around Donella. "You know I love you. I am tempted to take you back to my barracks and spend the night with you. But I want to do what is right. I am going to ask Joel for your hand in marriage."

"You are going to ask my father for my hand in marriage, and you have not even asked me. Maybe I don't want to marry just yet," she teased.

Asher again kissed her on the lips and she melted into his arms. "Maybe I will take you to my room after all. So I am asking you. Will you marry me?"

King Joel sat in his room. When he arrived he had hoped that Kira would be waiting for him, but she was not. Things were a mess with Kira and her daughter. He so much wanted to hold her in his arms and tell her that things would work out, but he really did not know if they would. Maybe he should slip down the secret passage and see her. *Would she want to see me?* He decided to go to her room. He went through the passage and knocked on the panel that opened into her room. He heard her acknowledge that he was there and entered. She was in her robe. He really did not know what to say. "So you have been to Reflection City. I hoped that I could have been the first to take you to the magic city."

"Brumble tried to prepare me for what I would see or should I say, what I wouldn't see. It really is a strange place. When we entered, the outside air was cold but just inside the giant door the air was warm and pleasant. It was difficult for me to talk to people through mirrors. I worry about Kala there. I know she is safe there, but she really is all alone."

"Don't worry, we will go get her in a few days." Joel walked over and put his arms around Kira. "We will deal with problems as they occur. Neither of you can go back to Rhodes. I think what I will do is to send both of you to Winter Castle. I need to get away and rest for a while. I want go with you to Winter Castle, but I will join you there about a week after you arrive."

Kira laid her head over on Joel's chest. "I love you so much, but I don't think that amount of time will allow people to forget that Kala was a spy."

"I have a plan if things fall into place. I think Asher will ask Donella to marry him. If he does, there will be so much excitement here that Kala will get lost in the mix. She just has to agree to spend about a year at Winter Castle."

"So you think Asher is the key. If he had not solved the mystery of Reflection City and Clive had not tried to destroy Regstar, the wedding might have been between Asher and Kala."

Joel reached down and lifted Kira's chin toward his face. He then kissed her. He opened her robe and let his hands slide to her back. "I don't want to make love but I want you to sleep with me tonight. I need to feel your warmth." The robe dropped to her feet and Joel quickly undressed and got into her bed. Kira got in next to him and wrapped herself in his arms. They did not say anything for a few minutes and then Kira said, "Do you think that you and I will ever be able to go public with this romance?" She waited for his answer but could tell by his deep breathing that he was already asleep.

The next morning in the dining hall, Asher and Donella were seated together having breakfast. Donella said with a smile, "You should have carried me off to your room last night. I could be preparing you your breakfast in bed."

"Give me something to look forward to. When should I talk to your father?"

Donella looked down and then up at Asher. "I hope you will understand my request. I will talk to father first, but I want you to first ask my grandfather Rue when we go to Reflection City. I want him to meet you and get to know you. He was expecting Evan to ask for my hand. Please understand this. They both will be in Reflection City together."

"What if I ask them together? They can say yes together."

Donella smiled. "Or they can say no together."

As Donella and Asher continued their breakfast, Kira came over to the table where Donella and Asher were eating. "May I join you for breakfast? I don't see Joel anywhere."

She sat down and a servant came up with a tray of food. Asher stopped eating. "Has King Joel been here and already eaten?"

The servant continued to serve the food to Kira. "I have not seen Joel this morning."

As the three continued to eat, a messenger came into the hall and quickly looked around. He spotted Asher and came to the table. "Sir, I received a message from Arsi last night. It was marked to King Joel urgent. I went to his room and knocked, but no one came to the door. I went into the room. He was not there, nor had his bed been slept in. I decided to wait until morning and breakfast-time, but I still can't find him."

Kira was turning a little flushed, but Asher quickly said, "King Joel came to my room last night and wanted to talk about the coming days and how to best use our troops now that we are at peace. He was worn out and fell asleep in a chair. I moved him over to my bed, and I slept on a cot. He was up and gone this morning when I got up. Give me the message, and I will see that he gets it."

The messenger handed the message to Asher and quickly left the room. The flush in Kira's cheeks left, and Asher excused himself and left to find Joel.

Asher walked outside and saw Joel coming from the barracks. *At least he was in the barracks,* he thought. When the two men faced each other Asher said, "Good morning, Sir. I have two messages for you."

"Good morning, Asher, what are the messages?"

"The first is if anybody asks, you fell asleep in my quarters last night and didn't return to your room. The second is that a pigeon came in last night with a message from Arsi."

Joel took the message from Asher. "Your bed is hard," he said with a grin. "I got up early this morning to check on the men. The past several days have been hard on them." Joel then opened the message. "It is from Bailee. He has been to High Yellow Pass. All the men who were there have been killed. That will include your good friend Trent. I am sorry. Bailee says he will see that all the men are buried. Assemble the men in the courtyard. I will let them know. We have all lost good friends at the pass. I will go and tell Para."

After all the men had been assembled and Joel made the sad announcement, he and Para walked inside and went to the throne room. They sat down at the meeting table. Para spoke first. "I need to get back to Arsi. They need to see me as a queen."

"I understand, but how is your strength? If you don't feel up to the trip right now you could send Dorian back and explain your absence. The people of Arsi need to know that King Geoffrey tried to have you killed."

"They will know. I feel okay but my magic is not going to come back. I need my magic to contact Epson. I am worried about him. He should have contacted me by now."

"When do you want to leave?"

"I am going to leave when you leave to visit Reflection City. By the time you are in Reflection City, I will be back at my castle."

Joel reached over and patted his sister on the arm. "Well I guess everything turned out okay. Our kingdoms are still intact. I gained a daughter, and you lost a husband. We both lost many good men."

Para put her hand on Joel's. "I still think something is wrong. It may be that Piper is still out there. If only I had my magic."

"I have an idea. Why don't you come to Reflection City with us? It is a magical place. Maybe you will get your magic back there."

Para thought for a moment. "It may be worth a try. We could leave together. My men could stay at Centerville, and I could meet them there in five days. I could spend one day at the city. I do want to see it."

"I am afraid you will have to do your looking through a mirror. So, it is settled. We will leave in four days."

The days passed quickly. On the morning of the fourth day, they assembled in the courtyard. Arsi had about twenty-five knights and Regstar about twenty. They planned to make Centerville by night fall. The trip went fast and the conversation among the three women was light. Donella liked Kira, but she could see that there might be some mistrust between her and Para. They made Centerville by nightfall. They decided to stay in tents instead of in Centerville because of the size of their party. The three women stayed in one tent while the men split up. Brumble and Joel stayed in one tent, Dorian and Asher stayed in another.

The next morning Dorian stayed with his men while the rest of the party moved on toward the village at Reflection Lake. By nightfall they were at the village and Joel and Silas greeted each other like old friends. Joel did not want to tell the old leader that they were going to Reflection City. He just told him that they were going to explore around the lake. Silas recognized Donella, Brumble, and Asher as having been in his village before. He looked at Donella and spoke to Joel. "Who is this pretty young lady?"

"This is my daughter, Donella."

The old man thought to himself, *Several days ago she was the niece of Brumble, and now she is the daughter of the king. Something strange is going on here.* "Several years ago you came to my camp, and you asked for my key to Reflection City. I know you were able to get in. It was said that you married a princess from the magic city. Your wife died about twenty years ago. You daughter belongs to the city, doesn't she?"

"She does. It is a long story, but you will have to trust me. When I get back from this trip I will tell you about the time I came here and you gave me a key. Right now, you will just have to trust me. We are going to visit the lake."

"What happened to your key?"

"It was lost. I gave it to a friend who thought he could find a way into the city, and he never returned it."

Silas rubbed his chin. "Looks like you are going to have to wait another five or so years to see the reflection again. I don't think I will ever see it again."

The next day, the three women and three men left the village and traveled along the northern edge of the lake. It took only about half a day to reach the magic city. While the others were looking at the mighty door, Brumble got the key that he had hidden in the rocks. With the key in the lock, the door slid open and the six travelers walked inside. Donella had warned Kira and Para they would need light clothing and the women quickly changed. They took off their heavy tops and stored the clothing in a bag in the rocks. They mounted their horses and started to ride. All could see the people in the city ahead, with the exception of Para and Kira. It was not long until they were spotted and an alarm was sounded. Brumble moved to the head of the group so all could see that they were friendly and would cause no harm. When they rode inside the castle, Rue was waiting in the courtyard. Kira looked for Kala but did not see her.

She reached over and touched Joel's arm. "I don't see Kala. Has she turned invisible?"

"No, I don't see her either." A crowd of people was gathering in the courtyard.

Donella dismounted from her horse and ran to Rue. She threw her arms around him, and they embraced. She did not want to let go until he said, "Easy young lady. Don't forget that I am an old man." They stepped away from each other, and she quickly hugged him again. "Let me meet this father of yours." Letting go of Donella he turned away from her to face Joel. "We have never met. I have never left this kingdom, but Brumble, who has, has told me much about you as a king. He says you are a kind man who is a good king."

"I am sorry that we have not met sooner and that I took your daughter from you. I wish we had known about the secret of the city sooner. I know that my daughter loves you very much, and you have done a fine job being a father to Donella."

"I am sorry too."

"I wish that I could have contacted you about the death of Phylass. I just didn't know of any way."

Tears formed in Rue's eyes. "We will discuss many things at our meal tonight. Who are your guests?"

Joel looked to the left. "This is Asher. He has been here before."

Rue looked at Asher. "So this is the young knight who stole Donella's heart and stole her from Reflection City." The two men embraced.

"I have two other people with me. You can't see them, but Kira is with me. She has also been here before. She is looking forward to seeing her daughter, Kala. Where is Kala?"

"She and Evan have gone riding. Welcome back, Kira. They will be back soon. You said there was someone else."

"I have brought my sister. She is the queen of Arsi, a kingdom to the west of Reflection City. Her name is Para."

Rue looked at Joel and Asher but spoke to all. "Welcome all to Reflection City. My servants will show you to your quarters." He then turned to Donella. "I assume that you can see Kira and Para."

"I can Grandfather. I will take them to my room. We should stay together." She turned to the two women. "This is going to be difficult for you. You will have trouble seeing, but I will guide you to my room." Once the two ladies were inside they could see that Donella was greeting servants and letting go of their hands to hug someone. Inside Donella's room they felt somewhat safe.

Para sat on the edge of Donella's bed. "I am going to stay in the room all the time that we are here. It is so strange that this castle is full of people, but we can't see them."

"You mean *you* can't see them. What about you, Kira, are you okay?"

Kira was looking around Donella's room. "Yes, I am okay. I have been here before. It takes some getting used to, but it will be fine."

Suddenly there was a knock on the door. Donella opened it, and there was a young servant holding two pairs of strange looking glasses. "Rue was having these glasses made for Kala. When you put them on, it looks like two small boxes in front of each eye, but the boxes contain two mirrors. It will allow you to see the people of this city." He put on a pair, and he could see the two women with Donella. "Gee," he said. "Are all the women outside this kingdom as beautiful as you two? If they are, I may want to leave." He then took off the glasses and handed both pairs to Donella. "Asher is in the side garden. He wishes to speak to you." The young servant then left.

Donella turned to the two women. "You two take the glasses. Give them a try. Walk up and down the halls and see what you see. I will be back shortly. I need to see what Asher needs."

Donella walked down the hall and out the side door to the garden. There she saw Asher sitting on a bench. He stood up, and they embraced. "Don't tell me you have already gotten into some trouble."

"No, or maybe yes. I am in love with you, and I have a problem."

"You are saying that being in love with me is a problem."

"Well yes, this girl I am in love with has a father who is king and a grandfather who is king. You said I should ask Rue for your hand in marriage first, and then ask Joel. I don't want to do it that way."

The smile on Donella's face faded away. "What is the problem?"

"I don't know Rue. I think he is a great man, but Joel has been like a father to me. I have more respect for him than any man alive. If I ask Rue, he is going to make a big deal out of it. The meal tonight will become a celebration. Joel is going to be hurt."

"I see your point. How do we solve this problem?"

"I am meeting with both men in a few moments. I think that I should talk to your father first. Once I have talked to King Joel, I will ask your grandfather for your hand in the presence of your father. It will appear that I am asking them both at the same time."

Donella's smile returned. "My, aren't you the problem solver? I agree it is a wonderful plan." She quickly kissed him on the cheek and returned to the castle.

When she started down the hall, she saw Kira and Para. She couldn't help but laugh. The two ladies were coming down the hallway wearing their glasses. "I am sorry, but you two look like I don't know what."

"Don't laugh. As funny as we seem, we can see people, and we have already had some wonderful and strange conversations." Kira turned to

Para. "She is right, we do look funny, and it is strange talking to people who can't see us."

Asher was right. Rue did make a big deal out of the announcement. He immediately started planning a banquet for that night. The whole castle came alive. Joel took Kira and Para for a ride so he could tell them the announcement. Asher and Donella stayed around the castle and just enjoyed themselves.

Later that afternoon, Evan and Kala returned from their ride. "What is all the excitement?" Evan asked as they rode into the castle. He saw a worker, and he and Kala dismounted from their horses. "What is going on?"

"Donella has returned. She is with her father and other guests. Donella is going to be married. There is going to be a celebration tonight."

Evan turned to Kala. "I guess we both should pretend that we are happy. If things were different, you might be marrying Asher, and I might be marrying Donella."

"If things were different, I would have never met you. It seems things have a way of working out. I wonder if King Joel plans to take me back to Regstar?"

"Rue would never let him do that and neither would Brumble. This is your home. We will just go to the celebration tonight and pretend that we are a part of the family. I need to go get ready. I will see you tonight."

As Evan walked off leading the two horses, Kala went to her room. She had enjoyed her time at Reflection City, but at first it had been a dread. She had grown to love Rue like a grandfather, and she was liking Evan more each day. *Perhaps it will turn to love,* she thought. When she got to her room she lay, across her bed. *I am not sure I will go. Donella will see me as a rival. Joel will see me as a spy, and Asher will see me as a former girlfriend or a spy or a traitor or someone who tried to have him killed. I am really not sure how Asher will see me.* Then she lit up. *I wonder if mother is with them.* She jumped from the bed and ran into the hallway. She saw a maid and stopped her. "How many women are here from the outside?"

"Well Donella is not from the outside. But there are two others. One has an unusual name, something like Para. The other is Kira. She was with you when you came to our city."

"Do me a favor. Go to wherever Kira is staying and bring her to my room. Tell her that Kala wants to see her. She will come."

In just a few minutes, Kira was knocking on Kala's door. Kala opened the door and standing before her was Kira wearing the mirror glasses. Kala laughed out loud. She gave her mother a hug. "You can take off those glasses. King Rue was making them for me. I am glad he found a better use for them." The two women took their seats at a small table next to the window. "We heard the news about Donella and Asher."

"Are you okay with that? I know that you and Asher had grown close."

"I am. It was over between us some time ago. There was no way it was going to work. Things went so horribly wrong. King Karnac being killed. Regstar and Rhodes going to war. Father being killed by his own men. Here I am, an outcast from both Rhodes and Regstar. Could it get any worse? Is Joel going to take me back to Regstar to stand trial?"

"I don't think so. This wedding is going to be a great diversion. Joel and I have talked about this. How did you know that your father had been killed? You were already in Reflection City when that happened. I didn't find out until Joel returned from Rhodes."

Before Kala could answer there came a knock on the door. A maid came into the room carrying a tray with some wine and glasses on it. "Thank you, May. Just set it down on this table. That will be all we need." The maid quickly left.

"You could see her and she could see you. How did this happen? Have you fallen in love in the short time you have been here?"

"No, I have not fallen love. The fact that the people of the kingdom can see me was a gift from an old man who lives here. I will tell you more about it later. You said that you and Joel have talked about this. What did he say?"

"He says that if you come back, you and I could live in Winter Castle, which is down on the southern coast. He says that after about a year, when things are calm, you and I could come back to Regstar Castle."

"We will just have to wait and see. I was not coming to the celebration tonight, but I just found out that Para is here. I need to see her so I changed my mind. I am going. There is a wonderful little shop in the village near the castle. Let's go there and get some simple clothing. Something light and gay but simple. We will help celebrate tonight."

That night the dining hall was filled with people. They were all eating and drinking and having a wonderful time. Music was being played from the back of the hall. At a long table, King Rue and Donella were seated together. To Donella's right was Asher, and to Rue's left was King Joel. Next to Joel was Para, and next to her was Kira. Brumble was at the end of the table. Evan was at a side table waiting for Kala, who was late. As the night went on, guests started to dance. Asher and Donella had the first dance by themselves, but after that everyone started to dance.

Kala had slipped into the hall unnoticed. She thought if she just gave the hug that Epson had asked of her, things would be okay. She thought to herself that this was a strange request, but she trusted the old man and his magic. As she watched, she saw Asher go to Para.

"Queen Para, or should I call you Aunt Para, would you like to dance?" Asher led Para onto the floor, and they started to dance.

Kala made her way through the dancers until she was standing next to Asher and Para. "May I cut in?" she asked. Asher was caught off guard. He assumed that Kala wanted to dance with him, but when he stepped back from Para, Kala stepped between them and hugged Para.

Para was caught off guard, and when Kala touched her, she became light headed. She felt a wave of shock coming from Kala's body. The room started to spin, at first slowly, and then faster and faster. When Kala released her everything went black, and she fell to the floor unable to move. Her eyes were closed, but she could hear people talking.

"Kala what have you done?" Asher was kneeling beside of Para. The room became a roar of unintelligible sound as while Para appeared to be dead, she was now visible. She heard Joel come to her side. She could not move, but she could hear everyone. Joel carried her from the room to a nearby bedroom and laid her on the bed. As they made her comfortable in the bed, she still could hear the conversions around her, but she could not open her eyes.

Rue, Joel, Asher, Donella, and Kira were all in the room. Joel look at Asher. "What happened? I saw you and Para go onto the dance floor, and the next moment she was lying on the floor." Joel said this with tears running down his cheeks.

Asher looked at Para. "We were dancing, and Kala came up and asked to cut in. I thought she wanted to dance with me, but she gave Para a hug, and she passed out and fell to the floor."

At first Joel didn't say anything. "Then she has accomplished what her father could not. She has poisoned my sister." Joel turned to Kira and then to Rue. "Will you confine Kala to her room, and post a guard until we find out what has happened? Do you have a physician?"

Rue took Para's hand. "Her hand is warm, that is a good sign. Her heart is beating very fast, but it is strong. I will send for the court physician."

Rue left the room. Joel took a seat next to his sister on the edge of the bed. Kira and Donella were crying. Donella came over next to her father. "Maybe things will be okay." He turned to her. "I want you and Asher to leave me and Kira and Para alone. I will let you know if there is any change."

After Donella and Asher had left the room, Joel turned to Kira, who was still crying. "Why would Kala do this to Para? Do you have any idea?"

"I don't know what has happened here. I do know that Kala has been under a lot of stress with all that has happened, but she seemed content today. She gave no indication she had murder on her mind. Something did happen to her here. Did you know she could see and be seen here? She told me that it was gift from an old man."

The door opened and Rue and the physician came in. The physician started his examination of Para. When he finished he turned to Rue and Joel. "She is resting easy. Her heart has slowed down. I would say she is in a coma. If she has been poisoned, it is like no poison I have run across. Have someone spend the night with her, and if she changes, send for me. I will check back in the morning."

Joel spent the night sitting with Para. Para did not move, but her breathing was smooth. She was aware that Joel was with her but could not move or speak. Then she started to drift as if she were going to sleep. She felt at peace, and she started to feel her strength return. She wanted to move but could not. She wanted to tell Joel she was okay. Then everything went black. Joel could tell that her breathing had increased. She was no longer aware of what was around her. Then things began to get light. In the light she could see Epson. "Don't try to talk, just listen. Your magic has left you, but it is coming back. When you awake your magic will be with you, but not only your magic, you will also have my magic. I am old, and it is time I moved on. You will know things and you will be able to do things, you have never known how to do before. Having magic makes you a lonely person. When people found out you had your magic, you became an outsider. People did not know how to take you. When you awake, don't let anyone know you have power. This way you can be a queen and still live a normal life. Use your magic only in secret. Kala has done what I asked her to do, but right now she is paying a price. Right now you are hidden from Piper, the wizard who tried to kill you. When you awake and leave this kingdom, he will have the power to find you. You must take precautions to protect yourself. You will sleep for about a day. When you awaken, you will have more power than you can imagine. Use it to protect yourself."

The light began to fade and the darkness returned. Joel could tell that her breathing was again smooth. He sat with her the rest of the night, and in the morning Donella came and sat with him. "You need to go get some rest. I will stay with her, and if anything changes, I will send for you." Joel patted his daughter on the shoulder and left the room. He went to see Rue.

Rue was with the physician. When Joel entered the room he asked, "Is there anything we can do?"

"No, she is stable. She does not seem to be getting any worse."

The physician looked down and then up. "If it is some type of poison, I am afraid to give her anything. If we don't know, anything I do might make it worse."

Joel looked at Rue. "I am going to have to force Kala to tell us what she did. I don't know how, but somehow I have to find out."

Rue walked over to Joel. "Nothing like this has ever happened in this kingdom. Love brought you to this kingdom, and love brought Asher to this kingdom. Everything about Reflection City is safe. Now we face a possible murder. I will not let you torture Kala, not even to save the life of your sister. You said your sister was stable. If she starts to get worse, I will reconsider, but I don't want to sanction any torture in this kingdom."

"Can I talk to Kala? Maybe she will tell me something, or maybe she will tell her mother something."

"Yes, you can see Kala, but only with the Great Knight Brumble present. We will protect Kala until we know the truth."

Joel left Rue and went back to Para. He knocked and Donella came to the door. Her eyes were red from crying. He quickly stepped inside the door. "I am so sorry. I am so sorry," she said.

"I am going to talk to Kala, and I want you to come with me. We have to know what she did to cause this sleep to fall over Para. If we can find out what poison was used, maybe we can save Para."

"Of course I will come with you. I just can't believe that Kala would do this. There has to be some other explanation."

"I wish there was, but I don't see how anything else could be there. Para was fine, and when she was hugged by Kala, she fell to the floor. Let's go talk to her."

When Joel and Donella arrived at Kala's door, Brumble was already there. He was accompanied by four other knights. "When you go in, I will be with you. If I ask you to leave, you must do so. If you don't, I will call upon these men and they will force you to leave. We don't want it to come to that. Do we understand?"

Joel agreed, and they walked into Kala's room without knocking. Kala was lying on her bed, but her bed had not been slept in. Kira was sitting in a chair next to her daughter's bed. Joel spoke first. His voice was calm. "Kala, we have to know what happened when you hugged Para. Did you stick her with a pin or something sharp?"

Kala was now sitting on the edge of the bed. She was like a little girl. She looked at her mother. "I did nothing. I just gave her a hug."

Kira took a seat by her daughter. "Why did you give Para a hug? You were not friends. In fact, you barely knew her."

"I was outside the castle the other day when I met an old man. He seemed kind, and I stopped to talk to him. He told me things that I did not know. He told me that my father was dead, killed by his own men. He gave me the gift of vision so I could see and be seen. He only asked one thing in return. He asked me to hug Para when I saw her. He made me believe that this would save her life. I thought I was doing something wonderful. I thought that this would bring me back to the good graces of you and King Joel. It seems that everything I do has hurt someone that I love."

Joel did not say anything. Kala's story was so compelling he did not know what to do. He motioned to Brumble. "I want to go back to my room now. I don't have any more questions." When he got back to his room, he lay on his bed. He tried to go to sleep but could not. Had some wizard gotten into Reflection City and tricked Kala into trying to kill Para again? Why did Para become visible to everyone when she passed out? Why was she now in what appeared to be a peaceful sleep? The afternoon passed slowly. He knew that Donella would be getting tired so he went back to the room where Para was. When he got there, Rue and the physician were also there. Donella got up when her father entered the room. "There is no change. She is exactly the same."

The physician echoed the same. "There is no change. It can't be poison. If it were poison, she would be getting worse. I am baffled. One thing I have noticed by watching her, it is almost like she can hear what we are saying. She seems to have rapid movement in her eyes when we talk. I am not sure, but she might respond to people talking to her. I will check back in on her later." He then left the room.

"I wish Dorian were here. He is her right hand man, and she cares a great deal for him as he does for her. She might respond to him." Then he thought for a moment. "Go and get everyone who came here with us and bring them to this room. Also bring Kala. I have an idea." It was not long until Brumble, Kira, Donella, Kala, Asher, and Joel were standing around Para's bed. Joel told everyone to say something to her, and they would see if they could observe any reaction from her.

Donella went first. "Aunt Para, I have been with you all night. I love you so much. Please come back to us." Para did not move, and she continued her steady breathing.

Brumble was the second to talk to her. His words were soft for such a large man. "I am going to hold your hand. If you can understand what I am saying, just give my hand a squeeze." Again there was no response from Para.

Joel took his turn. "My dear sister, I wish I had let you return to Arsi instead of insisting you come here. I love you, and please give me a sign you can hear me." He watched for any reaction but got none. "This is not working, I guess I was just grabbing at straws. Thank you for trying."

"Wait, I want to talk to her." Kala was standing at the foot of the bed, and she walked around and kneeled down on the floor as if she were going to pray. "Dear Para, I don't know how but somehow this is my fault. I only want to help you, and did only what Epson told me to do."

Kala was going to say more, but Para opened her eyes and repeated the name Epson. She then looked at the shocked faces of those gathered around her bed. "Epson is dead. I want to thank you Kala because you allowed him to visit me one last time. While I have been asleep, he has been with me." She looked at Joel. "He has told me many things. I will no longer have my magic, but I will be a good queen." She then turned and sat up on the edge of the bed. "It is strange, but I don't feel like a day has passed, except that I am hungry." She then stood up. She felt strong. She hugged and thanked everyone in the room. "I want everyone to leave except Kala and Joel. After I have talked to them, I will get cleaned up and join you for some food."

After the room was cleared she turned to Kala. "I know you are an outcast in both Rhodes and Regstar. You are not an outcast in Arsi. I want you to come and live in my castle for as long as you want." She then turned to Joel. "Do you understand what I am offering Kala? She can become a citizen of Arsi and have the protection of my kingdom."

There was a smile on Joel's face. "I understand, Sister. There will be no charges against Kala in Regstar. If she wants, she and her mother can take up residency in Winter Castle. It can become their home."

Kala felt free. "I cannot tell you how much I love what you have offered me. I am not sure what I am going to do. I went from having no home to having three. I might just stay here in Reflection City. I have a very good friend here named Evan. I might like to see where that friendship leads." Kala got up and started out of the room. "I think I will go see that friend now."

Joel looked puzzled. "I have a question. When Kala hugged you and you passed out, I could tell that the people here could see you. How did that happen?"

"It was a gift from Epson. He gave Kala the same gift."

Joel went to see Kira and Para got up and started to dress. She knew she had her magic back but decided to give it a test. There was a vase of flowers on the window sill. Some had bloomed and others had not. She just waved her hand and all the flowers were in full bloom. She felt strong and alive. When she arrived at the dining hall, she found that none of her friends were there. A servant came up to her and said, "King Rue is in the private dining area. If you will follow me I will take you there." When she walked into the small dining area, she saw that everyone was seated around a large round table. At first they did not see her come in but when they did, they all stood up and clapped their hands. Para came over and took her seat next to her brother. Rue had been talking to Donella but turned to all the guests at the table as he stood up.

"We have decided to have another celebration. The last one was cut somewhat short. Tomorrow night, which will be the last night for our guests, we are going to celebrate outside. Everybody will be welcome, and we want everyone in the kingdom to meet Asher and Joel. We want to make our guests so tired that they won't want to leave the next day. I also want to point out that Kala has decided to stay in Reflection City, and that makes us all happy. We thought the room we gave her in the castle would only be temporary, but now I am glad to say it will be her home. Kala will be family."

Para stood up and addressed everyone at the table. "I want to thank all of you for caring about me. Yesterday while I was unable to move or open my eyes, I could hear you talking, and it is great to be loved and have a family. Tomorrow when we leave, I will not be going back to Regstar. I am going to Arsi. When I left Arsi, we were under siege. During that time Arsi lost many good men. I have to be concerned not only with Arsi, but I also have to be concerned with Salados. They lost more men than Arsi. These men were victims of evil. When I get back I am going to visit Salados and see if we can't fix all the problems that exist between our kingdoms. Reflection City is a model for what a kingdom should be. I look forward to the celebration tomorrow and thank you King Rue for your hospitality."

When the meal was over, Para asked Kira and Joel to come to her room. When they arrived, she asked them to sit at her small round table. Para was smiling. Joel looked at his sister. "Why are you smiling so much?"

"Because you two are lovers but pretend to be just friends. I bet it has been hard trying to keep a secret that everyone around you and already knows."

At first Joel didn't say anything. "I love Kira very much. I want to make her my queen, but this is going to be difficult. Do you think Donella knows and will she accept Kira as queen?"

Kira was blushing. "I think she knows. Asher covered for us the other day before we left Regstar Castle. Donella picked up on it right away because she didn't say anything. I can't go back to Rhodes, and even if I could I would not. I want to be with Joel."

"What do you plan to do?"

"We are going to let Kira live in Winter Castle for a while. When Asher and Donella are married, she will come back for the wedding, and then we shall have an open courtship which will lead to our marriage."

"Sounds like a good plan, but why doesn't she come to live with me at Arsi until the wedding. She won't be so lonely at Arsi. You need to visit your sister more often, and you might just get to see Kira."

Joel looked at Kira and saw the approval in her eyes. "Sounds good. When we get back to Centerville, Kira can continue on with you back to Arsi. I will continue on to Regstar."

"Donella and Kala are in the garden. I suggest you go see them and tell them that in the future they are going to be sisters."

When Kira and Joel told them that they were in love neither girl was surprised. In fact they were delighted with the idea of being sisters. Kira told Donella that she was going to live in Arsi but would come to Regstar for the wedding and hoped that it would be okay for her to stay.

The next day the engagement celebration was wonderful. Food and dancing was provided from mid-afternoon until past midnight. Para was the guest of Rue and sitting together they talked of the history of Reflection City, the wedding, and a variety of other topics. They even danced several dances. As they were eating Para, noticed that Kira was still using her glasses on occasion to see the dancing and games going on around the courtyard. She seemed to be having a good time, but maybe it could be better. *I will just make her visible to everyone*, she thought. She concentrated and used her magic. Slowly Kira started to become visible to the people of Reflection City. Para moved away to a place where she could watch Kira, but Kira could not see her. Kira's face lit up when she could see all the activities going on around her. She reached over and touched Joel's arm. Para could tell she was telling Joel all about her new gift. Kira and Joel got up from the table, and Para could tell they were looking for her. She came up to their table as though she was just coming from the dance floor. "Isn't this a grand party?"

Kira didn't say anything. She wanted to see if Para had her magic back. Then she blurted it out. "I am visible, and I can see everyone. Did you do this?"

"That is wonderful, but I didn't have anything to do with it at all," she lied.

Joel spoke up. "I wish you did use your magic, but it must be all the love of this city which we have become a part of. At one time my heart was filled with hate for what Brumble and Rue did, but now I am content. I love this city, and my love for Kira, and your love for me and Kira must have done this. Regardless of how it happened, I am so pleased that Kira can enjoy our last night in this magic place."

The Fear of Piper

* * * * * * * * * * *

The next day, Rue, Evan, Kala, and Brumble went to the door to see Kira, Joel, Donella and Para off. Donella, was crying as she said goodbye to Rue and Kala. She gave Evan a hug. "Take care of my new sister," she said. Kira gave Rue a kiss on his cheek and thanked him for taking care of Kala and his hospitality. Donella gave Brumble a hug. "You know you are a second grandfather to me. I love you very much, and thanks for all you have done for me. I hope to see you at the wedding." Joel also told Brumble that he would see him at the wedding. "Para didn't say anything. She just smiled at her friends and led her horse through the large door. Once outside, the air seemed bitter. They quickly opened the bag that contained their warm clothing. Then they mounted their horses and started down from the rocks toward the lake. Once they reached the edge of the lake, they turned west toward the village.

Suddenly Para felt a deep penetrating cold. She knew what it was. Piper. He was somewhere either in Regstar or Arsi. She could sense his being. She could feel the evil that was inside him. She knew that he was going to find her. *Maybe,* she thought, *I should find him first.* She would deal with Piper when she got back to Arsi.

Piper had stayed in Edgewater for several weeks after he had been paid in gold for killing Para. He did not know he had not killed her and that Epson had saved her. It was not until news of the battle of Midway Bridge started coming to Edgewater that he found out that Para was still alive. He learned she had not taken part in the battle and concluded that even though he had not killed her she had no magic. That was the same as killing her, he thought. He had spent much of his gold on wine and women. He loved the river district. He could drink, gamble, and have any woman he wanted.

All the women of the river district could be bought. Every night he would spend money on the tables and the women. His gold was almost gone. With all his magic, he could not make gold. It was one thing he had never mastered. His only way to get gold was either to steal it or hire out his skills as an assassin. He did not like to steal gold, but he liked being an assassin. *I will spend a few more days here and when my gold is gone, I will find a way to milk more money from one of these kingdoms.*

The only two men that could use his skills were now dead, and the four kingdoms were at peace. As he sat in the tavern he started to formulate another plan. He would become a kidnapper. He had learned that King Joel had a daughter and Regstar was a rich kingdom. Joel would pay much to save his daughter. He looked down at his ale. *Queen Para is Joel's sister. Arsi and Regstar would both be willing to pay to save her.* Yes, Para who had escaped him once would be his target in his kidnapping plan.

All the way back to the village, Para thought about Piper. She wondered how much power he had. She knew he had to be able to turn himself into a bird to make the distance between Centerville, where he had killed Karnac and then poisoned her so quickly. They reached the village just past noon. As always Silas was happy to see them. They had a meal with Silas and his family, and then decided to move on toward Centerville. Their plan was to ride until it was dark, and then they could reach Centerville by around noon the next day. When it became too dark to ride on they left the road and moved off into the trees. Suddenly Donella spoke. "I know where we are. There is a cave nearby. I just can't see or remember just where it is."

Para discovered with just a thought she could turn her eyes into those of an owl and could see everything. She looked toward the rocky cliff, and a few yards to the left she saw the cave opening. "Let's look over here." She quickly led the group to the cave.

Once they were inside, Asher gathered some wood, and they had a fire going. As he sat down he said, "This is good. No one can see our fire from the road. How did you know about this cave?"

"When Brumble, Evan, and I left Reflection City to find you and Father, it was snowing very hard. Epson met us in the road and brought us here. We stayed here until the snow stopped and began to melt. This is just like home," Donella laughed.

The fire soon made the cave cozy and warm. Silas had given them a bag of food, and they opened it. Inside they found a couple of bottles of wine and food. Once they had finished their meal, they stretched out on their blankets. Kira yawned. "This mountain wine is stronger than I am used to. It is putting me to sleep." In fact, it was not the wine putting her and the rest of them to sleep. It was Para using her magic. When they were all asleep she walked to the cave entrance and said, "Let's see how this works." She quickly turned herself into a night hawk and flew out of the cave. There was a full moon, and she soared high above the trees, and in the distance she could see the night fires of the village they had left. She turned and flew back to the cave. Once back inside, she thought to herself. *This is wonderful, I have never had a sensation like this. It is going to be hard to keep my magic a secret because I am going to do this quite often at night.* She lay down on her blanket and started thinking about Dorian. She quickly fell asleep. In her sleep Piper, was killing Dorian and placing her in some type of prison cell. When she awoke, she knew that Dorian was in danger and that Piper planned to kidnap her.

The next day when they emerged from the cave, it was lightly snowing. Para held out her hands as if to catch the snowflakes. "This is strange. Last night it was clear, not a cloud in the sky."

"How would you know? We were deep in the cave. Did you take a midnight walk?" Joel laughed.

"No, but I did get up to put some wood on the fire. I walked to the cave entrance and looked outside."

The little lie seemed to satisfy Joel, and they mounted their horses and rode on toward Centerville.

They talked very little, and as they had planned, they were in sight of the city by noon. They made their way to their camp. When Para saw Dorian, she felt warm inside. *This man is good for me,* she thought. She had an urge to get down from her horse, run to him, and give him a hug. *No, that not is the way a queen greets her first knight,* she thought. She could tell that Dorian was both pleased and relived that they were back. "I am going to take a nap. I am tired. In about an hour, I will come to your tent. There is much we need to discuss."

Dorian seemed to be a little disappointed that her first words were about tending to business. Nevertheless, that was the relationship he had to accept. "Do you remember where your tent is located?"

"I do. Have some food and drink sent to my tent. I want to eat something before I sleep."

Dorian motioned for a young man to get some food. "Bring a bottle of the local wine they make in Centerville. Our queen will find it to her liking. Will there be anything else?"

Para could sense Dorian's frustration. "On second thought, you bring the food, Dorian."

He was now angry. He wanted to say, "I am the first knight of Arsi. I am not a common servant." When he spoke there was anger in his voice. "Go to your tent, my lady, I will bring you your food."

She turned away from him and started toward her tent. She was smiling. When he came to her tent he was talking to himself. "What does she expect of me?" When he entered her tent a she was standing next to her bedroll. "Where do you want this?"

"Place it on the blanket over there."

"Will there be anything else?"

"Yes." She then moved to him and gave him a big hug. "I have really missed you. I am so happy to be going home."

He was completely caught off guard. His natural response was to put his arms around her and return her hug. Without thinking, he lifted her chin and kissed her on the lips. Her lips were soft; he felt his body grow weak and she seemed to melt into his arms. He then quickly released her and stepped back. "I am sorry my lady, I forgot my place."

Para quickly stepped back to him. "No, I forgot mine." She then kissed him again. This time he did not step back. He held her for a long time.

"I am so happy you are back, but what just happened? When you got back, you seemed to care very little about me. I was caught off guard, and when I enter your tent, I am now caught off guard again. I am perplexed."

Before Para could answer she got another cold feeling. Again she knew it was Piper. *That wizard can sense my every move. Dorian will be in danger if he stays around me. I must find a way to save him until I can deal with Piper.*

"I am sorry, but I have a problem with you, my first knight. I care a great deal for you. You have saved my life and my kingdom. The problem is that I am still queen, and I have only been the ruling queen for a few months. I have only been a widow for a few months. I don't know how my people will react to me and you. I am not sure I can fall in love right now." She knew she was falling in love with Dorian, but she felt she must keep him at a distance. If they got too close, Piper might harm Dorian. If they became lovers, the people of Arsi might condemn her for not giving Alnac a suitable mourning.

"I notice that you did not say you loved me. You said you cared for me. The problem I have is that I am in love with you. I don't want to keep that love a secret."

"Like I say, we have a problem. You are going to have to give me some time. I can't promise you anything. When Alnac was alive, all I had to do was manage the castle. Now I am queen. I not only have to deal with Arsi, but I am not sure what needs to be done with Salados. I would love nothing better than to make you king, but not just yet. You have to be patient. The first thing we need is to make sure that the two kingdoms are stable."

"I am not sure I can work with you every day as first knight, seeing you every day with the way I feel about you."

"I know that you have loved me for some time. Not once have you ever crossed the boundary. It was I who crossed the boundary today. I am not sorry. I wanted you to know that your feelings for me were being returned. You should understand the problems here. We need time. When we get back to the castle one thing that will be expected of me is to honor my late husband and king. I will be expected to go into mourning for at least a year."

"The pain will be too great. When we get back to Arsi, I want you to send me to South Castle. Move Gaylord to Arsi to be first knight. He is a good man and knows how to manage an army and a government. He will serve you well."

"You are not making sense, Dorian. If you love me like you say, you will not be content living at South Castle. I will not make such a move. I need you beside me to help me get Arsi back to the way it was. I know Gaylord, and yes, he is a good man. Be content to know there is a chance for us. But you and I will have to wait." She then went back to him and this time she gave him, a quick kiss on the lips. He started to speak, but she put her finger to his lips and said, "Don't say anything. You are my first knight and there are many things I need to discuss with you. I want you to help me with the problem we have with the government of Salados. I want to meet with you and Joel tonight. Right now I need to rest." *Sending Dorian to South Castle might solve their problems.*

Dorian started out of the tent. "I have a question. Back in Arsi you lost all your magic. Am I now dealing with a queen or a wizard?"

"My magic has not returned. Epson has died. I am just a woman trying to be a queen."

Para, Joel, and Asher met with Dorian and brought him up to speed on the things that happened in Reflection City. The next day the two groups parted with Joel leading his group toward the castle at Regstar and Dorian and Para headed on the road toward Midway Bridge. A hard day's ride would put Joel and Donella back at their castle, but it would take three days for Para to reach her home. During the ride back Para, and Dorian kept their relationship very formal. The three days seemed like three months to Para.

That night Para was tired and had gone to sleep quickly. In her dream she had a visit from Piper. She could see him. He was dressed in dark clothing, both a black shirt and black pants. He had medium-length black hair and a mustache. Even his eyes were dark. He had a sinister smile on his face. "Where have you been, my lady? For several days I could not find you. I thought you were dead. Then just a few days ago, I felt you again. I don't know how you survived my little spider bite, but I now have other plans for you. I will be seeing you in the coming weeks." He then laughed and was gone.

Para awoke covered with sweat. She got up and poured water into her bowl and washed her face. Her heart was beating fast. She began to calm her fast beating heart. *Well I now have seen the face of my enemy,* she thought. She did not go back to bed but took a seat in a chair next to the fireplace.

Para stayed in her room the entire first day, but on the second day she came out and met with Bailee and Dorian. "Tell me what has happened while we have been gone," she asked Bailee.

"Things from Salados have been quiet. I did receive a message that they are sending a delegation to meet with you. They should be here tomorrow. I have accounted for the men we lost at the two battles. I went to South Castle and brought Gwen back to Arsi Castle. Her baby is not long away."

"How is she doing?"

"It is really hard to say. She enjoyed being at South Castle. I think she would have stayed if I had let her. She is really unsure of her relationship with you. When she found out you had lost your power, she seemed relieved. There is some talk among the staff as to who she is. I have stayed with the story that she is your cousin, but for some reason there is doubt."

"Send an escort to meet the delegation from Salados. Bring word to Gwen that I want to see her. Do you have anything to add Dorian?"

"No my lady."

Para watched Dorian as he left the room. She knew that she was losing him. He could not continue being her friend and first Knight. Not the way he felt about her. As she sat in the throne room she wondered if there was something she could do to make things better between them. Perhaps he was right; she should send him to South Castle and bring Gaylord here. At least he would be safe from Piper away from her.

It was not long until Gwen came into the throne room. "It is good that you are back my lady. Everyone has been so worried."

"You need to address me as Para. It is not necessary for you to be so formal. I want you to relax and talk to me like we are just two women. After all we are cousins, or that is what the staff thinks. We should continue our act."

Para watched Gwen's face. She was afraid of her. Then she said softly, "We can't be just two women. You are the queen of this kingdom; I am just a poor woman from Pan who was your husband's mistress. You are a woman who could put me to death. I keep thinking you might."

"Think how long you have been here Gwen. You have talked to the staff and other people who live in the court. Has anyone told you how many people that I have put to death? I really don't know what to do with you and your baby. Whether you like it or not, this baby will be in line to be the next king of this kingdom unless I have a child. When the baby is born, you can go back to Pan, but the baby stays here. I will not take a chance of anything happening to the child. I want you to stay and raise the child here. I want this child to have the best education possible. When the child is born, I will explain this child to the people of this land. In the future, if I should marry and have a child, I would want you to remain and be a part of Arsi. I hope that in the future you and I might become friends. We have had this conversation before. Have I made myself clear?"

"You have..." Gwen hesitated, "Para"

That night Gwen, Kira, and Para were talking and giggling like three little girls. They felt relaxed. Dorian and Bailee were eating together at a distant table. "Has Bailee treated you well?"

"He has, and I like him very much. I believe if I wasn't carrying this child he would be courting me." The three women laughed.

When they finished, Para sent a servant to Dorian's table to have both men come to her table. When they arrived, Para said to Bailee, "Will you escort my friend back to her room? She does not need to be alone. Have the servants come by and check on her from time to time."

Para watched Bailee and Gwen as they left the room. *I could use a little magic to bring these two together, but I don't think that will be necessary.* She then turned to Dorian. "Dorian, I do not wish to hurt you, but tomorrow a delegation from Salados is coming. I don't think the meeting will be long. They should get here by noon, and the meeting will last only a short time. We will give them a banquet tomorrow night, and they will most likely leave the next day. I want you to conduct the meeting. If you think what they ask is fair, you have the power to make the peace permanent. I will be there but will not say anything. I will take part in any signing that needs to be done."

"Is there anything else my lady?"

"There is. I thought this arrangement might work but I was wrong. You can't function around me, and I am much the same around you. I have thought about it, and you're right. After we have concluded our business with Salados I want you to move to South Castle. Send a bird tonight and tell Gaylord that he is needed here in two days. I am going to make Bailee first knight. I prefer Bailee over Gaylord because he has more knowledge about what has been happening the last several weeks. In two days I am going back to the cabin in the swamp. I am going to stay there a couple of days. I want to honor the memory of my good friend Epson. I am going to move his books to my private library."

Dorian was completely caught off guard. He did not want to go to South Castle, but it had been his suggestion. He just thought of Para's safety. "Are you sure you need to make that trip into that swamp? I'm not so sure you will be safe. Who knows what is in that swamp?"

"I will take an escort and go by coach. I will be safe. Do you have any other questions?"

Para could see the disappointment in Dorian's face. "Don't worry, this is for the best. We won't leave you there too long. Trust me. I have a plan."

I wish you would share it with me, he thought. He turned and left the room.

The next day as planned, Dorian conducted the peace settlement between Salados and Arsi. The minister from Salados caught everyone by surprise by asking to become part of Arsi. "The people of Salados are tired of war. We have been fighting far too long. We feel the best way to ensure peace is to join the great kingdom of Arsi. We hope that you will appoint someone who understands the needs of Salados to be your vassal and to serve the interest of both."

Dorian was unprepared for the request. He turned to Para. "Queen Para, do you accept the terms of this request and are you prepared to make Salados a part of Arsi?"

It was almost like she knew in advance of the request. "Minister Julian, I accept your request, but you must approve our choice as vassal. I am going to send a knight of great experience to your castle at Salados. He will conduct the affairs of Salados for a period of six months. At the end of six months, your council will decide if he meets your approval."

Dorian held his breath. He was almost sure that Para was going to send him north to Salados.

"I am going to send Gaylord to serve you as advisor and leader. He is from Odell. Odell is on the northern border between Arsi and Salados. He will understand the people of Salados and serve you well. I will come to Salados in three months to check on things. You can keep me informed of how things are progressing."

That night Dorian was packing to leave for South Castle when Bailee came to his room. "What is going on? I was just with Queen Para, and she named me first knight. What is happening?"

"I am going to South Castle to replace Gaylord. The queen thinks I need some rest or something. She doesn't explain herself to me."

"We have been friends a long time Dorian. I need to be honest with you. I thought that you and the queen where becoming very close. Do you think that she thought that perhaps you were becoming too close?"

"Maybe so. I know I have strong feelings for her. For the last few days, I have been with her a lot. I thought that she had strong feelings for me, but when she came back from the magic city, she seemed changed. She seemed to be content with the loss of her magic. I thought the loss of her magic would mean she would have to depend more on me, but it seems that it has been just the opposite. She is more independent than ever. She has this crazy idea of going to visit Epson's cabin. You have to promise me that you will take care of her. Who knows what dangers lie near that swamp."

"She has already told me of this. She plans to leave tomorrow. She has asked that she be escorted by three knights. Perhaps you can be with them on the first part of the journey. I understand that the first day of the trip is on the road to South Castle."

"Okay it is. I will check with her. If she leaves early in the morning, say before dawn, she could be to the swamp in a day and a half."

The next day the five travelers left Arsi Castle before daylight. Para had changed her mind about going by coach. She decided to ride her big gray horse. She had one pack horse for the trip. By noon they were at the split where one road went to South Castle and the other turned toward the swamp. When they got to the fork in the road, they dismounted and Para surprised them all. "I am going onto the swamp by myself. I want you four to go on to South Castle. I am taking the pack horse with me. I will need the animal to carry Epson's books."

Dorian was in disbelief. "There is no way in hell I am going to let you do such a dangerous thing. You have got to be kidding."

"I am going to do what I am going to do. You are going on to take charge of South Castle. If you say another word about stopping me, I will strip you of your rank and have you arrested and taken to South Castle by force. Do I make myself clear? Now you four get on your horses and go. I will expect you three to be back here at noon in four days."

The four men got on the horses and continued on to South Castle. Para turned west toward the swamp. She rode about a mile and stopped and got off her horse. She led the horses off the road and unpacked the other horse, "You two stay here. There is plenty of grass and a steam nearby. I will be back in four days." She then turned herself into a hawk and flew west toward the swamp. When she got to the swamp she went into Epson's cabin.

She looked around. She remembered the time she had spent with Dorian. Then she thought of Epson. He was her friend and now he was gone. Tears formed in her eyes. *I owe you so much,* she thought. *I loved you so much.*

She quickly built a fire and went to his shelf of magic potions. She mixed up a potion using knowledge she had gained from Epson's gift. When she was finished, she drank down the potion and thought, *Piper my friend, you won't be able to find me now.* As the cabin started to warm up she stretched out on the bed. *This flying makes you tired.* She quickly fell asleep.

Donella, Asher and Joel

Joel had settled back into a routine at Regstar. He was busy seeing to the day by day running of the castle. Asher and Donella seemed to be going through a courtship of sorts. They took daily rides, and when the weather was not so cold, they would pack a lunch. Joel missed Kira and wanted to come up with some reason go to visit his sister so he could see her. He planned to communicate a couple of times with Para and he could write in code to find out about Kira. He was walking across the courtyard when he saw Donella and Asher returning from a ride. "I guess we need to sit down and start making plans for the wedding. We can't do anything until we set a date."

Asher and Donella dismounted from their horses and a stable boy took them away. Donella hugged her father. "It has been difficult to come up with a date, but we think the spring is best. We are not sure if Rue will come out of Reflection City so we need to plan two weddings: one here and one in Reflection City. We thought we would get married here in the spring and then go the visit grandfather and have a second ceremony there if he doesn't come to Regstar. We thought we would spend some time in Winter Castle, after we were married but now we think we will just stay with Grandfather for a while. If the weather permits, I think we will go visit Grandfather in about a month and tell him our plans so he can make his plans for our visit after we are married here."

The three of them walked back toward the chapel. "It seems like a good plan. After the wedding and you return from Reflection City, why don't you live in Winter Castle? It will be a good home for you and Asher. Besides, I need someone taking care of that part of the kingdom."

Donella turned to Asher. "I believe that Father is already trying to get rid of us. What do you think?"

"I believe you may be right."

The three opened the door of the chapel and went inside. Donella looked down the long aisle. "I believe this place gets bigger every time I come here. How many will it hold?"

Joel starting walking toward the front. "Somewhere around eight hundred, but if we open the balcony we could seat one thousand."

"I wish that we could just be married in the small chapel. It only holds about twenty. We could just have family and a few friends like Kira and Kala.

"That's a wish that I cannot grant. The wedding needs to be a public one. The people of Regstar need to see their future queen and king. It will be just fine. But don't worry about running this kingdom too quickly. I plan to stay around a while longer. By the way, Rhodes has chosen Hector to be their next king. He has sent a message, and we are going to meet at Centerville in about a month. It would be a good time for you and Asher to visit Reflection City to see your grandfather."

Asher was scratching his head. "Do you think it wise to allow Hector to become king of Rhodes? Are we sure we can trust him?"

"Hector was caught between a rock and a hard place when Clive was king. He was caught between doing his duty and doing what was right. I think he will be a good king. I talked with him several times before I left Rhodes. He is tired of fighting. He will be alright. Enough politics, let's get back to the wedding."

Asher and Donella agreed. Everything seemed set. As they sat quietly on the first pew, Joel had a cold feeling. The man that killed Karnac and tried to kill his sister was still at large. *Was he going to go back to where he came from or was he going to be a future problem?*

Piper at Edgewater

* * * * * * * * * * * *

Piper was indeed going to be a future problem. Rumors about a possible wedding to take place in Regstar had already reached Edgewater. Piper had thought this would be a good time to take Para. Everyone would be too consumed by the wedding planning and the excitement to expect anything. Besides, it would be fun to make such a happy event turn into such a sad one. Instead of celebrating a wedding, they would be wondering if Para was still alive.

Piper was sitting with his back to the wall drinking an ale. The tavern was filled with loud seamen from the dock. They were there to drink and enjoy the many women of the night who made their living from the sailors who came into port. He was going to enjoy one such woman tonight himself. As he drank his ale, he looked across the room and saw a tall redhead leaning against the wall. He had not seen this one before. He got up from the table and started walking toward her. She was wearing a loose dark brown full skirt and with a white top which was off the shoulders. It had a drawstring which could be adjusted to keep it from exposing too much breast. In this case, the string was not tied. He could see almost all her breast from the side. As he walked up to her she pulled the top up to keep it from falling down.

"You don't have to pull that up because of me," he said.

She looked at him and started to tie the string. "If you are going to see more, I believe you might have to dig into your pockets for a piece of gold."

He looked at her breasts. The white top did very little to hide them. "I have not seen you here before. Where are you from?"

"From Centerville. Well, I am really from a small village north of Centerville but no one has ever heard of it."

He moved closer to her and let his finger trace the edge of her blouse along the top of her breast. "I have a room upstairs. Would you like to come up for a while?" He reached in his pocket with the other hand and took out a gold coin. He let it drop down the top of the white blouse between her breasts.

"Does this offer include something to drink?"

"It does. If you will come with me, we will stop by the bar and get a couple of bottles of ale. My room is at the top of the steps."

When they arrived in his room, he set the bottles of ale on a table next to his bed. She was leaning back against the door. He came back to her and kissed her on the lips. She quickly turned away from him and he pressed her against the door. He reached around and pulled her top loose from inside her skirt and put his hand underneath the top to feel her flat tight stomach. Moving his hands upward he cupped one breast in each hand. He released her and pulled the top over her head letting it drop to the floor. He kissed down her back. She turned and faced him. She held her hand out toward his face and opened it to reveal a yellow powder in the palm of her hand. She quickly blew the powder in to his face and pushed him away. "You have seen and done too much. This should close your eyes, and I don't think you will want to make love for a while."

The powder was burning his eyes and inside his nose. He was on fire and the room was spinning. When he was completely asleep, she opened his shirt and with some blue paint, painted a symbol on his chest. She said a couple of magic words and the paint seemed to go into his skin. She then walked over, picked up her white top and put it back on, then went to the door and opened it to let two men come inside. "When he wakes up he will be a very able sailor for your ship. I only ask one thing. Never bring him back here."

"Oh we won't. When we get him to our ship, we are going to chain him to an oar. When he is no longer able to row we will either drop him off on some small island or let him feed the fish." They were laughing when they dragged Piper out of the room.

The redheaded woman left the tavern and walked down by the river. She turned into a hawk and flew across the river heading west.

The next day, Piper awoke chained to an oar. He was next to another man. He pulled on his chain but found he could not get up. "Where am I?" he said.

The man seated next him said, "Relax. You are on The Gold Servant. You won't have to work hard today. We are under sail. It has been a great breeze since last night. We are making great time. We are at least a hundred miles from Edgewater."

Piper sort of laughed to himself. *I will shake off these chains and be back in Edgewater before night.* He looked at the chains and cast a spell. The only thing that happened was a sharp pain in his chest, but the chain did not move. He repeated the spell but got the same results. His magic was gone-- taken from him. He was just a man, and he knew he would die on this boat.

Para was flying high above the kingdom of Arsi. As a hawk she had great speed, and it was not long until she had reached South Castle. She flew right into the window of her living quarters which she knew would be locked and private. She was tired and the room was cold. She would not risk a fire because she did not want anyone to know she was there. She cast a spell that heated up the rocks around the fireplace but produced no smoke or fire. She spread a blanket out in front of the fireplace and lay down on it. She had never felt so free before. She quickly fell asleep.

The next morning, Dorian was inspecting the castle. *I am glad that we are not at war,* he thought, *This castle is not very defendable.* He rode his horse to the front side of the large summer home that stood in the middle of the castle walls. He looked at it. It was three stories high with the ground floor almost underground. The second floor had two sets of steps that started on the ground and curved opposite each other meeting on a balcony at the top of the second floor. The second floor was designed for grand parties and meetings. Across the front were large windows and a very large door which opened into a large room, the great hall. It could be used for meetings or dances. To the left of this great hall was a very large library, and opposite the library was the official office complex. Behind the great hall was a hallway that ran the length of the building. The back side consisted of a very large kitchen and rooms for storage and some living quarters for staff. Upstairs on the third floor was the living area consisting of about twenty rooms. The royal room for the king and queen was on the end. The ground floor had several rooms for storage and area living for more of the staff.

The castle was small. In the back, there were two barracks which housed about fifty men each. If need the barracks could hold another one hundred men but they would be crowded. There were a few living areas inside the castle walls, but most people lived in a nearby village across the lake.

Dorian knew he could live inside the main residence but chose to live with the men in the barracks. He did have a private area, but he loved to visit with his men. As he looked up toward the top floor, he noticed someone looking out the window of the royal living area. *No one is supposed to be in that room. Maybe it is just the staff cleaning it.* Then he looked again. The person just kept looking at him, and for some reason, he thought of Queen Para. He decided to see who was there, and he dismounted his horse and entered the residence from the rear. He climbed the steps and soon was standing in front of the door which led into the royal living area. He started to knock and then noticed the door was open. He pushed open the door and walked in. Then he saw her. She was standing next to the fireplace and was wearing a blue robe. He was almost speechless. She look so beautiful with morning light coming through the large windows. "I thought you were going to spend some time at Epson's cabin."

"I have been to the cabin. I had to take care of something first. No one knows I am here."

"I saw you from the outside looking out the window. If I could see you then others could see you." *She has not had time to go to the cabin and make it back here.*

"Only you could see me. There is much I need to tell you."

For a moment he did not say anything and then he spoke. "Why have you come here?"

She looked at him and tears came into her eyes. "As I said, there is much that I must tell you. I am going to tell you things that you cannot tell anyone else. I am going to trust you with my heart. When I came back from Reflection City, I knew that I was in love with you. But I was not free to give you my love at that time. There were things that were expected of me."

He interrupted her. "You have told me all this before. You sent me here so you could mourn Alnac and not be distracted by your feelings for me. What has changed? No time has passed, and you have to mourn whether you are here or at Arsi Castle. I will be just as miserable in both places with you present. Every time I see you, I want to hold you and you don't make it easy for me. When you came back from Reflection City, you let me hold you in my arms, and then the next moment you pushed me away. I am not sure how you feel about me. If you loved me as much as I love you, there would not be any problem here."

He started to speak more but Para stopped him. He had left the door ajar, and with one movement of her hand, she closed and locked it. "As I told you, I don't want anyone to know that I am here." She walked over and put her hands around his neck. "I said there is much I need to tell you. My magic is back. When I was in Reflection City, Kala had met Epson. He transferred his knowledge and magic to me by way of Kala. I have told no one. When I left Reflection City, Piper could feel my presence. He contacted me in a dream almost immediately. He told me that he planned to do me harm, and worse, to do you harm. I could not let that happen. I have been to Epson's cabin, and there I created a potion that would hide me from Piper."

He put his arms around her. "Why did you not tell me all of this? You did not have to bear this alone."

"One of the reasons I moved you to South Castle was for your safety and another was for me to deal with Piper alone. You would not have let me deal with him."

"Does this mean you have dealt with him?" He could feel her breathing and the warmth of her body as he held her.

Para looked up and into the face of Dorian. "I have, and he is no longer any threat to anyone. When I took the potion that kept him from knowing where I was, I could feel where he was. I turned myself into a hawk and flew to Edgewater. I did not kill him, but took his power and sold him to the captain of a ship headed for who-knows-where. There is more. I can fly from Arsi Castle to South Castle in about a half day or less. I want you to move into one of the rooms up here. I do not want to be without you during the next year. No one but you can know that I am coming here and I plan to tell no one, not even Joel, that my magic has returned. In six months, I will send for you. In less than a year, we can start our life together. I want you as my husband, and being king is just something you will have to accept if you want to marry me."

He looked at her and smiled. "I care very little about being king. I only want you in my life." He kissed her and she returned his kiss, pulling him even closer.

"I have to fly back to the crossroads in the morning, but today and the rest of the night I just want to be with you."

Joel Reflects

* * * * * * * * *

Sitting atop the South Tower of Regstar Castle, King Joel could see some of his kingdom but not all. He enjoyed coming to the top of the tower, and he loved so much the small garden in one corner of the tower next to the inner wall. He had built a fire and was just about to sit down with his wife and have a glass of wine. He then thought to himself about how much had happened in the two years since the battle at Rhodes. His daughter had been married for about a year. Para had come to the wedding and when she returned to Arsi had married Dorian. Gwen and Bailee were married and living in South Castle. King Rue had adopted Kala to be his daughter. He then sat down next to Kira. "I have news. A pigeon came in this morning. It was in a code that only my sister and I share."

"Why are you and your sister sending coded messages to one another? All four kingdoms are at peace. What could she possibly want to keep a secret?"

He looked at her with a big smile on his face. "Gwen's child is no longer first in line to be the next ruler of Arsi."

Printed in the United States
By Bookmasters